THE SECRET LIFE OF TRYSTAN SCOTT COLLECTION

THE SECRET LIFE OF
TRYSTAN SCOTT
VOLUMES 1-5

By

H.M. Ward

H.M. Ward Press
SexyAwesomeBooks.com

COLLIDE
THE SECRET LIFE OF
TRYSTAN SCOTT
VOL. 1

col-lide: to come together with a solid or direct impact.

CHAPTER 1

~MARI~

The stage wing was thick with shadows. I sat in a metal chair in the alcove between the curtain and the wall, my finger trailing down the pages of the play. They just about knew their lines. The one guy who fumbled was getting chewed out by the director, Mr. Tucker. He was a young teacher, but he wanted perfection from day one. Since this was day twenty-seven, I supposed he was within his right to be agitated. The cast didn't seem to be into this production.

Leaning forward, I looked out past the stage and into the rows of seats. Trystan wasn't there. That guy had chronic time issues. It didn't matter that he was the lead in this production. His mind was a sieve when it came to learning his lines, so Tucker appointed me to run them with him on a daily basis. This daunting task should have been done prior to practice, but Trystan was late. Again. If he didn't have charisma and a shockingly beautiful face, someone else would have been given the lead. But, when the guy finally learned his lines, he would make a room full of people swoon—especially the women.

There wasn't a girl around who didn't want to be me. Every single actress and stage-hand offered to help Trystan learn his lines, but Tucker chose me. Why? Because I wasn't interested in hanging out with a guy who couldn't keep his lips to himself. That made me the best candidate, so I've been badgering the hottest guy in school for the past two years. Thank God he was a senior and this was the end of it. If I had to put up with his friend Seth much longer, I'd cut my ears off.

Pushing off my chair, I took the play book and went to find Trystan. If he still didn't know his lines, Trystan would be a dead man. By extension, I'd also get slammed in the crossfire. Public humiliation wasn't my thing. I'd shove the play book down his throat if Trystan still didn't know the second act in full today.

Careful not to make any noise, I pushed past the black curtains that stretched floor to ceiling. Several more rows of black curtains hung behind the stage concealing the cinder block wall at the back. The set wasn't finished yet, so they were still practicing with bare bones on a half empty stage. I moved quietly and tried to stay out of sight.

Trailing my fingers against the cold walls, I felt my way through the darkness to the back of the stage. Inky shadows covered everything with only slices of light shining through. At the back of the stage there were three doors. Two led to dressing rooms and one led down into the prop room. The prop room was an oversized basement that spanned under the stage. It contained half a century worth of flats, props, and wardrobe. I felt for the metal doorknob and wrapped my fingers around it. Mr. Tucker's voice was growing more agitated by the moment. If he saw me, he'd scream for

Trystan—then we'd both be screwed. Turning the knob ever so slowly, I pulled the basement door open, careful not to make a sound and stepped around it.

As I stood on the landing, I could hear voices below. Trystan was down there, probably sitting on the couch with his feet kicked up. His voice lacked the normal playfulness. It actually sounded uncertain. "No, it's not like that. You don't get it. Everything about her is just—" he sighed as he trailed off.

Another voice cut him off. This one was more self-assured, more confident. He spoke with the authority only a jock could fully manage. "The girl's a tease, Trystan. What's the point of chasing after her if she won't put out?" That was a typical Seth question. Talk about poor choice in friends. I expected the conversation to stop. I wasn't that quiet, but the landing was high above the stairwell and tucked at the top of the staircase behind a wall of unused flats. They didn't seem to realize that I was there.

"I can't stop thinking about her," Trystan sighed, "Every time I close my eyes, she's there. I can't get her out of my head." His voice sounded haunted, like this girl had really gotten to him. Which was something since Trystan dated everyone and was serious about no one.

As the door clicked shut, I remained motionless—silent—but the metallic click echoed through the room. My heart rate shot up into being-chased-by-a-bear territory. I wanted to hear who she was, who made him sound like that, but the longing in his voice made me feel like a voyeur. I shouldn't be standing there. I shouldn't be listening. This was a private conversation, but I was already there.

Acting like I just walked through the door, I bounded down the metal stairs. I walked around the corner and stepped in front of the flats. Both of them looked up at me.

Seth was saying, "You need a college girl. Forget these high school girls," as I rounded the corner.

Seth was the size of a football player with a toned muscular body, but never seemed to do anything to get that way. His sandy hair was buzz cut, like he had enlisted. He was sitting on a chair across from Trystan, who was slouched back on an old leather couch with his hands behind his head. When Trystan looked up at me, he dropped his hands and straightened a little. There was something in his eyes, something about the way he glanced at Seth, that made me uneasy. He probably thought I heard what he just said.

Seth turned and looked at me, then back to Trystan. His voice grew louder, more cocky, "Besides, high school girls don't know how to give a decent blowjob. Do they, Mari?" Seth the pig liked to pick on inexperienced girls and make them blush. It was a pastime for him. From hanging around Trystan, I had become accustomed to his crass questions. My face no longer flushed, although he never stopped trying. The guy talked about sex so much that it no longer shocked me. It was like his brain was swimming in a lust serum. Seth wasn't hard on the eyes, but his mouth made him repulsive.

Trystan's eyes flicked up to mine after Seth spoke. He had no idea what my experience was with guys, if any. Sometimes it felt like everyone thought I was celibate, as though I'd taken an oath or something just because I didn't want to make out with every guy I met. This confused Trystan. He'd said things in the past, but I didn't feel the need to explain myself.

I tossed the play book on the battered coffee table and sat down next to Trystan. Answering Seth, I said, "I'm not planning on giving you demonstration." Trystan's blue gaze was on the side of my face. His lips parted slightly like he was surprised. I turned toward him. "What?"

He shook his head smiling, "Nothing. Just didn't expect you to say that." He folded his arms across his chest. The black shirt he was wearing made his eyes look like sapphires. They were such a dark shade of blue.

"So, who's a tease?" I asked, assuming that they heard me on the staircase. "Do I know her?"

Trystan was usually perky, like he'd eaten a case of Pixie Stixs, but he seemed uneasy today. His gaze lowered and he didn't speak.

Seth shifted in the old plaid chair. His fingers picked at the threadbare fabric, working a hole into the arm. "You know her," Seth said, grinning. "You see, Trystan here seems to think she's worth chasing, but there's no way in hell she'll put out. She's a tease. He just doesn't see it." Trystan shot Seth a look.

"She has no idea you like her?" I ask genuinely intrigued.

Seth replied for him, "Absolutely none. He can be sitting in the same room as her and she has no fucking clue. It's pathetic." He turns to Trystan, saying, "There's other pussy out there that's much easier to get. Forget about her man."

Seth's words irritated me on so many levels. "Why should he forget about her? Because she doesn't sleep with every guy that blinks at her? You're such a jerk, Seth. Besides, if Trystan found someone he actually likes, why assume anything?" I glance at Trystan. He hasn't moved. "Maybe she just hasn't found the right guy yet. Maybe a relationship means something to her."

"Waste of time," Seth says shaking his head. "Relationships are the fastest way to make sure you never get laid. That's why

Trystan here never dates anyone, and neither do I."

"How romantic," I roll my eyes. "And that's why you're going to end up alone."

Trystan sits up and gives Seth a look that clearly says STOP. Then he turns to me and asks, "What's with the play book?" He nodded his head toward it. The movement made his dark hair fall into his eyes. With a sweep of his hand, he pushed it back. Trystan's hair had that carefully messy look. It's kind of long on top and cut shorter around the bottom. When it's slicked back for the play, he'll look pristine. In the meantime, he looks like a rock star, bemusedly sexy, like he knows how beautiful he is and doesn't care.

I glared at Seth before turning to Trystan, "Tucker is on the warpath. I thought I'd run lines with you so he doesn't slaughter us up there."

Trystan grinned at me, "What makes you think I didn't learn them, yet?" He ran his hands through his hair and stretched. That playfulness that was usually there appeared to be coming back. Whatever girl caught his attention did a good job. I hadn't seen him so out of sorts before.

"Yeah, right," I laugh. "That scene in the second act sucked yesterday. You were tripping over your lines like crazy."

Seth groaned and pushed off the chair. He smoothed his tee shirt. It clung to his broad shoulders. The guy looked like a giant. "Nerds."

Trystan threw a pillow at his friend and it nailed him in the chest. "Get out. I'll catch up with you later," Trystan sat up on the couch and reached for the play book. Handing it to me, he said, "Fine. Let's do it."

Seth had an odd look on his face. He shook his head and left without another word. When the door on the upper-landing clicked shut, Trystan's demeanor changed. He seemed softer without Seth around polluting his thoughts. I really wondered why they hung out together. Trystan was all smooth and subtle with his confidence. Seth was in-your-face about everything. There was no way to have a civilized conversation with that guy. It's like he was raised by giraffes or something.

CHAPTER 2

~TRYSTAN~

Why did he tell Seth anything? His remedies always included girls, which in this case was not helpful. Trystan stretched and ran his fingers through his dark hair. This was more than a crush. It wasn't that the girl had a hot body, even though she did. It was more than that. He connected with her in a way that hadn't happened before. Being around her made him feel exposed. It was difficult to maintain the endless smiles and witty banter that he was known for.

To his horror, Trystan didn't hear that girl—the one that he was so taken with—standing at the top of the stair case. He straightened when he saw Mari round the corner. Trystan tried to make it look like they weren't talking about her, but she had to know. Didn't she?

He didn't see how she couldn't. Trystan saw Mari every day. It didn't matter that she was a junior and he was a senior. Tucker had placed them together when she was a freshman, and they'd spent nearly every day together since.

The reason Trystan didn't act on his attraction initially was because she was too young. He was the eldest in his class, and Mari was the youngest in hers. That put nearly two years between them. For a while he told himself that he was just fond of her, like Mari was the little sister he never had. But as time progressed, he knew that was a lie.

He noticed her quirky mouth early on. That only made her more appealing. Then her body followed, sneaking up on him like a ninja in the middle of the night. Mari's smooth curves melted into each other, forming a body to match that beautiful face. One day he saw her as Mari, the next she was the most desirable woman he'd ever met. Maybe the transition in his mind was slower than that, more of a gradual change, but Trystan didn't see it coming. It completely blindsided him.

To make matters worse, he'd learned over the years everything she couldn't stand about guys. She had this notion that a kiss should mean something and Trystan made it blatantly obvious that he didn't share that opinion. He'd shot himself in the head in terms of ever having a relationship with her. That was what he had been trying to ask Seth about. Trystan wanted to know if his friend thought it was possible to backtrack, to fix things with her so he had a chance.

Seth's response wasn't what he wanted to hear, and—as Mari descended the stairs—Seth saw her first and his over-the-top language came out. The guy only talked like that when Mari was around, almost like he hoped his nasty comments would chase her off.

Instead of running, Mari sat down next to Trystan. God, it was so hard to be so close to her and not touch her. Everything from that light floral scent, to her soft curls made him want her even more. Last night, in a moment of panic, he thought about telling her that he was in love with her. But she wouldn't believe him. He knew she wouldn't. Instead, he grabbed his guitar and recorded a song he wrote for her, before uploading it on a whim. He poured his heart out, never saying her name, only telling her that he loved her, and that he wished she noticed him. No one knew he sang or played. It was a secret he didn't even tell Seth. At times life was too hard. Too much happened, too fast, and it left him feeling paralyzed. Trystan found solace in his music. Now, in the light of day, he thought he should go back and delete that song before someone saw it and figured out it was him.

Mari leaned into him a little bit, her shoulder lightly touching his. Trystan stiffened, his smile faltered. As Seth and Mari argued, Trystan sat there with his insides lurching. He couldn't take Seth's crass mouth. He knew it was upsetting Mari, even though she didn't act like it. It was the little things he noticed, the way her fingers pressed into her jeans forming a little dent where the denim used to be smooth. The curve of her shoulders squared off slowly, her spine becoming straighter and straighter like she intended to fight Seth. After a moment, Trystan shot Seth a look that clearly said STOP.

Seth didn't hang around much longer. When he heard Mari wanted to run lines, Trystan groaned inwardly. It was that scene —the one from yesterday. Though he didn't let on, every fiber of his body protested. The end of that scene had a kiss, and Trystan didn't think he could resist.

CHAPTER 3

~MARI~

"So you just think she's waiting for the right guy?" Trystan's question caught me by surprise. I was flipping through the book, looking for the right page.

Stopping, I looked up at him. "Yeah, most girls want the right guy. They aren't looking for a one-time thing."

"That includes you?" The way he said it, the way his eyes bored into me made me squirm.

The corner of my mouth pulled up and I shook my head, "What I think doesn't matter. You want to know what she thinks." The movement made my hair fall over my shoulders. I pushed it out of my face, tucking a few stray curls behind my ear.

"How am I supposed to find out? Every time I get a second alone with her, someone interrupts us. And it's not the kind of question you can just ask."

I glanced over at him, "You asked me."

There's a lightness to his voice, "And you didn't answer." He smiled at me and looked down at his hands.

For some reason I was hyperaware of my heart. I felt it beating inside of my chest. I shouldn't have told him, but my tongue was moving before my brain realized it, "Yeah, I want the right guy. I'm not interested in screwing around with a bunch of randoms. I want it to mean something. I want the connection, the relationship." Something inside my chest swirled as I said it and my throat tightened. I couldn't help but notice his eyes and how closely he watched me. His gaze was so intense that I looked away.

Trystan nodded slowly and then says, "You want him to love you."

I wondered if I should respond, but I was up to my neck in the conversation already, "Is that so wrong? I mean, wouldn't you want that too?"

"If it were real, yeah. But there's no such thing as love. Love's a concoction of the Hallmark Channel." My mouth fell open as he said it, but he didn't stop. "At least I thought there was no such thing. Now I'm not so sure." His voice trailed off, like he was thinking, considering if it could be true—if that was what was making him so crazy.

My shock changed from offended to surprised, "Oh my God," I breathed. "She's really gotten to you. The great Trystan Scott is in love."

He didn't answer. The way he looked at me made me know I was right. Instead of teasing him, which would have been normal, I sat there in silent awe. "Are you going to tell her?"

He shook his head and leaned back, "No, I don't think so."

I lean toward him and pressed my hand to his knee. "You have to tell her. Damn, Trystan. If she's gotten to you like this, you should at least give it a shot." When his gaze lingered on my hand too long, I pulled it away. I wasn't a touchy feely person, so it was kind of strange for me to reach out and do anything.

"If she realizes it, I won't deny it, but I can't tell her." He looked at the ceiling as he spoke, his voice uncharacteristically soft. When he looked at me again, he sat up, breathed deeply and said, "Come on. Run lines with me. Help me forget about her for a while."

CHAPTER 4

~TRYSTAN~

"Are you going to tell her?" Mari asked. Her big brown eyes remained fixed on his face, waiting for an answer that he couldn't give.

It doesn't matter if I tell her, she won't believe me. You see Mari, it's you. You're the one I can't stop thinking about. You're the one who makes my heart race and my mood soar. You're the reason that I can't sleep, can't eat. The pain inside my chest, that ache that longs for your touch, devours me.

Trystan thought these things. They raced through his mind like a swirl of wind. The words were stuck to his tongue. He couldn't tell her. It had to be something she saw for herself or she'd never believe him.

Shaking his head, Trystan leaned back against the couch, "No, I don't think so."

Mari twisted toward him, her slender hand extended forward. When she placed it on his knee, Trystan nearly crawled out of his skin. As she spoke, he stared at her hand, mesmerized by how much power she held over him. The simple act of patting his knee was too much. Being in the same room as Mari was too much, and here they were alone. Again.

I did this, he thought to himself. I'm the one who sent Seth away. His gaze was still fixated on Mari's hand. She lifted it slowly, like she'd made a mistake. When he looked up at her, their eyes locked. Trystan was completely screwed. He couldn't hide it much longer, and telling her would only make it worse. Ironically, she was sitting there telling Trystan to confess, but she didn't understand. She didn't know it was her.

Trying to put some distance between them, Trystan stretched and looked up at the ceiling. Mari's gaze was burning a hole on the side of his face, but he'd kiss her if he looked at her again. His heart raced inside his chest. He couldn't slow the frantic pace. She was too close.

When he spoke, his voice caught in his throat, "If she realizes it, I won't deny it, but I can't tell her." He managed not to look at her as he said it. He knew she had a puzzled look on her face, like she didn't understand, especially since she could tell how miserable he was. At times Trystan thought she could see right through him, but right now she was blind. And he intended to keep things that way.

The thought of her rejecting him after confessing how he felt about her made him feel sick. He couldn't bear it. As it was, he could barely bear this. Thank God Mari didn't date a lot. If she did, there'd be no way to hide his feelings. They'd come rushing out.

Trystan looked at Mari again, resisting the urge to run his finger across her cheek. He blinked, clearing the thought from his head and sat up. "Come on," he sighed.

"Run lines with me. Help me forget about her for a while."

But running lines didn't help him forget about her. When they started, Trystan was acting like his character, seeing his lost love. But as they got into it, as they headed toward the end of the act, all he could think about was Mari's lips on his.

CHAPTER 5

~MARI~

Trystan knew his lines. He sat on the edge of the couch, facing me. Everything from the tone of his voice, to his inflections, to his expressions was perfect. Trystan had a way of looking at a girl that took her breath away. He used every skill he had in the scene, making it difficult to remember that it wasn't real—that the words weren't his. Before I knew what was happening, our eyes locked. Every muscle in my body tightened. While we were practicing, he moved closer to me. His knees faced mine. He was close enough to touch me, but he didn't.

Still running lines, he continued, "Then when I saw you again, I couldn't believe it was you. I watched you that night, trying to get up the nerve to talk to you. After everything that happened, after everything ended the way it did, I—" he breathed in and closed his eyes. When he opened them again, he lowered his lashes and looked up at me, "I couldn't risk ruining that moment. But it was a mistake..."

"Why?" I said the line, unable to look away. My pulse was racing even though I knew it wasn't real. Trystan was so intense, and when he looked at me like that, it was impossible to notice anything but him.

His eyes were dark as sapphires. They drifted to my cheek and a moment later, his hand was there touching me lightly. "Because it haunts me. Every moment of every day is filled with regret. I wonder if I had said something, if we could have had another chance..." his voice trailed off. He brushed my cheek lightly with his thumb before pulling his hand away. Looking down, he breathed, "But I didn't. I was a coward."

Our gazes locked, and Trystan was so close to my face, that I felt the warmth of his breath on my lips. My voice barely came out, "If you had it to do over again, what would you do?"

This was the spot where he messed up yesterday. The scene had no passion and he totally bumbled his lines. There was no connection with the actress. But today it felt so intense, so real. Heat flushed my body. I wondered what he would do, when he would stop. The scene ended with a kiss and Trystan didn't break character. Instead he leaned closer to me, slowly, hesitantly. His lips were a breath from mine.

He whispered, "I'd do this." The sound was soft and seductive passing over his lips, making butterflies erupt in my stomach. My body felt hot. Every inch of skin seared like it was on fire, pleading for his touch. He lingered, withholding the kiss, watching me through lowered lashes.

There was nothing but him and me in that moment. We weren't in a dank prop room, we weren't running lines. The way he looked at me, the way his eyes pinned me in place and stole my breath, made my heart race faster. It banged into my ribs as his lips moved painfully slow toward mine. When his hand touched my face and slid back into my hair, I thought I'd die. Every part of my body was on fire.

Trystan's lips brushed lightly to mine. The soft caress sent a spark through me that kept me from pulling away. Instead I savored the sensation, the feel of his full mouth against mine. The heat from his lips, the softness of the kiss would be burned into my mind after that. That kiss would come unbidden when I least expected it.

After he swept his lips across mine, he pulled back just enough that the sensation of his lips on mine ended. It pulled me toward him like a magnet tugging wildly at my insides. Shock held me in place as it crashed into me in a relentless wave. His kiss was bewitching. It felt real. The way my body responded to him—to his voice and his words—was real. I'd denied it over and over again. I didn't want to be like every other girl that was infatuated with him. We were friends. There was nothing there. I kept telling myself that, but right now, the way my stomach twisted to have him so close, I knew it was a lie. I liked him.

Trystan sat there watching me, his eyes locked on mine. His palm rested against my cheek as he gazed at me. It was like he was too stunned to move. At least I thought he was. When the door clicked open above us, he winked at me. His hand slid away from my cheek. The air felt cold with it gone. I repressed a shiver, and slumped backward like he had no effect on me.

A voice called down, "On stage, Scott!"

Trystan stood and looked down at me. I stared at his shoes, wondering what kind of crazy I had to be to let him kiss me.

"Be right there," he replied and the door shut again. "What'd you think?" There was a question in his voice. I glanced up at him.

"Better than yesterday," I replied, trying to sound normal. "Assuming Brie doesn't jump on you when you kiss her like that, you'll be good."

He grinned, "I thought that scene needed some tension. That worked, right?"

"Yes," my voice came out in a breath. "It worked perfectly."

CHAPTER 6

~TRYSTAN~

That kiss. He didn't want to stop. Her lips tasted like strawberries and when he pressed her mouth to his, Trystan felt whole. There wasn't another word for it. He needed Mari like he needed air. When his hands tangled in her hair, she didn't protest. As he kissed her, he waited for her to pull away. When she didn't, when she ran the lines through the end of the scene, he didn't question his good fortune. Instead he concentrated on the taste of her lips and the shape of her mouth, the smoothness of her skin and the softness of her hair in his hand. It would be like this, he thought, if we were together. His body burned hotter than it should have with such a chaste kiss, but it was the closest he'd ever gotten to Mari.

Reluctantly, he ended the kiss by pulling away slightly. He tried to control his breathing, still holding her face in his hands. Her breath rushed over his lips as he lingered there. Trystan didn't want to stop. He had no idea why Mari let him do it. It should have gotten him slapped. When the door above them scraped open, he released her face. Immediately his hands felt empty, like they'd been holding the most valuable thing they'd ever touched and now it was gone.

"Be right there," he replied. He waited a beat for the door to click shut. Heart racing, he looked at Mari and asked, "What'd you think?" It was brazen, especially after deciding not to tell her, but he had to know.

"Better than yesterday," she said coolly. "Assuming Brie doesn't jump on you when you kiss her like that, you'll be good." She smiled as she spoke, like she wasn't affected by his kiss. Like it hadn't meant anything to her. Swallowing hard he realized that he wanted it to mean something. He didn't want to touch her, taste her, and kiss her—no, he wanted more than that. He wanted her to want him. He wanted more than the physical act. Inwardly he cringed. That thought was so unlike him, so foreign, but as he gazed at her, he longed for it. He wanted something with her, but her reply made it obvious that the feelings weren't two-directional. Swallowing hard, he forced down a lump of regret that was nearly choking him.

He grinned to cover his real feelings, putting on the fucking mask that hid his real thoughts. He didn't want things to be like that with her, but that was the way things were.

Playfully, he said, "I thought that scene needed some tension. That worked, right?"

"Yes," she said softly. "It worked perfectly." Her dark curls were fanned across her shoulders. It was impossible to look at her and not touch her. Every instinct in his body was wrong. She didn't care for him, not like that.

He nodded toward the stairs, "I better get going." Without another word, he turned and walked away from her. It felt like something inside of him ripped.

I shouldn't have kissed her, he thought, climbing the stairs two at a time.

When he walked out onto the stage, he acted. Trystan was everything he was supposed to be, and no one knew any different. None of them knew him at all.

CHAPTER 7

~MARI~

"You let him kiss you?" Katie asked. Her mouth was hanging open, her burger positioned in her hands like she was going to take a big bite, but instead it just hung there. A piece of lettuce fell to her plate. Finally she cocked her head to the side, which is Katie's look for *are you crazy?*

Pushing around the fries on my plate, I shrugged, "We were running lines. I thought he'd stop, but he went to the end of the scene."

Katie and I had made plans to meet up at the diner for dinner. There was a scattering of people surrounding us and

Katie's voice was a little too loud for my taste. There hadn't been many other kisses to report, but this one seemed to blindside her. It was completely unexpected and according to her, completely stupid.

She blinked big brown eyes at me, "But he kissed you."

"But nothing. It meant nothing. He was practicing," I said, raising my hand and pointing a French fry at her. "It's called acting."

Her mouth was still suspended open. She snapped it shut, shaking her head and put down the burger. Her hands tugged at her long dark hair when she said, "This is going to screw with you. I can't believe you let him do that. You can't get him out of your head when he smiles at you and you frickin' let him kiss you!" I knew that she only acted like this because she cared about me.

Katie was the only one who had a clue about my feelings for Trystan. I hated that I liked him that way. He literally had a gaggle of groupies that followed him around. I didn't want to be one of them, but the guy got to me. There was no way to ignore it. I leaned back in the booth and looked around the diner to make sure no one we knew was near-by. This was my biggest secret. If Trystan found out, I'd die.

"Shhh!" I hissed, whipping my neck around. The movement made my hair fall over my shoulder and into my ketchup. "Awh, man."

Katie swallowed a laugh and tossed me a bunch of napkins. I dabbed the condiment out of my hair. When my brown curls seemed okay, I tossed my hair back over my shoulder again. Finally Katie asked, "So how was it?"

Her question took me by surprise. I glanced up at her with that deer in the headlights look. Squirming, I replied, "Fine, I guess." Better than fine. He made me feel every inch of my body. I flushed thinking about it.

She shook her head and picked up her burger again, muttering, "Yes, I can see that it was marginal at best. You're such a bad liar, Mari."

"Fine." I leaned closer to her and lowered my voice, "You know how I told you he gets to me? Like we can be standing there talking, and it's like he can read my mind or something?" She nods. I'd told her this before. Trystan had a weird way of knowing what I was going to say before I said it. When his gaze bore into me, I felt exposed, like he could read my mind. I avoided eye contact with Trystan, which was part of my mistake today.

I continued, "It was like that, but more. It felt like he could see through me in that moment, like all my thoughts were just spread out for him. And his lips were so soft. The way he did it made me want him even more." I grabbed the sides of my head, placed my elbows on the table and leaned forward. With closed eyes, I uttered, "What a disaster." When I look at Katie again, she's grinning. "What?"

"You did this to yourself, you know. You're the one who says a kiss has to mean something for it to be real, and it seems like this fake kiss made your brains blow up." She sips her soda and leans back in the booth. If someone else had said it, the words would have felt mean. But the way Katie mentions them, made it as confrontational as saying, please pass the milk.

But I won't back down on this issue. I was right. "A kiss is supposed to mean something. I just—"

Katie cut me off, "Do yourself a favor and stay away from him. You know he's a love them and leave them kind of guy. That's not your kind of guy. Hanging around with Trystan is just going to get you hurt." Her voice was beseeching, like she doesn't want me unhappy.

I can't avoid Trystan. He's at the theater every day with me, but I know what she means. "I'll try."

"Good," she said, smiling. She plucked a fry off her plate and popped it into her mouth. For a moment neither of us said anything. Before taking another fry, she said, "Did you see that video, yet? The one on You Tube of that guy singing?"

I shook my head, "What are you talking about?" I'd been at practice all afternoon. It was after 7:00pm and I was eating dinner on the way home.

Katie always knew what was going on. She pulled out her phone, flicked a few buttons, and handed it to me. A video loaded. It's hard to make it out, but a guy was sitting on a stool with a guitar on his lap. His fingers moving up and down the instrument as he played. There was a strong light behind him, obscuring his face. I could tell was that he's young, maybe my age and a little taller than me, with dark hair. The song he was singing wasn't something I'd heard before. It was a love song about a girl that doesn't know he's alive. He sounded so bewitched by her that I couldn't look away. The tune was catchy, but it was the haunting lyrics that mesmerized me. When the song ended, I stared at the phone immediately wanting to hear more.

Blinking, I looked up at Katie, "Who is that?"

She grins, "No one knows. He uploaded the song last night and it went viral."

His voice echoed in my mind. The lyrics said he was completely taken with a girl who didn't know he was alive. She called to him like a siren; and he couldn't help but love her. It was tragic and beautiful. I wanted to know who the singer was. I glanced at the phone again and pressed play. The words flowed through the tiny speakers.

Someone passing by stopped and said, "Great song, right?" It was a senior I'd seen around but never spoke to before.

Katie beamed, "It really is. Have you heard anything? Did they figure out who he is?"

The girl shook her head, "No, but it won't be long. I bet the guy goes home tonight and sees that his video got all those comments today and we know his name by tomorrow. At least, that's what I'm hoping for." She laughed and Katie told her thanks.

"God, I hope so," she said, turning back to me. "I can't see a damn thing with that light in the way."

"Me neither," I said, staring at the screen after the video stopped. "Did you see all these comments? There are thousands and this hasn't even been up for a day yet."

Katie snapped the phone away and scrolled through the comments, then handed it back to me. "That one is mine," she said, tapping at a spot on the screen.

I read it and gasped, "You did not type that!"

"Yup," she said, grinning, snatching the phone back. "He's too hot not to."

"You can't even see him!" I laughed. "How do you know he's hot?"

"I just know. With a voice like that and the way he sings about her…" Katie sounds like she has a bad crush on the mystery guy, which wasn't like her.

"It could be anyone. This guy could be a troll. Or a stalker."

Katie's eyebrow darted up, "You really think that a stalker made a video?"

"No," I admitted and quickly added, "but it would make it easier not knowing who it is if he was some kind of deviant."

"Well, I'm going to find out." She took one more bite of her burger and waived at the waitress to get the check. "I'm going home and surfing the web until someone forks over a name."

CHAPTER 8

~TRYSTAN~

When Trystan arrived home, the small condo was empty. He sighed a sigh of relief and tossed his books on the kitchen table. Trystan looked around at the dilapidated furnishings and the graying walls. In the back of his mind, he hoped it would burn and burn all the memories with it. This place wasn't a refuge, it was a nightmare.

Trystan pulled the fridge open and stared at empty shelves. "Fuck," he muttered running his hands through his hair. Empty. Again. He slammed the door shut. Shaking his head, Trystan grabbed his books and went back to his bedroom. Once inside he locked the door with a slide bolt.

He'd have to grab groceries, but there was no way Trystan would risk running into his father for food. Besides, his stomach was still in knots from kissing Mari. Eating was a necessity, but he wasn't particularly hungry.

Trystan pulled an old laptop he'd purchased second-hand out from between his mattresses. It booted slowly, its small screen flickering to life like it wished it were dead. When it finally was up and running, Trystan borrowed a neighbor's unsecure Internet connection. He had to take down that video. If Mari heard that song... The pit of his stomach dropped just thinking about it.

Trystan navigated his way toward the YouTube page, Day5705. Shock lined his face when the page finally loaded. Before he could click delete, he saw comments—tons of them. They loved his song. He scrolled down, recognizing several kids from his school. Hope and fear flooded his chest. If his classmates saw it, then Mari might have seen it. She'd know. She'd recognize him.

Trystan played the video again, frantically trying to see if it was possible to tell who he was.

With his hand keeping the curser hovering above the delete button, Trystan stared at the page. Should he erase it? Make it like it never existed? What would happen to the swarm of people who demanded to know who he was?

The only reason to delete it was Mari, but she was also the reason he wrote the song. Maybe he could ask her about it. Maybe that would be a way to approach the subject of them—a way for her to know he was sincere. Trystan scrolled down through the comments, and made a short post before shutting down the computer. He slid the black plastic under his bed and pulled off his shirt.

The front door slammed shut. Trystan killed the light quickly and jumped into bed with his jeans still on. He could hear his father through the apartment. His voice echoed back to Trystan, "You ungrateful brat! There's only one thing I ask you to do, and you can't even do that!"

Something hard thunked into Trystan's door and shattered. He closed his eyes tight. It was only a matter of time, he reminded himself. The yelling and screaming would stop, his father would pass out, and Trystan could rest safely for a few hours.

CHAPTER 9

~MARI~

Later that night, I surfed the web, as I listened to his song over and over again. It was addicting. Once I heard it, I wanted more. And not knowing who sang it made me want to know who he was to the point of insanity. The user account was Day5705. It wasn't even a name. The more message boards and tweets I read about him, the more people started referring to him as Day Jones, the anonymous lone musician.

The way he sang was sexy, but it was the words and his voice that captured my attention. I felt like that about Trystan. He saw me as some junior nobody, the girl assigned to read lines with him. This was the second year we worked together and it was always the same. Trystan would talk to me at practice, but that was all I saw of him. The cold hard truth was that he didn't know I was alive. And with friends like Seth shoving college girls down his throat, why would he?

There was a soft side to Trystan, something that only came out when we were alone. The arrogant swagger that he had melted away and he seemed vulnerable. It felt like I was seeing something that he didn't show to anyone else, but I knew that couldn't be. He didn't think of me like that. Trystan was pining over someone else; some girl that Seth didn't think was worth his time. Knowing Seth, he'd try to keep Trystan away from her. I thought about it, but there was no way to figure out who Trystan's crush could be. Before and after practice, Trystan was surrounded by girls. It'd always been like that. All the girls loved him and every guy wanted to be him.

I pulled up Trystan's Facebook page and gazed at his picture. Those perfectly pink lips—the way they felt would be seared into my mind forever. It wasn't my first kiss, but no kiss had ever made me feel so much before. I closed the page and pressed play on the song again. I went to bed that night thinking that someone would sniff out the mysterious Day Jones' real identity by morning, but when I woke up they still didn't know.

During the night he posted a comment and it made them love him even more. The guy seemed humble. He made one comment—that's it—and said:

Thank you for listening to this song. I don't really play very well and my voice isn't exceptional. The only reason I posted it was because I thought someone might be going through the same thing. Thanks for listening. –Day

After he posted that, the comments section of the video went nuts. Everyone wanted to know who he was, who she was, and they begged him for more songs. Day didn't post anything else. He didn't seem to want the fame, or the attention. It made me admire him more.

CHAPTER 10

~TRYSTAN~

He barely had five hours of sleep. Trystan showered and pulled on clothes without worrying about rousing his father. Dear old Dad was passed out cold on the living room floor. Trystan grabbed his books and ran out the door. The morning air was cool and damp. He breathed it in like he couldn't get enough of it.

It didn't matter how much his life sucked, there were times—little things really—that he took joy in. They were reliable, dependable like the sunrise.

Trystan walked into the high school and headed directly for the cafeteria. His stomach growled, reminding him that he skipped dinner last night. Today after school, he'd have to run into the deli and grab some things. That meant more odd jobs, less time at school. Trystan bartered with the deli owner, doing odd jobs for him once in a week in exchange for groceries. If he hadn't done that, he was certain he would have been taken away from his father and placed into foster care a long time ago.

Trystan smiled at the cafeteria lady, "Good morning, Miss Bensly. Is that a new pin?"

Miss Bensly was close to seventy years old. Every day she came in with a different broach pinned to her lunch lady uniform. They were usually too large and garishly awful. Trystan beamed at her, holding up an apple and a roll for her to ring up.

Miss Bensly, swatted at him, "Oh you. Save your sweet talk for someone closer to your age, Trystan." She hit the no sale button and waved him through.

"You're an angel, Miss Bensly. What would I do without you?" It was the truth.

This matronly figure had fed him breakfast for the past four years.

Miss Bensly shook her head, and waived him off. Trystan crossed the room and sat at a table by the windows. The sun was barely over the horizon. The bell would ring in about five minutes. Trystan watched students pour out of cars and buses. He ate his breakfast while waiting for her. Mari would arrive any minute, scurrying through the door like she was late even though she wasn't.

When he saw her, his heart stopped. The apple he was about to bite was midway to his mouth, but it hung there suspended in motion as he watched Mari run into the building.

"You seriously need to get over her," Seth said, slapping his books down on the table.

Trystan flinched, bit the apple, and threw the core into the nearby garbage pail.

Mr. Tucker chose that exact moment to walk in, "Detention Scott. Throw something else and it'll be a week. Come to my classroom during study hall. You can serve it then." Tucker scribbled on a pink piece of paper instructing the study hall teacher to excuse Trystan since he was serving detention with Tucker.

Trystan smiled, "Thanks. I didn't have one of these yet today," and snatched the pink paper and shoved it into his pocket.

"You're pushing your luck, Scott." Tucker waved a fat finger at him and walked away quickly, like Trystan irritated him and he didn't want to behead the kid before first period.

Seth stared at Trystan until he finally said, "What the hell is wrong with you? It's like you want to get busted. You keep doing all this stupid shit and it's like you know you're going to get caught."

Trystan folded his arms over his chest and slumped back into his plastic chair, "Like what?"

"Hello? Were you somewhere else five minutes ago? Apple core, right when Tucker walked in. That's sloppy man. You used to pull crap, but you didn't get caught. Now, well, look at you."

Trystan didn't feel the need to say why he'd grown sloppy. The lack of sleep from trying to avoid his father's fists was slowing him down. "Gee, thanks, Seth."

"I'm serious. You're falling apart, and I know why."

Trystan shot up from his seat, "Don't even go there. The only reason I told you about her was so you could help."

Seth ran up behind him as Trystan exited the cafeteria and walked into the hallway. It was packed with kids carrying books, still wearing coats, racing to get to their lockers. Trystan shouldered his way into the crowd, forcing his way across the hallway. Seth followed close behind, "I am trying to help you, but you won't listen. You never listen!"

Trystan spoke firmly over his shoulder, "She's not the problem."

"Then what is? Clue me in, what's making you so reckless?" Seth stopped in his tracks. Kids swarmed around him like a rock dropped in the middle of a pile of ants.

Trystan leaned his head against his locker. Seth didn't know about his dad. No one did. Taking a deep breath, he turned toward Seth and said, "I'll stop, okay? Just leave her alone." When Seth tilted his head with a try-to-stop-me look on his face, Trystan added, "I know you can't stand her, but that doesn't mean—"

Shaking his head, Seth cut Trystan off, "Not true. I just can't stand what she does to you. When you've been around her, you act like a fucking lunatic. I'd understand if you were thinking with your dick, but you're not. You're chasing some nobody that hates your guts. Face facts, Trystan. There's no future with her in it. You two aren't compatible."

It was the thought that was always drifting at the back of his mind. When Seth said it, Trystan felt like someone punched him in the stomach. All the air was forced out of his lungs. It felt like someone was strangling him.

"It doesn't matter. I can't let this go."

"You have to. It's like handing her a loaded gun aimed straight at your heart," Seth said in a low voice. He leaned closer to his friend, "Don't do it. Once those words come out, it's like pulling the trigger. You can't undo it."

———

Trystan went through the rest of the day looking for Mari. She wasn't at her locker at the usual times, and she seemed to alter her normal path through the hallways. Was she avoiding him? Trystan instantly knew why—that kiss. He shouldn't have kissed her. At the time, he didn't think it upset her, but it must have. There was no other explanation as to why she was avoiding him.

Trystan went into Tucker's room during his free period. "I'm here." His voice was distant, distracted. He wanted to find Mari and fix things.

Tucker glanced up from under an overgrown monobrow. He pointed at the first desk in front of him, "Sit." Tucker didn't bother to watch Trystan find his seat, instead he went back to the stack of papers in front of him. When he finished marking up the one he was working on, he lifted it and put it into a folder, leaving the pile of papers out on his desk.

"Want to tell me what's going on?" Tucker asked. He walked in front of the desk and stopped in front of Trystan.

Trystan stared straight ahead, "I threw an apple core and got busted." Glancing up, he said smirking, "I believe you were there. It was a pretty good throw. Crossed the room and sailed straight into the center of the can."

"Scott, you threw it when I walked in. Did you really think I'd let it go? This little cry for help?"

Trystan straightened in his chair and looked directly in his teacher's face, "What? That wasn't a cry for help. It was piss-poor timing."

Tucker's head tilted to the side. He folded his massive arms across his chest, "Yeah, right. And I'm the Toothfairy. Listen Scott, if you're in trouble there are people who can help. I know your dad—"

Trystan shot out of his chair. "You don't know shit about my dad, so don't try your psychobabble on me." Some emotion he couldn't identify reached out and crushed his gut. After a second, he realized it was fear mingling with shame. If people knew the beatings he'd taken, he'd die. Trystan was stronger than his dad but he never fought back. He took his punches. Maybe it was some distorted sense of reality. Maybe he just wanted a father like everyone else had, someone who watched over him and played ball on the weekends. Instead he got the drunken mess, the shell of what used to be a great man.

"Trystan," Tucker said, turning toward him as Trystan made a beeline for the door.

But Trystan didn't stop. No one could know. And Tucker was wrong. No one could save him. That was one fact he knew for certain. The last person who tried— shaking his head, he pushed the thought aside. He didn't want to think about it. His life was what he made it. As soon as Trystan crossed the stage at graduation and got his diploma, he was out of here.

But Mari, a voice said in the back of his head.

The jaded part of Trystan silently responded, If Mari doesn't come around by then, she never will.

CHAPTER 11

~MARI~

After school Trystan found me sitting alone in the theater, waiting for practice to start. I avoided him all day, and he noticed. "You weren't at your locker." It was a statement, but there was a question in his voice.

I shrugged, like it was normal. I had my math book open on my lap. "Just trying to finish some homework."

A lopsided grin lined his lips. Great. I knew that expression. He knew I was lying. Damn it. When did he get to know me so well?

"Mari, at least tell me what I did."

"You didn't do anything," I said, without looking up, starting another equation. He took the book from my lap and closed it quietly. When I looked up at him, he took my notebook and my pencil, too.

"I know you. Something's bothering you."

I was impaled on his gaze as soon as I looked up. It darted through me, and I couldn't look away. His eyes searched my face and I felt naked. Somehow he'd learned to read me. Two years of running lines had taught him too much. I looked away before he saw how I felt about him. I sighed and threw my head back like I was annoyed. "Trystan, I'm not mad at you, but I will be if you don't give me back my stuff."

He took the pile of books off his lap and held them out over the aisle. Watching me, he dropped them on the floor. The pencil rolled away as the slap of the books echoed through the empty auditorium. I jumped up to push past him, but he blocked me. Trystan was a full head higher than me. I couldn't look at his face; those eyes would make me say stupid things. Instead, I stared at his chest and the black tee shirt that clung to him.

Trystan tensed. I could feel his gaze on my face. "It was the kiss, wasn't it?"

I lifted my eyes and when I met his I knew I was screwed. I felt the truth about to tumble out of my mouth, but I bit it back. Pushing my curls out of my face I shook my head, "No, of course not. It didn't mean anything. Besides, you kiss everyone." The expression on his face faltered when I said it and I instantly regretted my words. He looked like I kicked him in the stomach.

But, Trystan recovered quickly. Nodding he said, "Sometimes. Mostly girls." He grinned to cover the effect of my words. "Still, I shouldn't have done it. I know how you feel about that stuff, and I just got caught up in the moment." He pushed his hands into his pockets, and looked up at me. His eyes were so blue.

I tore my gaze away, "It's fine." I tried to ignore the fact that my ribs felt like they were going to crack. My heart raced when he looked at me like that, making my pulse pound like I'd been running. I wanted to turn away, but I couldn't. My arms folded against my chest.

Trystan watched me do it. Then he reached out and touched my forearm, gently brushing my skin with his fingers. He had to know how crazy he was making me. That had to be the reason why he did it. Smiling, he looked up into my face and said, "I wanted to tell you something. Every time we get a second, someone comes and drags you away. Listen—" he swallowed hard, his dark lashes lowering. He paused like he can't figure out how to convey what he wanted to say. When he looked back up into my eyes, I felt like I couldn't breathe. The sensation of his palm on my arm, the way he looked at me, made me want to throw my arms around his neck, but I couldn't. The only actual thought registering in my mind at that moment was that Katie's going to kill me.

"Scott!" Seth yelled as he walked into the auditorium. The sound bounced around the empty room.

Trystan didn't turn toward him. Instead he stared at me like he wanted to say something else, but he couldn't. He finally blinked and turned toward Seth.

Seth sounded agitated, "I've been looking all over for you."

"I'm right here," Trystan said flatly. All indications of the seriousness of what he was going to say had washed away.

When Seth walked up, he looked at my books on the floor and then back up at us. "You peg him with your books? Nice." He grinned widely, his eyes sliding over me appreciatively.

Trystan bent over and picked the books up. He handed them back to me and our fingers brushed, sending sparks through me when I took them. "Can we finish talking about this later?" I didn't trust my voice, so I nodded. "I'll catch up with you after practice."

CHAPTER 12

~TRYSTAN~

When he saw Mari sitting alone in the dark theater, Trystan walked in and quietly sat beside her. He'd been thinking about this moment all day. He was going to tell her that he was Day Jones. Dropping a big enough hint should help her figure out that she was the object of his affection.

Then Seth bounded in and kept him from saying it. Part of Trystan considered blurting it out in front of his best friend, but he knew the guy wouldn't let him. Seth effectively ended the conversation. He pulled Trystan out into the hallway like nothing happened.

"What the hell?" Trystan finally asked. He stopped at stared at Seth.

Seth smiled carefully, like he knew he was on cracked ice. "I can't let you do it."

"It's not your call," Trystan's voice was cold. His eyes narrowed as he stepped toward Seth.

Seth could tell that this was going to be a fight, but he wasn't letting Trystan make this kind of mistake. He'd seen it before. The guy is completely in love with some chick and then she shoots him between the eyes and bats her eyes like he was nothing. Seth knew Trystan was secretive about his life, and he never pressed him before, but he had to know now. "Something's up with you, man. If it's not the girl, then what is it?"

A redheaded teacher stepped out of her classroom, "Get out of the halls, gentlemen. You know there's no loitering after school."

"We're waiting for Tucker," Seth replied.

Since we were standing in front of the auditorium, she didn't force the issue. "Well, he should be here any second. If he isn't, come and get me and I'll turn on the lights for you."

Seth nodded and said, "Thanks." When she was inside her classroom, Seth turned to Trystan, "I don't nose into your life, but something's going on. It's obvious. If it's not the girl, then what is it?"

Trystan was fuming. Did everyone see it? Did the dark circles under his eyes give him away? He couldn't tell anyone. Not even Seth. He wouldn't understand. Maybe it was a mistake, he wouldn't know until later, but he lied. "It's the girl."

Tucker raced past them, and into the theater. He didn't say anything to Trystan about his earlier outburst, or that he walked out of detention.

Seth nodded curtly, "That's all you had to say. I'll catch you later."

Trystan walked into the theater and slipped into a chair while Tucker went over the things he wanted to work on that day. A group of girls sat down behind him, like always. Sometimes he wished they'd follow someone else around.

Trystan couldn't focus; he couldn't keep his mind here, until he heard Monica whispering behind him. She was one of the actors that were always around, but he didn't really know her.

"Did you see this? Someone offered Day Jones a contract." She held out her phone and the girl sitting next to her took it.

"Holy shit. What'd he say?" Chanel spoke too loudly and Tucker glared at her.

After a small pause, Monica whispered, "Nothing."

CHAPTER 13

~MARI~

Something was up, but I had no idea what. The way he looked at me was curious. There was something in his eyes that reminded me of panic, but it was more subdued. I couldn't place the emotion that darted off his face as soon as Seth called his name.

Looking down at the play book in my lap, I followed along. I no longer fed people their lines. Instead, they waited next to me in the wings, waiting for their prompt to enter the stage. Brie stood next to me, her arms folded across her chest like she was bored. Her blue eyes were watching the actors on stage, completely ignoring me. When I heard her line, I motioned with my hand for her to enter, but she just stood there.

"Go," I whispered. She should have started walking two seconds ago. The pause will result in a gap in the on-stage banter. She'd mess up and I'd get blamed for it.

"I think I know my part better than you," she snapped. Before I could say anything, she stepped away from me and onto the stage. The lights shone down on her making her crown of golden waves look ethereal.

Brie was a classic bitch. She had the cheerleader Barbie body and all the guys fell all over her. The way she swung her hips when she walked made her impossible to ignore. Today she had on thigh-high boots coupled with a short skirt and a tiny tee shirt that showed her midriff when she moved her arms. The outfit barely met the school dress code. All eyes were on her as she walked on set.

Tucker yelled, "You're late, Levetto! Who the hell is prompting that wing?"

Brie replied sweetly, "Mary Jennings. I think she zoned out."

"Mari," I muttered to no one. That girl never said my name right. It wasn't Mary. It's Mar-e. The muscles in my arms twitched. I wanted to strangle her. Brie glanced back at me and smiled like this was funny.

"Get out here Jennings!" Tucker's voice boomed across the stage from his seat in the first row.

My cheeks flamed red as I walked out on stage with the play book in my hands. I shot Brie a nasty look. Trystan was across the room. When I walked on stage, he looked up at me. He was sitting on a kitchen table, his legs dangling. His eyes flicked to Tucker.

The teacher's chest puffed up like he was going to explode. I hated public humiliation. If I could run, I would have. Trystan stopped swinging his legs and straightened, as he watched Tucker have an embolism.

"Everyone listen up!" Mr. Tucker yelled. "A play is only as good as its weakest link and right now that link is Miss Jennings."

My face grew hotter, but he didn't stop. Brie was smiling like a demented doll. "Take note. Anyone who doesn't pull his or her weight will do double time. That means no lunch, no free periods." Some of the students groaned. He waved his meaty fist and they fell silent again. "Let this be an example to all of you. Miss Jennings," he said tartly, his fat face pinched into a scowl, "you will report here every day for the next week. If you don't come, I'm throwing you out. And since this isn't an elective, you'll have a serious problem come graduation." By the time he finished screaming at me, my face was bright crimson. Every inch of me was stained. I stood there, pulse pounding taking a beating that should have been dished out to Brie. Instead of protesting, I nodded. Everyone was watching me and the sooner I was in the shadows again, the better.

"Good. Now that that's cleared up... Scott, on stage with Brie. Pick it up from the second half of the second act." Tucker leaned back in his chair, visibly deflating.

Everyone cleared off the stage, except for Trystan and Brie. As people poured out of the wings, no one would look at me. I sat down in my metal chair and flipped the book open to the page Trystan rehearsed with me yesterday.

Brie sashayed up to him and folded her arms across her chest and threw out her hip. Bitch is the only role she can play, I thought to myself. God, I hated her.

Trystan took a deep breath and they started. He said his lines with efficiency, but they didn't sound the way they did the other day. Something wasn't right. I leaned forward, trying to see him better.

Trystan's voice carried across the stage, "But I didn't. I was a coward."

Brie sighed and switched her weight to her other foot, "If you had it to do over again, what would you do?" Instead of sounding like he was winning her over, she sounded annoyed, like he was wasting her time.

I didn't want to watch, but I couldn't look away. Everyone was watching. The wings were filled with actors and the stage crew. Each one was silent, wanting to see that kiss.

Trystan leaned closer to her, slowly, hesitantly, his lips nearly touching hers.

He whispered, "I'd do this." His hands shot out and grabbed her waist. He pulled her tight to his chest and dipped her backward over his arm. Her long hair dangled and she screamed. Brie's arms flailed before she slapped Trystan in the head. When her hand sailed into his face, Trystan lost his grip and dropped her. Brie fell to the floor and landed hard on one hip. Her short skirt flew up. Laughter erupted. It was comical. Everything from the slapstick way Brie went down to the floral granny panties she was wearing.

Brie fixed her skirt and jumped up, screaming in Trystan's face, "You did that on purpose!" She shoved him hard, but Trystan didn't move.

"I don't know what you're talking about," he said calmly, but his voice was a little too high, like he was trying not to laugh.

Tucker pinched the bridge of his nose, watching the shrieking Brie assault Trystan. When he stood up, the kids in the wings fled, and went back to whatever they were supposed to be doing in the first place. Tucker's deep voice boomed, "Scott!" Trystan squinted and looked past the stage lights at an irate Tucker. "For the next week, your life belongs to me. Every free period, every lunch, every day. And so help me God, if you show up one minute late, I'm failing you." Trystan's eyes went wide. He held up his hands, stepping forward like he was going to protest, but Tucker cut him off, "NO! That's enough from you today. Jennings!" he yelled, calling to me.

I wanted to die. When Brie fell it was awesome, but I didn't want more attention from Tucker. I stepped out onto the stage again. When Tucker saw me, he said, "You two. Get your act together or you fail. It's that simple." He tossed Trystan a set of keys. They arced across the stage and Trystan reached out and grabbed them. "My classroom. Both of you. Practice until I come for you."

"Now?" Trystan asked, intentionally goading the teacher who was about to blow a gasket.

If Tucker was a cartoon, steam would be screeching out his ears. "NOW!"

Trystan nodded his head at me, and I followed him off the stage. We walked to the back and escaped through a side door. As I followed him down the hallway to Tucker's room I had to ask, "You did that on purpose?"

He glanced over his shoulder at me, a small smile on his lips, "Of course not." The playfulness in his voice was tantamount to saying, Hell yeah.

"Thanks," I replied.

Trystan stopped and turned toward me. "Brie had it coming. Besides, you took a few hits for me over the years. I figured I owed you one." He smiled at me softly and shrugged his shoulders, like it didn't matter. "Come on. Better get into Tucker's room before he finds us out here."

"Wait," I said, reaching for his shoulder. When my fingers touch him, Trystan stopped. His back was to me, but I could see the tension shoot up his spine like a steel rod. He breathed in slowly, like my touch bothered him. I lifted my hand and pulled it back. I felt foolish, and didn't know why.

Trystan turned and looked down at me, "What's the matter?"

"I don't have the play. We can't practice anything."

The corner of Trystan's mouth pulled up, "That was never my intention."

CHAPTER 14

~TRYSTAN~

When Tucker chewed out Mari, Trystan couldn't stand it, but if he said something or did something right then, everyone would know he cared about her. Besides, it was better to flip things around and humiliate Brie.

Trystan and Brie had been an item over a year ago, and Brie never let him forget it. She hung on him, acting like they were still together, which pissed off her current boyfriend beyond belief. Brie must have fantasied about the two of them fighting over her. Although Trystan knew how to throw a punch, that wasn't going to happen.

The entire thing worked out perfectly. As soon as he started saying his lines, Trystan knew what he was going to do. Brie walked right into it. Dipping her back like that made the rest of the dominoes fall in rapid succession. It was perfectly played. And here he was walking back to Tucker's room with Mari. Alone.

He slowed his pace a little, to match hers.

"I don't know how you dated her," Mari said.

Trystan stared straight ahead, "She seemed different then."

"Every girl seems different before you go out. It's not until after a few months that you see who they really are," Mari picked an imaginary piece of lint off her shirt.

Trystan looked at her out of the corner of his eye, smiling, "Yeah, and you'd know this because..."

"I've dated before, Trystan." She didn't look at him. Shrugging she continued, "He wasn't who I thought he was either. He was really sweet at first, and then he turned angry—controlling." She laughed like it was funny. Trystan felt jealousy twist around his heart and squeeze. Mari looked over at him, "I'm enough of a control-freak for two people in a relationship."

"No?" he said sarcastically, grinning at her.

She leaned into his side, bumping her shoulder to his. "You already knew that. Why do you think Tucker stuck us together in the first place?" She pointed her thumbs at her chest, "Control freak perfectionist. He probably thought I'd beat you with the play until you learned it." She was laughing, picturing swatting Trystan with a rolled up play book.

Mari thought she was uptight, but Trystan thought she just liked things a certain way. Whenever they were together, she made him feel happy to be alive. Everything else, every other thing that was weighing him down flittered away when she laughed. He loved that sound, so he made her laugh as much as possible.

"That would have been far more enjoyable," Trystan smirked with a wicked gleam in his eye.

Mari's jaw dropped in a wide smile and she laughed. "Only you would say that."

"Only you would offer."

Mari shook her head. The smile on her face was aching like it did when Trystan was around. "God, you're so—"

He stopped and turned toward her, "So what?"

They stood motionless for a moment. Trystan's heart raced in his chest, faster and faster as she stood there with her shiny pink lips pulled into that shy smile he loved. When her big chocolate eyes looked up at him from under those dark lashes, he wanted to kiss her. His eyes stayed locked on hers. The amused smirk he often wore around Mari lined his lips. Trystan put his hands behind his back, clutching them at the wrists so that he didn't try to kiss her again. Every inch of him was drawn to her. Smiling, he rocked up and down on his feet, his dark brow inching up his face waiting to hear what she had to say.

"Do you ever think about anything else?"

"Does this have something to do with the innuendo?" he grinned.

Mari's smile was perfect. She laughed and shook her head as she said, "You're starting to sound like Seth." She glanced up and down the hall and then leaned closer to Trystan. "We have a nickname for him, you know. Me and Katie call him Seth Sexbot." Trystan snorted, a wide grin spread across his lips. He watched Mari try to repress a giggle, but she couldn't. "When he's done, he says, I'll be back." She lowered her voice and said the phrase like the famous movie line.

Trystan burst out laughing. It made the grip on his wrists loosen and his shoulders hunch. He tried not to laugh too loudly, but he couldn't help it. The way she said it cracked him up. Mari touched his arm, leaning into him, and she said it again. And if it wasn't hysterical before, it was now. Trystan and Mari leaned into each other laughing so hard they thought they'd fall over.

Mrs. Collen came out of her classroom down the hall, "No loitering in the halls, Mr. Scott. Get to where you're going. Now."

That only fueled their giggles more. Trystan and Mari started to walk down the hallway again. They staggered along, trying to swallow their laughs. When they got to Tucker's door, Trystan could barely get the key in the lock.

Mrs. Collen was watching down the hall. Finally the key slipped in and the door opened. Mari pushed in first, followed by Trystan. They both laughed until they couldn't   breathe.

CHAPTER 15

~MARI~

After our laughter was spent, Trystan made himself comfortable on top of Tucker's desk. His long legs dangled off the sides. I sat opposite him on top of a student desk. For a moment neither of us said anything.

Then Trystan slumped and breathed in deeply. He leaned forward on his hands, which straddled his legs on the edge of the desk. "Can I ask you something?"

When people ask that question, it's never something simple. And from the weight in his voice, I knew it was something major. I nod, "Yeah, sure."

He looked up at me, his blue eyes somber. It makes him look older than he is. No smile lined his lips. "Have you heard of Day Jones? That Internet guy."

"Yes. Who hasn't?" He nodded slowly, like he was collecting his thoughts. Since that wasn't the question I expected him to ask, I was even more intrigued. I leaned forward, mirroring his posture. "What about him? Did they find out who he is yet?"

Trystan shook his head, "No. I don't think so. But it's not about that. It's about the song." His voice was too somber for this conversation. I didn't know where he was going with it, but it felt like something was wrong. Running his hands through his hair, he said, "I know it's just another guy with a guitar, but that song—the words— they're hard to ignore."

I nodded slowly, watching him watch his shoes nervously. "I know. I heard it once and the words were burned into my brain. It's haunting."

He looked up at me from beneath dark lashes, "I know. That's what I wanted to talk about." His voice was soft, quiet. I could barely hear him. This was so unlike him that he had my full attention. If a pin dropped right then, it would sound like a sonic boom. I didn't even breathe. It was too loud and before I knew it, I was leaning closer to him. Trystan didn't look up at me. Instead he stared at the floor, saying, "If you were… if you—"

Before he asked his question, the door was thrown open and Seth walked in. "What the hell are you doing in here?" Seth blurted out. As an afterthought, he turned to me and said, "Hey Virgin." That was the genius nickname he gave me.

I stared at him without answering, irritated that he'd shown up. Someone always showed up. Just when things with Trystan seemed real, one of his friends walked in. The Trystan I got a glimpse of immediately vanished like smoke in the wind.

Glaring at Seth, I thought, Go away. Go away. Go away. Seth can't read minds. He barely has one, but Trystan seemed equally annoyed that he walked in.

It was too quiet. It's like we were talking about something that we shouldn't have been, and when Seth walked in all conversation stopped. My skin prickled like this was an omen. I repressed the urge to shiver and smoothed my hands over my arms.

Something was off. The way Trystan's shoulders slumped, like he physically deflated when he saw Seth made me wonder why. It was a tiny movement, one that Seth failed to notice, but I did. Trystan straightened quickly and that smile he always wore spread across his mouth.

"Dude, did you really flash the entire auditorium with Brie Parker's panties?" Seth asked, grinning, practically vibrating with excitement.

Trystan let out a huff of air and ran his fingers through his hair, "Crap. Is that what they're saying? She's going to kill me."

Seth laughed, "What'd you do man? Because I really liked the locker room version. It had Brie bending over and—"

I cut him off, "Trystan bent her back for a kiss and then dropped her on the floor. By the way, you're disgusting." I folded my arms across my chest. Maybe I hated Brie, but I didn't want to hear what Seth was going to say. It made my skin crawl. Sex was a game to guys like him, and I didn't want to hear about it.

Seth's smile faded. His voice was hard, "Why are you always here? Every time I go looking for Trystan lately, there you are—sitting right next to him. You got a crush on him or something? Hoping for a pity bang?"

Mortification choked me. For a moment all I could do was blink. Trystan sat, shoulders slumped, on top of desk until Seth said that. Suddenly, he sat upright. His tone warning, "Seth."

When I found my voice I said, "Hanging out with him would suck way less if you weren't around."

Seth laughed, "Funny. I was telling Trystan the same thing." He shook his head like I wasn't worth his time. Then he turned to his friend, "Come on, man. Let's get out of here. There's a set of twins working the 7-Eleven and they both have double Ds on the rack." He laughed like he was hysterical.

Trystan smirked, but shook his head. "Can't. Tucker has us in lock down."

"So that's why you're with her? Tucker's punishing you by strapping you to a boring chick?" Seth glanced at me while he spoke. His brows pinched together when he looked back up at Trystan.

"Something like that," Trystan replied. "Either way, if I leave this room, I don't graduate. And if you stay here and Tucker sees you, I suspect you'll be joining us. A week of in-school detention, Tucker style."

Seth's face fell. "You mean—?"

"No free periods, no lunch, no after school, nothing. For the next week I'm in here every day. Better run before he adds your name to the list."

Seth turned toward the door, ready to leave, but he still didn't seem to believe Trystan. Before pulling the door open, he stopped and asked over his shoulder, "What about the virgin? Did she piss Tucker off too?"

Before I could answer, Trystan slid off the desk. Walking toward his friend, he nodded and said, "As a matter of fact, yeah, she did. Get the hell out of here before he sees you. And if you head back this way before practice is over, sneak us some snacks."

"What makes you think I'm going without you?" Seth asked. He huffed like a little boy that was told he couldn't have more cookies.

"Please. Double Ds on twins. You're going to be there for the rest of the afternoon," Trystan slapped his friend on the shoulder and pushed him through the door.

Before Seth was gone, he hissed, "Don't do it. For god's sake, don't fucking do it." They stared at each other. Apparently Seth knew Trystan better than he let on. The two looked like they were having a showdown. I couldn't tell who won, but eventually, Trystan lowered his gaze and gave a nod before shoving Seth out the door. When he pushed the door closed, Trystan stood there with his back to me for a moment. He didn't turn around. He didn't speak.

Pressing my lips together, I slid off the desk and walked over to him. "What'd you want to tell me? About the song?"

Trystan turned. His plastic smile was firmly in place, his lighthearted nature on full display. It was disarming, but I knew exactly what he was doing. "It was nothing. Just curious if you heard it, that's all." He looked me in the eye as he lied to my face.

CHAPTER 16

~TRYSTAN~

Damn, he lied to her. Trystan didn't want things like this. He sighed, and ran his fingers through his hair.

"What's with you lately? One second your all intense and the next you're all smiles." Mari asked.

Trystan looked up at her, his eyes drinking in her face. What if Seth was wrong? What if Mari liked him? That look said she cared, but he didn't know what to do. Heart pounding, he said, "It's her. The girl. I feel lost, Mari. I can't take it much longer."

She was quiet for a moment. Mari watched him sitting on the desk. The smile fell off his lips as Trystan leaned forward, putting all his weight on his hands, and stared at the floor. His voice sounded strained.

"Then tell her," she urged.

Trystan glanced up at her from under his brow. The way she looked at him made him think he should. That if he said it, she would believe him. But Seth's words rang through his mind. The image of the bullet being fired from the gun, and the inability to take it back. Once he said it, there was no going back.

Silence filled the room. Mari finally said, "What do you have to lose? It's not like you're friends. It's not like you'd be risking one relationship for the other, so—" The way he looked at her when she spoke made the floor of her stomach fall. She stopped midsentence. "You already know her, don't you?"

"She's one of my best friends," he answered softly. "I doubt she even realizes it."

Mari's brown gaze was hypnotic. Trystan couldn't look away even though it pulled him in deeper. The feeling in his stomach, the alluring pull that made him reckless urged him to say it, but Trystan kept his jaw locked. She had to figure it out on her own. That's the only way she'll believe me, he thought.

But Mari didn't say anything. She remained lost in Trystan's gaze, her dark curls dangling over her shoulders as she sat on the desk across from him. It felt like time stopped. Trystan didn't want to blink. He wanted to remember this moment, everything about it. The way her perfectly pink lips were slightly parted, the way she leaned toward him like she knew, and the way her eyes locked with his—he could feel the connection with her in his core. It tugged at him at first, calling him back to her. But now it assaulted him day and night. There was nothing without Mari.

Pulse pounding in his ears, Trystan didn't notice Tucker until the door scraped open. Trystan quickly looked away, breaking the connection. The stirring in his stomach faded and it felt like he lost part of himself.

"Off," Tucker snapped at Trystan.

Trystan slid off the teacher's desk and walked around to sit a row over and behind Mari. She watched him pass, but he couldn't tell what she was thinking, if she knew he was talking about her.

"You two are pushing your luck. You are aware of that, right?" Tucker said looking at each of them.

"I didn't do anything to Brie," Mari said, but Tucker held up his hand and she stopped speaking.

"Your job, Jennings, is to get them out onto the stage at the right time."

"She did it on purpose," Mari muttered.

"So was Trystan's little stunt." He looked back at Trystan. "That little stunt should have been a suspension, Scott."

"There's no way to prove it was intentional," Trystan replied dryly. "She punched me in the head and I dropped her. Could have happened to anyone."

"That kind of crap doesn't happen to guys like you," Tucker replied. Beads of sweat lined his face, "Enough of this.

Whatever is going on with you Scott has to stop. Get back on stage and do it right this time." Trystan slid off the desk and walked out the door.

As he left the classroom he could hear Mari defending herself, but he knew Tucker wouldn't listen. Brie had him wrapped around her little finger.

CHAPTER 17

~MARI~

I left practice early, since Tucker said he couldn't stand the sight of me. The only reason he called Trystan back was because he was needed or they couldn't practice. As I left the building, Katie caught up with me.

"Hey, why are you leaving early?" she ran up next to me, smiling, happy to have someone to walk home with.

"Tucker tossed me." Before she could ask, I added, "Brie set me up, Tucker made an example. My life sucks. What else is new?"

"That was harsh. He threw you out?"

I nodded, "Yeah. Why are you still here?"

She grinned, "Math help. I needed a tutor."

"Jack King is the teacher's aide at the extra help session again, isn't he?"

"Yes, and I seriously need extra help when I'm around him." She fanned herself, and laughed, "He's so hot that I can't think. Oh, and his cologne. Damn, when he's standing over my shoulder... Well, you know."

"You're horrible, you know that?" I laughed as I said it.

Katie said, "So what's up? You avoid Trystan all day like I said?" I didn't answer. "Mari! What'd you do?"

"Nothing," I replied not wanting to talk about it. The truth was I had no idea what happened. One moment Trystan was going to tell me something about Day Jones, the next he says he's having girl issues. If I didn't know better, I would have thought he was talking about me. But that's impossible. I pushed aside the thought. It was a little too close to a dream to even consider. Things that raise my hope, that teeter on the edge of impossibility, only hurt harder when I smacked face-first into the ground.

Katie stopped walking. We were standing in front of the school where the buses drop off. There wasn't anyone else around. "Stop letting him screw with your head. The guy's a player Mari. Look at his best friend for chrissakes. Seth Sexbot." She shook her head, her eyebrows rising with her voice.

"He's not like that," the words slipped out of my mouth before I realized what I was saying.

Katie grabbed both my shoulders and shook me, "Do you hear yourself? He's not like that? Is there anyone in that entire group of theater girls that he hasn't nailed?"

"Me," I said softly.

"Exactly," she said forcefully. Katie had always been like a sister to me. She said what I needed to hear, which wasn't always what I wanted to hear. This time, I definitely did not want to hear it. It was like she could tell. Her hands flew as she spoke, "Wake up Mari. He's not that kind of guy. You're the only one. Get a clue. If he's paying attention to you, now you know why. Seth and him aren't that different, it just looks different for the girl. Trystan's seduction is more tempting, but in the end you're just another chick to check off the list." Her words smashed into me. I didn't want to hear them. It felt like she was throwing bricks at my stomach. I wanted to double over and cry. Katie wrapped her arm around my shoulders. I didn't shirk her off. Softly, she said, "He'll hurt you." The quiver in her voice was like being doused by cold water.

My first boyfriend hurt me. He was the only one I was serious about and Katie knew it. Trystan was not a step up. If anything, he was a step down and backwards. He'd hurt me. In the end, he would. It's the way he was. Katie was right. I'd seen it over and over again.

Sitting next to him in the prop room I'd asked him once, "Why is your life expectancy on relationships so short? They don't die that fast, you know. There's more there than sex."

He'd looked at me with those glittering blue eyes. A wicked grin lined his lips. "Not that I've seen."

"You haven't stayed long enough to find out." His answer had upset me. As if he could tell, he looked around to make sure no one saw.

When he leaned in close to my ear he said, "I haven't found anyone worth staying for."

"That's because you're dating the skank squad, Trystan." I rolled my eyes as I said it.

"And you'd be different?" he said amused. "How?"

I didn't answer him that day. I dated with my whole heart and there was no way I was giving it to someone who would tear it out of my chest without a backward glance. Katie thought Trystan was that person.

I nodded at Katie, "I know you're right. I'm just having trouble getting my head and my heart in the same place."

Katie slid her arm down and side hugged me, practically squeezing me to death. "Ah, I know how to fix that. Your heart is easily confused. Let's toss some chocolate at it and next time you get a free period, come and drool at Mathboy with me."

"Deal," I said, not bothering to explain that it wouldn't be for a week. If she knew I was stuck with Trystan for several additional hours every day, she'd insist that I transfer to a new school. Maybe it was inevitable. Maybe Trystan was destined to break my heart. I didn't want to find out.

CHAPTER 18

~TRYSTAN~

Trystan slipped away from practice as soon as humanly possible. There was no food at home. He'd have to run into the deli and hope Sam was still there.

The door chimed as he walked inside the small shop. The deli wasn't big, but the owner was great. Trystan called out, "Sam? You here?"

A small man with dark skin walked out of the back room, "Trystan Scott. What can I do for you?"

"Can we barter this week?"

Sam walked up to the counter and looked at Trystan. He knew the kid was on his own and had been for some time. Whatever so-called parent was supposed to be taking care of him deserved a punch in the face. Trystan was a good kid. "Sure, grab whatever you need and set it up here."

Trystan went through the shop grabbing what he needed, checking dates, and trying to pick up things that had been reduced. When he was done, there were two bags filled with food. Sam tallied the items as he put them in. "Not bad. Only $45. You can work that off in one day."

Trystan had done the math in his head as he picked up the items. "No charity, Sam. You shaved off nine bucks."

Sam's face reddened a little. He looked down at his pad and said, "It's not charity. I was going to throw those things out."

"We do this every couple weeks, Sam. I try to get as little as possible and you always forget to add something in. Come on, I don't want a hand out. I'm good for it. I'll work Saturday and Sunday, the 5:00am shift. I'll see you then." Trystan reached for the bags.

Sam pushed the groceries toward the young man. "You're a good kid. Don't let anyone tell you otherwise."

Trystan smiled at the old guy. It was a lopsided grin, filled with pride. Sam was one of the few people who could evoke that emotion. Trystan nodded and headed out the door.

When he arrived home, he swallowed hard. His dad was home. The lights were blazing in the windows, the sound of the television wafted out the front door.

Trystan pulled opened the rusted screen, balancing the paper bag on his hip. Nights like this made him what he was—an actor, a liar. His dad was a thin man well past his prime. He sat in a tee shirt and shorts in front of the TV with a beer can in his hand. It was still early. He'd move onto the hard stuff later.

"Where the hell have you been?" Dad grumbled not bothering to look at his son.

"School. Then I stopped at the store for some food. I got some of that pasta you like. I thought I'd make it for us for dinner." It felt like he was walking on egg shells. Dad worked to pay the bills, but he didn't bother buying food or cooking. Trystan learned how to use the stove before most kids could tie their shoes.

Dad scoffed, "You expect me to believe that?" Trystan didn't bother pointing to the grocery bags. He knew it was pointless. "I'm talking to you, boy. When are you going to stop lying to me?"

Trystan stepped in front of his father, blocking his view of the TV. One grocery bag was clutched in each arm. "I'm not lying."

"Then what the hell is this?" his dad asked, holding up a guitar. Trystan's heart clenched. For a second all he could do was stare. He'd hidden it, locked it in his room. "Yeah, I thought so. My son's a fag, singing fairy songs around a campfire. Perfect."

Trystan saved his money forever to get that instrument. It was an acoustic guitar with honey wood. It came from a second-hand shop, but it still cost more than he had. He saved his money for months to get it. Since then it'd been hidden in his room at the top of his closet. He'd put enough stuff around it to block it from view. But that didn't matter since it was sitting on his father's lap.

Trystan tried smiling. Ignoring the comments, he walked to the kitchen counter and placed the groceries down. Part of him hoped the guitar would be forgotten, but his dad kept it clutched on his lap. Trystan made dinner. It was a generic Hamburger Helper without the meat. He walked a plate of it over to his dad. Last time they'd eaten it, he liked it a lot. This time was different. Trystan would never forget this time.

When he reached out to hand Dad his plate, the old man swatted at it. "I'm not eating that shit. You stole it. Like you stole this!" Dad shot out of his chair. Trystan watched the plate go flying, the noodles stuck to the wall before they slid down leaving a rust colored stain in their wake.

Trystan took a deep breath, trying to brace himself. He knew it was coming. There was no reasoning with him when he was like this. It was one of the few times Trystan wished his dad was a sip away from passing out. But he wasn't and he was angry. "I bought it, Dad. I have a job."

"You think I can't provide for you? Is that it?" He advanced on his son.

Trystan stepped back. "No, that's not it. You work hard. You shouldn't have to cook and get groceries too." It's not what he thought, but now wasn't the time for that.

"Damn right," his father said, taking another step forward. "I take care of you. I give you everything I have. Everything. And you repay me like this." He pointed to the guitar. Shaking his head, Dad looked down at the instrument. One second he was calm, like he was going to hand it back, but Trystan saw the tell. His father's lips pressed together tightly, his biceps twitching as tension corded his muscles tighter and tighter.

The guitar swung forward and smashed against the floor. It made a cacophony of notes and cracking wood as it splintered. Wood flew through the room as the strings popped off one by one. His father held the neck of the broken instrument in his hands. A single string was still attached.

Trystan swallowed hard. Rage flowed through his body, barely in check. He wanted this to end, but there was nowhere else to go. He had to stay here until graduation. That was his way out. He'd already spoken to the military recruiter. He had to keep his nose clean until then. He couldn't fight back.

"Put it down," Trystan said, his voice deeper than usual.

Dad laughed, as he stepped forward, brandishing the piece of the guitar like a weapon. "Why don't you make me? Show me who's the man here, Trystan." Without warning, his Dad's arm swung. The piece of wood collided into Trystan's thigh, sending a sharp burst of pain through his hip.

Knowing it was pointless to talk, he turned and bounded down the hallway to his room. He ran inside and pushed the door shut. His hand reached for the deadbolt, but grabbed only air. It was gone. "Shit," Trystan said, panicked.

Just then his dad tried to crash through the door. Trystan kept his body braced against it to keep him out. With each slam, Trystan flinched. Just like old times, he thought. But now I'm old enough to keep you out, even without the lock.

Trystan knew the old man wouldn't learn. He'd keep beating the door until he passed out or Trystan did from lack of sleep. Hours passed. His father screamed at him for the first few, but eventually it grew quiet. Trystan slid down the door, but kept his body pressed against it, ready to brace himself if his dad tried to force it open again.

It was after 1:00am the next time he heard his dad's voice, "It was your fault, you know."

Pain shot through Trystan's heart, threatening to tear him in half. He'd always thought it was his fault, but hearing his dad say it was unbearable. He swallowed the knot in his throat and replied, "I never said it wasn't."

"You were too much for her. She said it over and over again."

He didn't remember his mother leaving. There were no pictures of her, only faded memories that he wasn't even sure were real. Trystan hung his head, lowering it to his knees. His arms were wrapped around his ankles, his back still pressed firmly to the door.

"Never fall in love, Trystan. It's the fastest way into hell. Once you're there, you can't escape." The sound of the bottle clunking against the floor told him that it was empty. Dad would pass out any second.

Trystan's eyes blurred, partly from weariness, partly because he saw himself in his father. Dad let love destroy him and Trystan was doing the same thing.

CHAPTER 19

~MARI~

Later that night, I tossed my backpack on my bed and went to my computer. Before I could turn on the screen, my mom popped up in the doorway.

"Absolutely not, young lady." I cringed. She only called me that when I did something wrong. It was the verbal equivalent of smacking a dog on the snout with a newspaper. She thinks that I crapped on the carpet.

"What'd I do?"

Tapping her foot with her arms folded over her chest, she asked sharply, "What do you think?"

Shaking my head, I said, "I don't know. There are so many things—"

She stepped toward me and the rest of my snark died on my lips. "Your English teacher called today. He said you weren't behaving in class. Is it true? Did you really fall asleep in class? How could you!"

I took a breath to steady myself, "I didn't fall asleep. Some girl missed her cue and Tucker took it out on me. She lied, Mom. I told her. I was awake and doing my part. You know the drama class has a diva in it. I pissed off the diva and she got me in trouble."

"How'd you piss her off?"

I shrug, "No idea, but I doubt her attack was random. She's a bitch, but she only does stuff like that when it makes her look good." I laughed, remembering the look on her face when Trystan dropped her. Brie is going to be gunning for him now. The two had been an item at one point, which was another reason why I shouldn't be infatuated with Trystan Scott.

Mom sighed and closed her eyes. When she opened them again, she seemed calmer. "You have detention all week?" I nod.

"Well, do whatever you have to and stay away from Brie. Her mother is equally mental." She turned and started to walk out of my room. Before she left she said over her shoulder, "Don't let this affect your other classes. Make sure you keep up with your homework, Mari."

"I've got it covered, Ma."

When she left I turned back to the computer and pulled up the YouTube video of Day Jones. I listened to the song again, loving it even more. He was perfect. Everything I wanted was in that song. The way he sang to her was so real. His voice was filled with so much pain, so much longing. His words stuck with me long after the music stopped.

"Who are you?" I asked the screen. I bet I sounded like every other teenage girl in America, drooling over Day Jones.

My gaze lingered on the comments, and I scrolled down. Day didn't say anything else, but there were agents on there saying they wanted to represent him. Scrolling further, I saw a post from a record label with instructions to contact them. Wow. I sat there in shock staring at the screen.

Day Jones looked like he was on his way to being a hit, but he remained hidden. I wondered if he was chronically shy or burned in acid or something. Most people wanted to be rich and famous, and from the look of it, that was where Day Jones' song would take him.

Lunch was my first free period. I walked to detention, rounding the corner just as Trystan did. We nearly collided.

Reaching out, he took my hand and pulled me towards Tucker's room, "His clock is fast. We need to hurry." Just as we stepped into the room, the class clock ticked.

Tucker's gut hung over his belt, "Cutting it too close, you two."

We both nodded, and for once Trystan was quiet.

Tucker dabbed beads of sweat from his forehead with a handkerchief and led us to his massive closet. It looked like a bomb went off. Papers, books, and plays were everywhere. There was no order, no way to find anything. The gruff man pocketed his hankie and walked into the closet and flicked the light on.

"The two of you will be doing this for the rest of today. Clean it. Make it look brand new. You," he said pointing to me, "Pay attention because Scott will forget." I glanced at Trystan, wondering if it bothered him that the teacher thought he was a moron. I wondered if the forgetfulness was an act.

Tucker pointed a chubby finger at the dusty shelves. "Novels there, plays there, and textbooks there. Roll up the posters and put them in that box. Just make it clean and organized with the rest of this stuff. Put the old stuff we don't use on the top shelves." I open my mouth to ask how we can tell which stuff is old, but Tucker cut me off, "You'll know. If it looks like something from a previous decade, shelve it. Funding is too dismal to throw anything out," he grumbled, walking out of the closet.

While he showed us where to put things, Trystan and I hung back in the doorway looking in. His classroom was empty since it was Tucker's lunch hour. The sound of the clock ticking filled my ears. When Tucker exited the closet, he shoved in a chair to stand on and held open the door. I walked through and surveyed the mess. When I looked up, Trystan was still standing on the other side of the door.

"Get in there, Scott," Tucker said, pushing on Trystan's back, making him step into the closet with me. "And if I find out that she did all the work, your free period tomorrow will suck even more. Get to it." Tucker released the knob and the heavy oak door closed. We were alone.

Trystan breathed in deeply, which made him sneeze. It was insanely dusty in there.

"It's not that bad," I said to him, trying to move the chair to the other corner. The closet was a walk-in. It had shelves that stretched floor to ceiling. There was just enough room for Trystan and me to move around without bumping into each other. If Tucker stayed we would have felt like sardines. Thankfully he left. Since it was his lunch hour, we wouldn't see him again until the bell rang. I ran my finger over a shelf and it came up coated in white dust. "Gross."

Trystan tossed me a damp towel that Tucker left behind with a small bucket. We wiped down the shelves, moving things around in silence. Eventually Trystan and I ended up shoulder to shoulder. He'd pick up something off the shelf and look at it while I wiped up the dust.

"What the hell does he use this stuff for?" Trystan was holding a record in his hands, flipping it over. He glanced around, "There isn't anything to play it on."

I shrugged, "Maybe his mom gave it to him. It's sentimental."

Trystan snort-laughed. "Yeah, I can see that." He cleared his throat and spoke in a girlie voice, "Here's your present for getting a teaching job at Dilapidated High." I smiled as he said it, trying not to laugh. When he did Tucker's voice, I couldn't help myself. "Oh! A linguistics record!" He pressed his hands together, "Just what I always wanted." He impersonated Tucker down to the last syllable.

"Stop it," I laughed, snapping the dirty towel at him. "I don't know about you, but I want to have time to eat something when we're done."

"You think we'll finish this in less than an hour? Are you insane?"

A tilt of my head said yes we will and no I'm not crazy. "This is nothing. It just looks messy." I took the chair and slid it against the shelves so I could reach the top. "How about you hand me stuff and I'll organize it and make it look nice."

Trystan handed me records, posters, and other archaic teaching aides. I put them on the upper shelves as neatly as possible while we talked.

Trystan handed me another poster. I reached, trying to get it on the back of the top shelve with the others. The chair started to slip, but Trystan stopped it. His hands shot out, gripping my legs as I lost my balance and clutched the shelves.

"Whoa. Easy, Mari." Clutching the shelf, I laughed lightly and looked down at him. Trystan's grip on my legs loosened, and he stepped back.

"Sorry, I'm a bit of a klutz." When I released the shelf my hands were shaking. I couldn't hide it from him.

"No, you're fine. Where's your lunch? I'll go grab it. You're probably just hungry." I told him where it was and he turned to the door to get it, but when he tried to turn the knob, it wouldn't twist. Trystan looked at the knob, still gripping it in his hand. His shoulders tensed. "It's locked."

"What?" I squeaked, climbing off the chair, and nearly falling into Trystan's back. I hopped a step to keep from falling and only smacked into Trystan a little bit. The room suddenly felt too small. My heart was racing.

When my hand touched Trystan's back, he jumped. He pressed his forehead to the door. I shoved past him to try the knob myself. When it didn't open I felt insane, "Oh my God!" I beat my hands against the door, hoping someone was out there. "Help! Let us out!" I screamed.

Trystan grabbed my wrists, and stopped me. "No one is out there. Tucker's at lunch. Don't bother."

I felt frantic. When I spoke, my voice was too high, too tense, "I can't be locked in here. I can't. There's not enough air."

"Awh, fuck," Trystan said pushing his hand through his hair. "You're claustrophobic?"

"No," my voice was wispy and light. It hardly came out as I stared at the door unblinking. "I just don't want to suffocate in a closet."

He grabbed my shoulders and turned me around, "You won't. Listen to me. It's fine. There's more than enough air in here. It's the same as before." I nodded slowly as he spoke, staring into space. Panic was licking at the inside of my belly making me jumpy. Trystan continued to speak in soothing tones. When I didn't answer him, he pulled me down to the floor with him. We both sat against the door, hip to hip. "Put your fingers here," he pulled my hand to the gap between the door and the floor. Cool air rushed over my fingers. There was a slight breeze, almost. The fear gripping my heart faded a little.

Looking over at him, I asked, "How'd you know that would help?"

"You wouldn't believe that I sleep in a closet under the stairs, would you?" I smiled a little and tried to fold my arms over my chest. Trystan held onto my hand, so I couldn't move it. "Keep it there. Feeling cooler moving air helps." I nodded and left my hands by the gap under the door. Trystan started to talk about other things, things that would distract me. While he spoke I wondered how much time he spent in small spaces. He was tense, every muscle wound tight like he hated it, but he didn't freak out the way I did.

Eventually I asked, "You have it, too? Don't you?"

Silence was my answer. Trystan smoothed his thumb over the back of my hand. Looking at the floor he said, "Maybe. I got stuck in the closet once when I was little. Spent an entire day there before they found me. At least we have light in here. For some reason it's worse when it's dark." He stroked my smooth skin as he spoke. His gaze was distant, like he was remembering something he wanted to forget.

I nodded slowly, and took a deep breath trying to steady my pulse. "He's going to kill us—Tucker, I mean. We didn't do much."

"He locked us in a closet and left the room. I don't think he'll say anything to anyone," Trystan said flatly.

After a moment, I ask, "How much time is left?"

"I don't know. My watch is in my locker. I took it off for gym and forgot to put it back on this morning."

I glanced down at our hands between us, noticing the gentle way he stroked my skin. Trystan watched me. When I lifted my gaze, his eyes met mine. My stomach twisted and suddenly the locked door didn't frighten me so much. Trystan's eyes bore into me. I could feel it. Combined with his touch, I couldn't breathe.

"Mari," he said softly, his eyes fixated on my lips like he wanted to taste them. When his blue gaze finally lifted to my eyes, it felt like I'd die. Every inch of my body was screaming for his touch, but my mind was chastising me, echoing Katie's words of warning to stay away from him.

A kiss meant something. Trystan's kisses didn't. But that wasn't enough to make me move. He turned toward me and lifted his hand to my cheek. His fingers slid across my face, slowly moving toward my lips. His gaze was intense, his breathing slow and steady. When his finger touched my lips, he leaned closer, closing the space between us. My heart pounded in my chest.

Frantic cries for help rang out in my mind. Where the hell was Seth when you needed him? I couldn't do this. I couldn't kiss him.

Trystan's thumb was on my lip, stroking it like he savored the sensation. He leaned in painfully slow, stopping when he was within a breath of my lips. His hands laced back into my hair and I couldn't move. Every inch of me wanted to feel his lips on mine. My mind was the only part warring within me. Trembling, I sat perfectly still, my eyes locked on his, watching him, waiting for the kiss I didn't want. It would melt my brain. It would make me want him more.

Instead of closing the space, Trystan stayed there. Blinking slowly, he said, "Kiss me." His voice was deeper than usual, his tone gentle. "Kiss me, Mari."

The request made butterflies swarm in my stomach. Trystan's hands were splayed on my cheeks. All I had to do was lean in. He was less than an inch from me. When he spoke those sexy words, his breath on my lips made me shudder. I didn't want the moment to end, but this wasn't real. This was Trystan locked in a closet with a girl and making the most of it. Kisses didn't mean anything to him and I'd already given him one of mine. He couldn't have another.

When the thought crossed my mind, I pressed my lips together and looked down. It broke the eye contact that had me paralyzed. My pulse roared in my ears. It felt like I couldn't suck in air fast enough. Trystan's hands slid down to my shoulders, and he pulled me to him, holding my forehead to his. He closed his eyes, breathing hard. Neither of us moved. We sat like that too long. I savored the feeling of his hands on my shoulders, feeling their strength and warmth, and pictured them holding me tight.

It felt like forever, but it could have been only a few minutes. I don't know. But when we heard footfalls coming toward the closet, we broke apart. There was remorse in his gaze, almost like Trystan didn't want this to end. It made my heart lurch, but I let him go. Trystan jumped up and sat on the chair. The way he looked down at me broke my heart. There was a haunted expression in his eyes. It was the one he hid at all cost. It only appeared when he was really upset and today it was crystal clear.

CHAPTER 20

~TRYSTAN~

When Tucker closed the closet door, Trystan's heart slapped into his ribs. He swallowed hard and tried to ignore it. Ever since he was a little kid, he didn't like being confined to small spaces. His father had thrown him in a dark closet too many times to not be affected by it. At least there was a light in here. And it's not like they were locked in. Trystan followed Mari's lead and helped her clean until she nearly fell. Things changed after that. Finding the door locked, Trystan tensed even more. It wasn't until he realized Mari was freaking out that he snapped out of it.

Sitting with her was bliss. Trystan tried to be content feeling the smooth skin on her hand, but he wanted more. He needed her. They'd be good together. If she gave him a chance she'd see it. But Trystan knew he'd said too many things too many times for her to give him that chance. She'd be crazy if she did.

After a moment, Trystan noticed her gaze on his hand. She watched him slide his thumb across her skin and when she looked up at him, Trystan couldn't help it. The way her eyes met his, like she was frightened. He wanted to protect her. He wanted to hold her close and tell her it would be okay, but all he could do was return her gaze. Every second he maintained that connection was another second he knew he loved her.

"Mari..." He breathed her name like it was life. Watching her, he felt the pull—the magnetic lock—that drew him to her. Those pink lips were so smooth, so perfect. He wanted to kiss her. He wanted to taste her. He wanted to learn the curves of her mouth and feel her kiss him back—and not because she was rehearsing some lines from a play. He wanted her to kiss him back because she wanted to, because she felt something for him.

Trystan's hand slowly floated toward Mari's face. She sat perfectly still, her eyes locked with his, her breath slowly filling her body again and again. She seemed as hypnotized as he was. Trystan leaned closer to her, but instead of kissing her, he rested his finger on her lips. He traced his finger along her lower lip, feeling how soft it was before tracing the bow on her upper lip. Mari didn't move. She seemed lost in his eyes. The fluttering in Trystan's stomach increased to intolerable when he traded his pointer finger for his thumb. Rubbing his thumb gently on her lower lip, he thought about tasting that lip. He thought about leaning forward, closing the short distance between them, and kissing her.

But he couldn't do that to her. She'd think he took advantage of her. No, she had to want him to.

"Kiss me," he breathed. His lips were so close to hers. She barely had to move, but it made all the difference. If she kissed him, it would be all right. His heart pounded wildly. Trystan's skin felt like it was on fire. He'd never done this before and any girl this close to his lips would have kissed him instantly, but Mari didn't move.

Lost in her gaze, he whispered, "Kiss me, Mari." His heart soared when he said it a second time. Saying her name, asking her to kiss him made him feel every inch of his body. He burned for her touch. There was nothing he wanted more. Thoughts of Mari filled his mind every waking moment, and when he dreamed he thought of her.

Mari seemed like she was going to kiss him. She didn't pull away. Her body was strung as tight as Trystan's. He could see it in her eyes and feel it in her breath as it flowed over his lips. When his hands tangled in her hair, he didn't think he could wait any more. Mari finally blinked, breaking the moment, and turned her face away from him. She looked down, but Trystan didn't release her. Instead he lowered his hands to her shoulders and pulled her forehead to his.

For the next few moments no one said anything. He kept his hands on her, steadying her, feeling the curve of her shoulders beneath her shirt. Trystan focused on the sound of her breathing, fighting the urge to pull her into his arms. When Tucker showed up, the moment shattered.

CHAPTER 21

~MARI~

My chest rose as I breathed in deeply, trying to steady myself. I remained seated against the door, and when Tucker pulled it open, I fell out backward.

"Miss Jennings," he started to scold me, but Trystan cut him off.

"You locked us in the closet. Correction, you locked a claustrophobic girl in a closet. With no lunch." Trystan didn't move from the chair. He was sitting forward, leaning on his elbows. He looked up at Tucker, his voice filled with unspoken threats.

Tucker's expression changed from fury to shock. He bent over to help me up, sputtering apologizes. "I had no idea. Why didn't you say something?"

Before I could reply, Tryst said, "I don't think the school board will care why she didn't say anything. I think they'll be more interested to learn why the door was locked with us inside." Trystan stood and faced Tucker after he deposited me at a desk.

"If you have something to say, Scott, say it." Tucker tensed as he spoke. This was the kind of mistake that would be severely reprimanded and Trystan knew it.

Trystan slipped his hands into his pockets and shrugged. "How about a trade? Mine and Miss Jennings' silence for free period passes for the rest of the semester."

"You're blackmailing me?" Tucker growled.

Trystan walked past him and stopped next to me. "No, it's a trade. Something that helps you for something that helps us."

Tucker turned to look at me, but Trystan stood between us. Trystan squared his broad shoulders like he needed to protect me. "You're lucky I was in there, or you would have opened the door and found her hyperventilated on the floor. The passes make up for it."

It was strange. The way Trystan acted, the way he flew between me and Tucker. I was slightly horrified by Trystan's demands, but I was too frazzled to interject.

"Where will you go? You can't wander the school." Tucker's hand was on his double chin like he was considering it.

"The prop room. Leave the door unlocked. You can check on us if you want." Trystan folded his arms over his chest. The way he said it was insane. It didn't sound like he was asking at all. He was telling Tucker what he wanted for his silence. I expected Tucker to say no.

But he didn't. Instead, he crossed the room to his desk and grabbed two passes. "If you get caught, I had nothing to do with this."

Trystan walked up behind him and stopped on the other side of the desk. They faced each other. "If we get caught, you'll tell them you gave us permission. This is an all or nothing kind of deal, unless you want us to mention parts of what happened today. There are several parts that sound kind of damning."

Tucker scribbled on the pass, taking in a deep breath as Trystan spoke. When he finished, Tucker handed Trystan the two passes. "It was a mistake."

"Yes, it was." Trystan took the passes, turned and collected me, and walked out of the classroom leaving Tucker behind.

CHAPTER 22

~TRYSTAN~

"Are you okay?" Trystan asked.

Mari hadn't spoken. She glanced at him vacantly, "Yeah. Yes. That was just unreal. I can't believe you did that."

Trystan didn't understand why. He walked next to her. As they rounded the corner, he pulled open the side door to the auditorium and walked to the first row of seats. Trystan held out his hand and said, "Sit down. Eat. You'll feel better."

Mari stepped past him and took her lunch out of her bag. She nibbled on half a sandwich as Trystan watched her. His heart was in his throat. He wanted to know what she was thinking, but she didn't speak. After a moment she looked over at him. "Where's your lunch?"

Trystan leaned back in the chair. "Lunch isn't until next period. I'll go grab something then."

Mari nodded and looked down at her sandwich. She moved slowly, like she was shell-shocked. "I have study hall next period."

Trystan smiled at her. "No you don't. Not anymore. You're needed in the prop room for the rest of the semester. Tucker's orders." He handed her the pass.

Mari stared at it before saying, "I can't use this. I can't be here with you... Trystan—"

"Of course you can," Trystan's heart was sinking. The more she came back to herself, the more mortified she looked.

"I can't. I shouldn't be here with you..." It seemed like she was going to say more, but Mari's voice trailed off. Her eyes looked everywhere but at Trystan.

His stomach fell into his shoes. "I understand. It's okay. Do what you have to do." He made sure his voice sounded light even though her words made him physically ache.

Shaking her head she said, "No, you don't understand." Trystan tried to say something, but Mari cut him off. "I can't do this. It's killing me and you're just playing me, and I'm falling for it." She stood as she spoke and rubbed the heels of her hands into her eyes.

Trystan tried to calm her. He didn't want her to think that. He wasn't playing her. He lifted his hands to her elbows as she rubbed her eyes. Touching her lightly he said, "This isn't a game. It's not, Mari."

She let out a rush of air and dropped her arms to her sides. Mari stared at him, her lips parted like she wanted to say something but she only shook her head. Grabbing her books, she swallowed hard, "I know what it is. It's the same thing it's been with every girl. It's never a game in the beginning, is it Trystan? She catches your eye and you can't fathom being with anyone else. That is until you sleep with her." A tear rolled down her cheek. "I've been burned before. I can't do it again. I won't. And not with you, so stop this charade or whatever you want to call it.

End this seduction scene you created. You're wasting your time. I don't like you that way. I never have. I never will."

Trystan absorbed her words, internalizing them until each one exploded inside of him. She thought it was a game. It was worse than he feared. Mari's words weren't sharp, they were pleading—begging him to stop, but he couldn't. He loved her. It wasn't random. It wasn't a quest. He didn't care if he slept with her or not. He just wanted to be around her, hear her voice, and feel the curve of her body in his arms. And now he didn't even have that.

He swallowed hard and sat in the chair facing the stage. Trystan didn't look at Mari. He didn't respond.

Mari's voice shook, "I'm serious, Trystan. Stay away from me." She turned on her heel and walked out the door, leaving him behind.

Trystan stared straight ahead, not blinking. He felt his heart shattering as she spoke, but there was no way to stop it. He let her leave, he let her walk away. She begged him to stop, to keep away from her.

Trystan leaned forward and put his face in his hands, knowing he just lost his best friend.

CHAPTER 23

~MARI~

It took me a while to calm down. I spent study hall in the girl's room trying to stop crying. Eventually Katie came in.

I heard her voice echo when she walked through the door. "I know you're in here. Melissa Drury saw you come in." Katie walked toward the stalls and bent over, looking for shoes. "Come on, Mari. Come out." She stopped in front of my stall. I was sitting on the back of the toilet with my feet on the seat so no one would see me. Katie rapped her fingers on my door. "What happened?"

I got down and unlocked the door. Blotting a tissue to my face I told Katie, "I'm in love with him." A sad, frightened smile laced my lips. It was the most pathetic, stupid thing I'd ever done, but I couldn't deny it anymore. It wasn't a crush. I loved Trystan Scott. Tears streaked my face.

Katie held out her arms and I fell into them sobbing. She hugged me hard, and then set me on my feet. "It's going to be all right. This isn't as bad as it seems."

Shock lined my face, "Not as bad as it seems? I'm in love with a guy that doesn't know what love is. How would you feel if you suddenly realized you loved Seth?" Katie flinched. "Same thing." I dabbed my eyes again. My make-up was toast, and I'd be lucky if I could stop crying before the bell rang.

Katie was supposed to be at lunch. She had a fifteen minute pass. After that, they'd come looking for her. "It's not the same thing. You guys have been friends."

"Well, we're not anymore," I sniffed. "I told him to stay away from me. That I'd never like him that way. It was like falling at his feet and begging him to love me. The way he looked at me, Katie," more tears ran down my cheeks, "it was like he couldn't even look at me."

"So, he told you he was just playing?"

"No," I said looking up at her.

Katie seemed confused. "I'm missing something. What made you tell him off? What'd he do?"

My lower lip quivered. "I thought he was going to kiss me, but he didn't. He stayed there, so close and asked me to kiss him."

"No way," she said wide eyed. Katie leaned back on a sink. "What'd you do?"

"I couldn't. I wanted to, but I can't. I can't let this happen again."

"Trystan isn't Greg. They aren't the same guy. You can't act like they are."

I stared at her. "What the hell is wrong with you? Yesterday you were telling me to stay away from Trystan and now you're on his side?"

She slid off the sink and stepped toward me. Taking my shoulders she said, "I'm on your side. Trystan has his own faults and it scares the hell out of me that you like him—"

"I love him, Katie. I feel it. It's in every inch of me and I wish it wasn't."

She released me. "Why are you crying? Because he asked you to kiss him?"

"No," I answered tugging my hair, "because I can't pretend anymore! I can't deny it and I can't let him play me whenever he wants. When his big blue eyes look at me a certain way, I'm toast, Katie." Sadness bled through me like I'd been fatally wounded.

Her arms folded over her chest. Katie was quiet for a while. She handed me another tissue and finally said, "Then tell him."

"What?" I squealed.

"You're stuck in the middle. You love him, but he doesn't know. He's flirting with you like you're a toy. That's why you're mad, right?" I nodded. "So tell him. He either runs away screaming, or takes you in his arms. Either way, there's no more in the middle."

Katie sounded crazy. The idea of walking up to Trystan and telling him how I felt scared me to death. But I felt desperate.

Without a word, I turned to the bathroom door.

Katie rushed after me. Grabbing my arm, she turned me around. "Wait! What are you doing?"

"I'm going to tell Trystan Scott that I love him."

Katie smiled sadly at me, and gave me a hug. "I'm across the hall. Let me know how it goes. I'll watch for you to come back." I nod and she released me.

CHAPTER 24

~TRYSTAN~

After Mari ripped his heart out, Trystan stared at the stage. A million thoughts ran through his mind but he couldn't focus on a single one. She's not coming back he thought, and ran his hands through his hair. Looking up at the high ceiling, he scolded himself for putting pressure on her, for telling her to kiss him.

If they hadn't gotten locked in that closet, he wouldn't have done it. But when he sat there with her, so close that he was breathing her in, he couldn't help himself. Mari was on his mind constantly, and it didn't matter what she thought—this wasn't a game. Trystan knew it. He felt it in his hollowed out gut.

Trystan's throat was so tight he couldn't speak. That's why he let her walk away. There was nothing to left to say. He blew it and she flat out rejected him. Hollowness consumed Trystan until he couldn't sit there another second. He sprang from the seat and bound up the stage stairs. Pulling open the basement door, he descended in darkness.

He felt his way through the room until he found a music stand. Feeling his way along the cold metal, he found the light at the top and clicked it on. Trystan crossed the room and grabbed a guitar that the music teacher offered as a prop a million years ago. He dragged a stool to the center of the room and tuned the ancient guitar, hoping the strings wouldn't snap. When he was done, Trystan took some pages that were folded in his pocket and smoothed them on the stand, spreading each on out so he could see the song he was working on—the song he didn't think he'd get to finish since his dad smashed his guitar. But since Mari left him here alone and Tucker was probably still fuming in his room, Trystan risked it. He put the pages in front of him and strummed the cords of an unfinished melody.

After a few moments, he hung his head, holding the guitar in his lap. One foot extended off the stool onto the floor. He turned himself around so that the light was to his back and before he knew it he was playing the song he always played when he was hurt. Mari's song.

At first he didn't sing. He couldn't. The knot in his throat choked him into silence, but as he played it melted and Trystan could breathe again. The tightness in his chest didn't release though. Mari's words echoed in his mind, I never liked you that way. I never will. Stay away from me, Trystan.

The guitar became part of him as he played. It was an extension of his soul. He poured his heart into his music and right then it was shattered. Trystan's fingers knew the song. They moved across the strings, pressing and sliding as he closed his eyes. There was nothing to compare this to. He'd never felt so broken in his entire life.

His hair hung in his face, but he didn't bother to push it back. Trystan played through the entire song three times before he found his voice. It broke through his sorrow and spilled over his lips. His fingers strummed as his mouth formed the words pouring from his heart. They were always the same, always equally haunted and adoring. He was foolish enough to fall completely in love with someone who didn't think he had a heart. Trystan pressed his eyes closed harder, willing himself to get lost in the song. And he did.

CHAPTER 25

~MARI~

Every fiber of my being was wound tight. My emotions were a total mess. I could barely think and the part of me that still could was screaming at me to reconsider my plan, but I didn't. I crossed the hallway and pulled open the auditorium door expecting to find Trystan where I left him, but the seat was empty.

I rounded the stage corner and climbed the stairs as I went over what I was going to say in my mind. It's dark and I had to feel my way along the wall until I found the door to the prop room. It was open slightly, like it didn't close right. When I looked down, I saw why. The rubber flap on the bottom of the door folded under and held it in place. Pushing through, I stood on the upper-landing ready to flip on the lights when I heard someone singing and the soft sound of a guitar.

The basement was normally pitch black, but there was a small burst of light cutting through the darkness. It was too dim to do anything but cast a narrow beam of golden light. Pulse pounding, I slowly felt my way down the stairs. Music drifted up softly and when he began to sing my heart twisted. It was that song by Day Jones. The melancholy tune, the longing in his voice, the way he played the guitar, the way his voice resonated on certain notes... A shiver ran down my spine as I came to the lower landing. The only thing separating us were the flats stacked next to the stairs.

My stomach twisted wildly as I stepped off the landing. Each note sank into me. Each word he sang pierced me whole. It made me move slower, breathe slower. It was like this wasn't happening, like it couldn't be real.

I stepped out from behind the flats and stared. It looked like the video. A guy sat in pitch black with a single light behind him. His head was bent forward, his fingers moving gently, strumming the instrument as he sang. He played a few more bars, singing softly before he noticed I was there. Suddenly, he gasped and looked up, startled.

I could barely breathe.

Trystan looked at me with those haunted sapphire eyes. "Mari," he said, his voice a rush of air. Rising off the stool, Trystan lowered the guitar from his lap. Yellow light poured from the music stand behind him. Handwritten music pages were spread across it like he'd been composing something.

"You're Day Jones," I whispered, pressing my fingers to my lips. Shock ratcheted through my body. Trystan didn't deny it. He stood there, beautiful and devastated, with his guitar at his side.

BACKDRAFT
THE SECRET LIFE OF
TRYSTAN SCOTT
VOL. 2

back ·draft: An occurrence in which a fire that has consumed all available oxygen suddenly explodes.

CHAPTER 1

~TRYSTAN~

There was nothing but sorrow and music keeping Trystan glued together. Mari was everything to him. He couldn't think about the void in his life or how it would be without her. Trystan's fingers slid along the neck of the guitar as he strummed, playing the song that brought him solace. When his world cracked apart the song always rose to the front of his mind.

The weight within him felt like it was too much to bear, crushing his bones while he still breathed. Nothing changed. Life continued down the same hellish path, beating him in every way possible. Maybe it'd be different if he gave up, but he wouldn't. That was Trystan's problem—he didn't stay down. It was like that with his father. It didn't matter how many times his father's hand flew, he got back up. It was the same with his life. It didn't matter how many bad hands he was dealt, he always got back up.

A numb tingling filled his body again as he played softly. There was no peace. No refuge. He was alone. There'd always been an ember of hope burning within him, but when Mari said she didn't like him, it felt like someone ripped his lungs out. The ember died, shriveling within his chest, leaving a dull ache in its place. Mari's words left him mute, unable to respond. It was the one time he didn't get up again. He couldn't.

Trystan sat silently on the stool, softly playing the guitar in his lap, and felt the familiar sense of loss fill him. When his voice finally came, he sang without realizing it. Barely whispering, Trystan's mouth formed the words that spilled from his heart. The lament, the song—Mari's song— it helped purge him. It gave him a false sense of control, which was something Trystan desperately needed.

In the moments when Trystan was weakest, it was like there was nothing else—no air touching his skin or filling his lungs. There was no stool, no music stand. He was just a voice, a heartbeat, and a breath of song. That was why he failed to hear the door, failed to hear her footfalls inching closer and closer.

By the time Mari was standing in front of him it was too late. She saw him. She heard him. She knew who he was and what he'd been hiding. Her slender fingers touched her lips as she said, "You're Day Jones."

Trystan's guitar slipped from his lap and slid to his side as he stood. Shock and fear twisted his stomach into a knot. His throat was too tight to speak. Instead of attempting an explanation, he stared at her with his pulse pounding in his ears. Mari stood there, looking at him with her jaw dangling open. She stared into his eyes, unblinking, waiting for him to speak.

A thousand thoughts flew through Trystan's mind, but he asked, "Why'd you come back?"

The shock melted off of Mari's face. She stood a few paces away from him. Uncertainty filled her eyes. It was like she'd never seen him before, like she never noticed the guy fighting so hard to survive that he'd do anything.

Her pink lips pressed together. The scent of strawberries filled his head as he remembered kissing those lips not so long ago. Mari's eyes darted away from his. She made a few false starts, before saying, "I was going to tell you something, but I think you might have something to tell me instead."

Trystan stared, his body tense. The grip on the neck of his guitar tightened, but he didn't put it down. The faint golden light doused Mari softly, highlighting the gentle curves of her face. He couldn't stop looking at her.

Taking a deep breath, he replied, "There's nothing to tell."

Mari stepped forward with an incredulous look on her face, "Are you seriously going to deny it?"

"No, there's just nothing to tell." Trystan's heart felt like it was going to explode.

The fame that Day Jones achieved wasn't something he wanted. He knew what would happen if he revealed himself—reporters would start digging into his personal life. It would expose everything his father had done to him. The thought made him sick. Trystan saw the offers and the endless requests to reveal his identity, but he couldn't. Now, it was everything he could do to keep it a secret. He considered deleting the page, but he thought that might give him away. If someone was watching when he did it, they could track him down. The risk was too great, so he left it there and watched the comments and likes swiftly grow to staggering numbers.

"Why didn't you tell me?" she asked softly. Mari's big brown eyes lowered like she was afraid he wouldn't tell her.

Trystan sat back down on the stool and pulled the guitar onto his lap. He looked down at the instrument, his dark hair falling into his eyes. "There are some things that are too hard to tell—you know what I mean?" He glanced up at her to see her nod and step closer. Trystan lowered his gaze to the strings and slowly began strumming again. He waited a moment before asking, "Is the door closed?" His voice was so soft he could barely hear it.

"Yes," she breathed, watching him closely.

Trystan nodded and started the song again. He didn't plan to sing, but as he played, the words poured through him and he couldn't stop. This was what he wanted, he wanted her to know. He wanted her to believe him. Trystan forced himself to look her in the eye as he sang and felt the bottom of his stomach lurch into a free-fall that didn't seem to end. Mari's big brown eyes locked with his as he sang. She breathed slowly, her slender fingers still pressed to her lips.

Suddenly, the song didn't seem melancholy anymore. It was Mari's song and Mari was here. The corners of Trystan's mouth pulled up slightly, giving him a ghost of smile. His voice and the music flowed together, mingling and conveying the things locked inside of his heart.

Mari watched him. She didn't move. Her beautiful body remained still, standing in front of him, her lips slightly parted. He took in every inch of her, every soft curve, and every twisting brown curl as she watched him sing. When Trystan played the last note he looked down at his hands. The music faded until the only sound he could hear was his breath.

Mari's body was tense, her slender arms rigid as her hands fell to her sides. She flexed her fingers one by one like she was nervous. Her voice was soft, curious, "Who is she?"

Trystan glanced up at her. He pressed his lips together and closed his eyes. He shook his head, indicating that he couldn't answer. The pit of his stomach lifted as his throat tightened. Trystan could feel the words in his mouth, the confession his lips that he wanted to bare, but he couldn't force it out. She had to see it for herself.

When Trystan looked up, Mari smiled down at him sadly. She sucked in a quick breath and it was like flipping a switch. Something changed, but he didn't know what.

"I won't tell, you know." Mari said. "I didn't mean to walk in on you." She stepped toward him, closing the gap between them and rested her hand on his shoulder. Even though it was only a moment, only a small touch, Trystan nearly jumped out of his seat. Her touch set his skin on fire. It made him want to touch her in return, but he couldn't. She didn't want him. She didn't like him that way.

Heart pounding in his chest, he tried to sound like his old self, but his voice was still too timid. Nodding, Trystan said, "Thank you. I don't want anyone to know. I thought I was alone..." His voice trailed off. Mari released his shoulder and moved to the couch. Sitting across from him, she remained on the edge of her cushion like she might jump up at any moment. Her hands were clutched in her lap, gripping her pointer finger like she was wringing it out.

"You were alone. I didn't hear anything until I stood by the door." She forced that smile again, the one that said her insides were being ripped apart, but he didn't understand why.

Glancing at her, Trystan stood and walked the guitar back to its place in the corner. He wished she would talk to him. He'd do anything to get that look off her face and make her laugh. Instead, he asked, "What'd you want to tell me?"

Mari stiffened, "What?" She startled, like there was a loud crack next to her ear.

Trystan watched her for a moment. Something wasn't right, but he didn't know what. His emotions were so out of whack. Maybe he was reading her wrong? Brow pinched, he said, "You said you were looking for me, to tell me something."

Trystan put the music stand away and stuffed the sheet music he was working on back into his pocket. When he was finished he walked to the couch and looked down at her. God, she was beautiful. Her skin was pale and perfect. The way her mouth curved made him want to kiss her. Trystan scolded himself. He had to stop acting like this around her. For whatever reason, she came back. He wouldn't chase her off again. Having her as a friend was better than not having her at all. That thought made his gut twist. There was no way he could deal with losing Mari.

"I was." She blinked up at him a few times like she'd forgotten something important. "I decided to take Tucker's pass. It wasn't upstairs and neither were you. I assumed you took it."

Trystan reached into his pocket and pulled out the pink paper. His eyes never left Mari's as he reached out and handed it to her. When her fingers brushed his hand, he wished he could pull her into his arms. Instead, he tried to capture some of his old swagger and hide just how much she affected him.

Trystan's lips pulled into a soft smile as she reached out, but Trystan didn't release the paper. She glanced up at him. "I thought you didn't want it," he breathed, stepping closer to her.

"I changed my mind," she whispered, tugging the pass, but he didn't let go.

"Your mind is usually a difficult thing to change." He grinned, looking down at her perfect face.

She smiled, "Not when there's a good reason for it."

"And what reason is that?"

Her brown gaze drifted over his face before returning to his eyes. She tilted her head to the side and her dark hair fell over her shoulder. "A sad song, being sung alone in the basement."

The way she said it gave him hope. Something inside of him came to life and told him to hold on tight. The way her lips wrapped around the words, the way she said them softly, glancing away for a moment like it was something she shouldn't admit, made it difficult to breathe and wiped the smug expression off his lips.

Trystan tilted his chin up, still watching Mari. Carefully, he asked, "You think you'll figure out who the girl in the song is, if you hang around me long enough?"

"I know I will," she said with a soft voice that was exceedingly confident. It made the corners of his lips curve up. "You wear your heart on your sleeve when no one is looking, but I'm always looking. I'll see it, even if no one else does. I'll figure it out." Her words sounded like, I want to figure it out. I want to know who brought you to your knees.

Her fingers were still touching his, each of them clutching the pass. As they spoke, their faces became closer and closer. Trystan could feel her breath on his lips. Every inch of his body was tingling. He wanted to say something great, reach out and take her face between his hands, and press his lips to hers. The way she was looking at him, the way her mouth was so close to his, made him think that she might be thinking the same thing, but he couldn't believe that any more. Before she stormed off, he would have thought she liked his attention, but now—he didn't know anymore.

Before he did something stupid and scared her off, Trystan smiled and released the pass. "I hope you do."

CHAPTER 2

~MARI~

Did I just say that? Did I actually confess that I was always looking at Trystan? I was so flustered. Trystan stood there, his warm skin brushing mine with that playful look in his eye. He tugged the pass hard and I tugged back. We were nose to nose by the time he said that. His lips were so close, so perfect. I sighed inside, wanting to fall into his arms, but I couldn't. He was lost in some other girl. If I threw myself at him now, it wouldn't end well. I'd be second to whoever stole his heart.

I heard myself say, "I'll figure it out," not knowing what I'd do after that. I just didn't want to leave. Part of me wanted to confess why I came back in the first place. Heart racing, I looked into his vibrant eyes, unable to look away.

Trystan grinned and released the pass. "I hope you do."

———

I replayed the whole thing over again in my mind as I walked to class in a daze. Trystan Scott was in love. As if that wasn't weird enough, he was also Day Jones. I didn't even know what to ask him about that, so I didn't ask anything. I cursed myself for thinking I could tell Trystan that I was in love with him. Naivety often blindsided me. I'd listened to that Day Jones song enough times to know that whoever wrote it was completely and totally lost to love—even if she didn't even know he was alive.

A spark of jealousy flamed to life inside of me. I knew Trystan was alive. Every inch of me knew Trystan was alive and wanted to know him more. Sighing, I put my books on my desk and slid into my seat. I'd walked so fast that I'd gotten to class early.

While many students still lingered in the halls, hardly any were at their seats, yet.

Katie arrived half a beat later. I heard her voice before I saw her face. She slipped into the seat next to me asking, "Did you tell him?"

I shook my head, not bothering to look up. "Couldn't."

"Why not?" Katie was pumped, ready to support me however I needed, but she couldn't tell what I needed. "You're killing me! Tell me." She shook my arms as she said it and I sat upright in my seat.

I glanced at the front of the room. The bell would ring in a second. Mathboy started to hand back papers. When he passed Katie's desk, she practically drooled a puddle on the floor.

"Later. I'll tell you later." Just as I finished saying it, a wadded-up piece of paper nailed me in the back of the head. Katie and I turned in unison looking for the source.

Brie Parker. She had that horrible smile on her face, the one she wore after she did something really bad. I was in advanced math and Brie wasn't. Since the school budget didn't pass this year or last, there wasn't an honor's class. Instead they combined a class of nerds with the class of burn-outs who were a year older than us. It had to be hell for the teacher. I didn't like it much either. It meant I had to hear about Brie and Trystan all last year while they dated. Sometimes he had come into the room and taken her in his arms. Every other girl was jealous, enviously watching Brie and Trystan. When they broke-up, there was a lot of chatter about who Trystan would date next. It drove Brie crazy. Trystan bounced from girl to girl, while Brie snagged the first thug she could wrap her pointy little fingers around. She made sure to slobber all over her new boyfriend in front of Trystan regularly.

I hated her guts before, but after Brie got me in trouble the other day I hated her even more. I figured out that I must have done something that pissed her off, but I had no idea what. Throwing stuff wasn't the normal backstabbing Brie-method of humiliation. She was usually more subtle, more devastating than that. It worried me that she seemed to have chosen me as her new target. There would be more crap like she pulled the other day. I'd hoped that Trystan humiliating her would have made her focus on him. As far as I could tell, she didn't change targets. Maybe it was because Trystan was already on her hit list.

Katie snatched up the paper and hurled it back at Brie's face, but Mathboy chose that second to walk in front of her. The paper wad nailed him in the back. He turned around and cocked his head, staring straight at Katie.

"Really?" he asked as a brow drifted higher on his face.

Katie flushed scarlet and she turned around in her seat. Mathboy picked up the paper-ball and stuffed it into the crook of his arm and continued to pass back papers. When he stopped in front of Katie's desk, he placed another of her tests in front of her, along with the wadded paper. Brie was sniggering from the back with her clones. When the hot guy finished passing out the papers, he left the room to do something else. The teacher walked to the front of the class and started the lesson.

On the side of the crumpled paper, there was a blue pen mark that looked like a number. It wasn't there before. I poked it with my pencil and glanced at it several times to get Katie to notice. When she did, she smoothed the piece of paper and saw Mathboy's phone number. The day got a lot more interesting after that.

———

As Katie and I walked to my locker after school, she leaned in close to make sure no one could hear her over the sound of slammed lockers and hallway chatter. The last bell had rung. There were ten minutes before I was supposed to be at practice.

"What's with you?" Katie asked, bumping my shoulder. "You've been out if it since lunch."

I was out of it. I couldn't stop thinking about Trystan, about that guitar in his lap, and the beautiful tone of his voice when he sang. I'd never heard him sing before. It was breathtaking and heartbreaking at the same time. Whoever caught his attention did a good job.

A jolt of jealousy shot through me, straightening my spine. I glanced at Katie. I couldn't tell her what happened. I couldn't say that Trystan was Day Jones. I promised I wouldn't say anything, even if I didn't understand why. Revealing that he was Day would have meant financial independence. He could leave this place and never look back, but Trystan left the agents' requests unanswered and kept his identity a secret.

Clearing my throat I said, "Nothing. Everything. I can't get him out of my head." I stared blankly ahead. I didn't want to lie to her, but felt I had to. "He doesn't feel like that about me, Katie."

The smile slipped off her face, "How do you know if you didn't tell him?" She leaned closer to me, clutching her books to her chest. Her eyes darted back and forth to make sure no one else could overhear us.

"Because he told me that he likes someone else." That wasn't a lie. Not totally. His song said he liked someone very much. He sounded like he was in love with her. I didn't understand how he could have written that, and sang that way, if he didn't. Swallowing the lump in my throat, I stopped in front of my locker and took a deep breath before opening it. I tossed my books in as Katie put a hand on my shoulder.

"I'm sorry, Mari. But at least you know now. You can move on. Find someone else."

I nodded and stared into the open locker like I was forgetting something. "I know." And I knew there would never be anyone else like Trystan. Every time I thought I knew all there was to know about him, another thing popped up—like Day Jones. It drew me to him more, making him too irresistible to forget.

CHPATER 3

~TRYSTAN~

Tucker sat in the first row like he always did, pinching the bridge of his nose as he watched the actors on stage. Everyone wondered why he taught all the theater classes, since he appeared to hate it so much. There were rumors that he was paying his dues, being the youngest English teacher in the school, but Trystan wasn't so sure. At times he saw the subtle smile on Tucker's face that said he enjoyed it. The man may have been new to teaching, but it also gave him passion some of the older teachers were lacking. Tucker didn't seem to think anyone was a lost cause, which was probably why he paid attention to Trystan when the rest of his teachers couldn't wait to shove him out the door.

Tucker stood and stomped up the steps, his gut shaking as he went. His voice was strained, "Brie, dear—" he started and she beamed at him, bating those blue eyes like she thought he was going to compliment her.

Trystan stood opposite Brie, his arms folded across his chest and rolled his eyes. Brie shot Trystan a nasty look when Tucker wasn't looking. She was still pissed about her skirt going over her head. Brie's expiration date on revenge was never. He'd been waiting, but so far she didn't seem to be plotting anything.

As Trystan watched Tucker coach Brie, he looked away. Everything about her irritated him. When she messed up, she'd pout and toss her golden hair over her shoulder. Her bottom lip would slowly push out until it looked like she'd cry. It kept her from getting the correction she needed.

Trystan couldn't believe how fake she was and that he failed to see it sooner. Brie smiled and said something. Tucker walked her through her lines again. Trystan stared into the stage wing, peering through the darkness, looking for Mari. Instead of seeing the girl who stole his heart, he only saw her empty chair. She was downstairs. They didn't need her to prompt anymore, and Tucker had sent her into the prop room to dig something up.

Trystan couldn't stop thinking about Mari. She consumed his thoughts to the point that he didn't hear his own name.

"Scott!" Tucker bellowed.

While Tucker coached Brie, he'd retreated to the other side of the stage and slid onto the table. He sat there, dangling his legs over the side and staring at his feet, while Brie played dumb. When people thought you were stupid, they didn't expect much from you. Trystan knew that trick. It was one of the reasons he'd been assigned someone to run lines with. No one knew the other reasons.

Trystan looked up slowly. He'd been so focused on the memory of Mari listening to his song, the way her face looked as he sang to her, that he failed to hear Tucker. Coolly, Trystan lifted his gaze and said, "Yes?"

Tucker folded his arms across his massive chest and looked at Trystan like he was crazy. Tucker jabbed his thumb at Brie, "Run through the end of the second act with her." When Trystan didn't move, Tucker added. "Now." The large man turned, huffed as he descended the stage stairs, and walked back to his seat. Clapping his massive hands, he bellowed, "Top of the second act people." Those who weren't supposed to be on stage cleared the stage, leaving Trystan alone with Brie under the spotlight.

As Trystan slipped off the table, he saw a sliver of light cut across the wall backstage. A moment later, Mari appeared. Her long curls dangled down her back as she rounded the stage, appearing next to Tucker below. She handed him something too small to see and went back to her metal chair in the wing.

As Trystan's gaze followed Mari back to her seat, Brie stepped closer and whispered with her ruby red lips a little too close to his face, "You'll never nail that. Her mom's on the school board and her dad's a doctor. There's no way they'll let their only daughter anywhere near scum like you."

"Good thing your parent's didn't care then, huh?" Trystan's gaze cut to Brie.

The snake-like smile that spread across her face fell as his words hit her. "Fuck you, Trystan."

"Anytime, Brie." Trystan smirked, as Brie's face contorted into a scowl that resided in evil bitch territory. Brie folded her arms across her chest and turned away. Venom radiated off of her. He'd pay for that later. He knew every jab, every insult he hurled at her would be repaid tenfold, but Trystan didn't care. Brie needed to be knocked down a few pegs and he didn't mind doing it, not when she kept trying to screw with him.

Tucker yelled, "From the top. Now, people."

They started again. The guy in the lighting cage changed the lights on the set so there was a single golden spot on center stage. Its broad beam was soft, spilling light across the stage like a streetlight on a dark night. Trystan moved to stage left and started his lines again. He had no trouble with this part. As the scene went on, they moved closer together. Romantic tension was rising steadily. Tucker didn't stop them. Brie played her part well, but not as well as Mari. Trystan said his lines with conviction. They were perfectly played, because he pretended Brie was Mari, the girl he wanted and couldn't ever have. It fit perfectly into that scene and made it easier to act opposite Brie and not puke on her.

They ran through the act perfectly. Everything was flowing at a steady rate toward the end of the scene. Trystan's stomach was pooling with dread. That act ended with a kiss, a passionate kiss. To make matters more awkward, Trystan could feel Mari's eyes on him, watching him get ready to kiss someone else. He couldn't think about that now. If he wasn't half way convincing, Tucker would have them start over.

With every ounce of charm he had in him, Trystan pulled Brie close, gently wrapping his fingers around her waist. Brie let him, and slipped into his arms like she belonged there. The scent of her perfume filled his head. At one time it had been attractive, but now the scent repelled him. He breathed through his mouth, inhaling as little as possible. Brie pressed against him, letting him feel her curves.

Trystan's voice was deep and seductive. He acted as though he were saying the line to Mari, "I'd do this." Trystan moved in slowly and pressed his lips to Brie's. Revulsion shot through him, but he didn't stop.

It's Mari, he told himself. Pretend she's Mari. Trystan closed his eyes and splayed his hands across Brie's cheeks, kissing her a second longer than he should have. The students in the wings got wrapped up in the steamy kiss. Trystan could feel all eyes on him, and for once, he wished they weren't. It was the emptiest kiss he'd ever had.

After all this time, he finally understood what Mari meant—that a kiss was worth something—that it meant something. This was the difference between a shallow kiss and one that he craved with every ounce of his being. When Trystan opened his eyes, he looked Brie in the face. For once, she was silent. Shocked. They both stared at each other as the spot light faded and curtain swung shut.

Trystan dropped his hands and stepped away. He felt sick, like he'd done something wrong.

"Trystan," she said his name like he had a tremendous effect on her. Brie stared at him with her red lips parted, waiting for him to respond. He'd never kissed her like that before. Sure, he'd kissed her plenty of times before that, but it never meant anything. It was purely fun, purely lust. This time was different, because he was thinking of Mari and her perfectly sweet lips. Apparently, Brie felt the difference. The look in her eye said she wasn't done with him yet, that he could have more.

Trystan said nothing. There was no way he was telling her what changed, why the kiss felt passionate. Instead, he turned to the wing where Mari was sitting and walked off stage. When he passed through the curtain, there were several stage crew members blocking his path. One slapped him on the back and said, "Holy hell! That was hot!"

Brie watched him walk away with her fingers to her lips like she never realized what she had while she had it.

When Trystan finally plowed through the kids, he found Mari's seat empty. It wasn't fair. It wasn't right. That was Mari's kiss and he gave it to someone else—someone he detested. Trystan sat down hard in Mari's chair and leaned back, running his fingers through his hair. Where was she?

Tucker's voice boomed from the other side of the curtain, "Take a break, Scott."

That was all he needed to hear. Trystan got up and exited through the side stage door. He walked through the empty halls toward the cafeteria and went to the vending machines. He normally didn't buy stuff like that. It was too expensive, but he wanted caffeine. He was shaking, his stomach churning inside of him like he'd be sick.

Fishing a dollar out of his pocket, Trystan fed it to the machine and then pressed a button. A Coke tumbled out of the bottom of the machine. He bent down and picked it up, lost in thought. Trystan walked back slowly, drinking his sugar quickly, when Seth ran up next to him. A teacher screamed at Seth to stop running, but he didn't slow until he reached Trystan.

"Hey man," Seth huffed. "You almost done? I have us a dinner date lined up." He waggled his eyebrows, very proud of his latest catch. It had to be the 7-Eleven twins. Seth had been hanging around them nearly every day.

Trystan groaned inside, but he didn't show any sign that he wasn't interested. He didn't want to fight about Mari again. Nodding, Trystan said, "Yeah. Give me about forty-five minutes. We should be done by then."

Seth grinned, "She's so hot, man. And her rack is like," he paused his hands cupping the air as a look of awe spread across his face, "so perfect."

"Which one?"

"Like it matters?" Seth laughed. "They're twins. They've got the same of everything." He elbowed Trystan, like his crass comment amused them both and then took off in the other direction. "Later, Scott! Don't be late!"

Trystan shook his head. He was starting to think that he and Seth had little in common anymore. At some point, Seth fixated on bodies and Trystan wanted more than that. A good body was great, but without a brain it didn't hold much appeal. Mari had a great mind, filled with tack-sharp wit and other awesome things. Plus she had the body, too. He grinned, thinking about it. Trystan started back toward the auditorium, chugging the rest of his Coke.

As he rounded the corner, Trystan saw Mari leaning against the wall by the stage door. Her head was tilted up, her eyes closed like she was upset. His heart twisted in his chest. He watched her for a moment, unsure if he should approach, but he couldn't help himself. His feet took him to her. It was like they were two magnets and when she was near, he couldn't pass her by.

"You okay?" Trystan asked, stopping in front of her.

Mari jumped when she heard his voice. She looked directly at him. There were no tears in her eyes, but he knew something was bothering her. Something had been bothering her all day. Mari seemed more agitated and jumpy than normal. "Yeah, fine." She waited a moment, then crossed her arms and sighed, "I don't get it."

Trystan leaned his shoulder against the wall next to her. The hairs on the back of his neck started to rise. He ignored the warning premonition. Looking down into her face, he asked, "What don't you get?"

"How you can do that. How you can make everyone believe your emotions are real, even when they aren't. That kiss..." She spit out the word kiss, shaking her head. Mari's soft brown curls moved as she did it, falling forward into her face. She pushed them back, her gaze skewering him in place. "It makes it hard to believe that you like someone else. That's all."

Trystan didn't understand why she was upset. Her reaction was strange considering what she'd told him earlier. She didn't care about him that way, and while kissing Brie made Trystan feel dirty, it shouldn't have had any effect on Mari. Unless...

Unless what, Scott? Take a hint, the voice inside his head scolded, she doesn't like you. Stop acting like she does.

Maybe his words were too clipped, but once he said them, he couldn't take them back. "Why does it matter, Mari? It doesn't affect you." And you'd tell me if it did, he hoped.

She straightened like he'd hit her.

Crap. That was the wrong thing to say.

"No, it doesn't." Mari looked at him once like he was cruel, and started to walk away.

He reached for her, grabbing her wrist, wanting an explanation. "Hey, wait a second. Mari, what is this? You know me." His heart throbbed harder as his hand gripped her wrist. Her skin was so warm, so smooth. When she looked up at him with those dark eyes, he was lost.

"I'm not so sure anymore." She looked down at his hand on her arm like she didn't want it there.

"What do you mean? Of course you know me." Trystan tried to strangle the pleading tone out of his voice, but it wouldn't budge. An icy feeling was pooling in his stomach as he watched her.

"I'm never really sure if the guy I know is the real Trystan or the act." She tucked a curl behind her ear and looked up at Trystan with those eyes. They said everything. She didn't trust him. She didn't know what to believe anymore and it was his own damn fault. "You can put on a dazzling show when you try. How I am supposed to know what's real and what's not?" When she asked the question, she couldn't look at him. Her gaze fell to the floor.

He took her shoulders in his hands. "Look at me, Mari. You know me. I wouldn't lie to you. About anything." Her gaze lifted and met his. Her brown eyes seemed incredibly vulnerable right then, and he didn't know why. Trystan knew this was important to her, that she felt misled and he wanted to fix it. He lifted a hand to her face and tucked a stray hair behind her ear, letting his fingers linger in her soft hair. His voice was soft, beseeching, "You know me better than anyone else. You always have."

Mari swallowed hard, her eyes locked on his. She didn't look away. She didn't shirk him off like she usually did. Instead she stood there, barely breathing, looking for the truth in his eyes. His gut twisted like someone was wringing it out. The way she looked at him said so much. Did she really not see it? Of course not. She saw the guy on stage, the one who kissed Brie—the one who was never serious about anyone.

Finally she said, "I don't know."

"Come to the prop room tomorrow with Tucker's pass. I'll show you that I'm serious. Acting is acting. Brie doesn't have my heart." He paused, willing her to see it, to feel it. Squeezing her shoulders, he said, "Someone else does."

Mari broke the intense gaze, nervously tucking her hair behind her ear, and stepped back. He smiled at her. The way she tucked her hair behind her ear was a tick that he hadn't noticed before. Something about the way she did it, like she was trying to hide from him, made him adore her even more.

"We'll see, I guess. I want to believe you. I really do. I just... I don't know anymore, but I'll come. I'll be there because of what happened today. All of it." Mari gave him a weak smile and turned on her heel to leave.

Trystan's eyes slid over her curves and landed on her hips for a second. The black top she wore wasn't tight, but it wasn't loose either. Coupled with those jeans and that sexy hair, she looked like a goddess— and just as far out of reach.

Mari was too good for him and he knew it.

CHAPTER 4

~MARI~

I didn't want to watch that part, but the end of the second act drew me back to my seat. No one blocked my line of sight, so I had the perfect place to watch Trystan give Brie a perfect kiss. The tension in the air was so thick, the way he looked at her made my stomach twist. It was like watching the lines when he ran them with me. Nothing seemed real in that moment. The guy I loved was inching closer to someone else, his lips pressing to hers, his hands gently touching her face. It was like hitting replay and watching him kiss me. Suddenly it felt like there was no air. The room grew hotter as my heart slapped into my ribs, banging inside of me like I was going to die.

That was my kiss. It was the same kiss he gave me in the prop room. I'd known it was fake, that he was acting, but somehow seeing it in front of me was too much. I felt sick and couldn't stay there for another second. My stomach churned like I ate glass as I staggered to my feet. My head was caught somewhere between being crushed in a vice and floating away. Anger surged through my veins, but not at Trystan—at myself.

How could I be so stupid? I'd come to think that the kiss we shared meant something to him. The way he looked at me, the way he leaned in so slow that my heart felt like it would burst, even the way he gently pressed his lips to mine—it was all nothing. Out on the stage, it looked like Trystan hit a replay button. The entire thing played out, just as it was done to me, but he was with another girl and it was right in front of my face. It didn't matter that he was acting. I couldn't get control of myself. My eyes stung as I tried not to blink. Tears would roll down my cheeks. I looked insane as it was, shoving my way through gawking kids and running away like there was a fire.

My kiss was nothing to Trystan. Our kiss meant nothing.

Irritated with myself for being so naive, I hurried through the hallway to my locker. Pretending that I forgot something gave me a moment's peace. I darted from my chair while everyone else watched the lights fade to black. It was like the air was charged with hormones and I imagined Trystan would get a fair amount of high-fives and crass statements for delivering such a smoking-hot kiss in front of so many people.

I fumed as I raced to my locker, trying to calm down. The teachers wouldn't say anything as long as I didn't linger, and as long as I didn't run. I opened the door and leaned my head against the shelf, feeling the cold metal against my skin. The scent of paper and musty textbooks filled my head.

How dumb am I? I wondered.

For a moment I thought that Trystan actually liked me. When I heard him sing, it made me feel like there was a part of him that I couldn't see. There was genuine pain and longing in that song. Could he have concocted that song and all its haunting beauty like he concocted that kiss? Could he toy with a girl's emotions as easily? I felt sick. How could I be so stupid? And what about everything else? All those looks, the way he brushed my hand when I was close, the way he looked at me—I swear, if I didn't know better I would have thought he liked me.

But I did know better. I knew Trystan Scott and this was one-hundred percent Trystan behavior. Damn, the guy was like a total sociopath. He wore so many masks, way more than I've ever even tried on, and each one fits him perfectly. He can become what he needs to be, what people expect, at the snap of a finger. The guy I saw so rarely was hidden somewhere beneath layers too deep to fathom.

Why does he do that? Why does he change when different people are around? The version of Trystan that sat in the basement and played the guitar, the earlier version that wasn't Day Jones even, those were great. What's not to like? Why hide when everyone loves you? There has to be a reason for it, but I had no idea what it was.

Yeah, you know. He likes getting what he wants, my inner-voice chided.

Oh God, was he that shallow? Did he really change to suit who he was with to get what he wanted? Trystan couldn't be that shallow. Deep in my bones, I knew he wasn't like that. There was something else. Something more that damaged him. There had to be. Trystan had that lost puppy thing about him. It made girls flock to him and want to be with him. That was always there. It never went away. He wore it like a scar. It was a piece of him that he couldn't hide no matter how much he smiled and flirted.

I checked my face in my mirror and pressed the locker closed. Walking back to the stage door, I stopped for a second and leaned against the wall trying to blow off what I'd just seen.

It doesn't matter what he does with Brie or anyone else. Trystan and I are nothing, but friends. I kept telling myself that, but it didn't take away the sting. Pressing my eyes closed, I took a deep breath. When I opened them again, I saw Trystan standing in front of me with a can of Coke, asking me a question that I barely heard.

"You okay?" Trystan asked. His eyes found mine and held my gaze gently, like he knew I was close to tears.

Irritation and anger mingled together and vaporized my resolve. It floated away like I never had any. Trystan's gaze was so convincing, which made it harder not to fall for him. I spewed out the words before I could stop them. "Yeah, fine." My teeth bit into my bottom lip. I tried to shut up, I tried to stop talking, but I couldn't. "I just don't get it," I said, arms flying around like a crazy person, my tone too clipped to be fine.

Trystan leaned next to me and looked down into my face. Those startling blue eyes were like twin pools. I wanted to get lost in them. I wanted them on me and only me. "What don't you get?" he asked.

"How you can do that?" I squeak, unable to keep my mouth shut. "How you can make everyone believe you're emotions are real, even when they aren't? That kiss..." I shook my head. My brain was telling my mouth to shut up, but it kept going. My heart overpowered my head, like it usually did. Taking a deep breath, the rest of the thought rolled out, "It makes it hard to believe that you like someone else. That's all."

"Why does it matter, Mari? It doesn't affect you." His words struck me like a blow to the cheek. I never expected him to say it. Not to me. Not so callously.

"No, it doesn't." Sickened, I turned away. I had to leave. Now. I couldn't stand there another minute. Trystan was all talk, all smooth lips, and smoother lies. I didn't want that from him. I thought I knew him and I didn't. It felt like someone was strangling me. I couldn't stand it another second.

Trystan's hand shot out and grabbed my wrist, stopping me, "Hey, wait a second. Mari, what is this? You know me."

Heart pounding, I looked down at his hand and then up at Trystan's face. I wanted to say so many things, but the only one I could manages was, "I'm not so sure anymore."

He looked offended, dark hair falling into his eyes, his lips curving into a confused expression, "What do you mean? Of course you know me."

"I'm never really sure if the guy I know is the real Trystan or the act. You can put on a dazzling show when you try. How I am supposed to know what's real and what's not?" I couldn't stop the words flying out of my mouth. It was like I was running straight into a freight-train and hoping it would miss smashing me to bits when it hit. I knew what he thought of me, how he felt for me, and yet—I was standing there doing what? Demanding more?

He's not mine, I reminded myself. I shouldn't be so upset. It shouldn't matter if he can photocopy a kiss and give it to every girl in the school. Trystan isn't mine. His heart belongs to someone else, assuming he has a heart at all.

Trystan shocked me out of my thoughts when he placed his hands on my shoulders. A current ran through me. That jolt laced around my throat, traveling down into my stomach, and froze me in place. I couldn't breathe. My brain was fighting it, screaming for him to let go. I couldn't take his touch and his false sincerity.

Panic clutched me harder until I heard his voice, "Look at me, Mari." But I couldn't look at him. Those eyes, that gaze would knock the sense out of me. He continued, his voice pleading with me, "You know me. I wouldn't lie to you. About anything. You know me better than anyone else. You always have."

I couldn't help it. As he spoke, my gaze lifted to meet his and once I did, I couldn't look away. Trystan stole my heart and I couldn't take it back. Hope and dread mingled together as his words washed over me. They were too easy to believe. I wanted to believe him, but I couldn't.

By the time I spoke, my voice was small, "I don't know."

"Come to the prop room tomorrow with Tucker's pass. I'll show you that I'm serious. Acting is acting. Brie doesn't have my heart. Someone else does."

His words were like a foot to my stomach. There was no air. I tried to cover it up. I looked away even though I felt his gaze burning a hole on the side of my face. Tucking a piece of hair behind my ear, I pressed my lips together trying to find an answer that wouldn't hurt me more.

Brie. He gave Brie my kiss. He kissed Brie before. He slept with Brie, I reminded myself. Closing my eyes, I wished he was gone. I didn't shirk him off this time. His hands felt too good. They were strong and warm, holding me in place, demanding something from me that I was afraid to give.

I babbled a few words that I couldn't remember saying even if I tried and then added, "I don't know anymore, but I'll come. I'll be there because of what happened today."

Because of what you did for me. Because of your gaze in the closet. Because of the way you defended me to Tucker. Because of the song that poured from your heart. Because I heard it from your lips. Because I'm not sure who you are anymore and I think I'm more in love with this version of you than the last.

Oh God. Katie was right. He was going to hurt me and I was giving him every means possible. I couldn't stand it anymore. Turning, I freed myself from his grip. When his hands fell away, it felt like someone ripped off a piece of my heart. I walked away leaving Trystan behind. For once, he didn't say anything. He didn't bound up the hallway chasing after me. Instead he stayed there, staring, speechless.

CHAPTER 5

~TRYSTAN~

"Well, that couldn't have gone worse," Trystan mumbled, as he walked back into the theater. Running his fingers through his hair, he pressed his eyes closed. There were so many things he did that totally screwed his relationship with Mari. It was like the whole relationship went up in a ball of flames before he even realized he liked her—before he fell in love with her.

Regret snaked through his stomach, as he walked to a few rows behind Tucker and slouched down into a seat. Within a matter of moments, girls he didn't really know filled the seats next to him. They fell from the sky like rain. They were always there chattering. He was never alone, but he always felt isolated. Trying to block out the chatter, he watched the beginning of the third act on stage. Brie was sucking-up her lines and trying to cover it by blaming someone else.

That's when he finally zoned in on the conversation going on around him.

The girl was saying, "I know, right? I heard there's a reward for the person who outs him."

Trystan's gaze snapped toward her, "Outs who?"

Regan beamed, glad that he noticed her. Her inky hair gleamed in the dim light, falling over her shoulders as she leaned closer to him. "Day Jones. Who else? The guy's a shadow. Every time someone thinks they got a line on him, he vanishes. Poof." She lifted her hand, making the fingers of her fist fly open. Her dark brows rose as if it were impressive.

Another voice spoke and Trystan turned to see Jamie, a coppery-haired girl with olive skin. "There's a reward, and it's huge. That rich dude said he'd offer a million bucks to the person who finds him. Something about wanting Day to sing at his kid's birthday." She shrugged like it was a normal thing to do. Trystan never celebrated his birthday. Actually, he spent it as far away from his dad as he could manage. It was a reminder of everything they lost, of everything he'd never have.

Trystan's skin prickled as ice filled his stomach. He shifted in his seat, hiding behind that cool smile he always wore. "Are you serious?" he was shocked, but he hid it like he hid everything.

What the hell was wrong with people? Why couldn't they admire a song and leave a guy alone?

"Totally," Regan replied. She laughed and turned toward Tessa behind her. "Did you see that Day-Tracker site? The one with all the leads and how they panned out?"

Tessa laughed, "Yeah, that was awesome," she leaned forward. "That last guy they tracked seemed like a good fit, but in the end, it wasn't him. I was totally hoping they'd find him. I can't wait to see what he'll do—and what he looks like. With a voice like that, he has to be hot. The shy thing just makes him more appealing."

"I know, right?" Regan smiled, nodding in agreement.

"Hey, did you see the Facebook page for Find Day?" Tessa continued, "It's hysterical."

Regan nodded, smiling huge. "I know right? And the pictures were an awesome touch." She turned to look at Trystan, adding, "It's like the ultimate Where's Waldo of hot guys. Girls have been uploading pics of what they think Day looks like and where they think he is. I'm totally uploading my guess later."

"And, what's that?" Trystan asked, a smirk on his face. He folded his arms over his chest while they were speaking and sat up a little bit. His stomach was tangling into a knot. They were looking for him.

Regan giggled, "Well, with a song like that there's no question that he's been playing for a long time. His accent sounded a little Cajun, and based on the way he plays, I'm thinking New Orleans." She turned quickly and pointed a finger at the others, "You better not steal my idea. Post your own city."

"He's not in New Orleans," Tessa whispered as Tucker looked back at them, a clear signal to shut up, but they kept talking. "Cajun accent," she mimicked and rolled her eyes. "What the hell is wrong with you? He's clearly from Long Island. Did you hear the way he said his G's?"

Regan contested, "Yeah, but he didn't put W's in the middle of everything. There's no way he's from around there. You'd hear it."

"Scott!" Tucker yelled. "Silence your posse or get out."

Trystan stood, heart racing, all too happy to flee. The girl's looked up at him as he rose. "Mr. Tucker, you know as well as I do that there's nothing that will get them to stop talking, short of the apocalypse, and even then I imagine that they'll be pointing out which zombie is wearing what, so I'll take you up on your offer and leave." The girl's watched him slack-jawed, admiring him and then bursting into giggles at the zombie fashion reference.

Trystan headed out the back door, his head spinning. People were looking for him, trying to discover Day Jones' identity. The thought never occurred to him, not in his wildest dreams. Dread pooled in his stomach as he walked to his locker and opened the metal door. Staring into space, he wondered if there was anything telling on the video—any signs of who he was or where he was. Trystan admitted he wasn't very careful. When he made the video he was only thinking of Mari. He leaned his head against the cold metal and took a deep breath. He'd have to watch the video later to make sure there was nothing identifiable. Although he'd done it already, he felt like there was something there, something that would lead them to him. Trystan was certain that their only real clue was the YouTube account and his user name. Even if someone managed to track the IP address, it would show his neighbor, not Trystan's home. The thought still made him squirm. That was too close.

Trystan grabbed his leather jacket and slammed the locker door. As he headed outside, a cool burst of wind caught his jacket and Trystan tugged it shut. Night was falling. Practice was running longer and longer, as it normally did, up until the day of the dress-rehearsal. Trystan walked down the street. Car horns blared on the busy road next to him. The scent of exhaust mingled with the crisp autumn air filled his lungs.

Passing store fronts, he walked to the diner to meet Seth and his date. Trystan cringed inside. Maybe it wouldn't be so bad. He laughed hollowly. Yeah right. Knowing Seth, there wasn't really another option. He sighed, his breath coming out in a white cloud. Sometimes he wished he had a different life, a different father, a different past.

Maybe it wouldn't be so bad if people knew he wrote that song, but the thought made him cringe. What would his life be like if people knew he was Day Jones? What would they think when they found out his mother ran out on him and that his dad hated him? Trystan hung his head, his gaze intent on the sidewalk in front of him. He could see it, picture it in his mind's eye— everything everyone ever thought about him was a lie. He wasn't anyone special. He wasn't anyone at all. Revealing Day Jones' identity would destroy him. It would strip away the little parts of his life that mattered.

Frustration shot through Trystan. Moving his feet faster, he came up with a plan for the date. He'd have dinner with Seth, so he didn't get grilled with more Mari questions, and then get rid of the girl. There was no way he could feel okay. Not tonight. Not after today. Everything had started off so promising, before it derailed and turned to ash in his hands.

CHAPTER 6

~MARI~

Katie got my text and met me at the diner in ten minutes flat. She must have hitched a ride, since she didn't have a car and there was no other way she could have arrived so quickly. I didn't expect her to get there so fast.

She slipped into the booth across from me, gasping like she was out of breath, "What the hell happened? I ran out after stuffing dinner down my throat. My parents think I'm a lunatic as it is. After tonight, they're gonna have me committed." I was near tears. "Awh, damn. It's Trystan, isn't it?"

I nodded and started spilling my guts, telling her how that kiss felt—the way it seemed like it was tailored just for me. Seeing him kiss Brie like that in front of everyone, giving her my kiss, shattered the illusion.

"It was a lie," I finished up, slumping back in the booth, folding my arms over my chest. I let my dark hair fall forward to hide my face and cast a shadow over the pain in my eyes. "He used me. No—he was running lines. The entire thing was fake and I was too stupid to notice."

It felt like Trystan wrapped his fingers around my heart and squeezed. I couldn't stand it. I didn't know what I wanted to do, but suddenly sitting in the booth felt uncomfortable. I wiggled in my seat, trying to slink out of sight when some girls who knew Brie walked by. Katie shot daggers at them and they passed without comment, which was good because I couldn't take anything else today.

A waiter came by again and asked for our order. When I first sat down, he tried to get my order, but I said I was waiting for someone. He huffed and walked off, like I screwed up his night. It's not like I was rude. I didn't understand people sometimes.

Katie ordered for both of us. "Two sides of fries and two chocolate milkshakes—tall with extra whipped cream. And she wants a cherry on top." Katie winked at me and the strangle-hold on my heart lessened. She always knew how to make me feel better. She dug through her purse and pulled out a ponytail holder. She pulled back her hair as she spoke, "I'm sorry this happened, that you found out this way, but at least now you know. Before you couldn't tell what he was doing. Now you know he's a goddamn liar."

"An actor—"

"Same thing," Katie said. When she finished tugging the ponytail tight, she leaned forward saying, "Listen, if anything, that thespian genius makes it harder to see through his little flirtations. There's no way to know if things are real with a guy like that. He's always acting." Her head tilted to the side and her eyebrows crept up her face. It was her uh-durrr face, she was just too kind to actually say it to me.

Some of what she said seemed true, but my mind rebelled against it. My voice was flat. I wasn't defending him, but I had to point it out, "We're all always acting. What the hell do you think high school is? You really think I strut around being myself all day? Come on, Katie. You have to do better than that."

She cocked her head at me like I was retarded. Leaning forward she said, "You don't get it. Actors don't just hide who they are, they manipulate people. They carefully construct a false facade and use emotions to do it."

"Nice alliteration," I interrupted.

She smirked. Katie was always a poet and totally bent on making her point. "People like that make you love them. They make you laugh. He's an expert at pulling emotional strings and he pulled all of yours. He did it knowing that a kiss meant something to you, and he stole one. He's an asshole."

I didn't know what to think of that. It was true. Trystan could make anyone love him. He had that ability, which was why he was such a good actor. It was throwing me off, because the time I spent with him felt real. They weren't conflicting versions of Trystan, and I'd seen how he acted around other guys and love-struck girls. He didn't change over the years. Actually, scratch that—the first major change I'd seen was that Trystan was in love. Descending the staircase and hearing him tell Seth that some girl had turned him inside out was the first change. The second was the revelation that he was Day Jones, and that he wrote a song that said he was in love.

Something changed Trystan, no, someone changed him—that girl he loves—she altered him.

The waiter put the plates of fries and milkshakes down in front of us. Sighing, I looked up at Katie. Sitting up straighter in the booth, I pushed my hair out of my face. I felt less fragile and more like I could handle this, and whatever else was thrown in my face tonight. "Thanks for meeting me here so fast."

She plucked a fry from the plate, swiped it through the whipped cream, and popped it in her mouth. "Sure, what are friends for?" she grinned at me.

"That's so gross." My lip pulled up a little bit, as she swiped another fry through ketchup and then dipped it into her shake.

She laughed, "Creative cuisine was never your thing."

"That's not cuisine. It's seeing how many things you can put on a fry before shoving it in your mouth." I reached for the pepper shaker and said, "Try this and maybe some jelly next time."

"Twit," she laughed, and then added a heaping amount of pepper to her fry that was already covered in milkshake. This was why guys loved to watch her. She stuck anything in her mouth. I cringed, watching.

Before I had a chance to unwrap my straw, the diner door swung open, and Seth walked in with a girl on his arm. My face must have shown my distain, because Katie turned and looked. She started to open her mouth to say something, but she was half-choking on pepper. Turning fast, she sloshed half a cup of water down her throat, before turning around and seeing Trystan and another girl follow Seth inside. The four of them stood, waiting to be seated, just inside the door.

Trystan had on his leather jacket. It looked so soft. It was the same one he wore every year once there was a chill in the air. There were tiny white lines in the leather, showing its age. It must have belonged to someone before him. The jacket didn't look new, but it sure made him look good. When he wore black, his gaze always seemed more intense, more vivid. More blue.

They didn't see us. Trystan had his hand on the small of the girl's back. She was pretty, all curves and hair, with big eyelashes with lots of make-up. She was the kind of girl who dated for fun.

I was her polar opposite. I was looking for love, which apparently was not fun.

Katie swung around before they saw her, "Holy shit. Is he frickin' serious?" She blinked at me like she couldn't believe it, and then glanced back at Trystan and Seth.

"Let's just go," I said softly, feeling the rest of my heart shatter and fall into my shoes. "I can't watch this."

Katie shook her head, "No. We're staying. Something's up with him." A waitress led them to a booth on the other side of the door. There was a long counter with silver stools with thick padded red seats between us, along with a scattering of booths. I was in their line of sight. As soon as they sat down, Trystan would see me.

When their backs were turned, Katie jumped up, "Quick, switch sides with me." I did as she said, my heart racing way too fast. I clung to the table, slipping silently into the booth while she passed behind me. "I'll watch them for a while and let you know what's up."

I nodded slowly, wishing I were somewhere else. I didn't really feel like eating, but I picked at the fries and sipped the shake. I couldn't tell Katie about the other side of him, the Day Jones side that was hiding from fame. If that part didn't exist, I would have thrown him out of my life. But I couldn't. It didn't make sense. Katie thought he was a glory-hog, but that wasn't it. I didn't know what the truth was, but it hurt to watch, trying to figure it out.

Katie told me about Mathboy. They shared a phone call earlier and some texts. "He's so hot, Mari. Look what he said."

I took her phone and read the texts, as she beamed back at me. It appeared that he had quite the crush. "So," I said, "it was a good thing Brie pegged me in the head. Just think, if she hadn't done that, and you hadn't tried to protect me, you and Mathboy would have never connected."

The corners of her mouth curved up. She cradled the phone in her hand, looking down at the messages. "He has a name you know."

"Sorry. I figured we'd be calling him Mathboy until you guys got married. Then we'd call him, Mathman. That'd make you, Mrs. Mathman." I smiled at her, but was distracted. Her eyes kept flicking over my head, back to Trystan's table. After a little bit, I said, "Can we leave now? He's on a date. You don't have to protect me. I know what's going to happen. He'll leave with her, they'll screw around, and I'll cry. I really don't want to know all the details, Katie."

Katie ignored me, her gaze still over the top of my head. "Trystan isn't acting like himself. He's sitting next to her, but they aren't touching at all. Weird, right?"

I nodded. Okay, that was weird for him. Every time I was around him, it was like he found some excuse to touch me. I'd seen him do it to other girls, too. Not touching was weird.

Katie continued, "Sexbot, on the other hand, has got some heavy hands for a public place." Her face scrunched up, "Gross. He's feeling her up and sucking her face off. Where does he find these girls?"

"Hoes-R-Us, aisle 4." I said deadpan, not really thinking about my words. There was no explaining, Seth. Katie snorted. I continued, "How someone could find him appealing, with that mouth, is beyond me."

"Maybe that's why she hasn't stopped sucking his face—to shut him up."

I laughed a little too loud. I smacked my hands over my mouth and grinned.

Katie's eyes went wide. "Holy friggin' frack. Just sit there. Smile and laugh again." When I started to turn around she hissed at me, "Just do it!"

I had no idea what was going on, so I smiled uncertainly and laughed again. It was a weak haha that sounded totally fake. Katie stomped my foot and I made a strangled sound, as a grin spreads across my face. Then, I kicked her back, laughing louder, not realizing that someone was approaching behind me.

"I thought I heard you," Trystan said, as he stopped in front of our table. His leather jacket was gone. The shirt he wore clung to his body and his scent filled my head. Trystan slipped his hands into the pockets of his jeans and looked from Katie to me.

Katie had a plastic smile on her face. She raised her eyebrows at me, but made no other indication that she thought this was unusual.

Every hair on the back of my neck stood on end when he spoke. My heart stopped. Don't turn, don't turn. If I look at him, I'm toast, I thought to myself. I continued to smile at Katie, tilting my head back like I looked up at him, but I didn't. My glance grazed his shoulder, not his face.

"Hey," I replied, sounding as normal as possible. When I glanced up, I didn't catch his expression until the memory of his face registered in my mind. The look in his eyes was soft, like he was fragile. God, I wanted to die. I couldn't take this.

As if Katie could read my mind, she blurted out, addressing Trystan, "So, double date with the boobie twins?"

Trystan glanced back at his table. Running his hands through his hair, he sighed, "Yeah. Seth needed a wingman. Personally, I'd rather be over here."

Katie had her foot on the bench next to me, keeping him from sitting down. She pulled her foot down, and said, "Then sit, actor-boy, but don't steal Mari's cherry. It's kind of important to her," Katie smirked evilly at her innuendo, as she glanced at my bright red Marciano cherry, still sitting on top of my spoon. "She saves the best for last."

Instantly, I flushed head to toe and promptly kicked her in the shin.

Trystan grinned deeply, showing off a set of dimples that made me die. He slipped into the booth next to me, his shoulder brushing mine. God, he smelled good. "I'm aware of that." He glanced at the cherry, and then looked at me. "Plan on demonstrating any cool party tricks? Tying the stem in a knot?"

I started to answer, but Katie cut me off, "I'm afraid that's privileged information."

Trystan smirked at her. "Really?" He folded his arms across his chest and stared Katie down.

"Mmm. 'Fraid so."

Trystan turned to me, "You're a bottomless box of surprises."

"I'm not a bottomless anything. Not around you," I said dryly. Katie had her straw in her mouth, sucking up some milkshake and promptly choked.

Trystan raised a single brow at me and smiled. Leaning in closer, he breathed, "I wouldn't bet on it."

A tingle shot through my stomach. The way he looked at me, the way he said it, made my heart slap into the sides of my ribs so hard that I thought they'd crack. I did everything humanly possible to not react to his words, to his charm—because that's what it was, charm. Flirtation. There was nothing else there.

Holding my gaze for a moment, he smiled softly. Heat spread through my body and I couldn't look away. Trystan might as well have been holding my face in his hands. I couldn't move. I couldn't think. The power he had over me scared me to death, especially, because he didn't seem to care. Every part of me reacted to him, was drawn to him. Trystan was beautiful—like a wisp of flame—and I knew trying to hold him would only get me burned, but I was mesmerized.

Trystan slipped out of the booth and stood, leaving me there with my jaw hanging open like an idiot. "See you around, Jennings."

CHAPTER 7

~TRYSTAN~

"Where'd you go? The food's getting cold." Seth glanced around after Trystan excused himself, but he didn't see who he was talking to. The diner was full of the dinner crowd and he could barely make out the top of Trystan's head across the room.

"Nowhere," he said. "Just thought I saw someone."

Seth groaned, "Oh, God. Seriously? You're on a fucking date." Exasperated, Seth dug his fingers into his scalp before letting out a huff of air.

The blonde next to Seth recoiled a little, "What's the matter? What'd he do?" She glanced around as she said it, and then looked back at Seth.

"I didn't do anything," Trystan said, ignoring his own date, who didn't seem to care one way or the other.

"You didn't tell her?" Seth scolded, his gaze narrowing on Trystan.

"No," Trystan hissed. "Drop it." He slouched back into the booth and put his arm along the top of the seat, not touching his date.

"I will when you stop acting like a lovesick dick. You can't live like that, man. She'll rip your goddamn heart out of your chest."

Trystan held his temper in check. That was one good thing about having a father like his—he could hide his feelings so that no one had a clue. Trystan dropped his arm down onto his date's shoulders. Grinning at Seth, he said, "Not planning on it. I've got Beth here—"

"Betsy," the blonde corrected.

Trystan didn't bother correcting himself. "—and nothing is distracting me from her beautiful face."

Seth stared at him from across the table. A plate of half eaten food sat in front of him. The guy's arms were wide, made to hit stuff. Trystan could tell that he pissed Seth off by looking for Mari, but when he heard her laugh, he had to see her. Trystan did it without thinking and didn't plan on giving Seth, or anyone else, an explanation. Besides, he was gone less than five minutes. There was nothing to tell.

Seth's tongue moved over his teeth under his lips, as his jaw tensed. "I thought you were into this," he hissed, pointing at the girl next to Trystan.

"I am," he insisted even though he wasn't. He pulled the girl closer. "You guys go do your thing. We'll do ours."

Seth watched him for a moment. Uncertainty clouded his eyes. Or maybe that was lust. Either way, Seth was frozen in place. He wanted to keep Trystan from doing something stupid, but the girl sitting next to him was a sure thing. "You're a pain in the ass, Scott," he said and scooted out of the booth. Twin number one—Bess— followed. Bess and Seth threaded their fingers together. She leaned into him and threw her hip out, annoyed that Seth stopped again.

"You sure?" Seth asked.

"Leave," Trystan urged. "We're fine. Right, Betsy?" Trystan said, as he gently pushed a strand of golden hair away from her face. The girl giggled and nodded so furiously that Trystan thought her head might snap off. Turning back to Seth, he said, "See, we're fine. Go."

Seth didn't need more encouragement. He took the check, paid, and left. It was the normal agreement. Trystan was fine being the wingman, if Seth paid the bill. He stretched and placed his arm over her shoulders again. This part was going to suck.

"So, what do you want to do?" she asked snuggling into his chest. Her fingers played with the collar of his shirt, slipping between the buttons.

Mari chose that second to appear at the door and looked over at them. His heart clenched tight, but he didn't move. Instead they stared at each other. She was a million miles away, someone he'd never have.

Katie's warning was clear enough, even if it did embarrass Mari—keep away.

When his date's lips landed on his neck, Mari shot him a disgusted look and walked out. Trystan pulled his date off his throat, but Mari was already gone. Katie watched her friend walk out the door and looked back at Trystan. The way Katie looked at him made his balls jump up into his body. That girl would castrate him, if she could. He stared her down, refusing to look away.

Betsy, Beth, or whoever she was seemed impatient. She pulled on his shirt front and grabbed Trystan's face, pulling him to her for a kiss. Before the kiss connected, he saw Katie walk out. Betsy's lips pressed into his, but they were cold and lifeless. There was no passion there. It was a kiss without feeling. Trystan didn't want this, but Mari wasn't his. She never would be. He peeled Betsy off his mouth and they slipped out of the booth, walking out the door hand-in-hand.

The rest of the night passed in a blur. After making out with Betsy, he walked her to her sister's car in front of Seth's house. She tried to talk Trystan into more, but he wasn't interested. It was like part of him died. Trystan didn't think a single girl could have such control over him, but if he couldn't have Mari, he didn't want anyone. And, to his horror, making-out with this girl didn't help him forget. If anything, it made the realization that he didn't have Mari more painful. Trystan didn't know what to do. Part of him wanted to give up and give in—say yes to the beautiful woman in front of him—but her kisses left him hollow and cold. He could only image what sleeping with her would feel like. He ran his hands through his hair and walked away.

Frustrated, Trystan walked home alone. Carefully, he cracked open the front door and glanced around for his dad. The lights were still on, the TV blaring. Trystan slipped around the door quietly and saw his father passed-out on the couch.

Relief flooded through him. While he wished his dad would just snap out it, he knew that wasn't going to happen. He wasn't a little kid anymore. This was his life. This was all there was. He stripped off his shirt as he walked back to his room, wishing he had his guitar. The weight on his chest felt like it was going to crush him.

Trystan closed his door and slid the new bolt shut before lying on his bed. He finally had time to think, time to rest.

CHAPTER 8

~MARI~

I slumped against my bedroom door, tossing my book bag on the floor. Thoughts of Trystan filled my mind in an endless wave. It wasn't fair. Why'd he have to show up with a girl on his arm? He didn't seem like he was that into her, but when Katie and I left, the girl was going all vampy on his neck and he didn't seem to mind. Actually, he seemed comfortable with it. If I ever did anything like that in a diner, I'd die of embarrassment. The concept of a public-display-of-affection was foreign to me. I wanted my private life private, so what Trystan was doing with that girl, in front of everyone, made me feel sick.

That would never be me.

Before I had time to think another thought, someone pounded on my door. Pressing my eyes closed, I peeled my back off the door and opened it. Dad was home. That was his knock. I braced for whatever scolding I was about to receive. Pulling the door open, I said, "Hey, Dad. Home from work?"

"Yes," he said in a clipped tone, pushing past me into my room. He had that look on his face, the one that said I didn't measure-up, the one that made me feel like a failure. "You're progress report showed up today. Would you like to tell me anything before we discuss it?" Dad had the piece of paper in his hand. The school sent weekly progress reports via email to psycho-parents, like mine, who demanded them. That was one of the changes my Mom made while she sat on the school board. Dad thought it was a great idea, while I found it to be less than stellar.

Dad's dark hair was silvering at the temples. Wrinkles sprouted from the corners of his eyes making him appear older than he was. Dad had seen too much, first in the military, and then in the hospital. To him, getting good grades was a life or death thing.

I pressed my shoe to the floor, staring at the black toe. I'd loved these shoes when I'd gotten them. They were so cute, but now they seemed frivolous. Dad probably thought so, too. I shook my head, "No, sir. There's nothing to tell."

"It says here that you received detention this week? Mari, we've talked about this. You cannot have such childish things on your permanent record. College is next year. It's not three years away. It's only one year away, and you can bet they'll look at this year and see this blemish." He became more stressed as he spoke, slapping the paper into his fist. When I didn't look up at him, he snapped, "You're destroying your future, Mari. It's not something that can be undone."

My mind broke. Maybe it was Trystan, I don't know, but I couldn't take the emotional berating he was giving me. The guilt he dumped on me sank into my stomach and sat like soured milk. It curdled and I spewed verbal vomit at him, ranting like a lunatic, "It's one detention, Dad! Out of how many days of school? Like seven hundred and twenty! One day doesn't matter! They won't even look at it."

Dad laughed, but the sound was angry, "Young lady, so help me, I'm going to get through to you." He leaned close to my face, speaking deliberately slow, like I was too stupid to fathom what he was saying, "Everything you do, from now until graduation, matters—every grade, every test, every day—all of it. It's recorded and they'll see it. If you just blew your shot at Yale, so help me God, I will—"

"What? What will you do?" Tears streamed from my eyes. I couldn't hold them back anymore. "I made a mistake. It wasn't even something I did. Mom knew about it and she didn't do this to me."

"Because your mother doesn't know! Did she go to Yale? Did she attend an Ivy League school and have her parent's pay for medical school?"

"No," I said softly.

He was still up in my face. "That's right. I did. I know what they expect and this little stunt might have just cost you everything." He sighed and shook his head, like he knew everything and I knew nothing. Closing his eyes he inhaled hard and let it rush back out. "I only want what's best for you, Mari."

I stared at him. I wanted to believe him, but I didn't. I felt like a trophy child, someone he had around to show off. It felt like it was more important that his daughter was smart, that his daughter was perfect— but, I was his daughter and I was neither of those things. I worked hard to get my grades, and I tried so hard to meet his expectations, but I failed. Over and over again, I fell short. I didn't measure up. That feeling never faded. It's there every day when I got a test back.

School was not for learning, not to Dad. School was to demonstrate how smart I already was, but I wasn't. And I wasn't him—he just didn't see it.

I nodded, "I know, Dad." There was nothing else to say. He couldn't see me. It's like I was nothing more than that paper he held in his hands. That one blemish blinded him to all the A's. I knew it was coming. I knew he'd react this way. He always did, but today I couldn't just nod and take it. Tears streaked my face, and I knew he saw that as a sign of weakness.

He lifted my chin in his hand, and looked me in the eye, "Only the cream rises to the top, Mari. You're mother and I know you're cream. Don't disappoint us again." His grip felt cold and distant, his gaze was even more so. I swallowed hard and nodded. He released me and said, "Get in a little studying before bed." With that, he turned on his heel and left.

Every inch of me wanted to scream, but I couldn't. They couldn't know how trapped they made me feel, how smothered I was. I pushed the door shut and went to the computer not thinking about what I was doing. Before I knew it, I was on the Day Jones page and clicking play on his song, letting Trystan's voice fill my head. I laid down on my bed, clutching the pillow, crying into it, as the song played softly and drowned out my sobs.

There were so many things that I wanted to say to my parents, but I couldn't. They both worked non-stop trying to give me everything they never had. They acted like I was an adult with some things and a child with other things. I just wished they'd see Mari, their daughter. I wished they saw how much I liked art and how much I didn't want to dedicate my life to something I wasn't passionate about. It left me, their only child, alone. From the time I turned twelve, I'd spent more days alone than with them. Last year, their work schedules lined up and they were pleased. It meant they'd get more time together, but it also meant I saw them less. They worked four days on, three days off. For the days they were gone, I was on my own, and they were proud they had such a self-sufficient child.

Tears chilled my face, as they sank into my pillow. I couldn't stand it anymore. For once, I wished I wasn't me, that I didn't feel the way I felt about everything. I wished I could just hook up with a random guy and not hand over a piece of my heart. It would help me forget the things that I tried so hard not to remember. No matter what happened, in a year, I knew if I didn't fight for my life, I'd be stuck on this path forever, living the life my father wanted—not the one I wanted.

Pushing off the bed, I looked at the screen. More comments, more pleas for Day to play another song, reveal his name, post a pic, anything—and they all went unanswered.

Emotional insanity compelled me to do it. Staring at the screen, I typed in one word at a time. I watched as my fingers wrote something I would never say, something I never tried before. I wanted to know if it helped take away the sting, if that was why he did it.

WHAT DOES IT FEEL LIKE TO SLEEP WITH SOMEONE YOU DON'T LOVE?

My hands hovered over the keyboard. I hesitated to post it. Trystan would know it was me. There was no way he wouldn't, and since he didn't answer anyone, what was the point? But I wanted to know. Maybe his way of dealing with life was better. Maybe a random hookup didn't leave everyone feeling hollow inside. Maybe that was just me and I could get over it.

My pointer finger smacked the enter button hard. The key clicked and the message posted.

CHAPTER 9

~TRYSTAN~

By the time Trystan was safe in his room, it was late. Out of habit, he grabbed the old laptop and turned it on. The machine made a hissing noise, followed by something that sounded like Cookie Monster munching gravel. It came from inside his hard drive, and Trystan knew the laptop wouldn't last much longer, but the machine finally turned on. The screen flared to life and he checked his Facebook page, stopping by Mari's page to look at her picture for a second, and then moving onto the Day Jones' YouTube page. Although he vowed to stay away from it, he couldn't. It was too insane how quickly it'd grown, how many people liked the song.

He didn't read every post. Instead he read a handful of new comments. One post that was in bold type caught his eye. The rest of the comments were of the same vein, but this one was different. His heart clenched when he read it. It had to be Mari. It had to be. There was no way to know for certain, but he could feel it tugging on his gut like a guitar string. The girl who wanted every kiss to have profound meaning was asking for pointers on sleeping around? That didn't make sense. It pained him, cutting through his core, like he'd been cleaved in half. Trystan's breath was ragged, as he stared at the screen.

Answer her.

Trystan's fingers twitched, dying to respond. He wasn't sure if she was scolding him or asking him how to get started. A sick feeling crept up from his gut and lodged itself in his throat. He swallowed hard, trying to force it down, but it wouldn't go away. Every part of him said that this was Mari, this was her question.

Trystan's fingers tapped out a response on the keyboard. Carefully constructing his reply, he crafted each word so she'd know. His answer was plain and simple. There were no excuses or pleas, just the naked truth. Trystan's finger hovered above the button. He wanted to click, he wanted to post the reply, but it was so risky. There were ways to track things back to him. He knew that, and with the number of people trying to find him, Trystan couldn't click.

He deleted his post and closed the laptop, knowing that he had to wait until tomorrow. He'd ask her when he showed her what he was working on. The thought made him feel better. Lying back on his bed, Trystan pictured her face as he sang. The memory was burned into his brain and he loved it. Closing his eyes, he could see her face, her brown eyes filled with curious flecks of gold surrounded by a cascade of curls that were soft as silk.

Trystan closed his eyes and for once, fell asleep with a smile on his lips.

———

Trystan heard his dad moving around when he was finishing up in the shower. Damn it. He'd taken too long. Toweling off fast, Trystan pulled on a pair of tattered jeans and a tee shirt. His clothing had seen better days. He hid it by layering his shirts with a flannel or button down shirt. He let the front hang open, which still gave him that neatly messy look.

Before he could reach the door, his father's voice rang in his ears, "I've got tickets to the hockey game this weekend. I thought me and you could go." His voice sounded softer than usual. Trystan turned slowly, carefully, and looked his old man over. "It'd be like old times."

"What old times were those?" he asked, knowing he shouldn't.

Trystan's dad looked down and sighed. He was wearing a gray suit with a jewel-toned blue tie. It brought out his eyes. Damn, they looked alike. It made Trystan's skin crawl to think he was turning into his dad. He wanted nothing to do with him. Starting a new life somewhere else was a dream. He thought about it day and night. The only think holding him here was Mari.

How many times had Trystan wanted to run? How many times did he nearly walk away and leave everything? Too many, he thought bitterly.

"Don't be like that. I do the best I can. This was something I could do. Give me another chance, kid. I promise you—"

"Your promises don't mean much. Not anymore. I'm not the little kid who used to wait for your approval. I gave up on you a long time ago. There's no point in pretending... not anymore. As soon as I graduate, I'm gone and I'm never coming back."

"Trystan... ," Dad said, stepping toward him. It was hard to look his father over, hard to see how normal he seemed in the light of day. Wearing that suit, smiling that smile, he could be any nice guy, but Trystan knew better. He was the jaded drunk who'd hit him faster than he could blink.

"It's okay, Dad. There's no need to pretend anymore."

His father look genuinely confused, "Pretend what?"

Trystan was so disgusted that he couldn't even say it. Pretend you care about me—

pretend you love me. Instead, he closed his eyes and shook his head. Trystan turned on his heel and left without another word.

By the time Trystan got to school, he was late. He sat down in homeroom, but Tucker didn't say anything. No commentary on his tardy, no threat to dock his grade.

When the bell rang at the end of class, Tucker stopped him, "Mr. Scott."

Trystan stopped. He stared straight ahead, not wanting to look at the man. It was like Tucker had radar for screwed-up students, and he was sniffing out what was wrong with Trystan. The thought made his skin grow cold and clammy. No one could know that part of his life. Ever. And Tucker was getting way too close to the truth.

Tucker waited for the other students to pass, "Want to tell me why you were late today?"

Trystan shrugged, "Had better things to do."

Tucker hmmmfed, but didn't say anything else about it. Instead, he said, "I'll check on you and Mari later today. You're a good kid, Scott, but you need to be careful.

You're walking the line and it's too damn thin—too easy to fall on the wrong side."

Trystan's gaze lifted and met Tucker's. He wanted to say, You don't know what you're talking about—you haven't lived my life, but he was silent. Trystan nodded once and walked out, leaving Tucker watching his back as the room filled with the next class.

Trystan sat through his classes, not paying attention to anything. The lump in his throat didn't abate last night. It didn't fade while he slept. His concern over Mari's question twisted into worry. What if she was really asking? What if she intended to sleep with someone she didn't care about? What could he do about it?

Nothing, he thought, gripping his pencil so hard that it snapped. The crack was audible. Trystan ignored the looks of his classmates, including Seth who sat shaking his head next to him.

After the bell rang, Seth walked out next to him, "Thought you would have hit that last night, but obviously you didn't. What happened to promising to stay away from her?" he said referring to Mari. "Do your promises mean nothing?" there was a joking quality to his voice, but it hit way too close to home for Trystan.

Trystan rounded on his friend, shoving Seth's shoulders hard. Surprised by the sudden hostility, Seth flew back into the lockers, tripping several students in the process. When his back slammed against the metal doors, Seth's face pinched with anger, "What the fuck, man?" Seth stood and walked back toward Trystan, shoving him back. Trystan tried to keep walking, but Seth wouldn't shut up, "She's nothing but a bitch," he enunciated the word, spitting it at his friend's back, "a tease," he said it slowly, but Trystan still didn't turn. Seth's anger got the best of him and he added, "A little cun—" but before Seth could finish speaking, Trystan was on him.

The word made him snap. No one could call Mari that. Trystan threw his books to the floor and charged Seth, ramming his shoulder into Seth's stomach. The two slammed into a group of lockers. Trystan's fists punched into Seth's sides, one after the other. Seth screamed at him, returning every punch, but Trystan was a better fighter. After years of beatings, he knew how to take a hit. His body moved, taking Seth's shots in less vulnerable places or moving out of the way, so Seth's fists missed Trystan entirely.

It didn't take long for a group of kids to circle around them. They chanted fight, fight, fight.

Trystan thought that was stupid, standing around them in a circle and cheering them on to fight. What do they think we were doing? Dancing? Just as the thought entered his mind, Seth's fist connected with his stomach. Trystan folded in half and rammed Seth with his shoulder. Neither of them could breathe. Blood dripped down Trystan's lip and he wondered if it was his.

Before anything else could happen, Tucker stepped between them, yanking them apart. "Get to class!" Tucker yelled at the crowd. The kids groaned, slowly walking away when they realized there was nothing else to see. Tucker glanced at Trystan with a look of exasperation on his face, "Get to where you're going, Scott. Seth, my room. Now."

"You're just gonna let Trystan walk?" Seth argued, following after Tucker but looking over at Trystan with malice. His broad shoulders were tense, the muscles in his arms still taut and ready to punch something. This wasn't over. That much Trystan knew.

Tucker didn't look back. He walked at a pace that was fast for him, forcing Seth to keep up and release some that anger burning in his body. He snapped over his shoulder, "Scott's already taken care of; you on the other hand need some guidance. Not another word or I hand this mess over to the principle and you both get suspended. Rumor has it that one more suspension gets you expelled." Seth groaned dramatically and trailed behind Tucker and out of sight.

Trystan headed straight for the stage, rage still flowing through his muscles. He couldn't control himself. He'd never hit Seth like that before. They'd rough-housed, wrestled and that kind of thing, but this was a fight. Trystan threw punches not caring where they landed, as long as they did some harm. He couldn't process what was happening. Up until then, Seth had been his best friend. The guy always had his back, but this was insane. It was like he was forbidding Trystan to be with Mari, like Seth would make him choose between them.

What kind of friend would do that? Maybe he missed something. Maybe it wasn't what it looked like, because it looked an awful lot like jealousy—but that didn't make any sense. Seth didn't like Mari. Trystan's arms were still tense. His fingers clenched over and over again trying to work it out, as he bounded up the stage stairs and walked behind the wing. It was dark, as usual. He made his way to the basement door and pulled it open.

Descending swiftly, Trystan stopped at the bottom to see Mari with her legs hanging over the end of the couch and her dark hair fanned around her beautiful face. The little white tee shirt she wore clung to her body. He watched her chest rise slowly, as she drew in a breath. Mari's eyes were closed like she was daydreaming, thinking about something wonderful. The way her pink lips pulled up slightly at the corners gave her a ghost of a smile. Her foot swung and he was treated to a full smile, though he didn't know the cause.

Mari's eyes opened, and she saw him standing across the room. "Oh," she said startled. Her hands slipped to her sides like she was going to push herself up.

Trystan crossed the room quickly, before she could sit up. Grinning down at her, he asked, "Hanging upside down off the end of the couch, are we?"

Mari smirked, "Maybe." Trystan laughed and it was contagious. Mari's soft laugh filled his body and warmed him, chasing away the rest of the animosity he felt toward Seth. "Definitely. I wanted to see if my hair could touch the floor if I leaned over the side."

"Does it?"

She nodded, "Yup." Mari's eyes were focused on his mouth. Trystan squirmed a little wondering why she was looking at him like that. "What happened to you? There's blood on your mouth."

Trystan straightened and tried to dab it away. "Nothing. Seth and I don't see eye to eye on something. It didn't end well."

Mari slipped off the couch and stood up in front of him. She licked the back of her thumb and ran it over his mouth, removing the rest of the dried blood, before wiping her hands on her jeans. The touch was light, gentle. Trystan's stomach felt like it was floating. How she could do that, how she could reach out and touch him without thinking twice was... he didn't know what it was. The nurse wore gloves when blood was involved, but Mari didn't seem to think Trystan was anything to be worried about. She trusted him in a way that surprised him.

Mari looked down and when she met his eyes again, Trystan asked her softly, "What does it feel like to sleep with someone you don't love?" Her eyes widened and she looked up at him. Her lips parted like she wanted to say something, but her jaw just hung there suspended. Trystan became serious, all traces of humor stripped away by the question, "Do you really want to know?" Do you already have someone picked out? Did you give up on your dreams? Was I the one that pushed you to do it? He stared down at her, hating himself. Breathing hard, heart fluttering, he watched her. Her brown eyes didn't stray from his.

She didn't apologize, she didn't explain. She just stood there, watching him breathe like everything was normal. After a moment, Mari smiled sheepishly. "You knew that was me. I figured you would." She looked down at her fingers, as they twisted in her hands.

He stepped closer to her, "Of course I would. And I knew what you meant, too. I just couldn't write it there. Too many people are watching, looking for me." He wrapped his fingers around hers as he spoke, suspending the nervous wringing of her hands.

Mari didn't pull away. "So, what's it like?" She sounded curious and it killed him. It killed him that she asked—that she wanted him to tell her it was good. He could hear the hope in her voice.

Trystan watched her dark, rich eyes. There was a hint of something in her voice, like she'd given up on her ideal. Guilt gnawed at him, like he was the one who pushed her to it. What was he supposed to say? That sleeping around helped him forget about his life? That he used it to hide from reality for a while. In those moments, it felt like time was suspended, like there was nothing to fear—like he could survive the lot he'd been given. But now, seeing the look on Mari's face, he couldn't say that.

Sleeping with her would be different. He lowered his lashes, and glanced at her hands. Swallowing the lump in his throat, he finally said, "It's not worth it, not compared to what you could have." His thumb stroked the smooth skin on the back of her wrist. His heart pounded harder. It felt like a confession, like everything he'd done until now was wrong—like he knew his salvation was standing in front of him.

"Compared to what I could have?" she repeated. "And what's that, Mr. Scott?" One of her dark brows lifted. It made her look jaded and he didn't like it. Cynical was something Mari was not. There'd been a pureness that attracted him to her. The way she lived her life with her whole heart was brave. She put herself out there and was willing to take chances that he never took. That demanded admiration, even if she didn't realize it. Now, it seemed like she was thinking about chipping that away. The thought killed him.

"Love," Trystan's voice was deep and determined. "It makes everything else seem trite." He looked down, unable to meet her gaze.

"You sound like a little hypocritical, there Trystan. There can't be one set of rules for you and another set for me." She sucked in air and added, "I saw you leave with her last night. Ten bucks says you didn't even bother to get her name."

Fuck. Trystan ran hands through his hair, his heart sinking into his shoes, "You're right. I didn't know her name. And the truth is, I didn't know what I'd do until the moment came." It was a confession that he didn't plan to give, but if fell from his lips like drops of rain.

Mari's hands fell to her sides, her gaze locked on Trystan's face. "Oh, and what'd you do?"

"Took her home. Said goodnight." He glanced up at her from under his brow, "She's not the one I want." His eyes connected with hers and held. There were so many things he wanted to say. Trystan's body felt light and lithe. In that moment he wanted nothing more than to lift his hand and feel Mari's soft skin under his fingers, and taste her lips. The longing in his gaze made him feel exposed. He wanted her to see it. He wanted her to know she was the one.

But for whatever reason, Mari was blind—or worse—she didn't care. Mari looked away and nodded, "I see."

Trystan smiled softly, whispering, "No, you don't—but I wish you would." Glancing at her, Trystan's heart beat wildly in his chest. Every urge he had was wrong. He wanted to wrap his arms around her, pull her to him, and kiss her with all his might. The way her eyes darted away, the way her lips parted like she was disappointed, killed him. Part of him wanted to tell her—no, to show her, how he felt—but his mind kept telling him not to. There was only one chance for him to get this right, and now was not the time.

Before he could say anything else, Mari smiled weakly and leaned forward, her beautiful face coming closer to his until her lips met his cheek. Her soft lips brushed his face, pressing against his cool skin before retreating.

Shocked, Trystan stared after her, unable to speak. Bewildered, he finally managed to ask, "What was that for?"

Mari shrugged, and looked up at him out of the corner of her eye, with a grin on her lips, "What? You're the only one who can steal a kiss?"

CHAPTER 10

~MARI~

My heart was pounding in my chest, beating harder than I'd ever felt it as I leaned toward Trystan's face. It wasn't a conscious plan. I didn't think, hey, let's kiss Trystan on the cheek and then grin like an idiot. Instead, I found my body moving without my consent. I was so happy he didn't sleep with her. I was so glad that it flooded my body like liquid sunshine coursing through my veins. Before I could stop myself, I felt my lips brush his cheek. Wildly fighting every urge within me, I made sure it was just a peck. I made sure I didn't take his gorgeous face in my palms and pull his lips to mine. Breathing steadily, I looked up at him when I stepped away, trying to ignore the jitters that were making me giddy.

Trystan's voice was airy and filled with shock, "What was that for?"

The perplexed look on his face made me say it. "What?" I asked, looking at him from the corner of my eyes. I could feel the smile spreading across my lips and I couldn't hide it. "You're the only one who can steal a kiss?"

Trystan blinked like he didn't hear me right. It was a moment that I'd play over in my mind again and again. Everything about it was perfect. That look, that baffled look on his face, made me want to dance. Unable to hide my giddiness, I swallowed a giggle, but it sounded like a sultry laugh instead.

Trystan tilted his head to the side, eyes wide, like he didn't know what came over me. Before I could say anything, he stepped behind me and wrapped his arms around my waist. The vixen, that seemed to possess me moments ago, fled when Trystan's fingers started tickling my sides.

His lips were next to my ear. I could feel his breath wash over my neck as he teased, "Kiss stealer."

I laughed hysterically, my knees buckling from under me. Trystan scooped me up in his arms and tossed me in the air. I shrieked as I fell straight down onto the couch. Before I could breath, Trystan pinned me by sitting on my legs and continued to tickle me.

"Kiss ninja," I laughed, trying to get my fingers to wiggle in a ticklish spot on Trystan's lean body.

"Kiss ninja?" he laughed, moving his hands over my sides, applying the perfect amount of pressure to make me laugh the hardest.

Between hysterical giggles I managed, "Yeah, because you sneak up all stealthy like a ninja."

"Kiss thief," he said smiling, his fingers moving between my belly and my underarms. Laughter made me shake so hard I couldn't stop. The glimpses I got of Trystan were filled with pure joy. His eyes sparkled, brilliant blue as he laughed.

"Kiss cowboy," I blurted out. That one made him chuckle really hard.

"Kiss bandit."

Right then his hands were on both sides of my waist, applying enough pressure to make me squealing with laughter. "Kiss assassin! You're killing me! Stop!" I laughed, certain I was going to explode in a ball of giggles. As we wrestled on the couch, Trystan leaned into me. From trying to pull away my hair was covering my face, several curls stuck to my lips.

Panting hard, he stilled and brushed the hair out of my face. "A kiss assassin sounds kind of sexy. I'd like to see one of those."

"Grab a mirror, because I'm totally looking at one. He has bright blue eyes, a killer smile, and he's a closet musician." A wicked grin spread across my lips. "All the kiss assassins are—"

Before I could say anything else, his fingers tickled me again. This time when I stopped laughing, something changed. I was more aware that here he was, how he was laying with half of his body on top of mine, on the couch—the nearness of his mouth and his breath on my face.

Trystan looked down at me, still smiling softly. My heart hammered in my chest, but this time it wasn't from tickles or silly words. His gaze pinned me in place, those sapphire eyes stole my breath and my brains in one look. They swept over my face, moving slowly from my eyes to my lips, and back again. Trystan's mouth parted like he was going to say something, but he didn't. He froze like that, watching me beneath him with an unreadable expression on his face. Just when I thought my heart couldn't take another shock, the door above us banged open.

Tucker's voice bellowed down the stairs, "Scott, get up here. Now!"

As soon as we heard the door open, we shot apart. Trystan pushed himself upright, and stood as I rolled to my side and patted my hair, trying to make it look normal and not like we'd been doing something naughty. I glanced over at him. Trystan didn't meet my eyes. Instead, he shoved his hands in his pockets and walked away. Before he got to the stairs, he looked over his shoulder. "Later, kiss thief." He treated me to a dimpled grin and I nearly died.

Ignoring the fact that my heart was half way up my throat, I slumped back into the couch nodding and said, "You know it, ninja."

CHAPTER 11

~TRYSTAN~

"What are you plans after high school, Scott?" Tucker asked him pointe-blank. Irritation made Tucker's face a reddish, blotchy color. He stood with his arms folded, eyes narrowed, waiting for an answer.

"I'm enlisting," Trystan replied. He didn't look away.

"How do you plan to do that when you're arrested for assault?"

Trystan blanched. "What?"

"You're eighteen, Trystan. For chrissakes, use your head. You're not a child anymore. When you hit someone, it's assault. You should know this by now." Tucker used little restraint when talking to him. Trystan didn't understand why he wasn't dumped in the principal's office, why Tucker seemed to be watching out for him, but it seemed like he was.

Before another thought came into Trystan's head, he blurted out, "Seth's filing charges?" Worry and shock pinched the spot between his brows.

Tucker sighed and his arms fell to his sides. "What's it going to take to get through to you? This isn't a game. You get one shot at life and if you screw it up now—" he trailed off, not completing the thought. He let it linger there, allowing Trystan to fill in the blank.

"I'm not playing games, Mr. Tucker." Trystan looked away. The anger he had toward Seth was still simmering below the surface.

"Then what the hell is going on with you? Seth's your best friend. What did he do that made you react like that?"

Trystan stared at the floor. A quick shake of his head was the only answer he could manage.

Tucker's stance shifted. They were standing in front of the stage. The only light in the room came from the recessed lights that hung above the exit doors. It cast a faint yellow glow across the stage, illuminating the place where they stood.

Tucker took Trystan's shoulder in his hand, "I can't keep you out of trouble forever. I want you to have a shot."

"Why?" Trystan blurted out. He sounded bitter, jaded. It was like he couldn't believe Tucker's words. He felt his face pinch when he said it, and it didn't matter how hard Trystan tried, he couldn't hide it. He couldn't believe that someone would look out for him.

Tucker dropped his hand. He blinked once, slowly, his forehead pinching together forming rows of wrinkles that made him look much older than he was. He sounded remorseful when he spoke, "Someone told you wrong, Trystan. They lied to you." He shook his head sadly, as he said it and then turned to leave.

"What are you talking about?" Trystan said to his back. Turning, Trystan watched Tucker as he walked away up the dark aisle toward the exit at the back of the auditorium.

When he reached the door, Tucker turned back to Trystan and said, "You're worth something, Scott, your life is valuable. Right now, you have a chance to escape whatever you're running from, but if things keep up like this, you're going to blast your only escape route straight to hell." With that, he disappeared through the door leaving Trystan alone.

CHAPTER 12

~MARI~

I didn't mean to overhear what I heard, but when Trystan's voice echoed from the other side of the stage curtain, I stopped. I was no longer interested in exiting the stage door in front of me. Instead, I lingered, listening.

Did he say he was enlisting? My throat tightened. I couldn't breathe. I had no idea what Trystan planned after school. I assumed he would go to college, but now that I thought about it, I hadn't heard him mention applications and admission interviews. It felt like someone was crushing my heart. Frozen, I stood behind the curtain and heard everything.

Tucker's warnings rang in my ears. I peered through the stage curtain to see Trystan sitting in the first row with his face in his hands after Tucker left the auditorium. Trystan leaned forward so that I couldn't see his eyes. The light spilled onto the curve of his back before it mixed with shadow. Dark hair hung forward, blocking his face.

Paralyzed by fear, I stood there staring at him. If he enlisted, I'd never see him again. The thought made me shiver. Sickness crept up my throat and soured in my mouth. There were only a few months of school left. Then, he'd be gone.

Forever.

I couldn't breathe. I couldn't think. I didn't think. I walked down the stairs, quietly making my way straight toward him. I didn't care if he loved someone else. I had to tell him. I had to say it before he left or I'd regret it for the rest of my life.

Trystan lifted his head when he saw me descending the stairs. His eyes seem hollow, like he was weary and broken. He didn't speak. That dark brooding gaze followed my movements. There was a hardness to his gaze that usually vaporized around me, but this time it remained in place. I knew that he'd be angry that I heard. Trystan never told me he was running from anything, but Tucker seemed to have figured it out. Trystan looked like he'd been sucker-punched with the truth. Knowing that I was standing there, knowing that I'd seen it happen, made it worse. His eyes said it all.

Heart pounding harder, I reached the lower landing and stepped onto the floor. I didn't know what to do, what to say, so I didn't say anything. There were no words to comfort, no words to explain how I felt or what I wanted. Walking toward him with my shoulders back, my long hair swayed gently with each step. Trystan gazed at me with a desperate look in his eye, like he was drowning and I wasn't welcome to watch.

When I was two steps in front of him, Trystan abruptly looked away. He pushed out of his seat, making us stand nose to nose. "Mari, I don't think now is a good time—"

I didn't stop moving toward him. I didn't answer him. I didn't speak. Pulse pounding in my ears, I lifted my hands and curled my fingers in his shirtfront. Surprised flashed across his eyes, as I pulled his face to mine. I yanked his shirt hard, pulling him closer to me, fast. His lips pressed into mine and I kissed him.

I kissed Trystan Scott. And it was a real kiss. I didn't hold back and I wouldn't apologize for it later.

My lips moved against his and this kiss was my doing, not his. His hands lifted and tangled in my hair. I flicked my tongue against his lips until he parted them, and let me deepen the kiss. His arms tightened around me, embracing me harder. Breathless, I kissed him more, feeling every curve of his mouth and tasting every inch of his soft lips. My hands released his shirt and tangled in his silky hair. I didn't want it to end. The moment was perfect. The kiss was perfect and I knew without a doubt it was my kiss, that it was real, and that I meant every bit of it.

When we parted he looked at me with that soft smile on his face. Breathing hard, he said, "You have to stop doing that, thief."

"You have to stop letting me," I replied, smiling back at him. My fingers pushed through his hair and then fell to rest on his shoulders. He closed his eyes, feeling my touch, enjoying the sensation.

When he opened his eyes again, Trystan was more breathless than before. "I need to tell you something."

Icy fear crawled out of my stomach and up my throat. He wanted to tell me that he was in love with someone else. If he said it, I'd die. There was no way I could handle it, and once I knew the name, it would be impossible to kiss him and not feel guilty. I could barely speak, but I managed to shake my head, saying, "I don't need to know. I like things like this. I'm okay with things like this..."

Trystan was quiet for a moment. He reached for me, running his fingers through my hair. When he spoke, his voice was barely a whisper, "You deserve more..."

My heart was in my throat, ready to crawl out of my mouth. The words, I love you, were on my tongue. I was going to say it, but the way he looked at me, rendered me speechless.

Trystan's breath warmed my cheek. He was that close, his body against mine. When he pressed his lips to my face, I couldn't speak. My breath caught in my throat as Trystan slowly bestowed one kiss after another across my cheek. I closed my eyes, and enjoyed every second of it. Every bit of me felt light and happy.

When Trystan pulled back again, I couldn't hide my grin. "Assassin," I breathed into his ear. "You're killing me. You know that?" The warm playful tones in my voice let him know how much I liked it.

Trystan pulled back enough to see my face, his smile widening as he did so. "I could say the same thing."

"So, what are we going to do about it?" This confidence, this insane person who was speaking wasn't me. She was blurting things out that I never had the guts to say. But he's leaving, a voice in the back of my mind whispered. You don't have another year. You barely have another semester. He'll be gone after graduation. Take a risk, give a kiss. See what happens. I listened to that voice for once, finding resolve that was foreign to me.

Trystan released me and stepped back. Before I could ask what he was doing, he pulled a piece of paper from his pocket and showed it to me. "I wanted to tell you this for so long, but—" his voice trailed off.

I took the wrinkled sheet from his hands, my eyes scanning the page like it could devastate me. It was the song—the Day Jones song about the girl. My stomach clenched, as I tried to shove it back into his hands. Shaking, I said, "I don't need to know who she is. Having you like this is better than nothing at all."

He smiled sadly at me, but shook his head. "Not until you read the last line on the page. Flip it over, Mari." Trystan watched me, his eyes burning into mine.

My stomach acted like it was in a free-fall. I looked down at the page in my hands and flipped the paper over. It felt like time stopped. The rapid beat of my heart filled my ears. I could feel Trystan's gaze on my face, as my eyes trailed down the page looking for the last line. There were two lines of words filling the space were only one line belonged. It was an alternate ending, an ending that showed a name.

My skin prickled as I read it. I didn't understand. I looked up at him and couldn't stop shaking. "What is this?"

"The original ending—the real last line where I tell the girl I love her and call her by name." My chest swelled as my throat tightened. I shook so hard that I dropped the song, and tried to step away. Trystan didn't chase after the sheet with his music and words. Instead he chased after me. His hands slipped around my waist and he pulled me to him.

Looking down at me, he said, "The girl who inspired that song, the girl who stole my heart—she's standing right in front of me."

Riptide
The Secret Life of
Trystan Scott
Vol. 3

rip-tide: a strong current of swiftly moving water that flows away from the safety of the shore.

CHAPTER 1

~**TRYSTAN**~

Trystan's fingers skimmed Mari's cheek and then tangled in her soft curls. They stood at the foot of the stage, surrounded by empty seats. That kiss was still burned onto his lips. He couldn't step away from Mari. His eyes locked with hers, never blinking, never straying from her intense gaze. The moment felt so fragile that Trystan was afraid to breathe. Everything he ever wanted was standing in front of him, looking up in shock.

Mari's body shivered in his arms when he told her that she was the reason he wrote that song. Swallowing hard, Trystan breathed, "The girl who brought me to my knees, was you." Taking a breath to steady his voice, Trystan lowered his gaze and looked back up at her. "That song meant everything to me. It was as close as I thought I'd get to you. I've made too many mistakes, too many times. And then, like an idiot, I flaunted them in front of you." A smile lifted the corners of his lips as he allowed a curl to fall from his fingers. "Mari, I don't know what made you do it. I realize that you wanted someone for one night, but that isn't what I'm looking for anymore." His lips curved like he was trying to form a word that wouldn't come.

Mari shivered, unable to hold her body still. When she finally spoke, he could barely hear her, "You love me?"

It was a question that he wanted to answer every hour of every day, but when she asked, when her lips parted and those words tumbled out, Trystan felt a pang of panic pierce his middle. She wanted a plaything. She doesn't want you that way, he thought. It felt like fingers were pressing into his throat and cutting off the air. The way Mari looked at him—it was too much.

There was a slight tremor building in his hands. To hide it, Trystan slipped his fingers off her face and into his pockets. Looking at her through the pieces of dark hair that hung over Trystan's eyes, he said softly, "It's more than that. God, Mari." He sucked in air, and ran his fingers through his hair. "There's so much to say, and I have no idea how to say it. I wrote it down, because otherwise all those words, all those feelings, stayed trapped inside of me, in here," his fist banged on his chest as he lifted his gaze and met hers. Stepping toward Mari, he confessed, "I love you. Everything I am, everything I hope to be, is better when I'm with you. I don't know..." Trystan was breathing hard, like he'd been running from something terrifying.

Mari watched him, her beautiful brown eyes impossibly wide, with her lips parted in shock. As he stumbled over his words, lacking the normal Trystan Scott confidence, Mari stepped toward him and took his hand in hers. Brow pinching together, she looked up at him, asking, "Why are you trembling?"

Trystan worked his jaw, freeing the thought that was stuck in his throat, "Love destroys, I believe that—but I'm hopelessly in love with you." His head tilted to the side as he said it, his blue eyes so soft and vulnerable. "What am I—" he started to ask, but she cut him off.

Heart pounding wildly, he couldn't stand it. In that moment, Mari didn't say much. She just stood there shell shocked after he said he loved her, but Trystan had to tell her. She had to know. There was no way he could let her think, after all this time, that he was in love with someone else. But when he said he loved her, she didn't say it back. The center of his chest felt hollow, like a carved out pumpkin. He couldn't breathe. His mind was telling Trystan to make a joke and run—do what he always did—but he couldn't, not now, not with Mari.

The corner of Mari's mouth curved up. She held his hands tighter and pulled them to her chest, "Do you feel that? My heart's pounding in my chest like it's going to explode. You do that to me. You make me crazy. You make me better. You make everything better. You're the brightest part of my day and you always have been. I don't want a fling, Scott," he recoiled when she said his last name, but Mari pulled him closer, not releasing his hands, "I asked you that question last night, because I couldn't stand seeing you every day and sitting next to the guy that stole my heart, and act like everything's okay. When Tucker said you were enlisting—" she let out a rush of air, eyes wide, locked on his face, and continued, "I couldn't lose you. Not without even trying. How could you think I didn't love you?"

Trystan listened to her speak. His mind was trying to pull out of the conversation before his heart was blasted to bits and splattered across the auditorium walls. Mari could destroy him. One word and his life would never be the same, but as she spoke he couldn't help but smile.

When she asked that question, Trystan finally met her gaze. "You love me?" he asked.

Mari nodded, smiling up at him, "I love you, Trystan Scott, every bit of you; past, present, and future." A grin twisted her pink lips. Mari looked at him out of the corner of her eye, "Besides, it's not like I can turn it off. If that were possible, we wouldn't have had that kiss."

Trystan laughed softly. The sound filled his chest, making him feel whole. Leaning toward Mari, he used every drop of boyish charm he had, "I really liked that kiss."

Mari's cheeks flushed as she smiled, and she quickly tried to look at the floor, but Trystan didn't let her. Instead, he reached for her face and tilted her chin up. Smiling, he took in every inch of her red face and instantly wanted to cover her in kisses, "And I suppose you didn't like it as much?"

Mari smiled broader. "You'll just have to do it again and find out... see for yourself." She looked up at him through her lashes, her cheeks growing hotter in his hands.

"Is that so?" Trystan asked, a soft smile spreading across his lips.

She nodded, "Very much, I'm afraid." Mari glanced up at Trystan. He pulled her closer and lowered his face, inching slowly toward hers. Mari's head tilted to the side and he was kissing her again. Her arms wrapped around his chest and she held on tight. Trystan's palms stroked her cheek as he pulled her lips to his. She tasted like strawberries and sunshine. He couldn't get enough, he'd never get enough of Mari.

The bell rang and shocked them apart. Trystan stepped back, his gaze filled with mirth and his lips twisted into a perfectly boyish smile. He crossed his ankles, and bounced on the balls of his feet for a second, drinking her in like this was a dream. "I have more things I'd like to discuss with you, beautiful kiss ninja, but I have to get to class. I can't miss another or I won't graduate, because believe me—if that weren't the case—I'd stay here with you."

Mari looked at him, still beaming, "Go on, I understand." Trystan nodded at her, and grabbed his books. He was half way up the aisle when she blurted out, "Wait! Trystan,"

When he stopped and turned back, he saw concern on her face. "What's the matter? Awh, screw it. I can stay." He threw his books on a chair and walked back down the aisle. Mari met him halfway and laughed.

Grabbing his books, Mari shoved them into his hands, and said, "No, you can't. Besides, I just wanted to ask you if we can keep this a secret, for now. I'm not really supposed to date. If my Dad finds out, well, I just don't want to deal with it…"

Trystan fought back the urge to reach out and run his fingers through her soft curls again—to be that close to Mari, and to be able to touch her…

Trystan felt like he could fly. There was nothing that could bring him down. Leaning toward her, he touched his forehead to hers lightly, "My lips are sealed. I won't tell a soul." He smiled at her again, beaming with excitement. Pulling away from her was torture. He shouldn't have gotten so close again. Tearing himself away from Mari was the last thing he wanted to do, but Trystan couldn't miss another class.

As it was, he was on thin ice. Tucker saved his ass earlier and he knew it. Who would have thought that today would go this way? Trystan didn't. Grinning at her, he sucked in a deep breath, letting it fill his chest before turning away.

"Better get going," he said, his voice a little too high, almost like he was laughing. When did it become so hard to hide how he felt around Mari?

CHAPTER 2

~MARI~

"Yeah, you better go." My voice was soft. It was everything I could do to keep it from shaking. Trystan Scott loves me. He said it. He wrote a freaking song about it. A song that went viral. A song everyone knew. My heart lurched in my chest as he pulled away from me and turned to walk up the aisle.

He looked over his shoulder at me, those brilliant blue eyes gleaming. "The view's good coming and going, I hear."

At that point, the smile on my face increased to mega-wattage. I glanced down at the floor and back up at him, feeling the blush spreading across my face. Looking up at him from under my lashes, I nodded once and said, "Only you would say that."

"Only you would pretend you weren't looking." Trystan walked backwards up the aisle, one sneaker squeaking as he clutched his books tightly to his chest. The way he looked at me made everything else melt away. I didn't remember where I was or what I had to do next. The only thing that mattered in that moment was Trystan. He was like a beautiful black hole, and he absorbed every piece of me.

I teased, "I'll make a note to ogle you more openly next time."

He held out his arms, his books extended away from his body and balanced on the top of his palm. "Why wait?" Trystan was standing right in front of the door. I could hear kids moving through the halls, heading to their next class. Trystan turned in a circle slowly, keeping his gaze on me the whole time.

I laughed. Closing my eyes slowly, I opened my mouth, not knowing what to say. I wanted to look at him. I wanted him to see me do it. I don't know why, but the moment felt charged. Every spot on my skin was hypersensitive, and when his eyes passed over me, I flushed harder. I've never blushed so much in my life.

Breathing raggedly, I folded my arms over my chest to try and hide it. "Very pretty," came out when I finally spoke.

Trystan's arms fell to his sides, and his books slapped against his leg. He ran back down the aisle to me asking, "Pretty? Seriously?" His brows disappeared under his hairline, as his soft lips hung opened waiting for me to respond.

I grabbed his shoulders and twisted him around, pushing back up the aisle, shoving him toward the door. "You're such a drama queen. Get to class already!" Trystan allowed me to push him up the aisle. I could see the laugher in his eyes as he looked over his shoulder at me. When we were standing before the door, he dug in his heels and turned suddenly, which resulted in me smacking into his chest. It would have been sexy if I didn't have that just-walked-into-a-pole expression on my face.

Trystan wrapped his arms around me for half a second, and whispered in my ear,

"There are so many words to describe you. I plan on telling you all of them later." He pulled back and kissed my temple before releasing me. His eyes met mine and held. "I can't believe it."

"Neither can I," I replied softly. We stood a step apart, not touching, just gazing at each other. The bell rang again, but he didn't move. "You're late."

"So are you," there was no more laughter in his voice. Those radiant eyes bore into me, cutting past every defense mechanism I had. That gaze stripped me, causing me to feel everything at once, making me realize exactly how much Trystan affected me. My heart pounded harder in my chest, as a shiver worked its way down my spine.

After a second, I knew why he didn't want to leave. This felt surreal, like everything would vanish like smoke in the wind when he left. I didn't want to say it, but it was the only way to vanish the fear. "Everything will still be the same after class. Go. I don't want you to get in trouble because of me."

Reluctantly, Trystan turned and put his hand on the door. He looked back at me, like he was going to say something else, but he turned and pushed through the door instead. I watched the door slowly close, until I couldn't see Trystan anymore.

When he was gone, I sucked in a sharp breath of air. It felt like I didn't breathe the entire time he was here. The tension flowed out of my body, and I threw myself into the nearest chair. The theater was dark, save for the safety lights spilling off the stage.

I sat there, alone, in the darkness wondering what just happened. Staring at the empty stage, I felt like my life just took a turn. It was one of those moments that mattered, where I could feel it and I knew this incident was important. This wasn't a fling. No, it was more than that. Trystan loved me. Somehow, we finally came together.

Maybe living like a lunatic wasn't a bad idea. I would have never done anything like that a year ago. Crossing a room and throwing my lips on a guy seemed like something someone else would do, but I did it—and it worked out. It made my life better, it dramatically changed everything.

I stared at the spot where we stood, where Trystan told me that I was the girl in the Day Jones song. My gaze fell to the floor. A scrap of white poked out from under the chair. Rising slowly, I walked toward that piece of paper like it was my destiny. Those words were Trystan's heart poured onto paper. There was no mask, nothing hiding any part of him. That was what drew me to the song in the first place.

Reaching down, I picked up the paper and held it in my hands. The entire song covered the front and back of the page. Trystan's familiar handwriting lined the margins, along with codas and breath marks mingled amongst the lyrics.

Grasping the page in my hands, I looked down at the last line. Mari. My name was there, written in thick dark lines. Pressing my eyes closed, I shuddered and pressed the page to my heart. I was the girl who brought Trystan Scott to his knees. I was the girl he fell in love with.

CHAPTER 3

~TRYSTAN~

The rest of the day passed sluggishly. The clock seemed to tic slower, like it was stuck in tar. Trystan leaned back in his seat after taking a verbal beating for being late, like it mattered. He was out of there in a few months. These last few weeks were fluff, filled with busy work. Trystan hated busy work. It was a waste of time. He'd rather have a test than do another bunch of worksheets and endless essays.

Trystan's mind drifted back to Mari, the way her lips felt against his. Trystan got that far off look in his eye and totally missed that someone was talking to him.

"Mr. Scott, will you please share with the class your thoughts on the matter." The teacher was already beyond irritated with him today.

Trystan straightened in his seat like he was going to answer, but after a moment, he smiled sheepishly and shrugged. "I'm sorry Ms. D'Miagmo, but I don't know." There were a few sniggers from the girls behind him, but Trystan ignored them. He also ignored Brie. Her gaze was burning a hole into the side of his face.

"Mr. Scott, please take this class seriously or I will ask you to leave. You must have an opinion on the matter, and since opinions aren't right or wrong, I want to hear yours." She arched a gray eyebrow at him and folded her arms over her chest. The woman could have been a schoolmarm. She just needed a wooden ruler and permission to beat kids over the head with it.

Trystan smiled at her, but knew it was pointless to try and get any sympathy. D'Miagmo had it in for him. There were some teachers that decided on day one that they didn't like him. He had no idea why, but there was always one teacher who thought he had an easy life and needed to be taught a lesson. Ms. D'Miagmo was that teacher.

Trystan opened his mouth, but Brie cut him off, "Ms. D'Miagmo, I think it's obvious that Trystan feels uncomfortable answering this question because of his religion. Isn't it against school policy to discuss faith issues in the classroom anyway?" She flipped her golden hair over her shoulder and blinked her big blue eyes at the teacher.

Ms. D'Miagmo sucked in air through her nose like a horse. Now Brie was in the line of fire. "Brie dear, and what religion does Trystan practice that he can't discuss this matter?"

Brie looked up from her nail like she was thinking about getting a manicure. "He's a conservative Baptist," she said with utter certainty, and then added, "and everyone else here is Catholic or Jewish so it's not right to press him on this. Faith issues aren't open for debate in public school."

The teacher arched an eyebrow at Trystan. "So let me get this straight? You can't discuss women's rights because it makes you uncomfortable... because of your religion?"

Trystan smiled once like he was uncomfortable and nodded, "Yes, I don't want a pack of rabid women to attack me in the hallway because you forced my conservative beliefs out of me."

D'Miagmo looked like she might cry... or scream. She looked down her nose at Trystan, not breathing or blinking. Trystan couldn't tell if she was having an aneurism, and had never been so glad to hear the bell ring. Trystan knew not to stay another second. Scooping up his books, he bolted for the door, but Brie was right behind him. Trystan pushed his way into the crowded halls.

"Don't I get a thank you?" Brie said, chasing him down the hall.

Trystan wove through the crowd, stopping at his locker. He didn't look at Brie. Gripping the lock, Trystan spun the dial, and opened the metal door. "What for? You made me look like a sexist jerk. Some crazy chick is going peg me with a stiletto in the parking lot later, you know." He tossed in his books and slammed the door shut.

Brie grabbed Trystan's arm, and twisted him toward her. "Nah, a woman likes to be owned sometimes. If you were handing out..." her voice trailed off.

At that moment, Seth rounded the corner. Trystan's shoulders tensed at the sight of him. Brie stopped talking and turned around to see what made Trystan respond that way. "What the hell was that?" Her gaze followed Seth, noticing an equally tense look from Trystan's best friend.

"Nothing," Trystan said after Seth passed. They both glared at each other like old enemies. It made Trystan's guts twist. Why couldn't Seth be happy for him? Why'd he have to hate Mari so much?

Brie muttered, "Could have fooled me." When Trystan didn't respond, Brie stepped in front of him. "Well, I just wanted to say that rehearsal yesterday was fun. I'm looking forward to it later." She wrapped her lips around each word, saying them with such a sexy voice that Trystan forgot to glare after Seth.

Instead his head snapped back toward Brie, eyes wide. "What?" he tried to step away from her, but Brie had other plans.

She lifted her hands and draped them over his shoulders, playing with the hair at the base of his neck. "I know that kiss yesterday was real, and it's okay. I'm willing to pretend that we're not into each other, but I know the truth."

Trystan shook her off. "What are you talking about? That was acting and nothing more."

Brie's ruby lips pulled into a smile that said she disagreed. "I know what's real and what isn't, and I'm saying it's okay. We don't have to let anyone know." She winked at him before turning on her heel, "It'll be our little secret. See you later."

With that she was sauntering away from him, her hips swaying as she walked. The bell rang and several guys just stood there, staring at Brie's ass as she walked down the hall. Trystan stepped back and leaned against the row of lockers, slamming his head against them. She thought it was real; she thought that kiss was hers. Crap. Brie had the potential to make nothing look like a whole lot of something. Trystan took a deep breath and decided to deal with the fallout when it came. There was no point in trying to figure out what move Brie was going to make next. He'd have to wait and deal with it then.

CHAPTER 4

~MARI~

Trystan lay in my arms on the old couch. It was the last period of the day. We both managed to sneak away and meet in the basement before practice. The stage above was empty. I touched Trystan's hair lightly, pulling my fingers back, over and over again. His hair felt like silk.

"That's nice," he said sounding a little sedate. Trystan seemed like he was running on fumes lately, like he hadn't slept well in weeks.

I smiled softly at him, touching my hand to his cheek. "Can I ask you something?"

He looked up at me, and a playful smile twisted his lips. "What could you possibly want to know? I've told you about every stupid thing I've ever done." He laughed, "And for some reason, you love me anyway."

Hearing the word was new. Mari wanted to say love as freely, but it stuck in her throat. Give it time, she reminded herself. This is all new. "Yes, I do. And I always will. I'm good like that." My fingers stilled as I looked straight ahead.

Trystan felt the tension and took my hand in his. Stroking my palm with his thumb he said, "Ask me anything. I'm yours Mari."

Heart beating rapidly, I looked down at him. It wasn't something that I wanted to ask him, but it had to be done. "Trystan, I'm so glad today went the way it did. I mean, I couldn't have dreamed something like this would ever happen, but I'm not sure my friends or family will understand—or approve. It's not you, it's me, and it's selfish. I can't tell them about us. Not yet." My tongue felt like cotton as it crashed into my teeth, making my words sound harsher than I'd intended.

Trystan lifted his hand and ran his fingers gently along my cheek, making my stomach flip. "Anything you want. If you don't want to tell anyone, don't. I told you already and I meant it. We can keep this a secret, Mari. That's fine with me."

"You're not mad?"

Trystan laughed. Looking into her eyes, he said, "Mad? How could I possibly be mad? My dream girl is holding me in her lap, she steals kisses, and she's so beautiful that I can barely breathe when I'm around her. This is a dream for me, Mari. I'll do anything to be around you, to let me love you." As he spoke, his fingers tangled in my hair and he pulled me down for a brief kiss.

Everything about him made me feel like I could fly. My stomach lifted inside of me as my heart raced faster. His kiss was so soft and so hot at the same time. He pulled away before I was done, leaving me wanting more.

Trystan looked up at me. "It's a secret until you say otherwise. Okay?"

I nodded about to say something else when the door above us scraped open. Trystan jumped up and shot across the room. Trystan slumped back in the tattered old chair he frequented and dangled a leg over the arm like he'd been there all along. The click of female shoes descended the stairs and I knew it was her before Brie rounded the corner.

"Hey losers," she said, grinning at Trystan. Brie glanced at me once, her gaze sliding over my outfit like she thought I was a fashion nightmare. "Cutting? Really Trystan, and this close to graduation?" She folded her slender arms across her ample chest, "And you kept the thing with you."

Have I mentioned that I hated Brie? Bristling, I retorted, "Nice to see you too, granny panties."

Trystan snorted a surprised laugh. Brie glared like she wanted to kill me with her eyeballs. If she was a robot, Chinese stars would have flown out of her pupils and sliced my head off. "Don't you have somewhere to be, you little leech? Nobody wants you here. They just pity you, and humor Tucker, so they can graduate." She glanced at Trystan, but his expression remained impassive. I wondered if he wanted to punch Brie in the face. The thought made my fist clench. I didn't notice until my nails bit into my palm.

Trystan glanced at me for a second. His eyes were light, but the set of his lips let me know he was seething underneath. I shook my head carefully, so Brie wouldn't see. If he defended me now, everyone would know about us. I had to keep a secret. If my parents found out, I was toast. They'd lock me in my room for eternity.

Trystan's brow lifted ever so slightly as he regarded Brie. "If you're planning on starting a cat fight, let me run and get a few of the guys." He grinned wickedly at her and leaned forward like he was serious.

Brie's face contorted and she laughed one short burst, "As if I'd waste my time pounding Mary. Get real."

Before I could say anything else, Trystan cut me off, "Then why are you down here?"

Her ruby lips pulled up into a seductive smile, "I already told you. The bell's about to ring and I thought that we could practice the second act, alone, before everyone got here." Her voice dripped with sexuality, as she walked toward him.

I'm sure flames erupted from my ears, but my lips were locked. My fists balled harder, my nails cutting through my palm.

Trystan grinned at her, and tilted his head to the side as if he were admiring her. That was going to take getting used to. If no one knew we were dating, every single girl in the school would still be throwing themselves at him. If they knew he was dating someone, the normal girls would back off.

Brie wasn't normal. She was a no-holds barred kind of girl and wanted what she wanted. What I didn't understand was why she was hitting on Trystan like this. I mean, she has a boyfriend.

When Trystan answered, his voice was playful. "Thanks, but I already practiced it with Mari." He jumped out of his seat and stretched his hands over his head, which caused his dark tee shirt to hike up and reveal his flat stomach. It felt like I fell down a mine shaft, my heart jumped up into my throat as I hyperventilated. I stared. I couldn't help it. Trystan was hot and he was mine. As the thought drifted across my mind, a smile drifted across my face.

Trystan said, "Meet you upstairs," and walked away from Brie. He winked at me as he passed, his sapphire eyes glittering.

Brie stood there with her hands on her hips, watching him take the stairs two at a time. When she turned back to me, her smile turned rancid. "You need to stay the hell away from him, bitch. Do you understand me?"

The butterflies that were fluttering in my stomach moments ago were blasted away by Brie's words. While Brie was rank, she'd never confronted me like that before. I tried to act like she didn't bother me. Still slouching back into the couch with my feet kicked up onto the coffee table, I asked, "Or what? Or Tucker won't pass Trystan. I bet he'd be real grateful if you arranged that for him."

Brie stood in front of the table with her hands on her hips before her boot crashed into the cheap wood. It jarred my legs from the table top, jolting me upright on the couch. "You listen to me and listen good. You've been getting in my way, and don't think I haven't noticed, because I have. Whatever you think you have going on," she waved her finger in a circle, indicating all of me, "isn't working out for me. So stop, or you'll find yourself somewhere you don't want to be." Her eyebrows lifted as she cocked her head, making her earrings sway along with her golden hair.

Sitting on the edge of the couch, I gaped at her. Was she serious? Brie ruined people, but it was through rumors and carefully making their lives miserable. What could she do to me? At the same time, this didn't sound like that kind of threat. I wanted to stand up and punch her in the face. Everything she did, everything from the way she acted like she owned the school to the way she assumed she could claim Trystan whenever she wanted, pissed me off. Something inside my brain snapped. That fist that I'd been holding launched from my lap and pulled me to my feet, as it made a beeline for Brie's perfect nose. When my fist and her nose collided there was a crunch followed by a deafening shriek.

Brie's hands flew to her face as she screamed, "You heinous bitch!" Before Brie could do anything else, she turned and fled, running up the metal stairs as fast as her high-heeled shoes would carry her.

I stared at my fist in horror and pressed my eyes closed. I sat back down on the couch and leaned forward, burying my face in my hands. What have I done? As if I wasn't in for it before, Brie will kill me now. I'd be a smudge on the sidewalk by this time tomorrow. I punched her. I cracked her nose.

Noise filled the stairwell overhead and multiple pairs of shoes descended in rapid thumps like they were running. Katie's voice rang out, "I leave you alone for two periods and you punch Brie in the face?"

"I'm sorry?" I said, almost apologetically, looking up surprised to see her. "What are you doing here?"

Katie laughed, "What am I doing here? Saving your ass. Brie was ranting at the top her lungs to Tucker. I was passing by and heard her say your name, so I stuck my head in. He's coming. Sound sorry. And next time you break Brie's nose, I better be there to see. We could have had this up on YouTube. With that shriek, it would have gone viral."

"Oh God, don't say that." Panic was setting in. It wasn't until then that I noticed the owner of the second set of feet.

Mr. Tucker stood behind Katie with his arms folded across his chest. Neither of us realized he was standing there. Katie turned slowly, like the girl about to get killed in a horror movie.

Tucker breathed, "Get out." Katie nodded like a dashboard dog and ran up the stairs without looking back. Before I could explain, Tucker said, "You too, get out. I don't want to see you on set again."

"Mr. Tucker, let me explain."

"Explain what? That we're days away from a show and you broke my lead's nose. And for what? Because she was mean to you? Ah, I've got some news for you, Mari—get over it! You take everything to heart. You always have. Brie's Brie. She's got thorns around other girls, I know. I see it, but you don't see anyone else punching her in the face, do you?" He sighed deeply, his face returning to a normal color and shook his head. "What's with you kids today? It must be a full moon. Scott attacks his best friend and now you. You, out of all people, picked today to throw a punch." He breathed deeply as he looked down, his fingers pinching his nose.

"Mr. Tucker…"

"I don't want to hear it. Just go, Mari."

It never fails. When something totally awesome happens, something equally bad blindsides   me.

CHAPTER 5

~TRYSTAN~

Practice was weird. Trystan stood on the stage as the completed set was being erected around him. The stage crew raised the flats one by one, installed doors, and touched up some of the paint. Now it looked like a real room, filled with furniture and picture frames. As the stage crew did their thing, the guy in the lighting cage was muttering to himself. His voice carried to where Trystan stood a few feet away. The house lights were flashing on and off instead of dimming. The lighting cage was nearly fifty years old and due for an upgrade, but with the school budget the way it was, they'd never get one. Whenever a budget vote came up, people showed up in drones to vote it down. It didn't matter what was on the ballot. The roof could be caving in and the town would still vote against it.

Trystan kept thinking about Mari. A smile leaked across his face. He couldn't help it. That kiss. And the way she felt laying in his arms. For a small moment, his life felt perfect. Happiness was always something just out of reach for Trystan. Whenever it came along, it was swiftly yanked away. This time, Trystan would make sure he didn't mess up. Mari mattered too much to him. Everything about her made him better, made him think he had a chance. Trystan wouldn't be another statistic.

Waiting in front of the lighting cage, Trystan stood with his hands in his pockets wondering where Brie went. When Brie finally surfaced from the basement, she ran straight into the girl's bathroom at the back of the stage. Trystan turned to watch Brie flee with her hand over her nose. His heart sank when Tucker followed a few moments later, pointing one of his chubby fingers at the stage door. Katie and Mari left without looking back. Shit. What'd Brie do now?

Practice took too long. It was close to opening night. Brie acted hysterical. Tucker forced Brie on stage with her nose bandaged and an ice pack taped to her face, which severely screwed with her head. Brie couldn't get a line out without stumbling or messing up. Tucker didn't bother to try the second act. They skipped over that part like it didn't exist, which was fine by Trystan.

After practice, Trystan grabbed his books from his locker and looked around for Mari, but the school was deserted. He walked past the diner on the way home, hoping to find her inside, but she wasn't there. Sighing, Trystan pushed his dark hair out of his eyes. The wind blew harshly, flipping his hair over his head and into his eyes again. Trystan tightened his jacket, wishing he had something warmer to wear. The leather was nearly worn away in places, giving the frigid air a way to leak in.

It'd been a long day and it felt good to finally be out of the school. Trystan just wished he'd seen Mari before the end of the night. Curiosity was part of it, and Trystan wondered how Mari waked away without a scratch and Brie had a bloody nose. Hurrying, Trystan pushed on toward his house, crossing the train tracks, and walking quickly to his front door.

When Trystan walked into his house, he came face to face with his father. The old man's eyes were bloodshot. There was a piece of paper in his left hand. Dad was left handed, just like Trystan. God, they were too much alike, Trystan thought as he walked through the threshold and closed the door behind him. He ignored his father's eyes on his back as he went to the kitchen looking for something that would pass for dinner. Trystan was always hungry lately and there was never enough to eat. Placing his books on the table seemed to be what set his dad off. Suddenly he was yelling like Trystan did something horrible.

Dad stood behind him, his voice was sharp enough to cut glass. "You think you're too good for us. That's what's wrong with you, you know. Always walking around like you own the place." Dad slurred his words slightly, telling Trystan that tonight was going to suck.

Standing with the fridge door open, Trystan froze. It took a moment to recognize that the scrap of paper in his father's fingers was a picture. When Trystan did, his heart dropped into his shoes. Trystan grabbed whatever food was left, which wasn't much. He took a few slices of bread and the peanut butter he'd gotten from Sam's deli and made a sandwich as fast as he could.

His father droned on and no matter how hard Trystan tried, he couldn't drown out the words. "You're the reason she left. This," he said, pointing to everything, "is your fault. Me and my whole fucking life got reduced to this because of you, and you stand there like you're so damn proud."

Trystan couldn't help it. He knew that he shouldn't speak, but he did. His jaw was tense, the words fell out of his mouth before he could stop. "Maybe she left because of me, but you did this to yourself. Things didn't have to go this way, Dad. You did this. Not me."

Before Trystan could blink his father was across the room and screaming in his face. "You think I didn't try! You think I fucking chose this?" Dad bellowed and spit went flying, sticking to Trystan's cheek. His father laughed with such rage that Trystan stepped away. When Dad spoke again, his voice was low and menacing, "That's right, boy. Blame me. You did nothing." The old man's rank breath lingered in Trystan's nostrils, but his dad finally stepped away.

Trystan went to pass by his father, but was clotheslined. His father raised his arm at the last second, trapping Trystan, before grabbing Trystan's hair with his other hand, and yanking his son back to his chest. The picture of Trystan's mother was clutched under his father's thumb. Thrusting it in Trystan's face, Dad made him look. When Trystan tried to wiggle free or look away, his father only tightened his grip and forced him harder. "Look! Look at her! Look at those eyes, and how they seem so steadfast, like they'd never leave. You destroyed everything!" He shoved Trystan toward the hall that lead back to Trystan's room. "Get out of my face. I can't stand to look at you!"

Trystan's chest felt like it was ripped open with a rusty nail. Every muscle in his body was tense, ready to fight, trying so hard to hold back. Trystan's jaw locked tight to keep from speaking, but the one thing he wanted to avoid the most was that picture and he'd already seen it. Stumbling back to his room, Trystan pushed through the door. His mind screamed, protesting that he should fight back, but something held his rage in check. Taking purposeful breaths, Trystan walked down the short hall, trying to steel himself, trying to make his heart go numb before it shattered into a million pieces.

When Trystan swung his door open, he meant to lock it and throw himself on his bed, but there was no lock, no bed. The walls were barren. The nightstand was gone. His closet door was open and the only thing inside were shadows. Trystan stood there, his hands shaking slightly, as he realized that his father threw out all of his stuff. Trystan felt his dad behind him but he didn't turn around. Rage flooded

Trystan's body, making him want to act out, but he refused.

A hand shoved hard between Trystan's shoulder blades. Trystan didn't expect it and fell into the room. "Maybe this will teach you that you're no better than the rest of us." Before Trystan could turn around his father yanked the door shut. It wasn't until then that Trystan realized that the doorknob was turned around. The sound of metal sliding against metal alerted him to the lock closing.

"No!" Trystan screamed and threw himself at the door, but it was too late. His fists beat the door, but it was solid, the kind of door that was used at the entry of a house. Trystan knew, because he put it there when he traded it out for the thin particleboard version that had originally been there, in order to keep his father out.

"You never learned your place, Trystan. I swear to God, I'm going to teach it to you." The hallway fell silent.

Trystan felt the panic slide up his throat. The room was dark. The lights were gone and the fixture that hung from the ceiling had no bulb. Racing to the window, Trystan pushed it open, but the bars kept him from getting out. The cold air rushed in over his face. Trystan turned around and leaned his back against the wall, clutching his face in his hands. He slid down until his back was under the window, hoping that his father would see reason in the light of day, but there was no way to know. Dad had done stuff like this before, when Trystan was little and couldn't fight back. He'd lock Trystan away for hours, sometimes days. When it seemed like Trystan would die of thirst, the man finally showed his face and let him out. Trystan tried to be good after that, but it didn't seem to matter what he did or didn't do—he was never good enough.

Tucker's words rang through Trystan's ears like a gong, ebbing and pulsing. Someone told you wrong. You're worth something.

Lowering his head to his knees, Trystan fixated on the words, but they couldn't penetrate his heart. Tucker's words couldn't strip away years of being told he was the reason for his father's grief. Trystan's chest felt hollow and he let the numbness overtake him.

CHAPTER 6

~MARI~

"Have you lost your mind?" Daddy screamed. He'd been pacing in my room since he got that phone call from Brie's father.

There was nothing I could say that would calm him down, but that didn't mean I wouldn't try. "What was I supposed to do? She threatened me!" Tears streaked my face. I couldn't help it. I cried when I was angry.

Daddy turned on me, roaring, "What were you supposed to do? Get the teacher! Not punch the girl in the face. Her father is threatening to press charges. Do you know what that means? Do you have any idea? We could lose everything because of you!"

Sucking a ragged breath, I screamed, "There was no teacher, there was no help! Maybe I shouldn't have hit her, but why can't you even act like you care about me? You didn't even ask me what she did! You just assumed that everything was my fault!" I trembled with my hands balled into fists at my sides.

If there was ever a wrong thing to say, that was it. Daddy blew up. His eyes widened, before he started screaming in a blind rage. The verbal assault went on, but I couldn't process what he was saying, not when he looked so livid. I backed away from him, but he kept coming at me like he'd hit me. My heart pounded in my chest like I was running away from an axe murderer.

Things weren't supposed to be like this. Daddy was supposed to defend me. He was supposed to protect me, but instead, he looked like he was going to kill me. After what seemed like forever, my Mom came in. It seemed to calm Daddy down enough to realize that his hands were shaking, lifting toward me like he was going to do something. Dropping his hands, Daddy shook his head fiercely and walked away from me. He shoved past my mother and left the room, leaving a wake of anguish behind.

All the fright that had built up in my body exited my mouth in loud sob that sounded more like a scream. My mother stood there, staring at me with disgust. "You brought this on yourself, Mari. Clean up and go to bed." She turned away and left without another word.

After they left, I heard them arguing in the kitchen. The conversation was about lawyers and settlements. They seem to think that Brie's father had his sights set on their money. I wanted to scream and jump up and down in front of them. Since when does money matter more than people? I didn't realize I was so disposable. My entire life, I thought they'd stand up for me, but they didn't. The only thing they cared about was protecting their money and their precious careers.

I plucked my phone from my backpack, knowing it was insane to try and use it, but

I wanted to talk to Trystan. I needed him. He'd understand, but I didn't have any way to contact him. I sat on my bed sniffling as I stared at the phone. I didn't want to talk to Katie. She'd tell me to suck it up, that this was part of having the perfect family— so what if they flipped out once every sixteen years? She didn't understand. Her family fought all the time, but this wasn't a fight. This was something else. It showed me where my place was in this family, and I didn't like it.

The next morning my eyes were puffy. When I sat at the table my mother said nothing, handing me my breakfast like everything was normal. "Your father and I are on for the next four days. I made your dinners for each night. Come straight home after practice and eat. I'll check on you when I get home." She poured a glass of orange juice, smiling like a saint.

I nodded, not wanting to talk about it. It was fine by me if they worked seven days a week. I did my best to eat my breakfast, but I wasn't hungry. I just wanted to get out of there and go to school. When I cleared my half-eaten plate, my mother said, "You don't have to be so dramatic, Mari. I know you're upset, but you still have to eat."

I just looked at her. I couldn't think of what to say to make her fathom how betrayed I felt. She dropped me off at school without another word. As soon as she pulled away, I felt better. Four days on my own would help. They'd come home from work in time to drop me off at school. We'd barely see each other.

After going to my locker, I looked around for Trystan. He usually haunted this hallway before first period, but I didn't see him. I went to class, listening to the teacher droning on. I didn't get a chance to look for Trystan again until our free period. When I walked into the auditorium I heard Tucker speaking softly and rapidly to Trystan, "…is not okay. You can't skip class like this and then expect to walk at graduation in June. If there's something you need to tell me, some reason for your tardiness, tell me. You don't have to fight the whole damn world by yourself."

"I'm fine," Trystan used a tone that said he was finished talking about it. When

Trystan turned around, I saw an angry red gash marring his cheek.

The smile I had on my face faltered and slipped away. Tucker looked at me and then back at Trystan. When I was closer, Tucker said, "Talk some sense into him," as he jabbed his thumb at Trystan.

"What are you talking about?" I asked, not understanding.

Tucker sighed, "Ask him how he got that cut on his face and make sure he had a tetanus shot. He won't talk to me."

Trystan's shoulders tensed as he looked after Tucker, who was walking away, "That's because there's nothing to tell." Tucker walked through the door and left us standing in the aisle alone. The empty seats surrounded us on all sides, the stage lights dim and glowing golden. When Trystan looked back at me, his expression softened, but the slant of his mouth said he still thought he needed to defend himself, and I didn't want that.

Before he could speak, I said, "I only want to ask you one thing."

"Really?" the corners of his mouth tightened again. "And what's that?"

"Will you hold me?" Tears welled up in my eyes and streaked down my cheeks. Trystan instantly became the man I knew, and forgot about his worries. Stepping forward, I walked into his arms, and he held me tight.

CHAPTER 7

~TRYSTAN~

When sunlight poured into Trystan's room earlier that morning, he tried the door. Still locked. Glancing out the window, Trystan saw that his dad's car was gone. Shit. Trystan stretched, his back aching from sleeping on the hard floor. His dick of a dad turned the heat off so that he was freezing, too. Although it was cold, Trystan refused to close the window last night. It was better than being trapped in the darkness. It was a good thing Trystan didn't take off his jacket when he walked through the door.

Running his hands through his hair, Trystan looked at the door. He knelt in front of it wondering what time it was, if he was late for school yet. The teacher's would ride his ass, threatening to not let him graduate. Some tried to threaten him by saying he couldn't walk at graduation—like that was a threat. He didn't care if he walked or not. It's not like anyone would show up and clap for him. No one cared what happened to Trystan Scott. While the other kids got pats on the back and ushered off to college, Trystan got a psychotic parent who blamed him for everything.

Trystan stared at the lock, wishing he could remember his mother—at least a little bit—but there was nothing. No voice, no sense of safety, no warm memories of his mother cradling him in her arms or kissing him good-night. It wasn't something that he usually dwelt on. That was the past. There was nothing Trystan could do to change it. She left. No amount of wondering would bring her back, and Trystan had no plans of looking for her either. What was the point of chasing someone who left him behind? Trystan had had enough misery from the time she left. The thought of finding her and having his mom turn her back on him again was just too much. It wasn't worth the risk. Not now, not ever.

Staring at the golden lock, Trystan realized his Dad changed the knob. Trystan could have picked the lock if it was the old one, but not this thing. Rising, Trystan stood back. He took a deep breath, braced himself, and kicked his boot into the door. The door shook, but it didn't give. Trystan kicked it again and again, trying to weaken the frame, so that it would crack and let him out, but the jam was too strong. Again, another of Trystan's ways to protect himself came back and bit him on the ass. After a few moments, he was huffing and the door gave no indication of opening. Trystan sat down on the floor hard, and banged his head back into the wall.

"I have to get out here," he muttered to himself.

He stared at the black bars that shuttered him in. They were solid. There was no way he could bend them or slip out between, they were too narrow. Pushing himself to his feet, Trystan walked across the room to the window. If he drew attention to himself, someone might call the cops, and Trystan learned early on that cops were bad. If they showed up, he'd be in a worse situation than he was already in.

Trystan leaned on the windowsill and turned his head, making his cheek press into the cold bars. They were jagged with rust. The paint on the bars had blistered and peeled long ago. When Trystan pulled his face away, he felt the grime on his cheek and wiped it away. It left an orange smear on his fingers. Wonderful.

Trystan stared at the bars, wondering if he could manage to kick them. They were a little loose, like the mortar holding the bolts in place had grown weak. Trystan's hands clenched at his sides. Before he spent more time thinking about whether or not he'd get into trouble, Trystan kicked. His boot came up and punched the side of the frame hard. To his surprise, his foot kept going. The bars went flying to the ground and bits of brick flew back into Trystan's face. One piece of shrapnel collided with his cheek, raking a deep cut as it flew by. Trystan swore, but he didn't have time to look at the cut. The window was the only way out. He was wearing the same clothes as yesterday, didn't get to shower, and now his face was covered in rust and blood.

Trystan swung his leg over the windowsill and jumped out. He landed next to a dead bush on the other side of the wall, and ran to grab the bars. Lifting them, Trystan wedged the rusty metal back in place. To his surprise, it held. The only problem now was making sure the school didn't throw him out when he got there and then he'd have to deal with his dad later.

When Trystan walked into the high school, Tucker was in the lobby. Trystan stopped mid-step and swung around, ready to bolt, but Tucker grabbed him by the shoulder.

"You missed first period, Scott. What do you—" Tucker stopped speaking as Trystan whirled around. His chubby jaw slipped opened for a second, before taking a deep breath. "What happened to your face? Is that rust?" Tucker lifted his hand like he was going to touch Trystan, but stopped when Trystan flinched.

Trystan didn't mean to wince, but so much had happened. He was overly tired and his body was reacting without thought. Shit. Shit. Shit. Trystan tried to laugh it off, by saying, "If you're suggesting that I—"

But Tucker cut him off, "Save it, Scott. Nurse's office. Now." The smirk fell off Trystan's face. They walked down the hall in silence. Why did things have to be like this? Why was Tucker gunning for him? Trystan grew more defensive, which made his wit so sharp it stung. When he walked into the nurse's office, Tucker followed.

"I don't need a babysitter," Trystan said in a snarky tone, but Tucker ignored him.

"Glenda," Tucker said as he crossed the room to the nurse's desk. "This one looks like he was hit in the face with a rusty bucket, but he won't say what happened. Can you take a look at it and clean him up?"

"Sure," Glenda said, eyeing Trystan. She'd always been kind to Trystan, but he didn't want people fussing over him. It just made things worse. She told Trystan to sit in the chair next to her desk. When he didn't move, Tucker gave his shoulder a shove.

"How'd this happen?" Glenda's voice was kind. She bent over and examined the cut, careful not to touch him.

Trystan's insides were twisting. Fear clung to his throat in thick clumps, making it difficult to swallow. They're going to find out. They have to know. Trying to muster his charm, Trystan said, "I ran into a burning building and saved a few babies on the way to school. I must have stepped on a rake on the way in."

Glenda grinned at him, "Always a kidder," she leaned closer, her fingers pressing on Trystan's cheek. He forced himself to sit still even though it was sore. "So this is rust?" Trystan nodded. Glenda stepped away and got a brown bottle and some cotton balls.

She dabbed the cotton with the stuff in the bottle and then on his cheek. "It might sting a little," she said too late. Trystan didn't flinch this time. He sat rigid in the chair, staring straight ahead. As she patched Trystan up, she spoke about the weather and other things that nobody cares about.

At some point Tucker left, because he was alone with Glenda. That was when she said, "Did someone do this to you? It looks like you were hit in the face with a shovel."

"I wasn't," Trystan responded, his voice flat.

"Maybe it was a brick, then? Or something else that bruised your face? Trystan, when was the last time you had a tetanus shot?" It didn't matter what she said after that. He didn't answer. Glenda was young enough to still be patient. When Trystan wouldn't answer, Glenda touched her hand to her forehead and said, "I'll have to call your father and ask."

Trystan wanted to jump out of the chair and run from the room. Suddenly he was more cooperative. "I don't need one. I'm fine. And thanks for cleaning me up. You were always my favorite nurse."

Her hands were on her hips as she watched Trystan inch toward the door with a smile on his face. "Wait, I haven't bandaged that yet. When you smile, it's going to bleed."

"It's okay," he said over his shoulder, exiting the room. "I'm fine. I'll come back if it opens up again."

Trystan's heart was pounding. His nerves were like brittle old wires, ready to snap. When he turned down the hallway, Tucker was standing against the wall, his massive arms folded across his chest. There was no way to get away from the teacher. Tucker insisted on talking. They'd gone into the auditorium and Trystan found out that talking meant having Tucker question him for nearly the whole period and Trystan sitting there fuming, not saying much.

By the time Mari walked in, Trystan felt his sanity slipping away. Then, Tucker left and Mari had questions in her eyes. Trystan couldn't unwind. Watching his reflection in her eyes, Trystan saw a man that looked too much like his father. Trystan was ready to turn and leave her there if she pressed him for answers, but she didn't. Instead, she asked him to hold her and tears streaked down her cheeks. All the anger and fatigue melted away as Mari pressed her wet face against Trystan's chest.

His arms closed around her shoulders, holding her tight, wanting to fix whatever made her like this. Trystan ran his fingers through her soft curls, pushing it away from her tears, "What's wrong?"

Mari's body shook gently. When she looked up at him, he wanted to make her smile so badly. Tears didn't belong on that perfect face. Trystan's thumb wiped a tear away as it spilled from her eye and ran down her face. "I'm sorry. I just had a really bad night."

Trystan pulled her close and held on tight. "I know what you mean. Mine was less than stellar, too."

"I would have called you, but I didn't know what your number was. Either way, my parents probably would have gone postal on me if they knew I was talking to you." She sniffled, trying to smile. Trystan felt Mari's back rise and fall as she sucked in huge, ragged breaths.

After a moment, Trystan suggested, "Let's go downstairs for a little while. I'll hold you all you want and we don't have to worry about anyone walking in and seeing us together. Sound good?"

The pulled apart and Mari looked up at him, nodding. When they got to the basement, Trystan flipped on the lights and they descended the stairs. No one was down there. No one was ever down in the basement during the school day.

Trystan sat on the couch and pulled Mari onto his lap. She fit perfectly, like she was made for him. When Mari leaned back into his shoulder, Trystan felt whole. The emotions that flooded him earlier were gone and he found himself wanting to confide in her.

Trystan squeezed his arms, which were wrapped around Mari's waist. She slipped her arms around him and held on harder with her face buried in his chest. Trystan could smell her hair. The mingled fruit scents filled his nose.

When Mari pulled back, Trystan asked, "Do you want to talk about it?"

She shook her head. "Not really. I finally stopped crying and there's only twenty minutes or so until the period is over. I'd rather just sit here like this. You make me feel so much better, I can't even tell you."

Trystan kissed her temple softly, pulling away slowly, like it pained him. "You make me feel better, too."

She smiled. It wasn't full wattage, but it was a start. After a second Mari said, "I've been banished from the theatre after school."

He nodded, "I heard. You punched Brie in the face." He couldn't help it, a smile spread across his lips as he watched her.

"I didn't mean to. It just happened. One minute she was threatening me and the next my fist was crushing her nose." Mari spoke quickly, like she couldn't believe she was telling him this. Panic laced her voice, but he didn't know why. It was a hit, and from what he knew of Brie, she deserved it. "Anyway, Tucker banished me for the rest of the semester, so I won't be able to see you until after."

Smiling, Trystan asked, "You want to see me after?"

Nodding, she said, "Yes. I was thinking about things—about what I posted on your Day Jones wall—and I've decided something." Mari spoke slowly, her eyes drifted to the floor as she spoke.

Trystan's stomach felt like it was in a free fall. Was she saying what he thought she was saying? He tried to stay cool and act like he didn't know what she was talking about. "What'd you decide?"

Mari was silent for a moment as she looked at the floor, with those long dark lashes blinking slowly. When she looked up at him, Trystan knew he'd give her anything she wanted. Her brown gaze was intent, focused on his face, making Trystan's heart race faster. Suddenly, he was much more aware of her weight on his lap, the curve of her hips in his hands, and the way her chest swelled when she breathed.

Staring at her lips, he waited for her to say it.

"I want to be with you."

Trystan's mind erupted with conflicting thoughts, both warring to win. But the thing that came out of his mouth was Mari's thoughts on the matter, not his, "But, you said you wanted to wait until you were married. I love you, Mari, but don't change things for me. That's part of who you are."

She looked into his eyes, pinning Trystan in place, making him want to squirm. "I need you," she said so softly that he barely heard it. When he didn't answer, Mari rested her head on his shoulder and said, "Please, Trystan."

The please and the way she said his name made Trystan come undone. Before he could do something stupid, he kissed her cheek and slipped Mari off his lap. The look of horror on her face struck him like a bat.

Quickly, Trystan said, "I can't say no to you. I'll do anything you want, be anything you need. I promise, but I'm not doing it in the school basement. You deserve more than that and if you keep sitting on my lap and talking about having sex with me, we won't be talking about it anymore." Mari's face flushed and she looked away. Trystan put his fingers under her chin and pulled her gaze back toward him. "I love that about you. I love how you can blush like that. Actually, I uh... wrote a song about it." Before he knew what happened, Trystan grabbed the guitar and was tuning it, talking about one of the songs he wrote for her.

"You wrote a song about me blushing?" Mari asked, surprised.

Trystan looked up from below his brow and smiled at her. "Sort of. It's about all the little things you do; the things that make me love you."

Placing his fingers on the strings to form the cord, Trystan began to strum. It was a song that was Mari to the core. It revealed more of Trystan's heart, but he didn't care. He wanted her to smile and he knew this would help. Trystan sang, watching Mari, as he slipped his hand across the neck of the instrument, allowing the notes to fill the air. As he played, her lips lifted into a smile and her brown eyes glittered just for him. Trystan couldn't help but smile back at her.

Everything about Mari was magic. She touched him like nothing else could, and honestly, the thought of having sex with her was equally appealing and terrifying. If a look from Mari could produce that much emotion, Trystan wondered what sex would do. If Mari had her way, Trystan was going to find out. The song ended and Trystan remained where he was, across from her on a stool.

Mari stood with a sweet smile on her face and walked slowly toward him, her hips swaying gently as she came closer. "That was so incredible. The way you see things is so pure, so intense, and so vulnerable at the same time." Stopping in front of him, Mari took the guitar from his hands, making Trystan's pulse pound harder in his ears.

He watched her, saying nothing as she set the guitar down and stood in front of him. A smile spread across Mari's lips. "You think blushing is sexy?" She placed both hands on his thighs, splaying her fingers, leaning in close to his lips.

"I think everything you do is sexy."

"Kiss me," she commanded, and he did.

Trystan's hands threaded in her hair and pulled her mouth down on his, tasting her sweet, hot kiss on his lips. Heart hammering in his chest, Trystan let the kiss grow stronger and hotter, tasting Mari when she opened her mouth, and stroking her tongue with his. They were both breathing hard when the bell rang and shattered the moment.

Mari stood and stepped away, her hands shaking slightly. Grinning at him, she said, "You follow directions really good."

Trystan laughed. He stood and rushed toward her, snatching her up by her waist and spinning her around until she shrieked. When he set her down, Mari looked up at him smiling like everything was all right. After a second, Mari reached into her pocket and fished out a piece of paper and handed it to him.

"It's my address and my cell. Come by later, okay?" Suddenly, she was shy again.

Trystan looked at the address, and confusion pinched his face. "I thought you didn't want your parents to know?"

"They won't. They're working for the next four nights."

Trystan felt his heart speed up. The way she looked at him said she had plans for all four nights.

CHAPTER 8

~MARI~

After school, Katie sat with me at the diner. We ate a bunch of fried food and topped it off with ice cream. I was so nervous. I'm not sure what person took over my brain and invited Trystan Scott into my bed, but she was gone now and I was left with moody Mari who fretted over everything.

"What's with you?" Katie asked, dipping a fry in ice cream before popping it in her mouth. "You've been out of sorts for days."

I shrugged, "PMS?"

She laughed, "Yeah, right. More like boy-on-the-brain. Don't tell me that you're still pining over Trystan."

I shook my head confidently. That wasn't a lie. I wasn't pining over him at all. "No, of course not."

"Then what is it?"

I debated telling her what had me on edge. The question was could I tell her and omit names? I didn't know. And if Katie snooped, she'd see it was Trystan coming to my house later. I decided to risk it. I needed someone to talk to about it and I sure wasn't asking my mom. "You know how I was going to wait to be with someone? Well, I changed my mind."

Katie's jaw dropped open and the ice cream slipped out. It splattered on the table in one big goopy slop. Neither of us said anything for a moment. As she wiped up the ice cream glob, she asked, "What? Why?"

I shrugged, "I don't know. I thought it'd be romantic to wait for the guy who'd marry me, but now that just seems corny." Corny was the wrong word. The real reason was that I felt so alone and I thought that sex would make it better. I wanted to feel wanted.

Katie stared at me like I'd grown two heads. "Something's not right here, but I have no clue what it is. Who are you and what have you done with Mari?"

"Stop it, Katie. I wanted to talk to you about it." My voice was serious, pleading almost. I felt stupid for bringing it up.

Katie noticed and became serious. In a hushed voice she said, "Don't do it. Having sex will bind you to that guy for the rest of your life. Be picky about who you're with. Honestly, I used to laugh at you, but when I see him," she couldn't stand to say her first boyfriend's name, "now, well, I think you had it right. I wish that I'd waited for someone that I wanted to be attached to forever."

Katie's eyes darted away from mine as she spoke, as if she were ashamed of what she did. "But it felt right at the time, didn't it? How were you supposed to know he wasn't forever?"

Katie laughed bitterly, "I knew, Mari. He wasn't the one. I just didn't bother waiting. Maybe it was stupid, but I didn't think I'd get another chance. Now I've learned that there's always another chance, another guy willing to do it. They're not picky when it comes to sex, so I figure I have to be."

"You think I'll regret it?" I asked, my voice nearly a whisper.

She nodded. "You sound disappointed. What did you think I would say? You see the way I avoid my ex. Whatever amount of fun I had wasn't worth worrying about getting knocked-up or contracting something gross. It probably sounds funny, but you rubbed off on me. I'm waiting from now on. The guy has to prove he loves me and stick around for a while before he gets into my pants." Just then the waiter walked by and nearly tripped as he overheard Katie. She was blunt and gorgeous. Hearing her talk about sex made guys salivate.

My gaze fell to the table as I played with my napkin.

Katie asked, "Are you going to tell me who he is?"

"Not yet."

CHAPTER 9

~TRYSTAN~

Trystan looked at the piece of paper in his hands. Theatre practice had dragged on, mainly because Brie refused to cooperate with her face looking the way it did, but it was finally over and he was on his way to see Mari. The streetlights cast a yellow glow on the pavement. The night air wasn't as frigid as last evening.

Trystan walked past Mari's house, not stopping in front. His heart raced faster, as his mind repeated the words she'd said earlier. Lowering his gaze, Trystan shoved his hands in his pockets and walked on. Circling the block, Trystan came up behind

Mari's house, cutting through the neighbor's backyard to remain out of sight.

Although Mari didn't ask him to sneak up to her house, Trystan was too smart to be seen. No one wanted him around their daughter and Mari's parents were probably worse. She was smart, like really smart. They probably wanted to send her off to some Ivy League school next year and he'd never see her again.

Trystan sighed, pushing through the spot where the fences met. Neighbors might have looked cordial in this neighborhood, but they were cheap. That last inch of vinyl fence was an expense that no one wanted to pay, since it was covered by tall shrubs and trees. Trystan twisted sideways and sucked in to press himself between the gaps in the fence. No one saw him do it.

Within seconds, he was standing on Mari's back porch, looking up at the two story house, with his eyes fixated on the only bedroom with a light shining through the windows. Mari crossed the room, her hands stretched above her head, as she pulled her hair into a ponytail.

As if she sensed him, Mari stopped and turned toward the window. Slowly, she stepped to the sill and looked down. A smile slipped across her face. The window was already open and her curtains fluttered in the breeze.

Smiling down at him, she said, "You could have come to the front door." Mari had on a white cami and jeans. There was a patch of lace at the top of the cami, but the shirt was cut lower than anything she usually wore. It was the kind of tank top that Mari would have layered, but tonight she hadn't. Her arms were bare, her hair pulled up, and that smile on her face made Trystan want to climb up the side of the house to her.

"I didn't want to risk being seen. You know, by nosy neighbors and all that." Trystan had his hands in his pockets. He might have looked suave on the outside, but his pulse was pounding in his ears and the paper with Mari's address on it was getting strangled in his pocket.

Mari leaned on the windowsill. Her breasts curved beautifully, swelling, as she leaned on her elbows. "Are you sure this didn't have anything to do with, I don't know, being you?"

Trystan grinned. "What does that mean? Being me is pretty good, but you'll have to be more specific."

She laughed. It was that magical sound he loved. It reached deep into Trystan and he didn't want it to end. "The Romeo and Juliet thing, this little seduction scene you've got going on here. It's insanely romantic. If you showed up with your guitar and sang from below my window, I would have died."

Trystan snapped his fingers. His palms were so damp from nerves that they nearly slipped past each other without making a sound. "Damn it. I knew I forgot something."

Mari smiled down at him before straightening up. "I'll be down in a second. There's a door by the kitchen," she pointed the direction he needed to go, "I'll come down and open it up."

"But I was going to scale the wall."

"Don't you dare!" she said, still laughing and disappeared from the window.

Trystan walked in the direction she pointed and came to a leaded glass door made from thick wood. His heart dropped into his shoes. Not only was she smarter than him, but she was way richer. He was poor. Suddenly a rush of cold ran through his stomach and he wanted to leave. This was a mistake. There was no way they'd have enough in common, coming from such different backgrounds, but before Trystan could give it another thought, Mari threw open the door. She looked fantastic, her body all smooth curves and that bared neck was perfect for kissing. Trystan felt every inch of his body respond to her. If only his body listened to his brain.

"I'm glad you came," she said shyly, tucking a stray curl behind her ear. "I started to think you weren't going to show up."

Trystan walked past her and into the kitchen, trying not to gape. The kitchen looked like something that belonged in a showroom somewhere. His fingers found his pockets again and hid out in there to conceal the nervous twitch of his hands.

"Practice ran late." Turning toward Mari, he said, "I wouldn't have missed this."

"Good." She held out her hand and Trystan reached for it, hoping she wouldn't mind how warm it was. "I mean, I'm glad you came. Not seeing you after school was weird. We're always together. Did you notice that before?"

His eyes slipped over Mari's body and her face flamed red. "Of course I noticed. I notice every inch of you, every day." He tugged her hand, pulling her into his arms. This was where she belonged. He could feel it. Smiling that wicked smile of his, Trystan said, "For the longest time, I thought you knew, and that you were just playing me."

"Ha!" she blurted out, and wrapped her hands around Trystan's waist. "I was playing you? You made me so crazy that I couldn't think straight. I had no clue you thought of me that way at all, I mean, why would you?"

"Are you kidding?" Trystan asked, his hands tangling in her hair, as he tilted her face up to meet his gaze. "You have no idea what you do to me, how you make my heart hammer in my chest, until it feels like I can't breathe another breath, how one look from those dark eyes sets my skin burning, longing for your touch, or how your smile sets me on edge and fills my dreams until I see you again. I thought you were doing it on purpose, but then I realized that you didn't know—that you were just being you and I was the one with the problem."

"The problem?"

"Yeah. I was hopelessly in love with you." He ran his fingers through her hair as he spoke, brushing the back of his hand against her cheek. She looked up at him with such wide dark eyes, eyes that didn't trust what they saw. She was afraid he'd hurt her, and Trystan felt exactly the same way.

After a moment, Mari looked down, breaking the intensity of the moment. "Come this way. I want to show you something." Trystan followed her through the dark house, their fingers laced together. As they climbed the stairs, he knew where they were going, to her bedroom.

Stopping in front of the door, she turned to him. "I thought we could hang out and talk for a while, if that's all right?"

"That sounds perfect."

Mari pushed the door open and a smile leaked across Trystan's face. She stepped into the room and turned to watch his reaction. He glanced around at the white moldings and thick trim around the door and window. There was a flat screen TV on one wall along with a stereo and iPod dock. A Kindle sat on her night stand, with a computer screen glowing softly on the desk next to her bed. The bed made Trystan pause. It was larger than his—well, the one his dad threw away—and was covered in a white and purple bedspread that had a cascade of ruffles on the skirt.

Trystan turned back to her, an eyebrow rising on his face in surprise, "Ruffles? Really?"

She shrugged, "What's wrong with ruffles?"

"Nothing," he said grinning, "it's just more girlie than I would have thought you'd have. I thought you'd be practical, a solid colored comforter kind of girl."

"I got it when I was twelve. Everything was purple, white, and unicorns. The bedspread was too expensive to toss, so the ruffle monster remains." Mari folded her arms over her chest as she spoke, like she was embarrassed a little bit.

"It's sweet. I can't picture you at twelve, wearing ruffles."

"I never wore ruffles. My mom wouldn't let me. She said ruffles made me look fat." She shrugged like it didn't matter, but Trystan could tell it was more than that. There was a rift between Mari and her mom. He'd heard it before, the way her voice sounded weary, like she'd given up on her mom.

Trystan didn't comment. Instead he crossed the room to a board decorated with ribbons. In the center of the board was a piece of paper with familiar handwriting. Trystan pressed his finger on the page and turned to look back at her, "Day Jones fan?"

"You know it. He's dreamy."

Trystan grinned and looked down for a second before meeting her gaze, "I thought I lost this. Some much happened that I didn't know where it went." It was the song he'd writen for Mari.

"I picked it up. If you want it back—" she reached past him to unpin it from the board, but Trystan took her hands and stopped her.

"No, it's yours. It's your song. I want you to keep it."

Mari looked at his hands and Trystan released her wrists. Mari walked across the room and sat on the bed, patting the spot next to her. Trystan felt like his body had frozen and turned to ice. For some reason, he couldn't move. It felt like he'd shatter into a million pieces. It wasn't like he hadn't done this before, but Mari made it different. Everything was intensified to the point he could barely breathe.

Sensing his apprehension, Mari said, "Come sit with me. We can watch TV or talk." She meant, we don't have to have sex.

The pit of Trystan's stomach was in a free-fall. He breathed in deeply and ran his fingers through his hair. "I'm sorry. I've known you forever, but this is…" he paused reaching for the right word, willing her to understand him, "this is too important. I don't want to mess it up."

Mari smiled at him and shook her head. Pushing off the bed, she crossed the room and grabbed Trystan by the wrist, "Trystan Scott, I swear. If you act like this when I say I want to watch TV, what will you act like when I say I want to sleep with you? Come here and sit. You won't screw this up." She yanked his arm, pulling him to the spot in front of her bed. He watched her, thinking too many thoughts to speak, but Mari just smiled at him. Wrapping her arms around his waist, Mari suddenly sat down and pulled Trystan down with her. They fell to the floor with a thud.

Mari laughed when she hit the floor. Sensing Trystan's tension, she said, "Hey, I'm still me. This is still us. Nothing's changed."

Trystan's smile faded as he sat up. Looking at her eyes, he whispered, "Everything has changed, for the better. Every time something finally goes right, something comes along and destroys it."

Mari leaned in and kissed his cheek, "You'll always have me, Trystan. No matter what happens, I promise my friendship is forever. Don't worry so much. Let's just spend time together the way we used to, but maybe you could kiss me once in a while, instead of torturing me with those sexy lips." A wicked grin spread across her pink lips.

The taste of strawberry lip gloss filled his mouth. Trystan was worried, but that was only because he cared about her so much. "Anything you want, kiss ninja. But, you gotta realize that I'm in uncharted waters here. I don't want to fall off the edge of the map."

Mari laughed, "What, are you a pirate now?"

"I know how much you like those puffy shirts, so yes. My eye patch arrives tomorrow. I ordered it directly from Davy Jones, so it's totally authentic. It'll be kind of soggy, but his customer service wench assured me that it'll dry out and have a nice sea brine coating."

Before he could finish talking, Mari's fingers found his waist and she started tickling him. Trystan managed to finish saying the snarky sea brine thing before retaliating. God, everything about Mari made him want to be with her. He was just so afraid of screwing it up.

No matter how much Trystan tried to worry, he couldn't with Mari's fingers wiggling against him. Every thought in his brain flew away as a massive tickle war ensued. Mari rolled across the floor, her smile and laughter intoxicating him further. She jumped to her feet a few times and Trystan jumped at her, knocking her back down and slipping his hands under the hem of her shirt. Her soft skin felt perfect. When Mari looked like she was about to cry, he'd let her wiggle away, only to repeat the scenario again.

Holding Mari close and hearing her laughter made him so high. If Trystan could stay like that, with her forever, he would.

CHAPTER 10

~MARI~

The look in Trystan's eyes faded, as my fingers found flesh under his shirt and tickled. Trystan squirmed and wiggled, periodically laughing harder than I'd ever heard him laugh. The tickle fight went on until I'd rolled across the room twice. I had no idea how much time passed—a few minutes maybe—but when I looked at the clock it was past eleven. How'd it get so late?

Trystan reached for me, his fingers snatching at my waist and he pulled me closer. Positioning himself above me, Trystan held me in place, tickling me until tears leaked from the corners of my eyes, and I was screaming like a lunatic.

That's when I cheated. I totally lost. He had me pinned, but I couldn't stop looking at his lips. Trystan's mouth was so close and that smile was so sexy. I wanted to taste it. Trystan's grin dissolved when my lips pressed against his.

Without a word, the tickle fight was over and he was on top of me. Trystan's hands found my face and stroked my hair while his kisses grew hotter. Teasing me at first, Trystan's teeth gently nipped my lower lip like he was hesitant to do more. He lingered there, pressing small kisses to my mouth and gently nibbling my lip, teasing me until I couldn't stand it.

Heart racing, I slipped my hands under the bottom of his shirt and found his back. Trystan's skin was hot and smooth. Lifting my fingers, I held him closer, pulling him tighter against my chest. We were both breathing hard, like we'd been running for miles. I was so hot, so lost. I needed him so much. Trystan had no idea, but I decided I wouldn't mention sex again, not after the way he acted before. I expected Trystan to be happy about it, but instead he seemed skittish.

I lay in his arms and enjoyed Trystan's hot kisses and the sensation of his full lips pressing against mine. Heat seared through me, swirling in my stomach until my nails bit into his back. I didn't mean to. It just happened. That's when he finally kissed me. I mean, kissed me fully, deeply—the way he felt he should. The kisses up until that point were like he was holding back. Passion surged through us and things got hotter. If I could have pulled Trystan closer, I would have. I couldn't get enough of him. Everything from his scent, to the way his skin felt beneath my fingers, to the way his muscles rippled beneath my touch made me want him more.

I was kissing Trystan Scott. No, it was more than that. He loved me and he was showing me what that meant, how he wanted to tease me with kisses until I lost my mind.

"Trystan," I breathed his name. He broke the kiss and looked down at me breathing hard. We were both covered in a thin sheen of sweat. "I love you."

Dazzling me with a pure smile, he said, "I love you, too."

We stayed like that for a moment, both of us breathing hard, just staring at each other. The way Trystan's gaze moved between my eyes and my lips made me want to kiss him more. When his scorching look drifted lower, I knew I was toast. We had to do something else or I wouldn't be able to stop.

As if he was reading my mind, Trystan sat up causing a blast of cold air to rush between us. "I'm thinking that I don't have the self-control I thought I did." Trystan gazed at the window with a sheepish look on his face. It was so sweet.

Laughing softly, I pushed myself up on my elbows and looked up at him. "Neither do I." Scooting over behind him, I threw my arms around his shoulders and squeezed hard, hugging him from behind. Trystan nearly fell over, but I held him against me. After a second I released him, and Trystan turned around to look at me. I knew what he was thinking, that he should leave. It was insanely late. My parents would have killed me if I stayed out this late.

Before he could say anything, I asked, "Stay? Just a little longer? You have no idea how much better tonight is compared to last night." The smile slipped off my lips. I couldn't keep the bitterness out of my voice.

Trystan sat on the floor, his arm draped over his knee, with those sapphire eyes softly searching mine. Finally, he nodded, "I can stay a while longer. I just want to be gone by the time your parents get home. I don't want to get you in trouble."

"They're working the seven to seven shift and they usually get breakfast before coming home, so unless you stay all night, there's no way you guys will run into each other." I looked at him for a moment, wondering why he wasn't antsy about missing his curfew, so I asked, "What time do you have to be home?"

Trystan smiled. It was the one that said he was going to evade the truth, but not quite lie. "There is no time. I don't have a curfew."

Sitting across from him, I felt my head cock to the side like a confused Pomeranian. "Seriously?"

He shrugged. "Seriously." It felt like he was leaving something out, but he didn't say what and I didn't want to push him.

"Then, stay here as late as you want. Oh, and since you don't have a cell phone, I want you to have this." I crossed the room and opened my closet door. Fishing out a box from the top shelf, I turned around and handed it to him.

Trystan had crossed the room and was standing behind me. He looked at the box and bristled a little. "You're giving me a phone? Mari, I can't take this." He tried to push it back into my hands, but I shook my head.

"Yes, you can. It's one of those cheap throw away phones. I bought it a few months ago because I lost the super-expensive phone my dad had gotten me. I bought that one and forwarded my calls to it until I found this phone." I pointed to my smart phone on my dresser. "I can't use this one and no one has the number. I thought it'd work good for us, you know, so I can hear your voice at night—so you can get hold of me, if you need to." I felt fragile for some reason. I didn't want him to say no, but I could see it on his face. He didn't want it. After a second I said, "I'm sorry. I didn't mean to make you—" Pressing my eyes closed, I shook my head and snatched the box back from his hands. I turned to shove it into the closet, but Trystan's hands fell lightly on my shoulders.

His voice was level, but when he spoke there was an intensity there that I'd never heard before, "What happened last night? Did someone hurt you?"

I turned toward him. Tears stung my eyes but they didn't fall. I shook my head. His eyes searched mine like they were trying to find the truth. I wanted to tell him, but I couldn't say it out loud. My parents don't care about me. I'm alone. My throat tightened and I couldn't speak, even if I wanted to.

Trystan looked down at the box and took it out of my hands. "I'll borrow it for a while. I want you to call me if something like that happens again."

I couldn't help it. The tears flowed over my eyes and ran down my cheeks. I wrapped my arms around his neck and Trystan held me. I had no idea how much time passed, but when he stepped away I felt like everything might be okay, and it wasn't because he took the phone. That was symbolic. For some reason Trystan didn't want it, but he took it anyway to make me feel better. He put me first. No one did that for me before. I smiled and cried like a crazy person until Trystan's shoulder was soaked with tears.

Trystan kissed my temple softly and said, "Tell me what happened when you're ready. I'll always be here for you, Mari. And if anyone ever hurts you—" he left the threat hanging in the air. I nodded and pulled away.

I sat down on my bed and before I knew it, I was recanting what happened last night. Trystan stood for a while and then he finally sat next to me. By the time I finished, he had his arms around me. "It's stupid," I sniffled. "I'm crying because I got yelled at. I sound like a brat."

"No, you don't." He kissed my wet cheek and held my face between his palms. "And that's not why you're crying. I know you, Mari. I know what this is about." He stroked my hair away from my face, and then I leaned into his shoulder, staring blankly ahead, not speaking. It was silent for a moment, until he whispered, "We're more alike than I thought."

Lifting my head, I asked, "What do you mean?"

Trystan didn't meet my gaze. Instead he looked down and stared the floor. "Our fathers—they seem to have unrealistic expectations. That's all. It's kind of paralyzing." I nodded, wondering what his father did to him. Trystan seemed so hard, so cynical at times. He constantly had a wall up that blocked everyone out, but somehow I snuck through. "I was going to leave after graduation, but things kind of changed."

My heart beat faster as hope flooded through my veins. "You're not going to enlist?"

"And leave you?" he grinned. "Nah, I'll have to move onto plan B, which has something to do with staying here with you."

I threw my arms around him. Trystan embraced me and we stayed like that. I couldn't help the smile on my face. When he pulled back, I said excitedly, "You should go down the Day Jones path and see where it leads." Trystan didn't look convinced. "Your songs are powerful, they speak to people, and I've seen you on stage—you glow. People can't help but love you. You'd be really good at it."

Trystan's gaze cut to hers. His mood was a tad off, apprehensive maybe. "You really think you'd want to share me with all those people?"

"I want you to be happy."

"I'm happy here with you. You're all I need." Trystan's thumb rubbed the back of my hand. His eyes drifted to my lips and I knew he wanted to kiss me again. Trystan broke the gaze, like he was trying to control himself, and looked at the clock. "It's nearly 2:00am. You're going to be a zombie tomorrow. You should get to sleep."

I nodded. Lethargy had been pulling on my body like giant sandbags. "So should you."

He looked down, and ran his fingers through his hair. "Yeah. I will."

Liar. What's with him tonight? I thought about it for a moment, what it could mean, and stumbled on the answer. "You don't sleep, do you?" Trystan's blue eyes lifted to mine, nervous like I'd wound him. "It's okay. Listen, you can stay here until dawn, if your dad won't mind. If you don't want to sleep, you can watch TV downstairs, eat something—" He was staring at me with his lips parted slightly. I couldn't read his expression. Trystan seemed to be caught between terror and surprise and I had no idea why. "What?"

Trystan smiled sadly and shook his head. That haunted look slipped away like it was never there. "Nothing. You're just amazing. I'd like to stay longer, if that's okay with you."

"Of course it is. Let me get ready for bed. I'll be right back." I dressed for bed, pulling on a pair of sleep shorts and a cami. I crawled into bed, and pulled up the blankets. Trystan sat at the foot of the bed and smiled at me.

"Will you stay until I fall asleep?" I blinked slowly, barely able to keep my eyes open.

"Sure, that'd be nice. And then I'll sneak out so your parents don't skin me. I'll see you at school in the morning." He stood and sat down again, closer to me, leaning in to kiss my forehead. My eyes fluttered like they wanted to close. I didn't want the night to end. It was so perfect.

Trystan started to sing softly, as he stroked my cheek. The result was instant bliss. The sound of his voice washed over me, comforting me. There were few things in life that were certain, but I knew this was real. We were meant to be together. My breathing slowed as I snuggled into my blankets. Trystan's gentle touch and voice lulled me into a sleep coma. I didn't wake up until my alarm went off the next morning. The night passed, and when I looked, Trystan was gone. It was like a dream, a wonderful dream.

CHAPTER 11

~TRYSTAN~

Trystan pulled his jacket tighter and looked back at Mari's window one last time before darting between the houses. It was nearly 3:00am. His father should be passed out by now. It was possible his dad didn't even know Trystan was gone. The room looked the same from the outside, so unless his dad opened the door, there was no way to know Trystan wasn't there.

Trystan didn't want to think about that right now. His heart was still enraptured by Mari. God, he loved her. Her scent was still on him. He inhaled deeply, basking in it.

Mari's aroma made him lightheaded and giddy at the same time.

A smile snaked across Trystan's lips as he continued down the deserted streets alone. Porch lights flared on houses that were more expensive than anything he'd ever own. Glancing down the street, he caught the telltale silhouette of a cop car, and cut down a side street to avoid the police. A kid out alone, at 3:00am was looking for trouble. They'd haul him back home and all hell would break lose.

Trystan walked faster. Shoving his hands in his pockets he felt the phone Mari gave him. He didn't want to take it from her. It felt like a lavish gift that Trystan didn't deserve, but when he saw her face, he knew that she needed him to have it. It wasn't about stuff. It was about Mari. Trystan felt the edges of the little phone and wondered if he'd have to add minutes to it. He was totally broke, so unless it was prepaid for a while, that would create a problem. While Mari knew he didn't have a lot of money, no one realized how strapped Trystan was. He did everything he could to keep it hidden.

Arriving at the condo complex, Trystan walked past the group of older guys who were drunk. The night air was temperate so they were hanging out in front of their door, sitting on the front step like it was a patio. They tried to get Trystan to come over, but he'd rather die than get hooked on alcohol. That damn stuff was what caused of all his problems. It wasn't that his mom left them; it was that his dad refused to pick up the pieces and move on.

Trystan stopped at his front door and debated whether or not to go through his window. After a second, he chanced the door. Trystan slid his key in the lock and the door creaked open. Glancing around, Trystan didn't see his father, but he could hear his insanely loud snoring carrying from the back of the apartment.

"Thank God," Trystan sighed and locked the door behind him. That sound was music to his ears. It meant nothing could wake the old man, so Trystan headed for the shower. When he finished, Trystan unlocked the door to his room and closed it quietly, locking himself inside. Lowering himself to the floor, Trystan slept against the door to make sure his father didn't try anything.

The next morning Trystan awoke with the door slamming into his ribs. "Get up, Trystan." The door pulled back and slammed into him again. Trystan shook the sleep from his eyes and sat up and braced his back against the door to keep his dad out, but the old man didn't try to come in. He was just in a foul mood. "Go to school today, before they come looking for you. And I swear to God, if you ever do that again, I'll lock you in here and never come back."

Trystan's jaw tightened as his father spoke. If Trystan didn't have to come back, he wouldn't. There was nothing here for him. His life was ahead of him, but he couldn't leave. Not yet. Trystan swallowed his pride and said what his father was waiting to hear, "Yes, sir."

As soon as Trystan said those words, his father's footfalls headed away from his room. A few moments later the front door opened and closed. He was gone. Trystan sighed in relief. Sitting on the floor, he pulled his knees into his chest and wrapped his arms around them. Lowering his head to his knees, Trystan sat in the quiet wondering what he should do. If the army was out, then he had to find somewhere else to live, and fast.

—

Trystan sat in the cafeteria looking out the window for Mari. He had an apple in his hand and was about to take a bite when Seth sat down hard across from him. Trystan stopped and scowled. "I'm not in the mood, Seth."

Then, Seth did something very un-Seth-like and apologized. "He man, listen… I shouldn't have said that. I knew you wanted to hit that, but I thought she was just another chick."

Trystan rolled the apple in his palm, and lifted his gaze. He held his temper in check. Flatly, he replied, "I told you she wasn't, so don't try to bullshit me now."

Seth rolled his eyes, and slammed his hands on the table making the metal fittings underneath jingle. "I'm not bullshitting you. I'm sorry, okay? I said it. If she means that much to you, I won't go there again."

Trystan wanted to tell him about Mari, about how things changed, but he couldn't. He didn't know how Seth would react and he'd promised Mari he wouldn't. So Trystan nodded, "Fine. Enough of this crap. It's over."

Seth's face lit up. He reached across the table and slapped Trystan's shoulder just as Mari got out of her Mom's car outside. Seth's gaze followed Trystan's and landed on Mari. "You want me to help you get her?"

Trystan flinched. He turned back to Seth. "The answer to that would be, hell no. Don't even think about it. She's mine. I'll get her, eventually." Trystan's lips pulled into a grin. He already had her heart—she loved him. It made Trystan wish he could shout from the tabletops and dance across the hallways, but he didn't. Trystan was careful to leave his poker face in place.

"What is she? The only girl in the drama class that you haven't nailed?"

Trystan stood and glanced at the doors. "Something like that."

Tucker walked through, and turned his face at the two of them. It was as if he was looking for Trystan. Tucker waved Trystan over and Seth followed. "I need to speak with you, Scott. This weekend is the play and Brie refuses to go on with her nose the way it is. I told her we could cover it with stage make up, that no one would know, but she said she quit. Her parents pulled her out of the class. You have no co-star, Scott. Can you please go talk some sense into her? She listens to you."

Seth glanced at Trystan, but Trystan was still looking at Tucker. "Maybe, but I have a better idea." A sly smile lined Trystan's lips. He cut his gaze to the cafeteria doors just as Mari walked by and flicked his chin up. "Her."

Tucker's face pinched. "What? You can't be serious. Mari doesn't know all the—" Tucker stopped midsentence. His eyebrows shot up as a smile lifted the worry off his face. Looking back at Trystan, Tucker seemed amazed at the idea, "She knows all the lines."

"Yeah," Trystan nodded. "And she's been practicing with me longer than Brie. Mari can do it."

Tucker glanced at the hallway, and watched Mari walk away. "Fine. Talk to her. You both get A's for this. That might not matter to you, but it does for her. She's the one that caused this issue in the first place by punching Brie in the face."

Seth laughed and jumped from one foot to the other like a happy monkey. He pressed his palms together, "No way! Girl fight and I missed it? Little goodie-two-shoes took a swing at the slut?"

Tucker opened his mouth to say something and then snapped it shut again. He shook his head and walked away.

Seth turned to Trystan, "Seriously? Your new conquest bitch-slapped your old girlfriend? Ha! I didn't think Mari had it in her." Suddenly Seth seemed more interested in Mari, which wasn't good.

"Brie had it coming," Trystan snapped. "And now she thinks she can screw everyone else by not showing up on Friday." Trystan grinned, thinking about acting opposite Mari, and that kiss at the end of act 2. Oh God, he'd get to kiss Mari like that in front of everyone without anyone thinking anything was going on with them. "This is going to be awesome."

CHAPTER 12

~MARI~

"I'm not an actor, Trystan. I can't do what you do." He asked me to take Brie's role. Part of me wanted to, but the other part said there was no way I could pull it off.

Trystan sat on the table in front of me. We were in the prop room under the stage. He waited to tell me until we had some time alone. Trystan's hands found my shoulders and he gripped them gently. "Yes, you can. You already have, and you did it a lot better than Brie."

My mind raced. If I said yes, this would be the third time I'd pissed off Brie in a really short amount of time. It just wasn't smart. "Trystan, I wouldn't know where to stand or how to respond to the other actors. This isn't my thing. I'd suck it up."

"Tucker said you have a C in his class right now. He wanted me to tell you that you'll get an automatic A if you take her spot." He watched my face as he spoke the magic words.

My face pinched. I wanted to say no, but that was too tempting. "Damn him— Tucker, I mean. That C will cause as much trouble as Brie." I started thinking out loud without realizing it.

"What?" Trystan asked, confused.

"The C. My dad is a psycho with grades. I'll catch hell for it. But, if I take Brie's place so I get the A, I'm going to catch hell from her. I'm already on her shit list." I sighed and looked into Trystan's face. "It's not much of a choice."

"I can take care of Brie."

"Brie's suing me, well, my Dad—" I just blurted it out. I'd managed to leave out that part last night. The conversation skirted around it. I made it sound like a teacher tattled on me and not Brie's father.

Trystan's hands slipped off my shoulders, as his jaw dropped open. "because I punched her. That's what caused the fight the other night with my Dad. It was Brie."

Trystan pressed his eyes closed and shook his head, like he couldn't believe it. He stood and paced, thinking. The muscles in his jaw worked as he walked. Trystan crossed his arms over his chest. The dark blue tee shirt he wore showed off his sapphire eyes. I couldn't help but stare at him. He was beautiful.

When Trystan stopped, he said, "Brie is a pain in the ass, but we have a shot at handling her. Your father, on the other hand, we have no control over him at all. I'd get the grade and deal with the Brie, if I were you."

I smiled at him. That was what I was thinking, I just wished there was another option. Standing, I walked over to him, "And this decision has nothing to do with the kiss at the end of the second act?"

"Do you know how hard it is to stand in front of you and not touch you? Right now—" he shook his head, "I can't even tell you what I want to do right now. It's more than a kiss Mari. It's more time together, more kissing, and more you. Of course I want you to say yes." Trystan looked down into my eyes. He held my gaze making butterflies erupt in my stomach.

"Yes." My voice was light.

Trystan blinked at me, like he hadn't heard me right. "Seriously?"

I nodded and stepped closer to him, slipping my arms around his waist. "Yes. You're right. I know the part and I really don't mind kissing you, actually I look forward to it." I ran my fingers through his hair while I looked into his eyes. Trystan's gaze remained locked on mine.

"You're wicked, you know that? The only thing I can think about now is kissing you." Trystan's fingers pulled at my waist until my chest was firmly against his. The way we fit together made me feel tingles all over. It felt like I was blasted with a heater when he touched me. Suddenly I was hot and breathing like I'd run miles. He didn't even kiss me yet. We were just talking about it.

"All part of my plan, kiss assassin." I flirted back.

"I wonder if tha—" Trystan didn't get to finish his remark because I reached up and grabbed his neck, and pulled his lips down on mine. Trystan's hands held me tight as he kissed me back, his lips gently tasting mine before he lost all control and kissed me harder. I think I forgot to breathe at one point. The whole thing was perfect; the way he held me, the way he kissed me, the way he said my name like there was no one else and there never would be.

When we pulled apart, I sucked in ragged breaths and tried to calm down. Trystan smiled at me. I grinned back, and swatted his arm. "I'm wicked? That was supposed to be a little kiss?"

"I didn't see you keeping it little," he said, bouncing slightly on the balls of his feet. Trystan was happy, happy like I'd never seen him before. Every inch of Trystan was alive and resonating with mirth.

"Ha! Like that's my fault. It's kind of hard to do things half way with you. When you kissed me, while we were rehearsing, I almost died. No one's ever kissed me the way you do." I sat down hard on the couch, fanning myself. My heart was still pounding in my ears.

Trystan jumped onto the couch beside me. "And who else kissed you?"

My spine straightened and I turned slowly to look at him. I didn't want to talk about that. Instead of answering, a blush stained my cheeks. Trystan took my hands, his eyes glittering with curiosity, and said, "Or should I ask how many? Are you really a sexual deviant? Could I be that lucky?"

I laughed. I couldn't help it. "A sexual deviant?"

"Back on track, Mari, my love. How many others have there been?" When I hesitated, he said, "I'll tell you mine if you tell me yours."

"I don't want to know how many girls you've slept with! God, Trystan." I pulled my hands away and rubbed my eyes.

He was still smiling, "Are you sure? You might be surprised. I'm not the male slut everyone thinks I am. I'm only a little slutty." He pinched his fingers together, leaving a tiny space between.

That got my attention. "What do you mean?"

Trystan shook his head, still smiling, not offering more information. "You tell me your's first."

"You're evil," I laughed. Trystan waggled his eyebrows at me and grinned widely. "Fine...I had one serious boyfriend. We didn't do everything, but it didn't matter. He still crushed me when we broke up. He goes to another school, so at least I don't have to see him every day." Trystan kept his hand on mine, rubbing the back of my palm. I glanced up at him from under my lashes, feeling foolish. "I haven't been with anyone. Seth's nickname for me is accurate."

Trystan leaned forward and kissed me on the end of my nose. Grinning, he sat back slowly. "You're perfect, Mari. Holding out for the right guy isn't stupid, and guys who say it is just want to get in your pants."

"Like you?" I said, kiddingly.

"Like me," Trystan continued to hold my hand, his fingers gently brushing against the side of my fingers as he gazed at me. "Well, like me before I met you, and I've heard your chastity sermons for a few years now. Let's just say you weaseled your way into my brain and I didn't hook up with every girl I came across. The rumors of my conquests have been greatly exaggerated." Trystan lifted my hand to his lips and kissed it.

"Meaning?" My heart was racing. Was he saying what I thought he was saying? That couldn't be true, but I could tell from the expression in his eyes that it was—this was a secret that he was happy to share—one that he couldn't wait to tell me.

"Meaning, I'm still a novice at this. I only had one relationship and it was with Brie." He cringed. "Obviously I'm a total moron and have no idea what I'm doing. Besides her, I messed around and made-out, but…" Trystan looked at me for a second and then looked to the side, his lips curling into a bashful smile. "Are you really going to make me say it?"

I blinked at him, assuming I was dumb as a post and not following. "I think I have to. Are you seriously telling me that you were only with one girl? What about all that stuff Seth said?"

"Seth's a moron. He's all bluster, Mari. Have you ever seen him do anything but suck face with a girl?"

I cringed, "No."

"Well, same thing for me. Appearances are deceiving. I hope you won't use this information to tarnish my bad-boy persona at school. I like all the ladies drooling when I walk by." He was laughing now, watching me with laughter in his eyes.

Grinning, I swatted him with my hand, "Oh, gross! Now you sound like him!"

Trystan and I laughed and kissed until the bell rang. When I emerged from the auditorium, I ran into Katie. She instantly noticed my swollen lips and blotchy skin. "Sucking face? With whom might this suckage be occurring? Or should I go look for him?" She glanced behind me, hoping to see the object of my affection.

I yanked her arm and led her down the hall. "No one."

"Yeah, right. And that's why we're running away, so I can't see the invisible man who ate your strawberry lip gloss." Katie's tone was light, teasing. She kept looking over her shoulder like the guy would magically appear.

"Where's Mathboy when I need him?" I glanced around hoping he was nearby.

"He's my sexy nerd, and he's not going to save you from the slew of questions I'm going to hurl at your head." We walked into the classroom and Katie set her books on her desk.

I looked back to the spot where Brie sat. Her chair was empty. I swallowed hard wondering if I could really go up against her and walk away intact.

CHAPTER 13

~TRYSTAN~

Rehearsal was much more enjoyable with Mari in his arms and Brie god-knows-where. Trystan tried as hard as he could to live in the now, but he couldn't shake the feeling that it would all slip between his fingers at any moment. The more time he spent with Mari, the more they kissed, the more he realized he wanted her—and not in a temporary kind of way. There was something about Mari that made him come alive when she was around. All the years of jaded cynicism melted into giddy glee around her.

Tucker barely corrected Mari. She remembered everything, because she'd been prompting the entire time. She'd only lost a couple of days when Tucker threw her out. The cast had a different feel with Mari among them. She affected Trystan's performance for the better and everyone around him strove to be as charismatic as Trystan. It was a domino effect and it started with Mari.

When Tucker first announced Brie's replacement, no one though Mari could do it. She sat in the shadows, reading books— she wasn't an actor—but Mari proved them wrong by the end of the first scene. Tucker didn't stop the play, he let the entire thing run from start to end and when they finished, Tucker just sat there, staring at them with one eyebrow lifted too high.

The entire cast stood on stage, waiting for him to say something.

"Did he have a stroke?" Tia whispered out of the side of her mouth to the girl standing next to her.

Tucker laughed one sharp, "HA!" And then stood in his seat, clapping his beefy hands until they were all deaf. "I couldn't have imagined that a high school cast was capable of this skill level. Trystan and Mari, I don't know what it is, but there's something about you two that pulled the whole performance up a few notches. I didn't think this was possible." Tucker stood there, arms folded across his chest, shaking his head.

Trystan spoke to Tia out of the side of his mouth, "We must have really sucked before." All the girls instantly fell into a fit of giggles. Trystan waggled his eyebrows at Mari, who grinned at him in return.

Everyone looked around, wondering if they could take a break, or if they needed to do another run through. Tucker finally realized this and said, "We're done. It can't get better than this!" Murmuring to himself, Tucker turned and grabbed his folders and jacket.

The lights were turned off as Tucker made his way to the door. The stage lights remained on for another moment while the kid in the lighting cage got his books. Everyone ran from the room like rats from a sinking ship, except Mari who hung back in the wing, waiting for Trystan.

"You ready?" he asked.

She nodded. "Yeah."

They walked out of the school farther apart than either of them wanted to be. Mari looked over her shoulder and smiled at Trystan. Her dark curls blew like ribbons in the wind. Trystan and Mari already discussed walking places together. They decided that they'd act the way they usually did. He walked her to her block sometimes, before crossing the railroad tracks and heading towards his house. Mari knew he lived in the condos in the rough part of town, but she'd never been there.

"That went well." Trystan smirked at her. Mari smiled back, her dark eyes caressing his face as soft as a touch. His stomach dropped. God, he wanted to kiss her.

"I was surprised it went that well."

"I wasn't. I knew you'd rock it. I mean, you have a natural talent for this kind of stuff. You always have." Trystan stood at the street corner waiting for the light to change, when he felt Mari's eyes on the side of his face. "What?"

She shook her head, "Nothing, it's just every time I think I know you, something else comes out."

"I adore you. You know that."

"It's not that. It's your conviction. You said that with total certainty, like you knew I could do it when I didn't even know that. How can you talk like that?"

"How can I not? Did you see you up there? It was amazing. Why haven't you tried out for a part before?"

Mari shrugged, "Daddy doesn't think it's a productive use of my time."

"I know he thinks he's helping you, but he's holding you back." Trystan looked at her as they crossed the street. "You have so much potential and he's channeling it into this little tunnel that sucks the light out of you."

Mari's gaze was on the ground in front of her. "There are some things that can't be changed—like parents—I'm stuck with mine." She glanced up at him.

Trystan knew what she meant. It pierced him at his core. "No, you can't pick your parents, but you get to choose what life you live. Mari, I don't know what's going to happen, but I want you to know this… you're capable of so much more." They'd stopped walking and were standing face to face in front of Mari's house. Trystan wanted to touch her face and pull her in and feel her lips against his.

"So are you, Day Jones," she said, knocking him off kilter. "What's holding you back?" Those brown eyes searched his face.

Trystan tensed. "That's different."

"Is it? 'Cause it looks kind of the same. You get a choice. You're beyond exceptional. You're pure magic, Trystan, and yet, you hide it from everyone. No one really knows who you are. For some reason you let me see, and I can't look away. I can't understand why you'd leave your musical talent hidden. It's a solid future, enough money for college, and a solid way to get your life started, but you won't take it. Why won't you take it? What are you afraid of?" Mari said these things looking into his eyes. She spoke softly, like she was afraid he'd run.

Trystan's heart beat harder and harder as she spoke. Every truth she struck rang out with pristine clarity. She saw him clearly, which was both amazing and terrifying at the same time. He felt his hands shake and slipped them in his pockets. He wanted to tell her. He wanted to say that it was his father, that he'd been beaten and neglected his entire life, but he couldn't. Trystan's sardonic smile laced across his lips.

Mari's gaze narrowed in response. "Don't say something witty right now. You're asking me to do the same thing, to tell them that the life they picked out for me isn't the one I want, but you won't do it yourself. You're not a hypocrite, Trystan, so there's got to be another reason for it, one you won't tell me—one I can't figure out on my own."

Before Trystan had a chance to respond, Mari's front door opened and a man stood there. He was tall and thin with waves of dark hair slicked back neatly. He had on dress slacks the color of caramel and a dark silk sweater that did nothing to block out the cold. The man was covered in subtle status symbols. From the way he looked at them, Trystan knew this was Mari's father.

"Mari! Get in here!" His tone was clipped. Trystan watched him go back into the house, instantly disliking him. He snapped at Mari like she was a dog.

Mari looked over her shoulder when she was called, then said to Trystan, "I have to go. Come later, okay? After 7:00pm."

"I wouldn't miss it."

——

Trystan avoided his home at all cost, but he needed a shower and clean clothes. When Trystan arrived, his dad wasn't home. Thank God. It was still too early, but you never knew with him. Some days dad would show up early and Trystan didn't know why. The way Trystan figured it, he had just enough time to take a shower and get out.

Trystan washed quickly, happy to get clean before seeing Mari again. He pulled on the same pair of jeans he wore earlier, but he had no shirt. Rummaging through his dad's closet, Trystan pulled out a tee shirt and put it on. Trystan combed his damp hair, pushing it out of his eyes. Thoughts about Mari and what she said kept drifting through his head. When Mari spoke like that it was contagious. She believed he could make it as Day Jones. Her confidence made Trystan feel like he could do anything, be anything, that there were no limits.

The Day Jones phenomenon was still raging and getting more insane by the day. Rabid fans wanted more. They wouldn't let it die, and since Trystan's computer was gone, he didn't know what level of insanity things had grown to. Last he looked, the number of comments had more than tripled. Agents and record labels were begging him to contact them. There was no way Trystan could read the comments all in one sitting. It would take days.

Maybe Mari was right. Maybe confessing that he was Day Jones was the best option, the best way out of this hell hole. Trystan liked the idea of performing, of singing on a stage, and of everything that goes with being in the limelight—except the paparazzi. They'd dig into his past and find out everything. It was too much to even think about. Mari was right. There was something holding him back, something that prevented him from ever coming forward as Day Jones. His father.

As if he conjured the old man from thin air, Trystan heard the front door slam shut. Trystan swore and ducked into his room quickly. His dad wasn't supposed to be home for another hour, at least.

His father's garbled words rang out. "I busted my ass with the company for twenty years!" There was a loud crash, the sound of something heavy hitting the wall. "And how do they thank me for it?" Another crash, followed by the sound of shattering glass.

Trystan's eyes grew wide. He knew he had to get out now, but his father was blocking the exit. Trystan turned toward the window, wondering if the bars falling to the ground would make too much noise. Looking back at the door, Trystan decided that it was too risky. Besides, his father would know that he'd left his room if the rusted bars were on the ground. Like it or not, Trystan was stuck here for a few more weeks. He had to make it through. The sounds of things being destroyed suddenly stopped. The apartment was silent. The hairs on the back of Trystan's neck stood on end as a shadow stretched across the floor. His father stepped into the doorway, irate. His muscles were corded tight, ready to explode.

Glaring at Trystan, his dad growled, "You little shit, you're home? You hear me yelling and screaming and you didn't bother to come see what was wrong?" His father's bloodshot eyes locked on his. Dad was still wearing his dress shirt, but the tie and jacket were gone. It was unlike him to get plastered before heading home. That kind of awesomeness was reserved for Trystan alone.

Trystan didn't answer. There was nothing he could say that would make this better. His father's gaze swept over his son's damp hair and clean T-shirt. Recognition formed on Dad's face. "Who said you could take my shirt?"

Trystan knew his silence was being taken as defiance. Everything in his body told Trystan to run, but he was trapped in his hell-hole of a room with his dad barring the exit. "All my clothes seem to have been thrown out."

"So you steal my stuff? That's your solution to everything, isn't it? You see what you want and take it. There's no talking to you. Even now, with the way you look at me like your better." As his dad spoke, he walked into the room. With every step his dad took forward, Trystan took a step back.

Fuck. He was going to get trapped in the corner. Trystan had to get out of there. Every muscle in his body tensed, waiting for the old man's fists to start flying. Trystan had not seen his dad this irate before, not during daylight hours anyway. "I'm not better than anyone," Trystan breathed the words through his teeth, his chest tightening as he spoke.

"You're a goddamn lair and a thief."

Trystan stepped away again. "What happened today? Why are you even here?"

His father's face pulled into a grim smile. "That fucking company that I spent my entire life working for let me go. They merged with another office and decided to downsize. Did they bother to tell any of us that? No. We walked in today and guess what? Surprise! After working my ass off for two decades, I have no job." He ranted, anger surging through him as he spoke. His gaze narrowed on his son. "And then, I come home and find my kid stealing my stuff. What the fuck gives you the right?" He was yelling now, his hands flying through the air.

Trystan's back was nearly against the wall. He'd rather fly into his dad's fists than get trapped in the corner. Don't fight back, he chanted in his mind, over and over again. Get around him and run. But Trystan couldn't see how.

Swallowing hard, Trystan said, "No one gave me the right." Trystan grabbed the shirt and pulled it over his head as fast as he could and threw it at his dad. The shirt hit his father in chest and fell to the floor.

The anger in his father's face exploded. Dad's normally nice features contorted with rage. He lunged at Trystan, his hands open like he planned on strangling him.

Trystan dogged to the side at the last second and darted past his dad into the hallway. Quickly, he reached for the door and pulled it shut. His dad started screaming profanity at him. It was the worst verbal assault he'd ever had. It combined every failure, every short coming, and every fear that lurked inside Trystan's mind. Trystan tried to let the words slip past him, but every single one lodged into his skin like darts. By the time his dad tried pulling on the door, Trystan had the knob in his and was twisting the lock. When Trystan heard the metallic scrape, he knew the door was locked.

Resting, Trystan pressed his head to the door for a second, thankful that he made it away without getting hit, when something slammed into it and shook the frame. The plaster on the ceiling cracked and sprinkled on his bare shoulders like baby powder. Looking up, he saw thin lines spidering away from the doorframe.

Trystan stepped back before the second blow came. That shot was harder and shook the wall. A picture frame crashed to the floor and shattered. His father was cracking the doorframe. Trystan turned to run. He thought he was safe for a second, but he wasn't. From the look of it, Trystan only had one more hit to get himself out of harm's way. That door was coming down.

Trystan ran for the front of the apartment, cutting down the narrow hall as fast as he could. A loud cracking noise came from behind, as Trystan reached for the front doorknob. His father bellowed and fell through the rubble. He stumbled to his feet fast for a drunk guy. The expression on Dad's face was beyond livid, more like psychotically angry. Trystan never pushed his dad that far before. He never fought back, he never intended to. Locking the door didn't count, but the expression on his father's face said otherwise.

Fear snaked through Trystan, strangling him. This was something he couldn't undo. What happened tonight couldn't be changed. Trystan didn't mean for it to happen. He wished he never came home. Before Trystan could think another thought, his dad came barreling down the hall like a rabid bear, practically foaming at the mouth, with a thirst for blood in his eyes. Part of him wanted this to be a nightmare, to believe that his father wouldn't hurt him, but he'd been alive too long to think that.

Trystan yanked the door open, intending to run through and escape into the cold night air, but when he jerked the door open someone was there.

"Mari?" he gasped, taken by surprise.

Mari stood there with a red nose and eyes like she'd been crying. Huffing like she'd run to him, she looked past him and then back at his eyes, "Trystan, what's wrong?" The look on Trystan's face said everything was wrong. He couldn't believe she was at the door. Now.

"Run, Mari. Go. Don't come back." Trystan turned away from her just as his dad barreled into him. Their bodies collided smashing the door shut before Mari could blink. A bloodcurdling scream erupted from her throat, shattering the still night.

SHATTERED

THE SECRET LIFE OF

TRYSTAN SCOTT

VOL. 4

shat ter verb : to break suddenly into many
small pieces

CHAPTER 1

~MARI~

I run. I run out the front door of my house sobbing. I don't know what I think or what I need. I just know that I want Trystan, but when I get to his house, something's wrong. When Trystan pulls the door open, it seems like he is going to walk out, which is strange since he's not wearing a shirt and his hair is damp. I glance at his face—his blue eyes are wild. They're too big, like he has no idea what to do, like I'm the last person he expected on his doorstep.

Trystan hesitates. He looks over his shoulder with panic in his eyes. He tells me to leave in a rush of air. I can hardly make out the word. My heart is pounding. My skin prickles. Something is wrong, but I don't understand. Before I have a chance to ask, someone slams into Trystan. The door snaps shut as their bodies collide and fall into the wall.

I scream. My hands fly to my face as the sound rips out of the back of my throat. Someone is hurting him. Now it makes sense. Now the look on his face, the fear in his eyes, means something. Trystan was going to run out the front door, but I was standing there blocking his way. If he tried to run past, whoever is fighting with Trystan could have come after me instead.

Trystan threw himself in the middle. He knew someone was behind him.

Glancing around frantically, I try to figure out what to do. I'm tiny. I can't do anything, but I know what I saw. Someone is hurting Trystan. I pull my cell phone from my pocket and call 911. I'm not even sure what I'm saying. I repeat myself and say the name of the condo unit one more time. They ask me too many questions. They try to keep me in place, but I can't just stand there. I put the phone down without hanging up. They can find me.

That's when things get worse. I hear Trystan's voice through the front window. It's a strangled yelp and then a crash. Glass shatters inside the house. Horrors are taking place behind that door. My heart thumps in my chest so furiously that I think it might crack my ribs. My muscles tense. Every part of me knows that I'll get my ass kicked—maybe worse—if I walk through that door, but I have to. I can't leave him in there. I can't wait for the police. Trystan needs me. Someone's hurting him.

I can't just stand here and cower. But I have nothing to fight with. I glance around and see a busted up brick in the parking lot. I run and grab it. Then, I do the stupidest thing I've ever done in my entire life—I open the door and go inside.

The sight makes me stop in my tracks. My mouth gapes open. A man in a white dress shirt has Trystan by the throat and is pressing him into the wall. Trystan's hands are wrapped tightly around the man's wrists. Every muscle in Trystan's body is corded tight, like they could snap at any second. His face is a mixture of pain and terror, and is the wrong color. He can't breathe. Trystan doesn't see me. The other man doesn't hear me. He's screaming at Trystan, blaming him for something that I can't understand. Every time the man screams, he shoves Trystan back into the wall, harder and harder, choking him.

Rage courses through my veins. My muscles tense and I don't think. I feel the rock burning a hole in my hand. I feel the pull toward the man's back, as if the broken brick wants to collide with his head. I launch myself across the room and swing my arm. My hand comes down hard and the brick slams into the man's head. But, I realize my mistake too late. I'm too short, too weak. I didn't hit him hard enough.

Instead of falling to the ground, the man drops Trystan to the floor and rounds on me. His eyes burn like acid, overflowing with hatred. I know I'm going to die. The way he looks at me, the way his hands float up so slowly, makes every hair on my body stand on end. I slide one shoe back. My senses are all hypersensitive, but it doesn't help. I know what he's going to do. I see him coming toward me, slowly fixating his focus on my neck. I know he wants to snap me like a twig. My lips are parted, but I can't speak. Someone has stolen my voice.

"What the fuck gives you the right to attack me in my own home?" His voice is like gravel and nails. Venom is laced thickly through every word. His shoulders are hunched forward like he's ready to pounce and bury me in the ground.

My heart hammers harder. I don't understand. I blink, even though I don't want to take my eyes off the man. "You were hurting him." The words come out of my mouth in a huff of air as though he's already choking me.

"It's none of your damn business what I do to him." The man's jaw shifts back and forth. He steps toward me and grabs my wrist. I scream and he shoves me back into the wall. I claw at my arm, at that one wrist that he has pinned, but I'm not strong enough.

The man hisses in my face, "He's my kid, not yours. I should break your hand for this. You came into my home and attacked me. No one would blame me, you know.

No one would know what happened here. They'd say you were lucky that I didn't shoot you." He twists my wrist slowly, twisting it farther and farther.

My heart pounds frantically, as pain shoots up my arm. I try to pull away from him, but I can't. I scratch at his hand, the one holding me, and kick his shins, but he just laughs. It's like I'm a fly. I can't do anything to stop him. Fear makes my body shake. He smiles like he's enjoying hurting me, like he'll really do it.

I freak out. My brain snaps. Trystan is battered and bloody on the floor and this lunatic is his father. This is the person responsible. Before I know what I'm doing, my mouth lands on his shoulder and I bite. He screams and throws me back. The floor hits me hard and I roll onto my side. There's no time—there's no time to run or crawl away. Before I can blink, his foot connects with my stomach. Pain shoots through me as tears burst from my eyes. A raw scream rips from my throat. I try to curl into a ball, but the man doesn't stop. It's like he can't stop, like he has to finish this. I scream louder as the foot comes at me again, but it doesn't connect.

Trystan is yelling, his voice is mangled, but I still understand him. "Don't touch her!" He's standing. There are angry marks around his neck and his lip is split. A trail of blood runs down his cheek. That wound from the other day, the one that Tucker was upset about, opened up.

Tucker. Tucker knew something was wrong. My eyes dart to Trystan. His dad has been beating the shit out of him. I didn't know. Horror washes over me in a frigid wave. How did I not know?

Trystan's dad has a strange look on his face. I get to my feet even though my middle feels like it's been smashed to bits. Trystan stands between us. His shoulders are tense, corded with muscle, ready to fight. I don't breathe. I can't. Everything happens so quickly, but it feels like forever, like we're moving through a vat of Vaseline.

Trystan's dad takes a swing at his son. Angry words come pouring out of his mouth and his fist follows. Trystan remains between us, dodges the hit, and swings his arm straight up. Trystan's fist connects under his dad's jaw. The punch is solid. The man's bones make a cracking sound before he gets a strange look on his face and falls backwards. His body hits the floor.

Trystan stands over his father, breathing hard, his fingers still clenched into a fist. Neither of us moves. Trystan's shaking, looking at his hand like he's some kind of monster. When he turns back to me, I nearly die. His expression is horrible. All the anguish is plainly painted across his face for me to see.

We both stare at each other for a second. It feels like time stops, but in a bad way. I finally remember I have feet and lunge at him, throwing myself into his arms. Trystan's chest is slick, covered in sweat. I feel every muscle in his body as he wraps his arms around me. He buries his face in my hair and we stay like that until the lights and voices tear us apart. Trystan releases me and looks up confused. Their words sound like far away echoes. They say to drop to the floor, to let go of me. Neither of us moves. We both shiver as the men run at us. One pulls me from Trystan, while the other knocks him to the floor and pulls his arms behind his back.

A police officer speaks to me. "Are you all right? Are you the one who called? Miss…" he continues to talk, but I'm shaking. I can't understand why they're hurting Trystan. I can't understand anything.

I blurt out, "He didn't hurt me! That man did. What are you doing?" I try to pull away from the cop, but he keeps me back. More police are there. Another cop car. They say that I should calm down. They ask my name, my parent's names. They want to know what happened, if I'm all right. But I can't speak, they don't listen when I tell them that Trystan is hurt. They pull Trystan away from me and I can't see him. It feels like there's a foot on my chest and I can't breathe.

CHAPTER 2

~TRYSTAN~

Something inside of him snapped this time. When Trystan saw Mari fall and his father's foot connect with her stomach, his brain broke. Red hot rage ran behind his eyes, blinding him. Before Trystan knew what happened, his father was on the floor. He remembers the steps toward his dad. He remembers the way it felt when his fist collided with the old man's jaw. Maybe dad deserved it. Maybe, but that isn't the emotion rolling over his skin. Trystan looks at his hand, still clenched tight. That fist. Oh god. He didn't want to fight back. Fighting back makes it worse. Fighting back makes him like his father. Trystan's stomach twists as he stares at nothing.

After a moment, he sees her—Mari. She moves toward him. Shame covers him like a thick blanket. He didn't defend her fast enough. He didn't prevent this. He should have. When Mari falls against him, Trystan pulls her to him, touching her back and lacing his fingers through her hair. He saw the kick and knows how much she hurts. Trystan is careful not to make it worse, but he doesn't want to let go. Closing his eyes, he buries his face in her hair and breathes. It seems like hours pass this way.

His life is so fucked up, so far beyond repair—and Mari walked straight into it. She saw him when he opened the door, but she didn't run. Mari came inside. She must have done something after he blacked out. The last thing Trystan remembers is his father's fingers around his throat and the liquid fire filling his lungs.

Then, Trystan opened his eyes and the world was on its side. Mari was on the floor. It was too much. Trystan was too late. He didn't save her. He walked her into this mess, led her straight into it.

Mari's hands are warm and hold onto him tightly. She doesn't hold back. It isn't until the cops arrive that they part, and it isn't willingly. Before Trystan knows what's happening, he's forced to the floor with a knee in his back. They say things to him, but the pain is making it hard to focus. He can't swallow. His entire throat burns and aches at the same time. It's like his neck was in a vice, but it wasn't. It was in his father's hands.

They pull Trystan up and drag him into the kitchen. The wall blocks his view of Mari. Anger is coursing so wildly through his body that he can barely control it. The cops ask him questions, but he can't really speak. Each word is like a nail through his throat. The only things he can manage is, "It's not her fault. I did this." They shove paper at him. Trystan knows better than to write anything down. He shakes his head.

"Don't be a dumbass kid. Write down what happened." The cop pushes the paper back at Trystan, but he doesn't take it. "You're old man beat you one too many times. We know this story kid. The girl showed up and tried to help. Things got out of hand. I know how this goes. Tell us something." But Trystan is quiet.

The cop glances through the doorway to the cops in the other room. He shakes his head once, and turns his attention back to Trystan. Another cop comes into the room. He's shaking his head, like he can't believe Trystan's so stupid.

"Are you a minor, kid?" the new cop asks. Trystan shakes his head and wishes he didn't. It makes his head throb more. He mutters curse words under his breathe and looks back at Trystan's dad who is still lying on the floor.

A few minutes later the paramedics arrive. Trystan doesn't want them to look at him, but the cops insist. There's no way to pay for this, but they look him over anyway.

They tell Trystan that he'll be all right. They tell him that his father is awake and unharmed, but they are taking him in anyway. They repeat a question, "You sure you didn't pass out? Not even for a second?"

Trystan mouths no. He lies. He isn't going to the damn emergency room.

Trystan knows exactly where he's going as soon as the paramedics leave.

"Kid, we're going to have to bring you to the jail if you don't go with them. Blacking out would be normal. It's nothing to do with how much of a man you are." The cop looks at him. He doesn't understand. It isn't blacking out. It's that his private life is suddenly exposed. All those years of misery are out in the open. The only thing Trystan wanted was to get through the next couple of months and then go out on his own. This wasn't part of the plan.

Mari appears in the doorway. "I'm not pressing charges." Trystan perks up in his chair, but the cop places a hand on his shoulder to keep him in place. There are two officers with Mari, walking her out to the car. She screamed the words as she passed by.

Trystan says, "But her father will."

"Smart boy. Come on. Let's get going. You're going to have a long night." The cop gestures for Trystan to stand and hold out his wrists. Cold metal bites into Trystan's skin when the handcuffs tighten.

He blinks slowly, wondering how he ended up with this life.

CHAPTER 3

~MARI~

Tear stains streak my cheeks. When the cop car pulls up in front of my parent's house, I nearly die. One of the officers goes ahead to the door, while the other one fishes me out of the backseat.

"They aren't home," I say.

The two cops look at me. They're both young with no wrinkles around their eyes. One has dark skin and the other one is so pale that he's practically glowing. They're like a law enforcement ying-yang.

The pasty guy asks, "Where are they?"

"Work," I say. They're always at work. And if these guys call them, I'm going to get my ass handed to me. It doesn't matter that it isn't my fault. "My dad's a surgeon. My mom's a nurse. Is there any way you could take care of this with them in the morning?" They both shake their heads. I reach for the door and stick in the key. "Fine, come inside." I keep talking as I walk in. They follow me. Their heads swivel on their shoulders as they take in the house. Everyone does that. It's too posh, too pretty. It's a status symbol in the extreme.

"Do you want coffee or something?"

"No, thank you, Miss," the cop with the super-tan says. His name is Marcello. I squint to read it on his chest. "We'll just wait for your parents. What time do you expect them?"

"In the morning. They both work the night shift." I quickly add, "And if you call them, and I'm not dead, I will be when they get home." I can't say more. I hope to God that they understand what I mean and take me seriously.

The pasty cop furrows his brow. He steps toward me. "Is someone hurting you here?"

I say nothing. I just stare at them. No one is hurting me. No one is ever here. It's not like what Trystan was enduring. My God. My stomach clenches thinking about him, about the pain in his eyes. He hid it from me all these years. There were times he seemed off, but I couldn't figure him out. Now I know why. I feel sick.

Pressing my lips together, I ask, "What'd you do with Trystan?"

"He's been taken in for questioning. They should let him go, because of what it is. You're the wild card in this equation. Your parents need to be notified. If they want to press charges, we'll be forced to comply."

"What does that mean?" I ask looking at both of them. "Why would they press charges?"

Marcello takes a deep breath. His eyes shift and he looks at his partner. Neither of them wants to tell me, but they both know the answer. "Just be glad things didn't get worse, okay. And stay away from that complex. There's some low-life scum in that part of town."

"Trystan's not like that," I say, automatically defending him. "He's a good guy. His dad beat the shit out him."

Marcello doesn't want to say it. His eyes shift to the side and then back to me. "Listen, kid. Guys like that don't get second chances. His dad may have been the one that messed him up, but there's no saving him. You understand? There's nothing left to save. He's already gone. Stay away from guys like that if you want to be happy."

The cop stares at me like I'm his little sister, like he's remembering something. He blinks and looks away. His partner is at the door. They're leaving to find my parents. I hope to God that my parents aren't at work—that somehow they fail to be notified—because I know how this will end. My throat constricts and my heart pounds harder. I say nothing else. They nod and leave. Once again, I am alone.

———

The next morning, my parents sit across the table from me. They eat breakfast like nothing happened last night. They don't even talk about it. It isn't until I stand to leave that my father asks my mother about the lawyer.

I stop and turn with my plate in my hands. I'm worried that they're going to press charges against Trystan. "Lawyer for what?"

Daddy shoots daggers at me with his eyes. "For what? Oh, let's see. First of all there was that assault you were involved in with Brie and then there was the incident last night." His jaw twitches. I know he wants to scream at me until his eyes get too big for his head and that vein in his temple swells to spaghetti size.

"She had nothing to do with the incident last night. The officer said—" Mother is kind. She tries to defend me for once, but Daddy cuts her off.

"The officer was being polite. He didn't want to say that our daughter was with a derelict and his drunken father, doing God knows what, when things got out of hand." Daddy gives Mom a stern look and she lowers her head and goes back to her eggs. My heart falls inside my chest. I wish she'd defend me. Just once.

When Daddy resumes his rant, his voice is tense, clipped. "I'm not pressing charges. It'll cost more than it's worth." I hear *it'll cost more than you're worth.* It rings crystal clear in my head, like he actually said it. He looks up at me and asks, "Tell me, Mari— do you intend to throw away your life on someone so utterly beneath you, or do you intend to make something of yourself? Actions like this have consequences and from where I stand, you're throwing away your life. You're nothing but a goddamn waste."

His words cut me in two. I don't know what I expected him to say but that wasn't it. I move robotically to the sink and set my plate down. My chest constricts and turns cold. My eyes don't blink, they look but they don't see. I don't see Daddy go back to his breakfast like he wished me well today. I don't see my mother cowering, doing nothing to prevent his words from stabbing me in the heart. I've done nothing to warrant this from him, yet, this is my treatment. I'm an inconvenience. He makes that abundantly clear.

I'm a bill.

I'm an expense.

I'm an adverse risk, one that he would have rather lived without.

CHAPTER 4

~TRYSTAN~

The police don't know what to do with him. Trystan is too old or too young. The cops don't want to throw him in jail, but they haven't released him yet, either. Trystan sits in the police station after questioning that took too long. He didn't say much. There wasn't much to say.

The police station is busy even though it's getting late. It seems like the later it gets, the more stupid people become. Trystan is sitting in an old beat up wooden chair by the detective's desk. The cop sits next to him filling out paperwork, not saying much. Trystan's gaze is carefully placed on the floor where it can't attract trouble. His arms are folded over his chest and he's slumped back in his seat. There isn't anything that he wouldn't give to be somewhere else. This trip, this whole damn night, is going to ruin his shot at the army. Trystan stares at his toe, the once-white part of his Converse, as he thinks that plan was shot to hell anyway. Mari loves him. Mari wants to be with him.

And now this.

Trystan rubs his hands over his face and back through his hair. He stretches and looks over at the cop. "Can I go?" He's polite. It's a stupid question. After everything that happened, Trystan's sure they won't release him.

"Not yet, kid. Let me finish this and you can sign it. If the girl's family presses charges, we'll deal with it then. I don't want to throw you in a cell with the guys that are in there tonight. Too much shit has happened. They'll rip you apart before you even get a chance to turn around." The cop has a wrinkled dress shirt on. His tie is loosened around his neck. His face is covered in wrinkles and his skin weathered like old leather. There are too many creases and he has that smoky smell that comes from lighting up too many times each day. The cop doesn't look up at Trystan.

This is the first time anyone told him what was going on. Since they dragged him into the station, no one said anything to him. Trystan doesn't want to ask, but he can't help it. "Did they say if they're going to press charges?"

The cop nods, not looking up from his paperwork. "Not yet, but she's a minor. They'll probably talk to their lawyer in the morning and we'll hear back then." He glances up at Trystan and points a pen at the string of bruises blossoming around Trystan's neck. "From the look of things, it could have been a lot worse. You're lucky."

Trystan laughs. The sound is so bitter that he can taste it. "If that was lucky—"

The cop cuts him off. He looks straight at Trystan and narrows his eyes. "Damn right, it was lucky. Lucky she showed up. Lucky your old man didn't break her ribs. Lucky you're still breathing. You were lucky, Trystan. No one else stepped in. That parking lot was filled with people. They all minded their own business and let your dad strangle you. That girl saved your ass." His old eyes hold Trystan's for a moment and his expression softens. "If you've got some family you can stay with until you graduate, do it. These things don't end well. Once you pass that point, once you fight back, there's just going to be more of it." Trystan holds the cop's gaze for a second and nods.

Trystan gets what the detective is saying. Don't go home.

Trystan slides down further in the seat. His arms are flexed tightly across his chest with his head lowered. It's the only way to hide the marks on his neck. He swallows hard and waits, thinking. Too many thoughts, too many images flood his mind. Everything in his life sucks, everything expect Mari.

When Trystan thinks about what she did, how she raced in like she wasn't the least bit afraid—oh God. If there was a rewind button on life, Trystan would press it. He would go back and delete the whole thing. If he'd never went home, this wouldn't have happened. As it is, it kills him that Mari was hurt and he couldn't stop it.

There are too many things wrong with his life, too many things that he can't fix.

———

A noise startles Trystan awake. He rolls over on the old couch and flinches. His shirt is on the floor and he's wearing nothing but his jeans and a tattered blanket from the prop bin. When Trystan had nowhere to go, he decided to break into the school and sleep in the prop room. No one comes down there early in the morning, which is confusing him now.

Trystan blinks again and yawns. A pair of brown eyes and soft dark hair comes into focus. "Mari?" he asks, still half asleep. He wonders if he's dreaming. Trystan blinks again, but his throat is still aching. It feels like his body was ripped apart last night and reassembled. Add to that the shame he's feeling and Trystan can barely breathe.

Mari reaches for him and smoothes her hand across his cheek. Her touch is warm, gentle. "Did you sleep here?" Her eyes slide over his chest and then back up to his face.

Trystan stretches and sits up, letting the blanket fall from his body. He really doesn't want to answer. It isn't that he doesn't trust Mari, it's that he wishes that part of his life didn't exist. But, after last night he owes her. Trystan rubs the sleep from his eyes and says, "Yeah. I had to. I couldn't go home."

"What happened last night after I left? I tried to stay, but they wouldn't let me do anything. The police treated me like a child. It..." her gaze is on the side of his face. She lets out a sigh and closes her eyes for a second. When she reopens them again, Mari looks at the same spot on the floor as Trystan. They both have that vacant gaze.

"I was worried about you." She bumps his knees with hers.

"I'm fine," Trystan says, but deep inside he's not fine. Somehow Mari got sucked into his private hell, and that makes it worse. Trystan couldn't stop it. When he finally passed out on the couch last night, the whole nightmare unfolded again and again as he dreamed. That's the problem with his life, there is no escaping it, not even in sleep. Trystan glances past Mari, looking for his shirt. "What about you? Did your Dad..."

Mari stirs and sees his shirt. She reaches for it and hands it to him. Trystan pulls the fabric over his head as she speaks, but her eyes lift to his neck and lock there. She can't tear her gaze away. "Dad doesn't listen to me. He doesn't hit me, but sometimes I think he will. Oh God, Trystan. Why didn't you tell me? I had no idea—"

"There's a reason why you had no idea. I love you, Mari, I really do—but I can't talk about this. It isn't something that I want to share. I'm completely horrified that you walked into it. I'm horrified that he hurt you. I…" Trystan's jaw drops open and for the first time since it happened, he really looks at Mari. He meets her gaze and holds it. She's his refuge. Mari is his glue, his balm, his other half. Her brown eyes are wide. Her narrow fingers are gripped tightly in front of her waist, like she thinks she did something wrong. "I just want to get past it and now I can't even hide it. Everyone is going to see my neck and know."

Mari is wearing an oversized flannel shirt. Without a word, she unbuttons it, revealing the cami beneath. Trystan doesn't realize what she's doing until she holds out the flannel to him. "Take it. It has a collar. And I have access to the stage make-up. That will cover up the marks in front. No one will know. Everything will be okay." Even as she says it, Trystan knows Mari doesn't believe it. There's a look in her eye, but he doesn't press her about it. Instead he nods and takes the shirt, grateful.

Mari changes the subject and talks about other things while she dabs thick, cold, goopy, foundation on his neck. This will work. It covers everything. Her fingers are so soft and work so fast. Trystan waits until she stops talking and asks, "What made you come here this morning? School doesn't start for another hour or more." Part of him thinks that she was looking for him. The other part thinks something happened, something with her dad.

Mari's shoulders tense. She stands taller and her eyes dart away. He's right. Fuck, he didn't want to be right. She licks her lips and finishes covering up his mangled neck. "I had to get out of my house. You know how it is."

"Yeah, I know." He's quiet for a moment.

Mari is wearing one of those cami's with the lace at the top. It hugs her body, closely fitting to every curve. His eyes drink her in. In the back of Trystan's mind, he knows that he's going to lose her. Life isn't fair and he knows that, but losing her so soon is unbearable.

Mari's dark hair falls down her back in a cascade of thick curls. They sway and fall over her shoulder as she works. Mari moves around him, not feeling his eyes on her skin as she picks up the make-up and puts it back in the kit. Trystan feels so torn. He needs her, but she'd be so much better off without him. Trystan has nothing to offer her. He only brings pain and shame. He swallows hard, trying to ignore the guilt that's choking him.

When Mari turns around, she has a soft smile on her lips. She isn't afraid of him. She doesn't pity him. Mari acts like Trystan is the same guy he was yesterday, before she learned his secret. She sits down next to him and helps him pull her shirt on. It was too big on her, but it's about the right size for him. She buttons it up, a few of the top buttons she leaves open, and smiles at him.

Mari places her hand over his heart and says, "No one will know."

Their eyes lock. A rush of emotion floods through him. Trystan feels too much. After everything that happened, he just wants to hold onto her and never let go. Acting on the urge, Trystan leans in and gathers Mari in his arms and holds her tight. She winces as he does it, which makes him let go. "You're hurt."

Trystan's blue gaze slips over the cami. He doesn't see anything. Slowly, he inches his hand toward the hem of her shirt. Mari is very still, her dark eyes tracking his hands as he takes the bottom of her cami and slowly slides it up. An angry purple mark mars her perfectly pale skin. He can't breathe. Things can't be like this. She's hurt because of him. He shouldn't do this. He shouldn't be here with her and he sure as hell shouldn't be touching her, but he can't stop. It's still early. No one is here. Trystan could slide his fingers along her soft skin and press his lips to hers. She could take him away from here with a taste of those lips. Trystan could be higher than high in a heartbeat if he just leaned in and kissed her.

Mari's eyes drift to his lips. His hands are still on her shirt, his fingers are so close to her skin that it aches not to touch her. Mari takes a jagged breath and looks up at him. Her eyes are molten chocolate. They shimmer with golden heat. The way she looks at him makes Trystan's heart beat harder. Suddenly, he's hot all over. His body is responding to her. He wants to lean in. Trystan wants to be with her, but he doesn't move.

Trystan's lips are a breath from Mari's. The stay like that too long, impossibly long. Lingering thoughts tease him, telling him to take what he needs—that she'll let him— that Mari needs him just as much. But he can't. He can't drag her into this more than he already has. Guilt juts up between them like a wall.

Trystan blinks and breaks their gaze. He turns his face away from Mari without explanation. He sucks in air and runs his hands through his hair and down the back of his neck.

She deserves so much more.

CHAPTER 5

~MARI~

When Trystan pulls away, it feels like my lungs have been ripped out of my throat. I don't understand why he does it. My heart races frantically, and won't calm down. Trystan bends forward and lowers his head like he's praying. He doesn't look up right away. I want to take him in my arms and fix this, but I know I can't. There are too many things bottled up inside of him, too many thoughts that I don't know. So, I do the only thing that I know to do.

I stand up and smooth my shirt back into place. My middle is still sore as hell, but I'd rather die than pass up the chance to have Trystan's hands on me.

"Come on, Scott," I say, grabbing a pillow off the couch. The thing is old, huge, and heavy. Trystan glances at me from the corner of his eye. I waive the pillow at him. It nearly knocks me off balance. "I'm serious, Scott. We both have shitty lives. Mine is covered in glitz so people don't bother to notice, but I'm not stupid. And I'm not letting you give in to it. Get up."

When Trystan doesn't move, I swing the pillow at him. I try to do it gently, but there is no gently with these things. It's too big. The pillow hits him in the side of the face and makes a smacking sound. Trystan actually sways sideways. He glances at me with a shocked look on his face. The corners of my lips curl up. "You know you liked it." I waggle my eyebrows at him and he laughs.

Trystan stands and plucks a pillow from the couch, but not before I have the chance to whack him again. The pillow is too heavy. It pulls me forward every time I swing. When it smacks Trystan, it sounds like I hit him with a ream of paper. He rounds on me with that boyish grin on his face, and then nearly falls over. I laugh, but Trystan already has his footing back. He taps me lightly with his pillow, like I might break.

"What the hell was that, Scott?" I tease him and bounce on the balls of my feet. I taunt him and say, "Play like you mean it."

"You like it rough?" The corner of his mouth twitches.

"No holding back. Not now. Not ever." I say the words and know that I'm not talking about a pillow fight. I'm talking about us, about what's happening between us and to us. I don't want to give up and I don't want to lose him.

I swipe my pillow at his arm. It took a mega-swing to get momentum, but I manage. When the pillow collides with Trystan, he staggers to the side before dropping his pillow. His blue eyes are crystal clear. Trystan steps toward me, pulls the pillow from my hands, and slides his palms up my cheeks and then tangles his fingers in my hair.

A rush of tingles shoots through my middle. I can't breathe. Trystan looks at me like I'm air and that he can't breathe without me. He brings our faces closer, so slowly that it feels like I'm going to die, but then our lips touch and everything changes. Butterflies fill my stomach. They swoop inside of me, making me giddy. The spots on my face where his palms touch my skin are electrified. A current shoots through me and makes me tingle.

And his lips, oh God, his lips—they press lightly at first. His mouth is so soft, his lips are so full. It's like that kiss when we were rehearsing, and then suddenly it's not. Trystan stops holding back. His desperation hits me hard. The tension in his arms flows into his hands and onto my cheeks as he tightens his grip.

The heat from his body encompasses me and I'm lost, falling through space. My eyes close and little white spots flicker behind my eyes. His hands slip over my skin and carefully move down my back and under my shirt. I gasp and press my mouth harder to his. The kiss is urgent, demanding. It's like we both know our time together is limited and everything is going to change. I can't stop and I don't want to. Heat seers under my skin as Trystan's hands slip over me. His tongue licks the seam of my lips, teasing me. My heart beats harder, and drowns out every other sound. When I open my mouth and let him, I feel my body going limp in his arms.

Trystan holds me to his chest and kisses me harder, deeper. His tongue moves in my mouth and I'm floating and falling at the same time. I don't come up for air. I'm afraid he'll stop. I'm afraid of what will happen next. I'm afraid...

Trystan barely breathes as the kiss endures. It's seeking, giving, and hoping. It's everything that I though a kiss should be, but he pulls away too soon. Trystan's face is flushed. Heat fills his cheeks and he breathes like he's run too far, too fast. His fingers brush my cheek and rest on my shoulder. "I love you, Mari." His sapphire gaze locks with mine. We hold each other. We say nothing.

The moment remains perfect, as if it's suspended in time. We cling to each other, hoping to God that there's more for us, that there's a way I can hold onto him. But, Trystan is like a snowflake. I'm afraid that if

I try to close my hand around him, he'll disappear from my life. Trystan can't accept who he is, that it stems from where he came from. He won't forgive himself for this. Somehow I know it, but I can't let it go. I can't let him go. I love him with every ounce of my being, and I know that I always will.

CHAPTER 6

~TRYSTAN~

Mari is amazing. It doesn't matter what's wrong, she brings Trystan back to life.

He moves through the school and goes to his classes like it's any other day. Trystan smiles and jokes, but it's different now. That hollow feeling inside his chest has someone to fill it. Mari knows him like no one else. She understands him. Trystan wishes so badly that Mari didn't, but at the same time, he's glad she does. It's one of those things that he can't explain.

And right now he feels caught. Trystan can go on without her, but he doesn't want to. Love isn't like that, is it? Is it selfish? He didn't think so, and keeping Mari in his life is selfish. Things will only get worse. Trystan is falling down a pit, head first. He knows he's mid free-fall, and that he took Mari with him. The crap with his father isn't over. Add to the fact that he's homeless and his life is just getting worse.

But… but if he leaves Mari alone, her father will crush her. The light in her eyes will disappear. She'll give in and be what he wants, which is that demur version of Mari. Trystan brings out the other side of her, the real Mari. The one that is all vibrant and fantastic. The side she hides from the world.

Trystan glances across the stage. Mari is in the wing. The stage lights cast a golden glow on her skin as she waits for her cue. Her long hair is soft and totally touchable. When Mari woke him this morning, Trystan thought he was dreaming. Any touch from her sends him reeling. It's like she's his angel, his second chance, but somehow that isn't what's happened. Instead of pulling him up, he's sucking her down. Trystan swallows hard. The thoughts pummel his mind in a relentless wave. He'd give anything for her—do anything to make her happy. After last night—

His thoughts are cut off when Mari senses his gaze and looks up at him. She smiles. That soft, shy smile drives him crazy. He winks at her, knowing that it'll conceal his thoughts. Mari has a way of reading him that scares him to death. One glance at his eyes and she knows exactly what he's thinking. Hiding things from her is difficult.

Trystan honed in on things that set her off balance a while ago and uses them judiciously to set her off kilter when she gets too close. Damn it. He really needs to make up his mind and pull her in or push her away. You don't deserve her, a small voice reminds him. It's the same voice that said don't fight back. Trystan doesn't know what that is anymore. Last night, when the voice said to be still, he nearly died because of it. Maybe he's been listening to the wrong voice all this time? Maybe he should have fought back before now. He doesn't know and dwelling on it won't change anything.

Trystan takes his cue and enters the stage, while banishing the whole mess from his mind. He says his lines perfectly and it's all Mari's doing. When he enters the stage to act opposite her, Trystan can't help beaming. His smile is at full wattage. The acting is a reprieve, a chance to pretend that his horrid life doesn't exist. It's a chance to escape, and escaping it with Mari makes his time on stage even better.

They act—they fight, they banter, they kiss—it's as if this is a dream. If only life were this simple. If only saying a few well-chosen words could really fix his mistakes. Trystan grins and pulls Mari close. She has that shy thing going on. It drives him crazy. The stage lights make her more radiant than she already is. Trystan can't think about anything but kissing her when her eyes lower like that, and she looks up at him from under her lashes.

Mari says her lines, but it feels real. For half a second, Trystan is lost in the scene. He's not himself. His past is gone, his pain is gone. Mari holds his heart and there is nothing else. They're in their own world and there is nothing weighing them down, no one to hold them back or break them apart. Mari looks at his eyes and he's lost in her gaze. There's no place better than this. It feels real. It feels like this could be his life, like he could have Mari and make her happy. For a second, hope floats into his chest and it feels so real that he can taste it. Then, the lights fade into blackness. The moment fractures as the curtain swings halfway closed and abruptly stops.

Mari is breathing hard. She steps away from him. Their relationship is still a secret. She glances at him out of the corner of her eye and smirks before exiting the stage. Trystan watches her walk around to the back of the theater and out the door. His eyes trail her slender frame too long.

Seth is sitting in the empty auditorium with a few other people. They mill around while we try to run through the entire play from start to finish, with lighting, and sound. The mic guy is doing well. There are hardly any issues with him, but the lighting guy is having problems with the spots.

Working with the lights on is awesome, but they're really warm. Trystan is glad they shut them off when he walks toward the front of the stage. He lowers himself and swings his legs off the edge and sits, looking out at vacant chairs. Trystan pushes his hair out of his eyes. Tucker and the lighting crew are yelling back and forth. The guy in the lighting cage curses and the lights dim.

Then, the remaining stage lights turn off completely. Tucker is yelling at them to switch to the spot, but they turn on a set of lights behind him. Trystan looks back behind him at the golden light, blocking his eyes with his arm, wondering how many more times they'll need to run through it tonight before everyone leaves.

Trystan wonders how long he can hide out in the basement without going home, how long it will be until he's caught.

CHAPTER 7

~MARI~

I love this. It's a rush, so much more than I thought it would be. Standing on stage, feeling the lights on my skin. There's no way to describe it. Add to the fact that I'm Trystan's co-star and it feels like a dream. Everything about him is contagious. He's dazzling on stage. He connects with me, calls to me, like we're two ends of the same string. I feel him tugging by just listening to his voice. It's magic and it's all Trystan.

I want to run and throw my arms around his neck when we take a break. I want to have that comfortable feeling of being close to him, but I can't. It's easier this way, I keep telling myself. Katie will have a stroke and I really don't need more crap from Seth or Brie right now. It's better that no one knows.

I smirk at Trystan. He returns the look with his blue eyes sparkling, before I run down the staircase on the side of the stage and up an aisle. I need a drink. I don't know how Trystan does it, especially since I know his throat is still sore from last night, but he's talking like nothing ever happened. It makes me wonder how many times he came in to school broken and battered and I didn't notice.

That smile of his hides so much pain.

Blinking hard, I push through the doors and smack into Brie. She's instantly irritated. "Watch where you're going, heifer." Brie shakes her head and her golden hair settles onto her shoulders before she shoves past me and into the auditorium.

I glance after her, wondering what she's doing here. I decide not to overreact. She's not a threat. Her part was given to me. It's not like Tucker will just hand it back. I turn and walk the few paces to the water fountain and drink. The water cools my throat.

When I walk back into the theater, I stand at the back half-wall, draping my arms on it. It's right when you walk in and separates the seats from the back aisle and the doors. Brie is a couple rows in front of me. She's slouched in a seat, but when they mess up the lights and blind everyone, Trystan turns around. For a moment, there's a halo of golden light around him. I smile. He looks like his video. My eyes drift to Brie. I wonder if she notices. If she does, she doesn't say anything.

A moment later Seth settles on the wall next to me. His voice is low, his lips barely moving, "What's the tramp doing here?"

"I don't know, but I don't like it. She's messed with Trystan enough to last a lifetime. I wish she'd fall down a hole or something."

Seth turns his face toward me and lifts a brow. "Is that venom from Little Goodie Two Shoes? I'm impressed."

"It's not unjustified." I watch Trystan dangling his legs off the side of the stage. I watch Brie watching him. It makes me nervous. He has enough pain in his life. He doesn't need anything else to go wrong. "She's got Trystan in her crosshairs."

He nods and looks back at his friend. Seth's expression softens and he sighs. "You care about him?"

"I'm not going to dignify that with a response," I say, tightly.

"I'm just saying, if you do—help me keep an eye on that one. I got his back for most of the day, but when he's in here…"

I glance at Seth. He's staring at Trystan unblinking. I wonder if he knows. Instead of asking, I lower my gaze and nod. "Done." Before Seth can say anything else and ruin my new, higher opinion of him, I walk back toward the stage.

Brie stands at the same time and smiles at me. It's one of those smiles that's good and pure, but when it's coming from someone like her, you know it's an evil omen. I narrow my eyes into slits as I pass her. She's trying to spook me. What could Brie possibly do to make life worse?

Tucker claps his large hands and thunder booms through the empty room. "Back on stage. Let's repeat the end of that last scene so the lighting guys can get their glitch fixed. Come on! Let's go!" He waives his arm toward the stage in a sweeping motion.

I climb the stairs and go back to the wing opposite Trystan. My stomach does a free fall when I see him. In the shadows, across the stage, Trystan looks up at me through his dark hair. He winks and I feel the need to giggle hysterically. I hear my cue and walk on stage. We run the scene two more times until lights and sound are at one hundred percent.

Tucker is pleased. Instead of pinching his nose, he's smiling at us. He stands at the edge of the stage. "You guys should be proud. You worked hard and it's obvious. Mari, thank you for stepping in at the last second. You are a perfect fit for this part. I hope to see you in more productions next year." I nod and smile awkwardly. Everyone looks at me. Trystan is standing next to me and bumps my shoulder with his. It attracts Tucker's attention. "And you, Scott. Try to refrain from doing anything stupid. We need you here, in one piece, tomorrow night." He rubs his palms together. "All right! Get out of here. See everyone back tomorrow night at 5:00pm. Don't be late!"

Trystan and I walk away from each other. I glance at him over my shoulder briefly. He's laughing, talking to Sophie about something. God, could she flirt with him more? Just as I'm thinking it, Trystan turns back and grins at me. I smile, and roll my eyes.

After I collect my stuff from backstage, I realize that I forgot a book and head back to my locker. The hallways are empty and the lights are off. I'm not supposed to be wandering the halls. I stop in front of my locker and rest my head on the metal, wondering how to help Trystan. I wish I could snap my fingers and make everything better for both of us.

"Are you holding up the wall with that pretty head of yours?" Trystan says softly. I turn my face and glance down the hall. He's standing with his hands in his pockets a few lockers down.

I sigh and straighten. "Someone has to."

He walks towards me, and his smile slips off his lips. Trystan is serious and that makes me more nervous than anything else.

"Thank you. For not saying anything about last night. I know you're hurt." He's actually talking about it. When I tried to ask him this morning, he wasn't ready. But he is now.

"I know you're hurt. I wish I knew. I wish you'd told me." I can't look at him. Guilt is swallowing me whole. I'm the crappiest friend alive. I had no idea, none at all.

"There was nothing you could have done. Mari, this shit is normal. The cops don't even come anymore. I'm lucky they didn't toss me in jail last night. I'm eighteen. That arrest would have been permanent. I got lucky this time. There can't be a next time." He's next to me. His voice is soft, his breath is in my ear.

I know he wants me to turn to look at him, but I can't. Something is strangling me from the inside. I want to fix this. I know I can help him, at least a little bit. I know he can't go home anymore. I know he has no clothes. These are things I can offer. Before I even realize what I'm saying, the words are out of my mouth. "Then, stay with me. Hide out at my house until you graduate." I glance at him from the corner of my eye. My heart is beating too hard, too fast.

He laughs. "Your dad hates me—"

"My dad's never home. Last night after everything that happened, he didn't even call to see if I was all right. He stayed and worked his entire shift. The only thing he cares about is work and my mother." Trystan's eyes search my face. I turn toward him and press my back into the lockers. A sad smile lines my lips. Glancing at his chest, I say, "I shouldn't complain. Compared to you—"

He shakes his head. Dark hair falls in his eyes. Trystan's hands land on my shoulders. "Don't say that. Compared to me, you have your own hell. Compared to me, you're in just as much pain. I see it, Mari. It's written on your face and chiseled into your heart."

Trystan's eyes lower for a moment. His hand slips across my cheek, leaving a warm trail on my cool skin. "I wish I could take it away," he breathes. "I wish they'd see how wonderful and special and amazing you are. I don't know how your parents can't see that. They must be blind.

"You outshine the sun, Mari. And I'm not just saying that. It's true. When I look at you…" he breathes hard and rests his head against mine. "I see everything I ever wanted and more." By the time he finishes, his voice is a whisper.

I don't look at his eyes. I'll fall apart. Moving slowly, Trystan brushes his lips across my cheek. Every part of me reacts to his touch, to him. I'm breathing too hard. It's too hot. Trystan pulls back. There's a breath between us and no more. My heart hammers inside of me. We're like two magnets, slightly separated, pulling toward each other. When I lift my gaze to meet his, I melt. My lips part and I breathe. Trystan lowers his lashes and watches my mouth. I'm falling. I'm lost in his gaze.

Trystan is about to kiss me when a jarring voice slams through the hall.

"Oh, no. Not this shit again. Scott, you said you were over this." Seth walks toward us. His boots echo up and down the hall. He's as graceful as a gorilla with concrete sneakers.

Trystan gives me a look that says he's sorry and a million other things. Before

Seth gets closer, he leans in and whispers in my ear, "I'll come. After seven?" I nod. Trystan's eyes meet mine and the only thing I want is his arms around me.

He winks at me and turns away. Trystan is all swagger and charm. He struts away saying, "You know how much I like to tease her." He looks over his shoulder at me. I play back and give him a pointed expression. Trystan laughs and grabs Seth's shoulders, pulling him away from me. "Come on. Let's grab dinner. I'm starving."

Seth looks at Trystan and then back at me, saying, "We had an understanding Jennings and this isn't part of it." Seth gives me a hostile look and points his finger at me. "You're back on my shit list."

"I was never off your shit list," I huff and slam my locker door. I walk down the hall and shove past them, adding, "And I don't really care if I'm on your list or not, Seth. Have fun making out with yourself, Sexbot." I feel their eyes on me.

My heart is flying, soaring so high, so fast. Trystan said yes. He'll stay over. Nothing could ruin this night. Nothing.

CHAPTER 8

~TRYSTAN~

Seth doesn't drop it. As soon as Mari disappears from sight he hisses, "I thought you were over her?"

Trystan keeps that distant look in his eye. He never tells Seth much of anything. The guy panics. He wants Trystan's life to make sense to him, but it doesn't. Hell, it doesn't even make sense to Trystan. How is he supposed to explain anything to the guy?

"Maybe I'm just friends with her," Trystan says, "and maybe I don't want to rehash this whole thing with you tonight. Do me a favor, okay? If you still can't stand her on Monday, tell me and we can discuss it then." Trystan says, pushing his hair out of his eyes. "From the way your acting, it seems like you liked Brie better."

Seth's eyes get a little too big for his head. "You're into her, too? Damn man." He grins. "You think you can get 'em both at once?"

Trystan's fingers flinch. Instead of slugging his friend, he smiles and nods. Trystan says things he doesn't mean, wishing for things he doesn't want. Mari and Brie. As if that was something to hope for. Trystan shakes off the skeeved layer sticking to his skin and changes the subject. "I heard you were talking about enlisting?"

Trystan couldn't believe it. When they were in lab, he heard a teacher mentioning Seth's lack of teacher recommendation forms. The teacher from across the hall said Seth was enlisting. It was weird to find out that way.

Seth doesn't look a Trystan. Instead, he nods and says, "Yeah, I mean, it's not like I'm a nerd and can get into a good college. Besides, I haven't got cash for that kind of shit."

"I know what you mean." Trystan and Seth weave their way through the school as they talk, and then exit the front of the building. The air is crisp, like it might snow. There are about two hours until he has to be at Mari's house. Two hours to kill with Seth. He breathes in deeply and runs his fingers through his hair. "I was going to enlist, but I don't know anymore…"

Seth gives him a look. "Dude, you're seriously going to let me enlist by myself? Why do you think I went to the recruiter?"

Trystan gives his friend an awkward smile, "Thanks, but there is no way you should enlist to hang out with me. I'm headed nowhere too fast."

Seth laughs, "Well, it's better to have company along the way. I mean, who else is going to be your wing man when they send you to China or some shit?"

"I don't think we have troops in China." Trystan glances at Seth and tries not to smile. The guy is about to sign on the dotted line and has no idea about anything, which sounds about right for Seth. "Besides, I might not enlist anyway. I've been thinking about doing something else."

"Like…?" Seth asks, knowing as well as Trystan does that there aren't many options. Neither of them is exceptionally anything.

Trystan shrugs. "The hell if I know. I'm just saying, don't enlist because of me. There's a chance I'm not going to do it."

Seth is staring at a car full of girls in track uniforms. Seth and the girls are hollering at each other. The man isn't even listening anymore. The girls pull over to the side of the road. "Hey hotties! Want a ride?" One girl asks and they all start giggling. Seth's eyes go wide, like he's being called to the mother-ship.

Trystan grabs Seth's arm and waves them off, "Not tonight, ladies." The car full of girls takes off, leaving behind streamers of white smoke and giggles.

"What the hell was that for? What'd I ever do to you?" Seth whines.

"I want to eat dinner. Plus I gotta be somewhere in an hour, so get your ass moving or I'll have to eat without you." Trystan starts walking again. Seth waits a beat, and then follows. Trystan has eight bucks in his pocket. It's the last of his money from Sam. He'll have to go bust his ass after school next week and earn more.

"You have something set up?" Seth asks, his voice filled with innuendo.

Trystan shoves his hands in his pockets and stares straight ahead, wishing the diner would materialize and suck them through the front doors so he wouldn't have to take part in this conversation. "Something."

"Way to be vague, Scott. Come on, man, who's the lucky girl? You think she'll put out?"

Trystan smirks and laughs. That's the last thing that he expects to happen. The night will probably be filled with Mari's voice and lips, and maybe if he's lucky, her dad won't come home early and beat the shit out of him. Repeating last night is the last thing he wants to do. But still, it's worth the risk. Deciding to go to Mari's is one of the stupider things he's done.

"Come on, Trystan. Give names, man. Who are you gonna nail?" Seth yips like a dog, begging for scraps. He's relentless and doesn't stop until they walk into the diner. He scans the booths for girls they know. "Nicole's over there." Seth says, hopeful.

"So go sit with her if you want. I'll be over here." Trystan points, and follows the waitress. Seth seems to be stuck. You could see the guy getting pulled in two directions.

Seth finally follows Trystan to the booth and sits down. He grabs a menu and then something weird happens.

The girl sitting across from them says, "If it's not my two favorite idiots." Katie sweeps her long hair over her shoulder, tosses a tip on the table and walks over. "How's it hanging, Trystan?" She places her fingers on their table and cocks her head to the side. "Cuz if you mess with my girl Mari, I'm gonna make you wish—"

"Mari's at home, and I didn't do anything to her." Trystan says, tightly. He wonders what Katie knows, if anything. She's Mari's best friend. They're always together.

Seth is watching Katie a little too closely. "Hey kitten, you want me to make you purr?" Seth grins at her and sweeps his eyes over her body, lingering way too long on her breasts.

Katie's mouth falls open. When she snaps back to life, Katie swings her purse and pegs Seth in the side of the head. He makes a noise like a pig bouncing out of the back of a pickup truck, and then clutches his head between his hands. "What. The. Fuck." He glares at Katie.

Katie's pissed. Her jaw is locked and when she talks, she sounds like she'll rip his face off. "Don't talk to me, Seth. So help me God—"

Katie is interrupted by the waiter. "Is there a problem over here?" the waiter asks, looking at each of them in turn.

Trystan beams and shakes his head. "Nope. We're ready to order though." He goes ahead, ordering three plates of food, fries, and shakes. When the waiter leaves, Trystan points at Katie and then the booth. "Sit down, Katie Scarlett," he says with a thick Irish brogue.

She lifts a dark brow at him. The girl could eat them alive. She'd spit out their bones and ask for seconds. There's a fierce thing going on with her, that's for certain. "You think I'm that vapid skank from Gone with the Wind? Seriously?"

"No," Trystan replies with a smirk on his face. "I just thought you liked big hats.

Besides, that's the only famous Katie I know."

Seth offers, "Katie Couric."

Trystan inclines his head toward Katie. They lock gazes. Katie's expression is telling Trystan to piss off, but that look tells him that he's right. She'd happily slaughter them both with her purse. Seth got off easy. God help the poor bastard who dates this girl. "Katie Couric doesn't have the same spunk as Katie Scarlett."

"Who the fuck is Katie Scarlett?" Seth blurts out way too loud. That pretty much sums up dinner. Seth and Katie bicker for an hour and Trystan tries to derail everything by throwing them off their game. It works, but not for long. It's as though they like fighting with each other. Eventually, he just sits back and watches and develops a deep respect for Katie in the process.

CHAPTER 9

~MARI~

When I get home, I'm blindsided. I walk through the door and drop my book bag on the floor. I expect to be alone. My parents go out to dinner together on Thursday nights, but tonight they didn't go. Tonight they're home, waiting for me.

"Mari dear, pick up your school bag and put it away." Mom's voice meets me before I find her in the kitchen. I don't double back for my books.

"What's wrong? Why are you still here?" I glance around, looking for Daddy, but I don't see him.

Mother replies, "There was an important development with the lawsuit. That girl you punched in the face came by looking for you. Your father sent her away, but her parents called later." She moves through the kitchen getting a lunch bag ready. She puts in a sandwich and pours the coffee into a travel mug. She glances at me. "We worked everything out. If you apologize, they'll drop the suit."

"What?" I squeak. My hackles rise. I can't stand it. I can't believe she even said it. "You want me to apologize to her? You realize that this is the same person who bullied me every day for the past three years? This is the same person who—"

Mother gives me a look that makes me stop talking. It doesn't matter what I say. The decision was made without me. I press my eyes closed and sigh way too loud. I want to scream at her. I want her to act like she loves me and not like a goddamn robot all the time. She tries so hard to make my dad happy, like he's the only thing that matters. Why'd they even have me? I don't understand. I doubt I ever will.

Mother's voice carries a warning when she speaks. "Go upstairs and apologize. She's been waiting for you."

My eyes go so wide that they nearly fall out of my head and roll across the floor. "What? What did you say?"

"She's in your room, Mari. You've kept her waiting long enough already. Go apologize and you better be nice. If this blows up, your father won't like it." She glares at me and wipes down the counter. I stare at her. It's the only thing I can do. Screaming at Mother doesn't help. It's like she's a hollowed out shell. It doesn't matter how loudly I speak, she won't hear me. Mom would let me sign away my own life if it made my dad happy.

Gritting my teeth, I say, "Fine." I sprint-walk toward my room and fly up the stairs. When I pull the door open, Brie is standing in front of my desk. She was obviously looking through things.

"Hey, virgin," she beams and waves the tips of her fingers at me. "My daddy said you owe me an apology. So let's have it." She folds her narrow arms over her ample chest and tilts her head to the side, obviously pleased.

I want to pull her hair out. I want Brie to go away and leave me alone. I knew she was gunning for me and this is lightweight for Brie. I suppose I should be happy, but I still want to shove her down a well. I manage a fake smile, and say in my nice voice, "I'm so sorry I hurt you, Brie."

There's something about the look in Brie's eye that tells me that she already got what she came here for. My stomach falls into my shoes when she walks past me, her heels clicking on the floor. Leaning closer, she whispers, "This isn't over, Mary. I don't need my daddy to fight my battles for me. Watch your back." She smiles at me like she couldn't be more pleased.

My heart pounds harder. My fingers ball into fists at my sides. I'm so close to snapping. I don't care if my dad gets sued. It'd be worth it. But something holds me back. I don't clothesline her and shove her down the stairs. Brie leaves my room. I don't follow her out. Instead, I sit down hard on my bed and hold my head between my hands. How could they? Betrayal snakes up my throat and tastes vile.

Mother's voice carries up to my room. The door is open. I hear her thank Brie for her kind, forgiving, spirit and wish her a good evening. Then, Mother walks up the stairs. I hear her familiar footfalls and I wish so badly that she tried to help me, just once. I need her. I want her, but she's never there.

"Now, that wasn't so hard was it?" She's standing in my doorway with her jacket on over her scrubs.

"How would you know? You aren't the one who stood up for yourself and then had to apologize to the asshat that was harassing you. Was that you? Because I thought that was me?"

"Don't be so dramatic, Mari. This will end well, and before it wouldn't have. Be thankful that she was so forgiving." Mom walks into the room, and fluffs a pillow on the bed next to me. She doesn't sit by me, she doesn't offer any support whatsoever.

Tears are in my eyes. I shake my head and look up at her. "Yes, I'll remember how forgiving she is next time she hurts me. I'll remember how my mother liked Brie better than me, and I'll thank Brie for kicking my ass and invite her to tea!" I lose it. I'm standing, screaming in her face. I can't help it.

Instead of fighting back, my mother rolls her eyes and turns to leave. "Honestly, Mari. You're almost an adult. Such juvenile behavior is unbecoming."

She glances over my outfit, over the cami with no flannel, and scrunches up her nose. "And you are not to dress like this again. You look like a streetwalker in that shirt. The boys will think you're giving it away and then what will you do? You can't punch every person who offends you, dear." She looks back at me and smiles, like one of those TV moms that always knows best— the one with an apron and a pie in her hand—the one who is there when her children come home—the one who is there when they cry. My mom thinks she is that mother, and that all my cries for help are silly attempts to get her attention. It makes me crazy.

"Good night, mother," I say through gritted teeth. Too many thoughts race through my head. They are things I should never say, things I should never feel.

Mom leaves and I close the door behind her. Turning I press my back against the door and slide down to the floor. My hair sticks to the tears that refuse to stay in my eyes and fall down my cheeks. I push my tangled mess back and slide my palms over my eyes. When I look up, my gaze lands on the wall with the bulletin board. I stare for a moment. Something's different, but I don't know what.

CHAPTER 10

~TYRSTAN~

Ditching Seth is easier said than done. The guy doesn't want to part ways until he knows where Trystan is going. He wants specifics. Trystan won't give any. Seth finally caves in and follows some girls out of the diner, which pisses Katie off to no end. She abruptly leaves and says a few choice words to Seth. That breaks up their little party and Trystan is free of them.

It's dark and chilly out again, like it might snow, which is bad since Trystan is homeless. He takes his time walking along the streets, weaving his way past the pristine homes as he heads toward Mari's house.

When he arrives, he sees a light in kitchen. A woman stands at the window. She's tall and slender with Mari's dark hair. That must be her mother. Trystan glances at his watch. It's past 7:00pm.

He waits and the woman finally shuts off the lights and leaves. When her car travels down the street, Trystan pulls out the cell that Mari gave him. He keeps walking, not wanting to linger in front of her house. He walks down to the end of the block and turns the corner, planning on coming up to the house from behind, like last time. He texts Mari:

Can I come up?

A few seconds pass and then:

Yes. I'll b down in a sec

Trystan turns at the corner and heads back in the direction of Mari's house. He cuts through the backyard directly behind her house and squeezes through the gap in the fences. Soon he's standing on her back patio. Mari is in the open door, looking down at him. Light spills around her, creating a perfect silhouette. She looks so beautiful. Everything about Mari is so far out of his reach, so why is he reaching? Does it matter if she loves him?

Our lives are so different.

But they're so similar, too. Wealth doesn't get rid of abusive parents. It just hides the damage better. Trystan feels a flutter in his chest, like he shouldn't be here—like something bad is going to happen. He remains on the patio and holds Mari's gaze for too long.

"Are you going to come in?" she says, smiling at him. Tension creases the spot in the center of her forehead like something's wrong. Trystan can't leave her alone. Not now. Not when she needs him. Any second thoughts about being at Mari's vanish.

Trystan grins at her, wanting to see her smile. He wants that worry line pressed flat, erased like it was never there. "Do you always invite boys into your room when your parents leave, Mari Jennings? I had you pegged for a good girl. To think, all this time, I was totally wrong." He teases her with each step he takes, closing the distance between them. When he's in front of the door, Mari still hasn't opened it. She stands on the other side of the screen in a cami and a pair of jeans. His eyes drift to the bare skin at her neck and arms, then back to her face. "You look beautiful tonight."

"Flattery will get you nowhere, Mr. Scott." Mari looks at him from under those dark lashes and smiles. Every inch of skin burns for her touch when she gives him that look.

"I'm not so sure about that. Let me in and let's find out." Trystan grins and she breaks his gaze. Looking away, Mari tucks a curl behind her ear and opens the door. Trystan brushes past her just as Mari turns to the side. It aligns their chests so that they barely touch as he passes. The sensation shoots through him in a crippling wave that takes his breath away. Trystan sucks in air softly, trying to hide how much she rattles him.

Mari turns toward him. Those big dark eyes are filled with remorse. He can see it. He can read it on her face, in her stance, and the way she holds her fingers and twists each one. Trystan wants to ask what happened, but he doesn't want to invade her privacy. It's weird. There's a spot where he wants to be, and it is invasive. That spot is smack in the center of all her most intimate thoughts and feelings—the ones that no one else knows. Trystan doesn't speak. Instead, he steps toward her and pulls Mari to his chest. His hands find her hair and he just holds her gently. Mari's hands lift and slip under Trystan's jacket. She buries her face in his shoulder and stares blankly.

Mari looks up at him with that expression on her face, and Trystan feels like he's going to shatter into too many pieces. He kisses her forehead and whispers, "What's wrong?"

Mari's eyes fall to the floor. She doesn't let go of him. "My mom decided to humiliate me instead of paying a settlement to Brie's dad. It's nothing. I don't want to talk about it."

Trystan splays his fingers and runs them through her hair, forcing Mari to look up at him. A million emotions flash across her eyes. He doesn't press her. "Then, we won't."

Mari smiles softly. She steps away from him and walks away. Trystan remains frozen by the door, his eyes sweeping over her back and drinking in her curves. Mari glances back at him and extends her hand. "Come on. I have something in my room for you."

Trystan smirks and takes her hand, not bothering to contain his excitement. "That is quite a line, kiss ninja."

Mari laughs and bumps him with her shoulder. "I didn't mean it like that! You're so stupid, Scott. I swear—"

"Nah, you like me like this. Admit it." They walk up the staircase to her room side by side. "You wouldn't want me if I were all polite and proper. For instance, telling you that I intend to kiss every inch of your bare skin later is something that I would say. Telling you that you're pretty isn't something that would ever fall out of my mouth. Mainly because it's such a ridiculous understatement that—"

Mari releases his hand and turns suddenly, pushing him into the wall. She leans into him and presses her body against his. Mari's pink lips linger so close, but she doesn't close the distance between them. The sudden action makes his heart lurch. Her hand presses into his chest and remains there with her fingers splayed. Her breath is warm and sweet. Trystan wants to taste her so badly, but Mari doesn't kiss him. Her eyes only sweep over his face, and then land on his lips.

When she speaks, he thinks he might die and tumble down the stairs. "I admit it. I like you this way. I expect you to say the unexpected, to do things to knock me off balance and make me drop my guard. I know you do it on purpose, but for the longest time I didn't know why. Now I do, and I think things are going to get very interesting between us. Don't you think?" She smiles the sexiest smile he's ever seen and traces the tips of her finger along his jaw, barely touching his skin.

Breathless, Trystan says, "You know me so well." He tries hard to hide it, but he can't. His body hums when she touches him. Those perfectly pink lips are so close. When Mari spoke, they touched his mouth with a light brush. The sensation is still shooting through him. It makes him want more. "So, are you planning on having your way with me on the stairs?"

Mari's face flames red. She laughs. "You're such an ass." Mari releases him and walks up a step.

Trystan repeats her swift movement and pins her to the wall. His hips press into hers and she gasps. There's no question about what she does to him. His eyes meet hers. His heart pounds harder. He leans in and brushes his lips across hers so lightly. It's a ghost of a kiss, as subtle as a whisper. He pulls back and Mari gasps and grabs her heart. The smirk on Trystan's face says he's playing, toying with her, but he's not. He'd kiss her like that all night, if he could.

Mari's knees are shaky after that. She tries to push off the wall and stand, but one leg doesn't cooperate and she falls into him. Trystan holds her arm and grins. "Took your breath away, did I?"

"You're evil," she says, smiling, still breathless. "We seriously need to get you a long black cloak and a helmet."

"We could, but I think that'd just turn you on." Trystan laughs as they walk up the stairs together and reach the upper landing. He follows Mari into her room. On her bed are some towels and a pair of jeans and a shirt, folded and stacked into a neat pile.

The smile fades from Trystan's lips. "What's this?"

Mari walks over to the pile and thrusts it at Trystan before she turns to the little bathroom in her room. "I thought you'd want to shower and change." She's opening the bathroom door and flicks on the lights. "I can reapply the make up around your neck in the morning. I'm guessing the bruise is an awesome shade of green now. Mine is." She lifts the hem of her shirt. The bruise on her belly is purple with green tinges around the edges. She lifts her gaze and looks at him, still holding onto her shirt.

Trystan's mouth has gone dry. He steps toward her and sets the clothes and towels down on the counter before slipping his hand around her middle. "I'm so sorry for this. So sorry." His voice is soft, barely audible. Something creeps up his throat and chokes him.

Trystan's fingers trace the bruise slowly, gently. Mari takes a slow breath, but exhales jaggedly. When he looks up, he sees her eyes and realizes what his touch did. While he was mourning his previous actions, she was frozen by his touch. Mari closes her eyes and blinks slowly, like she's trying to snap out of it. But she can't. Not as long as he's touching her like this.

Trystan withdraws his touch and runs his hand through his hair. Mari's chest swells as she breathes in. It draws attention to her breasts. It makes him wonder what it would feel like to hold them in his hands. Trystan tears his gaze away. Although Mari said she changed her mind that one time, she hasn't mentioned sex again. Trystan already decided that he won't pressure her. He won't sleep with her no matter what happens tonight.

Trystan gathers his wits and picks up the clothes and towels. "Thank you for this. I won't be long." Trystan slips past her into the bathroom and closes the door. For a moment, all he does it stare at the knob. He wants her so badly. He can't stand it. Every thought that fills his head is more forbidden than the last. The way Mari pressed him into the wall before set him on fire. Trystan knows he needs to calm down and put some distance between them or they'll end up tangled in her sheets faster than he can blink.

Trystan turns on the shower, making it as cold as he can tolerate.

CHAPTER 11

~MARI~

My heart is racing too hard. I didn't think that I could feel more attracted to Trystan than I already did, but when he touched me like that—oh my God. It was like every inch of my body was burning. I couldn't stop staring at his hands, willing them to touch me. I still haven't moved. I'm leaning against the wall, and finally hear the shower turn on. I wonder what Trystan looks like in there with the water running over his body. I think about how much I'd like to run my hands over him. I don't even realize that's what I'm thinking. I just feel the palm of my hand grow hotter and more sensitive. I think about his bare skin and the water. I blink hard, trying to free the thoughts from my mind.

Scolding myself, I push off the wall. What's the matter with me? When did I become this hornball who only thinks about sex? I pad across the room and grab a pair of sweats from my dresser. I strip quickly with my back to the bathroom door in case Trystan walks out. The water is still running, but I'm too nervous to think.

I'm mad at myself for acting like this, for melting so fast. He barely touched me and I'm falling to pieces. I tug my sweatshirt over my head and pull on a pair of fuzzy socks. This is the least sexy outfit I own. The sweatshirt is way too big. It swims on me. I yank my hair into a ponytail and jump up on the bed and flick on the TV. I try to stop thinking about him, but I can't. I watch a show without really seeing it.

When the water turns off, my heart beats faster. I wish I were a sane person. I wish for a lot of things that I can't have. I decide that I'm not doing anything with him tonight. I want more time. Plus, the bruises on my stomach and the way it aches, I just would rather he saw me the way I usually am. I realize what I'm thinking and feel the heat burn across my cheeks.

Trystan pulls open the bathroom door. He's bare-chested, wearing the new jeans around his hips, with no shoes. His hair is so dark and still dripping. There's a towel in his hand. Trystan wraps it around his shoulders. He notices my blush and says, "I love it when you do that." He smiles at me, winks, and then runs the towel over his head.

"I hate it when I do that, which seems to be all the time. It's not becoming at all." I realize I sound like my mother and flinch.

But Trystan doesn't care. He steps toward me with that sexy smile he always wears. "It's sexy as hell." He tugs at the towel and adds, "I can't say the same for this, and unless I wear a towel all night, you're going to see bruises. The thing is…" he looks down for a second. When his blue eyes lift, he meets my gaze. "I don't want you to fuss about it all night. The past is the past. I can't fix it. I would, if I could." Trystan's breathing hard, his chest is rising and falling too quickly. It pains me to see him like this.

"You can leave the towel on, if you want. Or…" I smile. I have an idea. I jump off my bed and cross the room. My dresser drawer has exactly what I need. Without thinking twice about it, I grab a pair of scissors and slice through the bottom of my sweatshirt. Trystan looks at me like I'm crazy. He flinches, his hands lifting until he realizes what I'm doing. I cut off the front bottom half of the shirt. It reveals my rainbow bruises as if they were framed. The scrap of fabric falls to the floor. I put the sheers down and turn back to him. "Better?"

Trystan grins. It makes those beautiful eyes sparkle like the sea in the afternoon sun. "Is there any other circumstance where you'd cut your clothes off like that? No? Are you sure." He looks at the floor and then back up at my face. He finally answers, "Yes, it's better."

I nod toward his towel. "Good, then drop it."

Trystan glances at me from the corner of his eye. He pulls the towel away. The angry marks around his neck look worse than last night. I try not to react. I lift my eyes to his. I step across the room and slip my arms around his waist. Trystan's eyes lock on mine, but there's something there, like he has to protect himself from me.

My fingers trace the warm, smooth skin at his waist. I say softly, "We're the same. You know that, right?"

Trystan's gaze remains locked with mine. He inhales sharply as my fingers move around to his back. There's a small space between us, both physical and mental. "Mari, don't..." It's all he can manage. His jaw is tight, locked shut. The muscles in his neck are corded like he can barely swallow.

I want him to relax, to feel safe for once. My godforsaken parents won't show up until dawn. There's no one to hurt him here. I have a sinking feeling in my stomach. Maybe he thinks that I'll hurt him. My eyes lower. My gaze traces the curves of the muscles on his chest, but I'm not brave enough to lift my hand. My heart beats harder. I want him to understand. I feel the pull to him, like we're two sides of the same coin. The fact that I'm shiny and he's not doesn't matter. We're connected. We're the same.

I don't look into his eyes again. I know what I want to do. Tugging his arm, I pull him toward my bed. I flick out the lights as I pass them. We're encased in darkness. Trystan doesn't move easily. It's like he's holding back. I finally say, "I just want to hold you. I want to sleep with your arms around me. No sex."

Trystan's voice catches when he speaks, "Mari, I don't know. I don't want to do anything you'll regret—"

"I won't regret this. I'll never regret this." I slip back on my bed, but he won't sit. His eyes pierce through me like a sword.

"You said this was something that was reserved for marriage." He's still looking at me. I smile softly. It turns out that all those times I scolded him for taking sex so lightly, he was listening. I almost wish he wasn't. He runs his hands through his hair and looks at me. "I don't think this is a good idea. I don't want you to resent me. These aren't whims with you. It's part of who you are. I can't do this to you."

I'm kneeling on the bed, looking at him. My eyes sweep over his face. He means well. Trystan wants to protect me. I understand, and I know he won't change his mind. "You're too good for me."

He laughs. It sounds so haunted and bitter that it kills me. "I doubt it. I heard I'm made of snails and puppy dog tails." Trystan grins at me and winks, quickly covering the emotions that played across his face seconds ago.

I lay back in my bed and he pulls up my blankets and tucks me in. Then, he settles on my floor at the foot of my bed. The clock ticks off the minutes, but I can't sleep. My eyes are wide open. After what feels like forever, I say, "Trystan?"

"Mmm?"

My throat is tight. "How do you manage everything? I mean, no one has any idea and you never give the slightest indication that anything is wrong.

"Some days I feel like I'm going to fall apart. You never seem weak like that. How do you do it? How do you brush off the fact that the people who are supposed to love you the most, don't love you at all?"

My lip is quivering. Although I've thought it, I never had the guts to say it before. "I know they don't love me. I know they resent me, but I still can't accept it. I keep hoping that one day they'll really see me and love me for who I am, but that day never comes."

By the time I finish talking, I'm whispering. I don't want to admit the words to anyone, but I do. As I speak, the words crush me. The bitter truth is that I feel guilty that my parents don't love me. I feel like it's my fault. For a long time, I thought that if I was better or smarter—I thought that I could earn their love—but it didn't happen. Nothing changed. I stare at my ceiling without blinking. Thoughts stream from my head like rainwater down a gutter.

Trystan sits up. He's at the foot of my bed on the floor, looking up at me. His hair dried into that messy look he always wears. Pulling his knees into his chest, Trystan leans back against the side of my bed. "I think that's the key—admitting that the day will never come. It's the hardest part it. Hope just rips your heart apart with shit like this.

"There is no hope. There is no peace. Accepting it makes it easier to wade through the day to day stuff. But, I've done a crappy job at hiding it lately. My old man locked me in my room the other day after tossing all my things. He does stuff like that from time to time. It's supposed to remind me of my place. He says that over and over again, like it's a lesson that I need to learn. I know my fucking place."

Trystan takes a deep breath and runs both hands over the back of his neck, stretching as he does it. "Tucker figured it out. For the past few weeks he's been hinting, telling me it's okay to talk to him, but they don't get it. Dragging it out for everyone to see will just make it worse.

And I've got no right, but it makes me mad. Where was Tucker ten years ago? Where was he five years ago? It would have made a difference then. It won't do a goddamn thing now." Trystan startles and looks over his shoulder. His eyes meet mine. He smiles, sheepishly. "I didn't mean to say all that."

I shrug. "It needed to be said."

"How do you do that?" He stands and sits on the end of my bed.

"Do what?"

"How do you make me feel like this? I can be talking about the most horrible thing that ever happened to me, but with you here, the pain lessens. I feel like I'll get through it and everything might be all right after all."

I smile at him. I don't know what else to do. I'm lying back on my pillow. I cross my ankles under the blankets and tuck my hands behind my head. "That's what you do for me. Maybe it's magic. Maybe you're my yang."

"Yang?" He gives me a weird look.

"Yeah, like on a yin yang. We reflect each other, despite everything." I watch him for a moment. His eyes are on mine. I pat the bed next to me and Trystan finally gives in. He crawls toward me and lays his head on my pillow. I turn on my side to look at him.

Trystan kisses my lips lightly and sighs. A smile pulls at the corners of his mouth. "Good night, beautiful girl."

CHAPTER 12

~TRYSTAN~

A car door slams and jerks Trystan awake. Early morning sunlight pours through Mari's windows. Trystan sits up and looks down at Mari, still asleep. That noise woke him up, made him jump. Call it conditioning from his father, but if Trystan didn't jump up and grab his things that second, he would be thrown out the window.

Trystan peeks out the bedroom door and sees Mari's dad. He's still wearing scrubs and is setting his things down on table in the hallway below. Panicked, Trystan doesn't know what to do. He can't sneak out. Her dad is blocking the way.

Trystan goes back to Mari and wakes her gently, kissing her cheek. She smiles and stretches. "Trystan." The way she says his name makes him reel, but he can't afford to think like that. Not now. If Mari's dad catches him, he's dead.

Whispering next her ear, he says, "Your dad is downstairs. I need to hide."

Before Trystan has a chance to say anything else, the sound of footfalls reaches their ears. Mari sits straight up in bed, her brown eyes wide like dinner plates. She points to the closet. Trystan takes his things and ducks inside and closes the door just before Mari's dad enters the room.

He bangs on the door and shouts, "Wake up, Mari. You're going to be late." He flicks on the lights and it fills the crack under the closet door. Trystan can hear him enter the room. His heart beats harder, faster. He pulls on his shoes and shirt without making a sound. Trystan feels like a coward hiding. He should run out and stand up to the man, but he can't. He can't even take care of himself. And getting found out won't help either of them.

"Mother said you apologized to Brie last night. I was glad to hear it. No more of this, Mari. Now get dressed for school. And mind your mother. She said no more tight clothes. Do as she asks. I don't want to hear about my daughter looking like a street-walker ever again." The door clicks shut and he's gone.

Trystan cracks the closet door open and looks at Mari. The life has been sucked out of her. Her shoulders are slumped and her skin is sallow. The color in her cheeks is gone. There's no light in her eyes. He knows that look and wishes to God that he could take it away, but he can't. Even if they were older, Trystan doesn't have the money to save her from that man. Her dad crushed her just now and there was nothing he could do about it.

Mari glances up at him. She blinks slowly and smiles, but it doesn't reach her eyes. "You better go before Mom comes home and decides to go through my closet. You can climb down the trellis like you wanted to the other day. Dad is headed for the shower. Wait a second for the water to turn on and then go. I'll meet you in the basement at the school and fix up your neck."

Trystan doesn't know why he does it, but he does. He can't stand that flat listless voice. He can't bear to watch Mari like this. He crosses to her bed and pushes her back into her pillows while pressing his lips to hers. They both have morning breath, but he doesn't care. Trystan loves her. He wants her to be happy. He wants that smile on her face again. Trystan tangles his hands in her hair and lays on top of her, kissing her so hard that he can't breathe.

When he pulls back, she's smiling shyly. It's a perfectly Mari smile. "I love you," he whispers and bounces off her bed and heads to the window. Mari touches her fingers to her lips like she's dreaming.

Trystan sneaks out before anything else can go wrong.

CHAPTER 13

~MARI~

When I'm done pulling on my jeans and tee shirt, I bend over to find my boots. I kicked them under my desk the other night. When I pull them out, I see a piece of paper caught between the desk and the wall. I reach for it, instantly knowing what it is— Trystan's song. How'd it get on the floor? I go to pin it back in place, but decide that it shouldn't be where anyone could get it. If my parents took the song or Brie managed to get her hands on it, that'd be bad. So I take it with me, stuffing it into my jeans pocket.

I get to school early and head to find Trystan. The halls are empty. I pull open the basement door and run down the stairs. After that kiss this morning, I have a kiss of my own to give him. But when I reach the bottom of the landing, I freeze. He's singing softly. His back is turned to me, like he doesn't know I'm there. After a moment, he glances back at me and startles.

"Hey, ninja. Fancy meeting you here." Trystan's eyes sweep over me in a way that makes me feel beautiful.

"I heard there was a rock star living in the school basement. I had to see it for myself." I smile at him and drop my bag on the couch. Walking over to him slowly, I swing my leg over his lap and sit. We nearly fall off the little stool. He laughs and holds onto me with the guitar between us. "This was more romantic in my head."

He grins. Hard. "Kiss me, Mari."

The way he says it makes my heart jump. My stomach twists and that empty space inside my chest fills with warmth. I'm beaming at him, moving in slowly, crushing the guitar between us. My lips brush against his and then he's kissing me back. Trystan's hands find my face and he holds onto me, encouraging me, wanting me. My heart pounds harder and harder. I wish there was nothing but this moment now. I can understand this. I can deal with this. Everything else can fade away and I'd be happy. When we come up for air, I slip off his lap.

Trystan moans and puts the guitar back. "I wasn't done with you."

I'm still flushed. My lips are too sensitive. I can still feel his lips on my mouth. I smile and shake my head. I know how much it will devastate him if anyone saw the marks on his neck. "You need make-up first. Kisses later."

He gives me a funny look. "I never thought I'd hear that sentence."

I laugh. He tugs a loop on the waistband of my jeans and pulls me close. His hands lace through my hair and he kisses me again. I don't want to pull away. I moan and say, "We're running out of time."

He sighs and gives me a serious look. "What if we just said you gave me some really wicked hickeys?" That makes me laugh even louder. The smile that stretches across his face when I laugh is beautiful. It's Trystan without anything hindering him or weighing him down.

I shove him back down to the stool. "Sit. Let me do this before the bell rings."

"Fine, but you're going to have to talk about something else. A guy only has so much self-control, and your chest is right in front of my face. Honestly, I'm having a lot of trouble not jumping on you and covering you in kisses." He smirks, his eyes still way below my neckline.

The way he says it is so casual, like he might actually do it. Part of me wants him to. My pulse is racing, making it so I only hear the steady, swift, beating and my breaths. I reach toward him and take his chin in my hand and tilt it up to my face. His blue gaze is dazzling. It's like someone's lit a flame inside of him and it's shining through his eyes. Trystan grins at me.

"You are impossible. You do know that, right?" I'm breathing too hard, flustered beyond belief. Trystan loves it. I can see it in his eyes.

I dab and blend until the ugly marks around his neck are gone. They fading fast, but the colors are worse. Now there's an ample amount of green and yellow mixed with the blues and blacks. I finish his make-up and he stands and turns toward me. "I can't wait for tonight, for that scene that includes kissing you senseless on stage in front of dozens of people. I'm really looking forward to it."

I can't help it. The way he's looking at me makes me feel giddy. I slap his chest lightly. Trystan grabs my wrist and pulls me toward him, careful not to squeeze me too tight. "You would be—"

"So are you. I can see it in your eyes." I tear my gaze away from him, suddenly feeling very nervous. Trystan takes my chin and turns me back. "No one knows, love." He kisses my bottom lip. "They think we're acting." He kisses my top lip. "Only we know it's real."

CHAPTER 14

~TRYSTAN~

His heart is pounding. Mari is so close. Her lips are right there, but the bell is going to ring. Trystan settles for nipping her lip again. Mari slips off his lap and hands him another flannel.

"It'll help hide the marks if something happens to the make-up. Besides, I like the way you look in it."

"In that case," Trystan reaches for the shirt and tugs it on over his black tee shirt. He leaves the front open. The collar makes him feel more secure. Mari knew it would. That's why she brought it for him. Trystan wants to say something, but words escape him. Instead he leans his forehead against hers for a second and looks into her eyes. "You're too good to me."

She smiles softly, shyly. It's like two people are living inside of her—one is so demur, but the other is a firework, bright and beautiful. "Come on. Today's going to be good. I can feel it." Mari backs away and reaches out for his hand, taking it in hers.

They walk up the metal stair case together. When they exit the auditorium, their hands separate. Trystan steps away a little bit, making things look like they've always been. No one suspects that he's fallen in love with this girl. No one knows they've spent a few nights together. No one knows how much he adores her, or how she makes him feel so alive that he's humming. No one knows anything and he likes it that way.

They head toward Trystan's locker, talking about the play later that night. Mari laughs at something he says and bumps him with her shoulder, taking hold of his arms and leaning into him. The contact makes him feel like he can fly. It jars other memories and he can almost taste her lip gloss.

That moment, that relaxed shared moment, is why he likes her. Mari never expects him to be someone else. She accepts him, scars and all. Trystan glances at her out of the corner of his eye, wishing he could cut class and spend the day with her. Last night wasn't enough. He can't ever get enough of her. When Mari isn't there, he burns for her. She's everything to him. They're walking and talking again. Trystan glances at her, reaches over and brushes the back of his hand against hers. She smiles up at him. His heart is soaring higher and faster than he ever thought possible.

But when they turn the hallway that leads to Trystan's locker, everything changes. That tender moment shatters. It's like Trystan is shoved out a window and is falling too fast to stop. There are tons of people at the other end of the hall. Trystan scans the crowd and sees Brie, Seth, and too many people to name. There's a woman dressed in a suit with a microphone. A man with a large camera on his shoulder stands with her. Tucker is standing to the side of the crowd, along with other faculty members. Everyone is buzzing like a happy mob.

Trystan's heart slams into his chest, thumping harder and faster. His breathing becomes jagged as his body tenses.

They know.

It's at that moment that Brie sees him. She flicks her eyes in his direction and hustles down the hall, sashaying in her tiny skirt. The swarm of people follow in her wake. Trystan's frozen in place. He considers running, but he can't because there's no way to hide from this. Dread chokes him, rendering him silent. The confident smile that usually lines his lips is long gone.

Brie steps into the space between Trystan and Mari and wraps herself around his arm. "This is Trystan Scott," she says beaming. He can feel her hand on his arm and hear her voice, but it sounds like static in his ears. She pulls him closer to the crowd, either that or they form a circle around him, surrounding him.

Trystan breathes hard, his eyes darting between the excited faces and the cameras.

There's more than one. Trystan's heart lurches when he realizes that he's been cornered. He reaches for Mari's hand, but she's gone. He can't even see her face. The crowd has swallowed him and she's gone.

Dread creeps around Trystan's throat like a noose, pulling tighter and tighter. These people know his secret. He can feel the icy cold truth racing through his veins. That means they know about the other night, about how his dad strangled him. Everything he's been trying to hide for so long is about to be exposed.

There's no way to stop it.

A voice cuts through the noise, through the chaos of his thoughts. The woman in the suit holds out the microphone to him, asking, "Are you Day Jones?"

REVEALED

THE SECRET LIFE OF

TRYSTAN SCOTT

VOL. 5

re·veal : to make (something) known

CHAPTER 1

~TRYSTAN~

The words hang in the air before falling to the ground like lead. Trystan offers the woman a crooked smile as he steps away from Brie. "You're mistaken, although I've heard that I'm hotter than Day Jones." He winks at the reporter before turning toward his locker. Trystan's mind is reeling a mile a minute. All he could think to do on the fly was to deny the whole thing. There's no way they can prove he's Day Jones.

The reporter is momentarily stunned, but Brie laughs and catches his shoulder. "Trystan! Tell her the truth. Tell her that you're Day!"

"I'm not Day Jones." Trystan is wearing his most charming smile, trying to hide the knots in his stomach, and then he does what he always does when things get unbearable – he acts his way out. With enough charm and vibrato, no one sees what's real and what's not—well, no one but Mari. He scans the hall for her, but she's not in sight.

Brie laughs that high pitched giggle that drives him insane as her catlike claws drift up and down his arm. "Oh, come on, Trystan. Everyone knows. There's no reason to be shy about it anymore. Tell the reporter what you told me."

He gives Brie a blank look before responding to the reporter. "I have no idea what you're talking about. It was nice meeting you, but I need to get to class." Trystan intends to shoulder past the crowd. People are speaking in hushed whispers, trying to figure out what's going on. About half the group believes him. Good. Tucker catches his eye from across the hall. The teacher's arms are folded across his round chest while he watches the situation unfold.

Just as Trystan starts to leave, Brie catches his elbow.

"You'll have to forgive him for this. When he wrote that Day Jones song, Trystan swore that he'd never tell anyone about it, but it was for me. See, I have it right here." Brie holds up a piece of paper and waves it around.

The reporter takes it and looks down at the sheet. "Is this your handwriting, Mr. Scott?" She tilts the paper so he can see it, but Trystan already recognizes it. It's the song he wrote for Mari.

Brie is beaming and still tethered to his arm. She lets go and steps in front of Trystan, taking the paper and turning it over. "Look at the last line. That's the original version. He wrote it for me." Brie is all girlish charm and warm smiles.

Trystan can see the avalanche of crap hurling toward him but nothing will allow him to side-step it. It's too late. The paper has damned him. He could deny it, and say Brie's a lying whore, but what good will that do? They already know. The crowd of students and teachers grows louder. They sense it. The reporter is talking, but her words sound like noise in his ears. A teacher steps up and nods, confirming that the song on the paper is Trystan's handwriting. Someone shoves a guitar at him, as Trystan stands there unblinking. His mind is caught, reliving the worst parts of his life—and realizing that everyone is going to know. It's a matter of hours before they dig up the police report from the other night. Trystan shoves the guitar away and shoulders his way through the crowd without looking back.

CHAPTER 2

~MARI~

I've never crashed so hard, so fast, before. Trystan tenses next to me when he sees the people around his locker. Before we even make it to his locker, Trystan is engulfed in the mass of bodies, all of which are brimming with excitement. I stand there for a moment and feel sick for him. Trystan is going to hate this. I wonder how they found him, how they know.

At that moment, Brie steps between us. She takes Trystan's arm and pulls him forward. Just before she does it, she looks over at me with a sharp smile. Acid fills my stomach. I don't know how she figured it out, but she did. I feel my feet sliding backwards, moving away from the crowd. Suddenly, Katie is beside me.

"Holy shit, Trystan is Day Jones?" She's smacking gum in her mouth and staring. When I don't answer, Katie stops chewing and looks over at me. Bright blue eye shadow is painted across her eyelids. "What's with you?"

The mob seems to get sucked down the hallway. It forms a chasm between me and Trystan—a gaping hole is expanding and swallowing him—and there's nothing I can do about it. Katie's eyes are on the side of my face. Her gaze flicks toward Trystan and then back to me. I hate this. It's as if I can feel his skin crawl even from here. I don't see Trystan look up for me and there's no way to get to him. I turn back and duck around the corner with my heart racing like someone is trying to kill me. I'd pull the fire alarm if it would help him, but nothing will help him now. Maybe this was meant to be? Maybe he needs this?

Katie's knuckles wrap the top of my skull. "Hello? Earth to Mari."

Jerking my head out of the way, I manage to avoid getting my brain knocked again. "Cut it out, Katie," I snap.

"So let me get this straight. You were with Trystan this morning before he was ambushed by reporters, doing God-knows-what in the basement." She ticks off two fingers as she says it, acting like it's no big deal, even though it is. I know she wants to scream and giggle with me, but we can't right then because everything is falling apart. So, last night doesn't matter, not after this. She senses my worry and it makes her mood drop.

I have my back to the wall and suck in a huge breath. I keep telling myself that this isn't bad, but it feels horrible. I nod at Katie.

"So, you're still stuck on him and now Brie wants him back, right?"

"What?" I glance up at her and try to shove away the nauseous feeling that's making me sweaty. I didn't think of that. Is that what she's been doing this whole time? How did I miss it? Jaw hanging open, I manage, "You think Brie wants him back?"

She smirks at me and gives me a look that clearly says I'm an idiot. "Yes, for starters she's a whore and secondly, if Trystan is Day Jones, she's going to let everyone know that they were together. It's not like Brie to just be pushed aside, not when something this big happens. Trystan was her first and only long term relationship—well, long term for Brie. Add to the fact that she's a glory-hog and yeah, there's no doubt she's after Trystan."

Acid is creeping up my throat and no matter what I do, I can't calm down. No one knows about Trystan and me, nobody realizes we're together, and right now he's not with me—he's with Brie talking to reporters. I want to slam my head into the lockers, but I don't. My mind drifts to what things will be like without Trystan. I knew it was coming next year, but I couldn't picture it until this second. My heart flutters nervously as I realize what it means—no more Trystan to run lines with, no more teasing in the basement, no more friendship, no more anything—Trystan Scott won't be here, but I will. The hollow space inside my chest fills with dread. I'll spend the next year waiting to graduate, waiting for college, and trying to manage my craptacular parents without him.

I shove off the wall and dart down the hallway to the office with Katie on my heels. "Where are you going? Class is that way." Katie points behind us, but continues to follow me to the office.

I shove through the doors and hear the women chattering about Trystan, wondering if their golden boy is really Day Jones. They're excited for him, I can hear it in their voices.

"That kid needed to catch a break," one woman says. She's standing next to the humming copy machine, running off worksheets.

They look up and see me at the counter. The secretary doesn't get up from her desk. "Can I help you girls?"

Katie leans her hip against the counter and shrugs as she picks at her black nail polish.

Nodding, I say, "I'd like an application for early graduation." The idea has been bouncing around in my head for a while now, but I was too chicken to act on it. It means defying my father, and I didn't think I had the backbone, but at this moment I do. At this moment the acceptance letter at the bottom of my sock drawer looks like a way to escape and I plan to take it. The only obstacle is the application for early graduation. It was due weeks ago, so I don't know what the chances are of the school giving me my diploma early, especially since the principal has the final say and the guy is a stickler for the rules. He'll probably deny me without even looking at my transcript.

Katie's jaw drops and she stares at the side of my face. I never told her that this is what I wanted, or that I was even thinking about it. The truth is, leaving her early will suck, but staying here will suck even more. She gapes at me and a wad of gum tumbles out of her mouth. "You can't graduate early! Why would you want to do that? Senior year is almost here—it's time for fun—and you're going to cut out on me? Who am I supposed to hang out with at senior cut day? What about at lunch? We can finally leave campus. What about prom,

Mari?" Katie's shocked posture says it all—how could you leave me?

Trying to explain is difficult, but my senior year won't look like hers because of my parents. "Katie, my senior year is going to be all advanced classes. It's not going to be fun because my parents won't let me slack off, so what am I waiting around here for? I could go take the classes at college."

The secretary digs through the filing cabinet next to her desk, and then walks over and hands me the paper. She taps at certain parts, including the deadline. "It's already passed, honey, but it can't hurt to try. I'll add it to the stack if you get it back to me by the end of the day." She winks at me as she speaks. "And if it's accepted, you walk with this year's graduating class. You're cap and gown will cost extra because you'll be paying for a rush, you can't get a class ring because it's too late, and unless you already submitted your college applications I'm not sure who'll take you this late in the year."

Taking the paper, I say, "Thank you." I stand there filling it out with Katie burning holes into my head. After jotting down the reason, I thank the woman, and head out without another word. Katie trails behind me stomping her feet on the floor much louder than normal. She's mad, I know she is. "I can't stay. Not after this."

"But, why?" She races up to walk next to me just as the bell rings.

I can't say it. The words are in my head but I can't force them out.

Just as we round the corner, I see the mass of people standing there by Trystan's locker, but he's gone. Teachers are telling everyone to get to class. That's when I see Brie walking toward me. Her books are clutched against her chest and there's a triumphant smile on her face. As she passes, she says, "I couldn't have done it without you. Thanks for leaving that song where I could find it, Virgin."

I stiffen as she passes. Her words hit me like a steady stream of bricks. That's why Trystan's song was on the floor behind the desk. She must have taken a picture of it last night and printed it out. The reason they know Trystan is Day Jones is because of me.

CHAPTER 3

~TRYSTAN~

He shoves out the front doors of the school thinking that he's evaded the reporters, but walks straight into a mob of people. Awh, what the hell? How did Brie get his song and why is her name on the back and not Mari's? He was too dumbstruck to speak before, but now Trystan's angry. Without a doubt, he knows that this is Brie's fault, that she's the one who called the press, and she's the one who exposed him.

Trystan stands there for a second before turning back toward the building. Seth comes crashing through the door next to him. "Come on, man. Let's get out of here." Seth's voice is deep and demanding. It's like he knows that Trystan wants to run.

"Tucker will fail me if I cut," Trystan blurts it out without thinking.

Seth shakes his head. "No way. Not after this. Show up for the play tonight and you're golden. Come on, my car's around the side and I bet all these pussies parked out front." Seth is walking down the sidewalk and cuts toward the student parking lot. He ducks through a hole in the chain link fence and Trystan follows.

A few reporters trail after them, but the camera guy can't follow. The equipment doesn't fit through the fence, so they have to walk around. By the time that happens, Trystan and Seth will be driving away.

Trystan settles into the passenger's seat and presses his hand to his temple, shading his eyes. Seth starts the engine and they peel out of the lot, cutting into the busy road. Seth floors it, bobbing and weaving through traffic to put some distance between them and the reporters.

For a while Seth doesn't say anything, but then he explodes and once he starts talking the words don't stop. "How could you not tell me? I'm watching all these people gathering in the hallway this morning and thinking, there is no way in hell that Scott is this Day Jones guy because I would have known. He would have told me. I'm the guy's best friend and shit like this wouldn't be kept a secret, but what the fuck do I know? Because apparently, you're all about the secrets, Scott. Do I even know you?"

"You're an asshole if you think you don't." Trystan doesn't drop his hand from his brow. A queasy feeling has been surging through him since he saw the mass of people. His mind drifts to Mari. He'll have to text her and make sure she's okay as soon as he can patch things up with Seth.

"That's the only thing you've got to say? Are you shittin' me? After everything we've been through, you're seriously going to keep lying to me?" Seth cuts someone off and a horn blares behind them. Seth flips off the other driver and gives the car more gas.

Trystan looks up from under his hand. "What am I lying about?"

"Okay, Scott. You want to play it this way? Fine. I'll play. Tell me if you're Day Jones. Tell me you didn't write that song for that skank Brie. Tell me who you nailed last night. Or how about you tell me why the hell someone saw you at the police station." His gaze cuts to Trystan's, sharp as glass. The tension in his jaw is enough to make it snap. "Pick one, Scott. I know you've been making stuff up, and I figure that's fine—he'll tell me when the shit hits the fan—but since that happened, and you still haven't said two words—"

Trystan drops his hand and looks over at him. "What do you want me to say, Seth? That I'm Day Jones? Fine, I am. I wrote that song for someone else, not Brie. I don't even know how she got it. And yeah, I was at the police station, and no, I'm not telling you why, because it's none of your goddamn business."

Seth's grip tightens on the steering wheel, making his knuckles rise up under his skin. "I see. So where were you last night? Tell me who you fucked 'til morning, because I know you weren't at home. You used to tell me that kind of thing Scott, you know, back when we were friends. Choke up a name right now or I'll toss your ass out of my car—"

It's none of Seth's business, but the guy is in torch everything and ask questions later mode. Trystan's been keeping things from him, yeah, but he keeps things from everyone. Well, not from everyone. Mari knows. The vein on the side of Seth's head is about to explode. It's throbbing under his skin, making Trystan feel guilty. Maybe he is a shitty friend. So he answers, "Mari Jennings." But as soon as Trystan says her name, he regrets it.

Seth turns abruptly, and smashes his mouth shut. Taking the wheel hand over hand, making the tires shriek as the car skids into a parking lot. He slams on the brakes and they come to a quick stop. "Get out of my car, you lying sack of shit. You honestly think that I'd believe that? You didn't even try to—"

Trystan glares at his friend, resisting the urge to roll his eyes. Seth is so dense with this stuff. "You think I'd lie and make up Mari? Are you seriously telling me that you can't see it? I'm with her whenever I'm not with you."

"You spent the night at Jenning's house? You slept with her?"

Trystan nods slowly, even though he knows that Seth thinks they did more than sleep. "Yeah, I ducked out this morning after her dad got home from work."

Seth looks disgusted and disappointed. He tenses in his seat and Trystan's ready for the verbal onslaught that spews from his friend. "I told you to stay away from her. That family has enough money to bury you and don't think that her dad won't do it. The guy is—"

Rubbing the heel of his hands over his face, Trystan yells back, "I know what he is, but she's worth the risk."

Seth sucks in a deep breath, trying to rein in his temper. Trystan slips down in his seat and stares blankly out the windshield. "So," Seth finally says, "Everything changes now, right? You go and sign with some company and get rich, while I go and serve four years in some hellhole country that I can't point to on a map."

Trystan glances over at Seth and his stomach sinks. "You enlisted?"

Seth nods. "I signed on the line. They own me after graduation."

Horrified, Trystan sits up straight. "Fuck, Seth. Tell me you didn't! Why'd you do that?"

"Because I thought that's what you were doing! I thought we'd be shipping out together, but there's no way in hell you're doing that now, not with this opportunity. You'll be rich in a week and have a penthouse in Manhattan. You can leave this shithole behind and nail a different chick every night."

Guilt is choking him so hard that he can barely speak. Seth enlisted because of him. Damn it. There's no way to undo this. It's already been done. "That's what you would do."

"Nah, I'd have a different three-way every night. I pussied it down for your version of the American dream." Seth settles back into his seat and tilts his head back. "So what happens now?"

Trystan sighs and pushes his hands up over the top of his head and down the back of his neck, digging his fingers into the muscle. Every part of him wants to scream, but he can't. "No fucking clue. But I'm guessing that everyone finds out everything I've been trying to keep hidden, and my life becomes a living hell."

Seth snorts and smiles at him. "Only you would say that pussy and cash are hell."

"Only you would focus on that shit after what happened this week. Life is more than getting laid, Seth."

Seth laughs once, like he doesn't agree at all. "Then spill, Scott. What the hell happened?"

Trystan works his jaw, thinking about whether or not to tell Seth. In the end, Seth will find out—they all will—so he tells him now. Trystan tells him about his father, about Mari showing up and saving his life, and about the songs he wrote for her. "No one was supposed to give a shit about the video, no one was supposed to find out about my father, and I sure as hell didn't want Mari caught in the middle."

Seth doesn't react to anything Trystan says. For a moment Trystan thinks that his friend isn't listening, but there's not much to say after something like that. Being beat reminds them both that they're insignificant.

Seth finally smirks at Trystan. "Do you want me to mow down your old man?"

Trystan laughs darkly and shakes his head. "No, he's not worth it, and I have no intention of seeing him again—ever."

"Okay, so let me get this straight—you're homeless, kind-a, sort-a banging an under-age good girl, you've got a father who blames you for his life being shit, and a reporter that wants to publically out you. Did I forget anything?"

Staring straight ahead, Trystan adds, "Yeah, you forgot vengeful ex-girlfriend."

"Ah, yeah. The Skank. I need to make her up a tee shirt that says that in glittery letters. Ten bucks says she wears it." Seth laughs at his own joke, but Trystan is lost in thought. He needs to play his next move well, so that it cuts off all the crap and gives him a sure footing, but Brie and Mari create vulnerable spots in his plans. He can't figure out how to lose Brie or how to keep Mari from being found out. Damn, if the press realizes that she was there the other night...

"Scott?" Seth sounds irritated, like he's been trying to talk to Trystan while he's been lost in his own head. "There's only one way to play this hand. Live it. Own it. Claim that title and then the next move is yours. Tell the reporter about your shitfaced father, about how you worked your ass off to keep food on the table, and about Sam giving you a job. It'll make your fans love you even more."

Trystan is staring at the people in the parking lot and realizes that this is one of the last times he'll be able to move freely. Once they know he's Day Jones, his life will change. Folding his arms over his chest, Trystan mutters, "I don't want fans."

"Tough shit. Deal with it, Scott. This is your ticket out of this hell hole and the train's only going one-way. Get on or get run over." Seth puts the car in gear and drives over to a deli in the center of the strip mall. "I'll get us some breakfast, knowing you, you didn't eat. But when you become rich and famous, I expect a hooker or two for my troubles."

Trystan laughs. "You make your own troubles, Seth. Hookers are not a good thing to factor into the equation."

Seth flashes a ghost of a smile and he nods. After getting out of the car, he leans into the open window. "I don't usually say shit like this, but I got your back, Scott. Whatever you decide, I'm still your man." Seth lets out an uncomfortable breath and turns away, and walks into the deli.

CHAPTER 4

~MARI~

Katie fires off a slew of profanity at Brie's back.

"I can hear you," Brie snaps, as she sashays away from us.

"I know! I'm talking loudly!" Katie is seething. She grabs my arm and pulls me toward the side doors. "There is no way in hell that we're going to learn a damn thing today. Come on. Let's get out of here." Katie pushes through the metal doors and we're in the parking lot.

"If my Dad finds out that I cut—"

"He won't, Mari. Who's taking attendance right now? All the teachers are in the hallway buzzing about Trystan. No one is going to file a cut slip on you." Her venom for Brie drains as soon as we're outside. Katie tugs my arm. "Come on. Let's walk to the deli and grab some grub. Katie hungry." She says the last few words like Cookie Monster.

I can't help but wonder what this means for Trystan, but I bet he's dreading it. For someone that shines so brightly in the spotlight, he really doesn't like being in it. The main road isn't too busy right now. A few of the news vans drive past us. Others stayed and are interviewing Trystan's teachers. By tonight, it will be on every channel—Trystan Scott is Day Jones. They'll all think Trystan wrote that song for Brie and I'll get shoved aside.

Katie glares at me. "You planning on answering anything any time soon?"

"Sorry, what'd you ask?"

Katie makes an overly dramatic noise and stomps her combat boots. She's wearing a floral print skirt, knee highs with skulls on the side, and a lacy white shirt with a big sparkly belt. Her hair is slicked back into a ponytail and swishing high on her head. I feel frumpy standing next to her in my flannel shirt and jeans.

"I said what's up with you and Trystan?" All the color drains from my cheeks. I can't hide it. I've been blindsided too many times to mask my emotions and keep them off my face. "Okay, let's pretend I didn't see your reaction. Come on, use your words, Mari. Tell me what happened." Katie says it like she's talking to a toddler.

My gaze is on the ground when I answer. "I love him, okay. He spent the night last night. The reporters couldn't find him, because he was with me."

Katie stops in her tracks, and grabs my arm. When I turn, her eyeballs are still expanding in shock. "What the hell? You tell me you're over him and then you sleep with him? As in you guys had sex?" She makes a shrieking noise and spins in a circle. It looks like an angry chicken dance. "How could you not tell me that!"

"Shhh!" I shove her past the store front. There are people inside looking out at us.

"Damn, you're loud. And no, Miss Dirty Brains, it wasn't like that. He needed a place to stay. Trystan's been coming over for a while, but last night was the first night he stayed."

"And your parents—Mr. and Mrs. Rodup D'Ass—didn't have issues with this?"

I smile sheepishly. "They don't know. Trystan was in the closet when Dad came home this morning. I thought we were going to get caught."

Katie squeals and slaps her hands over her mouth. "Shut up! Mari Jennings turned into a bad girl. We need to stop at the pet store and buy you a big fat dog collar—the kind with the spikes. Your Dad would so shit himself when he saw you wearing it."

Katie makes me smile even though I'm a bunch of tangled nerves inside. "I can't even imagine what would happen then."

"You should totally do it. They take you for granted. It'd serve them right if you went all nutso on them for a while."

I tuck my hands under my arms. "Probably not a good plan. My Dad would sue me or something."

"God, your father is a douche. I need to tell him that the next time I see him. I'm pretty sure that your dad and my dad went to Douchiversity together, because they've both got that bastard thing nailed. Hey, isn't that Sexbot's car?" All of Katie's sentences flow together, but my gaze follows her finger to an old muscle car running in the parking lot when we finally reach the deli.

I smile to myself. "It is." I see Trystan sitting in the front seat with his arm over his face. "Go grab us something. I need to talk to Trystan."

"Fine, but if me and Seth come back and you guys are all making out, he's probably going to want to watch. He's a perv like that." Katie laughs and disappears inside before I can say anything.

I walk over to the car and wonder what I'm going to say. He's got to be coming unglued. Too much has happened to him, too close together. I walk over to his side of the car and tap on the window. "Hey stranger, or should I call you rock star?"

Trystan smiles when he sees me. He opens the door and pulls me into the car. I fall onto his lap and he holds on like I'm an anchor. "I prefer kiss ninja. I'll always prefer that." Trystan's hands wrap around my waist and he pulls me in for a hug. Being on his lap makes me so excited and nervous at the same time, but his hands feel good so I don't wriggle away. He kisses my cheek lightly and the sensation shoots a current through my veins and a soft smile spreads across my lips.

"So, I see that I've corrupted you. It's not even second period yet and you're already cutting class." The smirk on Trystan's face is so cute that I want to lean in and lick it off. That cocky arrogant smile excites the butterflies that are ravaging my stomach.

"Ha! As if I could be so easily manipulated by you."

"So, it's Katie that's the evil force at play here? Hmmm. I'll have to study her methods." Trystan beams and I swat at him, needing him to be serious for a moment.

"Are you all right?" I ask. After everything that's happened, I doubt it.

Trystan tried so hard to hide this, and now it's exposed.

"Of course. You're here, now. Everything will be fine." His confident smile falters and his voice loses the token Trystan Scott vibrato.

"Everything will be fine. You'll see."

He smirks at me. "It sounds better when you say it."

"Because I believe it. This can be a good thing, Trystan. You'll never have to hide from anyone or anything ever again. You just have to be brave this one time, and take whatever crap comes your way, but after that you can live your own life. You don't have to enlist. Your life is yours now." As I speak, Trystan's fingers run through my hair.

"They'll know you were there. They'll know what you did. People will talk, they'll say things about you and me. I don't want them to." His eyes are on the dashboard, like he can't look at me.

Tilting his chin up so our gazes meet, I say, "They're only words, Trystan. Let them say whatever they want. I owe you that much—"

His blue eyes lock onto mine, confused. "What are you talking about?"

"I'm the reason the reporters where there. They found out you're Day because of me."

Trystan stiffens and his hands fall to the seat. "You told them?"

"No, but I might as well have. Brie was in my room, she found the song and recognized your handwriting. I'm sorry. I didn't—"

He pulls me to his chest and it's all I can do to keep the tears from falling. I know Trystan didn't want this and it's my fault it happened. "Shhh, it wasn't your fault. You're not the one who called them. Why the hell were you hanging out with Brie, anyway?"

"I wasn't. I was forced to apologize so her dad wouldn't sue my father. My mother left her in my room for god knows how long. Brie saw the song."

Trystan holds me tighter. "Brie's my fault, I—"

Seth chooses that moment to materialize next to the open window with Katie in his wake. They say in unison, "Brie's a bitter skank." The two of them stop and this awkward thing happens. Seth looks down at the juice in his hands with a weird expression on his face.

Katie gapes at him like a docked fish. "Stop stealing my thoughts, perv."

Seth comes back to himself and snaps, "It's not like it's a novel idea, G.I. Hoe."

Trystan groans and slams his head backward into the seat. "I'll jump out of the car right now if you two are going to fight all day."

Seth sees me on Trystan's lap. "She is not staying. You got some, now you can get out."

Katie shoves Seth aside and slips into the backseat. "That's a suckie idea. I'm not walking home and Trystan isn't going to let you talk crap about Mari, so keep your disgusting comments to yourself." Katie opens the bag and holds it out to me. "Bagel?"

"No! You two are not coming with us!" Seth stands with the door open and is pointing, like we're bad dogs for climbing on his seats.

"Yeah, I'm not leaving." Katie bites into her bagel. "Did you guys get bacon? I swear to God, I smell bacon." She lifts her nose to the air and sniffs.

Everyone looks at Seth. He shifts all his weight to one foot and surrenders. "Fuck, yeah. I got bacon and if you get grease on the upholstery, I'll take it out of your ass." He holds the bag out to Katie.

She snatches it from his hand. "Yeah, I'm not into that, but thanks for the offer."

Trystan tries to hide a surprised smile, as Katie inhales a strip of bacon before handing us the bag. He asks me, "Is she always like this?"

"Only when she's wearing those boots. She goes all Combat Katie and thinks she can kick ass."

"She's got a great ass," Seth smirks and slips into the car.

Katie glares at him as she glances at her wooden handbag. "I should hit you with my purse."

"What? It was a compliment." Seth's smiles in the rearview mirror.

"Then, you suck at compliments. Why can't you just learn to secretly leer like everyone else? Damn, Seth." Katie smiles crookedly and munches another piece of bacon.

"Who said I wasn't doing that too?" Seth looks at her in the mirror again. I expect more pointed comments from Katie but she just eats her food like she doesn't care who's watching.

Seth grabs his breakfast, unwraps it, and takes a huge bite before looking over at Trystan. "Where are we going, Scott? The next move is your call."

CHAPTER 5

~TRYSTAN~

Mari tenses in his lap as soon as Seth and Katie get into the car. Trystan knows she wants to slide in the seat next to him, but he isn't ready to let her go yet. His fingers lace together around her narrow waist as Seth and Katie attempt to verbally castrate each other. The familiarity makes his raging pulse slow to normal—well, almost. Mari is in his lap. If he lets his mind wander, it'll go back to her bedroom and run through the things he could have done with her last night if he didn't have a conscience. Telling her no seemed like the right thing at the time, but now Trystan's worried that she'll slip through his fingers.

There's no way to hold onto Mari, not with the world going up in flames around him. He can't even bring Mari with him, assuming he signs with one of the deals that he's been offered. Mari's a minor and is stuck living with parents who don't love her for another year, while he does what? While he becomes famous and she forgets all about him. There's nothing Trystan can offer her, not if he doesn't step up and change something.

The idea of publically professing what happened at home makes him sick. Telling everyone about it seems unbearable, but it's one barbed hurdle and the reward on the other side is worth risking impalement. Trystan isn't accustomed to telling people his secrets, but he's guessing that everyone in the car already knows most of them.

Trystan looks over the seat at Katie. "What do you think I should do?"

Her jaw drops and she blinks repetitively, batting her eyelashes. Katie presses her hand to her heart and drops her bagel. Her voice drips with sarcasm as she speaks. "Are you really asking me? Oh my God! Day Jones is asking me a question!" She sounds like a crazed fan, and then laughs, falling back into the seat, and taking another bite of her bagel. "Seriously, Scott. Get over yourself. What do you think is going to happen if people know?"

Trystan realizes that he likes Katie more than he thought he did. She spars with Seth so much that he's hardly gotten two words in when she's around. He didn't expect her to react this way, and that's good. Mari needs friends like that. Hell, I need friends like that, he thinks, and grins at her. "Okay, wiseass, try again. What happens if I confess and sing? What happens when they know without a doubt that I'm the online legend?"

Mari cuts off Katie. She sees where he's going with this, and that he needs to think it through. "The agents that tried to sign you show up, the record labels do the same—"

Seth adds, "Except they go to your house, because they think your dad isn't an asshole—"

Mari nods and continues, "Then, they find out your stuff is gone. Your dad is a wild card—he could claim you or disown you and say you never lived there—and since he threw out all your stuff—"

Katie cuts her off. "Your dad threw out all your stuff?"

Trystan doesn't answer. Seth gives Katie the drive-by version. "Trystan's dad is a shithead and abused him, on and off, forever. Mari almost killed the old guy with a brick the other night, which is what has Trystan on edge. He thinks the press is going to find out and it'll ruin Mari's life."

Mari turns and looks at Trystan as Katie's jaw hits the carpet. "You're afraid for me?"

He nods, avoiding her gaze. "I can't keep them from finding any of that."

"They won't find it, Trystan. My files are gone, my dad probably had them all burned. You know how he is. He didn't want to sue because he didn't want to leave a paper trail that could come back and haunt him." The words stick to the back of her throat, but she manages to spit them out.

"What if they know we were together last night?" He takes one of her lose curls and tucks it behind her ear. "If someone saw me come or go, then you'd get in trouble and I don't want to make your life harder than it already is."

"Trystan, don't worry about me." Smiling kindly, Mari tilts her pretty face to the side. "The worst thing that I had to worry about was Brie, and if this is the best she can do, then I'm overjoyed. Go meet with the suits and pick one. You'll be good at this Trystan, but you have to want it. You have to own it the way you do when you're on stage. They'll love you—all of them—and you'll be unstoppable no matter what skeletons from your past are aired out." By the time she stops speaking, Mari has her head tipped in and pressed against his. "Your next move is to let the world know that you're Day Jones and that you have more songs that are even more awesome than the first."

Trystan's blue gaze is locked with hers. His hand is on her back with his thumb sweeping in slow circles. "I can't do it at your expense—"

"It's not. My path is already set. Trystan, I didn't mention this before, but I applied to a little college not too far from here. They accepted me. Actually, they offered me a full ride—full tuition, fees, room and board—everything. I didn't mention it because I didn't think I could go through with it, but…" her words trail off as a smile creeps across her lips.

Katie butts in, "But she's going through with it. Little Miss Secrets here just submitted an application for early graduation. She's ditching me."

"No shit?" Seth's breakfast stops half way to his mouth and he stares at Mari.

She nods and flashes smiles. "Yeah, I did."

Trystan asks, "What about your Dad?"

Katie's the one who answers. She's sucking on a piece of bacon and removes it from her mouth like it's a lollipop. "Her dad is going to shit bricks—"

"Katie!" Mari yells at her, but she's right.

"What? It's the truth." She chomps on the bacon and starts fighting over the remaining pieces with Seth.

Trystan turns Mari's face towards his. There are so many emotions flooding through him that he can't figure out how he feels. "Are you really going to do it?"

"I don't know. Are you going to admit that you're Day Jones?"

His eyes flick to Seth as the guy snort-laughs. Trystan says to his friend. "I walked right into that, didn't I?"

"Yup. She played you, lover boy." Katie uses the moment to her advantage. She grabs a fist full of bacon before Seth can stop her and shoves the slices in her mouth. "Ah! You bitch! You ate all the bacon!" The greasy meat hangs out the sides of Katie's mouth. She grins and waves the tips of her fingers at him, laughing. "Fuck it." Seth turns around and pulls a piece from between her lips and eats it.

"You're disgusting!" The words come out of Katie's mouth garbled as she blinks at Seth in shock.

Trystan laughs and squeezes Mari tight. "Yes, he is. And you—Mari Jennings—

you're diabolical." She laughs as Trystan tickles her. The little movements of his fingers make Mari jerk around on the front seat like a squirrel on a string. She tries to tickle him back, but Trystan has the better angle. There's no way to get away from him. Katie and Seth are busy telling them how disgustingly cute they are, and someone threatens to douse Trystan and Mari with juice so they stop.

Trystan is smiling wide, "So, we're both going to do it?"

Mari is grinning at him. "Apparently."

"Psh," Katie interrupts, "that was weak, Mari. Own it, woman!"

Mari clutches her hands and screams, "I'm going to college early! Wahoo!" Trystan laughs and hugs her.

"Wahoo?" Seth makes a face. "Isn't that what the fox says when he falls off a cliff?"

Katie kicks the back of his seat with her big ass boot. "You're such a moron."

They continue to bicker, but Trystan doesn't care. He can't keep his eyes off of Mari's. Seth notices. "You guys are going to get slobber all over the leather. I'm getting rid of her now. Where's your house, Mari?"

Before Mari can object, Trystan slides her into the seat next to him and gives the address. When Seth stops in front of her house, Trystan gets out first and holds the door. Mari slips out and before Katie can crawl out of the backseat, he closes the door. Leaning in through the window, Trystan informs them, "I'm hanging out with Mari. See you at the school tonight."

"Mari! You can't leave me with Seth!" Katie has her face in the little gap between the seat belt and the window. She extends her hand. "Save me!"

Trystan wraps his arms around Mari and presses a kiss to her cheek. Seth revs the engine. "Trust me, Katie, you don't want to hang out with them right now. They're going to be all lovey dovey and shit. Let's go find something else to do."

Seth hits the gas before anyone can reply. As the car travels down the street, Katie turns around and smooshes her face against the back window and gives them both the finger. Trystan laughs and waves at her. "She's going to kill you later."

"Me? You're the one who waved. She remembers stuff like that."

Trystan makes a mental note to never piss off Katie again. Then he turns to Mari and takes her hands. "So, we have an entire day to ourselves. What should we do?" Stepping closer, he slips his hands around her waist and closes the space between them.

"I might have a few ideas." She looks up shyly and then laughs.

In that moment, Trystan is so happy that his chest might combust. "Oh? I thought your parents were home during the day?"

"They usually are, but today there's a meeting and some other stuff that they told me about. The general gist was that they wouldn't be at the house today or the school tonight." She mimics her dad's voice, "Because acting is a waste of your talents."

Trystan leans in close enough to kiss her. "So, that means that we both have until six o'clock tonight with no parental supervision? That's a really long time." His eyes shift to her lips. "Got any ideas?"

Grinning, she pecks him on the lips, and then tugs him toward the front door. "I plan to kick your ass at Guitar Hero for the first hour. Your ego will be so bruised that you won't be able to look me in the eye after that—" The rest of her verbal jabs are lost in giggles as Trystan presses her against the front door and attacks her with tickles.

"Bruised ego, my ass."

"I like your ass." Mari spurts, between bouts of laughter. Suddenly, Trystan's body is pressed to hers. He steps closer, pressing her back against the door, before kissing her until she forgets to breathe.

CHAPTER 6

~TRYSTAN~

The bed is soft and it feels good to have Mari against his chest. She's laying on her side, snuggling into him on top of her comforter. They've been lying like this since lunch. Trystan doesn't remember how they got into the position. They'd been talking, sitting side by side, and now she's laying in his arms. Tightening his hold around her narrow waist, Trystan feels content. No, it's past that. For the first time in his life, he's happy. He can see a way out, a path that leads to something good, and he's glad that it includes Mari.

"So," Trystan says, "When were you going to tell me about the early graduation thing?"

She shrugs. "I don't know. I guess I was saving it for when you decided to tell everyone that you're Day. Have you thought about how you're going to do it?"

They talk about it a little bit and decide it should be after the play. Otherwise they fear that the cast will have worked so hard for nothing. Trystan doesn't want to overshadow them, especially Mari. Plus, kissing her on stage is a moment that he doesn't want to pass up, and there are several hot kisses in the little production. "Not really. What do you think I should do?"

"Mmm, as much as I hate to say this, I think Seth is right. You have to own it. Spill the whole thing."

"How? I know I should, but knowing it and saying it are two different things." Her long hair is draped over her shoulder. She shifts and looks up at him.

"What if we helped? Like me, Seth, and Katie. What if we each said something about why you wouldn't come forward, so that way when you say that you're Day Jones, it makes more sense? People are going to wonder why you're saying it now."

"Because they found me. If they didn't know where I was, I wouldn't say anything." Trystan rolls onto his side and leans on his elbow. "I wouldn't have risked this." He gestures between them. "It's too important to me."

Mari smiles in that girlish way, with the shy eyes, before she slips off the bed. She walks over to her dresser and pulls something out. When she comes back, she sits on the edge of the mattress, and takes his hand. Trystan sits up as Mari drops something cold into his palm—a ring. It's a thick silver band with strange letters etched onto it. Holding it up between his thumb and forefinger, Trystan asks, "What does it say?"

"It's ancient Greek. It says…" her cheeks redden and she looks away.

When she lifts her gaze, Trystan feels the pull to her. It starts in the center of his chest and travels deep into his bones. Those eyes, that hair, and her voice—there isn't a more wonderful sound. Leaning in slowly, Trystan lingers within a breath of her lips. He can feel the heat from her skin and although he longs to touch her, he doesn't. "What does it say, Mari?"

Her eyes lift and she tenses, seeing how close he is. If her heart is pounding like his, they're in trouble. Trystan leans in and closes the space, pressing his lips to the corner of her mouth. Mari's dark lashes close and when she lifts her gaze again, those pink lips curve into a beautiful shy smile.

"Tell me," he breathes.

"It says 'my soul is your soul.' It means you're part of me and that our friendship is eternal." She presses her lips together hard and adds, "And it means I love you. When you're famous and miles away, you can look at it and remember me."

"As if I could ever forget you," He pulls her against his chest and says in her ear, "I love it."

"Trystan, I know our lives are about to change and I want you to do what you need to do, to become who you need to be. But the thought of waking up every morning and not seeing you—"

He silences her worries with a kiss, and then pulls away. Both of his hands find her face, and slip back into her hair. "Come with me. Whatever I do, wherever I go— come with me, Mari. You don't have to stay here."

"I'm seventeen, Trystan. I can't—"

"You'll be able to leave for college."

"Yeah, but I can't leave to live with a guy. Add in the fact that you're a rock star and my dad will throw your ass in jail for kidnapping me." Her dark gaze falls between us and when she looks up again, there's pain in her eyes. "It works better this way. You can come see me and I'll start college. I can catch up with you when I'm eighteen or stay here and graduate. We'll have more choices then, Trystan. But right now, we both get to start over. We both get two shiny new lives and they're going in different directions. That's why I want you to have the ring. Remember me when things get rough, because they will. I'll always be there for you, no matter what happens between us."

Her words are like a stake through his heart. She's talking about them like they're already over, even though they've barely started. The idea of losing her, of going through his life without her, is more devastating than anything he's ever felt. But she's right and he knows it. Their time together is limited and he wants to treasure the few moments they have.

They stay like that, embracing each other, on the side of Mari's bed. He can't tell if it's seconds or hours, but the tug inside his chest is demanding. Everything within him is making Trystan want to kiss her senseless and hold her in his arms.

Suddenly, she pulls back and takes his cheeks in her palms. "Kiss me, Trystan." Her voice is soft. Mari doesn't have to ask twice.

Trystan lowers his lips and presses them softly to her mouth. Fighting to maintain control, he plans to kiss her slowly and take his time, but then Mari sinks back onto the bed and pulls Trystan down with her, which changes things. The kiss becomes all hot lips, and he can't get enough. His hands travel down the sides of her body, grasping her tighter, as he presses himself on top of her.

The moment is perfect, and his head is filled with the sounds Mari makes in the back of her throat and the way her nails scrape the back of his neck. Her scent fills his head and he's utterly lost, unable to think or focus on anything but her.

That's why he doesn't hear the door or the footsteps until it's too late. A hand is on the back of his neck and a second later, Trystan is ripped away from Mari. He's pulled to his feet and then a fist connects with his stomach. Mari's father manages to keep a hold on his shoulder. The man is screaming incoherently as he tries to throw another punch, but Trystan is ready this time. He moves at the last moment. Mari screams drown out her father's angry words, as his fist connects with the wall, and goes straight through.

Trystan steps back, and pulls Mari to her feet, shielding her. When her father pulls his hand free and turns back, his jaw is clenched tight and his fists rise again. Trystan thought the man was yelling at him, but he isn't. He's giving Mari a verbal lashing that's worse than anything his old man ever said.

Her father is growling, his back curved, his arms ready to strangle her. "I gave you everything and this is how you repay me? You cut school and sit at home, playing house with this piece of shit! You're a goddamn whore! And no daughter of mine is ever going to—"

Trystan knows he shouldn't do it, but his fist is already in motion, making a bee line straight for the doctor's jaw. On contact, the man staggers, and his back hits the wall. Hard. The picture frames that her mother so neatly displayed in a little row crash to the floor and shatter.

Broken glass glitters as Trystan steps forward, crunching it under his boot. "No one talks to Mari like that. I don't care if you're her father or if you sue me. Your daughter loves you, even though you don't deserve it. Your vicious words are destroying her and I'm not going to let you do it. So, go back to your ivory tower and complain about how the world doesn't recognize how smart you are, just like you don't recognize what you've done to your own child, you pathetic waste of life."

Trystan holds out a hand for Mari. Sweat drips from his brow as he sucks in air, trying to slow his heart rate back to normal. Every muscle in his body is tense, ready for an attack that never comes. Instead, Mari's father sits on the floor, glaring. He doesn't stand when his daughter walks past him with tears glistening on her cheeks. The doctor sits there, rigid, utterly still, like he's in shock. Trystan and Mari walk out of the house together in silence.

CHAPTER 7

~MARI~

I can't stop crying. Trystan's arm is around me as he guides me to a picnic table and sits me down on top. My mom took me to this park when I was a little girl. It's a few blocks from my house. Trystan's hands are on my knees as he tries to look up into my face. "Are you all right?"

Frantically rubbing tears out of my eyes, I look up at him. "I'm so sorry, Trystan. He wasn't supposed to be home. Dad never comes home. I—"

"Shhh," he pulls me against his chest and holds on tight, and strokes my hair. I can hear the steady beating of his heart and it soothes me.

When I finally pull away, I feel embarrassed. We weren't even doing anything, but that's not what it looked like. "I'm sorry." I say it again, because I don't know what else to say.

"You have nothing to be sorry about, Mari." I give him a weak smile and glance away, but Trystan doesn't let me. He takes my chin in his hand and lifts my gaze until our eyes meet. There's so much affection in those blue eyes, so much love. "No one will hurt you when I'm around, okay?"

I lean into him again, holding on tight. "No one has ever talked back to him before, and you yelled and punched him."

Trystan kisses the top of my head and rests his cheek there. "I'm sorry if I made things worse. I couldn't stand there and watch him rip you apart."

"He didn't get up, Trystan. I expected him to fight back, but he didn't. Dad seemed more shocked than anything." The look on my father's face when Trystan defended me wasn't anger, it was something else. It was almost like he was shocked that someone had the nerve to talk back to him. No one ever talks back to my dad. He's above everyone at work and at home. He's always right, and a teenage rock star just told him he was wrong, and followed it up with an undercut. "Oh, god. He's going to kill me later."

Trystan pulls away and takes hold of my upper arms. He lowers himself so we're eye to eye. "Then don't go home."

The thought brings a smile to my face. Stay with Trystan. I would love that, but I can't. "Trystan, I can't. They'll tear the town apart looking for me, and say horrible things about you when they find me."

His gaze falls to the ground as his hands slip down to mine. "I can't let you go back there alone. What if we figured out how to get you a room, so you're not with me?"

"A room?" What is he thinking?

Nodding, Trystan says, "Yeah, a hotel room. I'm kind of homeless and all of my regular go-to spots aren't going to be possible because of the media. Especially not after tonight." He takes my hands and pulls me to my feet. "I need to call one of those record labels about a deal. I'll tell them that they need to give me a place to stay, and I'll get a room for you, too."

I'm not sure I should do it. It feels like he wants me to run away. It's strange, but if I was a year older, I wouldn't be a runaway, I'd be a smart woman leaving an abusive home. Trystan knows what's going through my mind before I even speak.

The wind catches my hair and blows it across my face, leaving little strands stuck to my drying tears. Trystan reaches for me and yanks me to him by my waistband, before he smoothes away the stray strands. When he's done, his gaze lifts. The way he looks at me makes my heart race. Every pain, every piece of anguish that I felt a moment ago fades until there is only me and him. A tingling sensation starts in my chest and awakens the butterflies in my stomach as Trystan leans in and presses his lips to mine. I'll never get tired of his kiss, because I can't believe he's kissing me. And it's not fake, it's not from rehearsal, and it's not part of a play.

For once, I don't hold back. I trust him completely and it shows. The kiss changes somehow and becomes hotter and more breathless. By the time I pull away, my entire body is searing and I'm gasping for air.

He tilts his head forward and rests it against mine. Trystan's breathing as hard as I am. He laughs and smiles at me. "I've never had someone kiss me like that."

"What do you mean?"

"I don't know. It changed. It wasn't just kissing. It's like I could feel how much you care about me right here," his fist lands on the center of his chest. Trystan takes a deep breath and shudders, like it scares him. When he looks up, he adds, "It's like you're part of me and always will be. It's awesome, and utterly terrifying."

The way he smiles fills me with joy. There's vulnerability in his gaze, as if he wants me to reassure him, so I do. "I love you, Trystan. I always will." I pull him against me and resist the urge to continue kissing him since we have some practical issues that need to be figured out quickly. "I think you're right about calling someone, but I think it should be Tucker."

"Tucker?" Trystan looks at me like I've lost my mind.

"Yeah. You can trust him, right? The guy's been looking out for you, hasn't he? You should have him talk to the record label."

Trystan thinks about it and says, "You mean I should ask him to be my agent? He's an English teacher, Mari."

"I know. Which means he's underpaid and works his ass off. It also means he can read and parse stuff that makes your head spin. You could get a big name agent—I'm sure they're all trying to sign you—but it makes sense to ask Tucker, right?" I give him a lopsided smile.

He laughs and shakes his head as I hand him my phone. "You know, most people spend their life trying to get away from their teachers."

"Yeah, but good people are rare. He's good people."

"Who are you?" Trystan's smile is huge. He teases me for another second and then dials. "Here goes nothing."

CHAPTER 8

~TRYSTAN~

Trystan walks into the coffee house with Mari on his arm. Today has been so weird. He should be in school. Actually, he should be sitting in Tucker's classroom right now, but here they are in this little café.

Tucker is already at a little table that's jammed into the corner. His white shirt is rolled up to his elbows and his collar is unbuttoned. There's a cup in his hand that gets lifted to his lips. When Tucker sets it down, he sees them, and waves them over. When they stop in front of the table, he asks, "So, it's true then?" Tucker asks while dabbing his forehead with a napkin. The guy is covered in sweat.

Trystan pulls out a chair for Mari and then sits next to Tucker. "Yeah, it's true."

Tucker seems amused. There's a smile on his lips that he's clearly trying to hide. "Why didn't you want to tell anyone?"

"Because of my dad. I know you know," Trystan adds quickly.

"Actually, I didn't know for certain, Trystan. If I did, social services would have pulled you out of there. I'm sorry." Tucker takes a deep breath and leans back in his chair. "So, what do you need from me?"

Trystan glances at Mari. After everything they talked about, he suddenly feels shy asking. It's Tucker, the same man who he threatened to report, but he's also the same guy that let him nap in the school basement.

Mari speaks for him. "Trystan wants to take a deal. Several were offered, but he needs someone to negotiate things for him."

"And you want me to do that?" Tucker's caterpillar eyebrows crawl up his face.

"Yeah, I do."

"Trystan, I'm not an agent. Shouldn't you—"

Trystan cuts him off. "Maybe, but I'd like you to help me with this. You'd get the agent's cut. The thing is, I trust you. I can tell you stuff and it won't end up in the paper, you know? I don't know them."

"Trystan, there are people that would be much better at this. I can look over your contracts, but I'm not taking your money."

Trystan smiles and taps the table between them. "And that's exactly why I want you to do it." Trystan tells Tucker the plan for that evening. Mari interjects once in a while, filling in anything he left out. When he finishes, he says, "And since neither of us have any place to sleep tonight—"

Tucker glances at Trystan and then Mari. "Why not? I mean, I know what happened with your father Trystan, but what's happened to you? Why can't you go home?" He looks at Mari with concern.

"Well, her parents neglect her most of the time and when they're actually around, they lash into her. It's verbal crap for the most part, but when her dad went after her today. I thought he was going to strangle her, so I, uh, kind of punched him." Trystan realizes how bad that sounds. Now that the moment is over, it seems like an overreaction on his part, but at the time Trystan felt the need to defend Mari.

For a second he wonders how much his father messed up his perception of things. Maybe all livid parents don't beat the shit out of their kids. Maybe they yell and that's it, but things had already taken a turn when he grabbed Trystan. He can't afford to second guess himself. He did what he had to and he'd do it again.

Tucker pinches the bridge of his nose and presses his eyes closed. "You punched Dr. Jennings?"

"Don't make it sound like I'm the bad guy here—" Trystan bristles, but Tucker slaps his hand down on the table and cuts him off.

"Trystan, you're not the bad guy, but you can't punch people. You're eighteen—it's assault. We've already been through this! Did you think of that before you hit him?"

"He grabbed me and then he went at Mari. I thought he was going to hurt her. I..." His voice trails off as he looks over at Mari.

She takes his hand. "Mr. Tucker, I didn't like any of it, but Trystan didn't start it."

Tucker looks up at her and sighs. "What's done is done, but you two can't be in situations like this. It's not safe. Mari's a minor, for godsakes. If the police show up—"

"I know," Trystan says quickly. "They showed up at my house the other night when things got ugly with my father. I know what happens to Mari. They drag her ass back to her father, and we all know how that goes." Trystan swallows hard and leans back, running his hands through his hair. "I want to make sure she's safe, Mr. Tucker. That needs to be part of the deal."

Tucker looks at each of them and shakes his head. "I can't do that Trystan. Social Services won't intervene if she's not in immediate danger. Verbal abuse is frowned upon, and he never actually touched her. When there are kids getting beat within an inch of death, they just don't have the capacity to deal with the stuff Mari is living with. Even if I reported neglect, she's seventeen. She can feed herself. Her parents are wealthy. Do you see where this is going?"

"I don't want you to call social services," Mari squeaks, looking panicked.

Trystan takes her hand, "We won't. Besides, that's not what we need right now."

Mr. Tucker looks confused. "Then, what do you want me to do?"

"Make housing a provision of the contract with the record label. We both need a roof. At the very least, have them put her up somewhere until she can move into the dorm in the fall."

Tucker blinks and does a double take. "Come again? She's going to college in the fall?"

Mari finally speaks up. She loses the hitch in her voice and confidently tells Tucker her plans. "Yes, I applied to a little college out east. They accepted me and offered a full scholarship, but I can't move into the dorm until August."

Tucker's brow furrows as he thinks. After a few moments, he points at Mari. "I can fix your problem. We can get you into the dorm now instead of at the end of the summer. I assume your parents don't approve?"

"They don't know." Mari glances at her hands as she speaks, looking younger than she is. "Daddy wanted me at Harvard, pursuing something in the medical field. I don't want that life. So I applied. I was planning on disappearing one night and not telling them a thing."

Tucker closes his eyes. When he opens them again, he smiles at her. Tipping his head to the side, he says, "You're a good kid with a good heart and a brilliant mind. I agree that you should move into the dorm as soon as possible, but you need to tell them. Otherwise, they'll think you were abducted or something horrible. I assume that your application for early graduation was submitted?" She nods. "Good, then I'll make sure it goes through. As for you," Tucker glances at Trystan while his index finger traces the rim of his coffee mug, "I'll talk to the record labels for you and tell them what you want. We can go from there. You have a lot of potential, Scott. I want to see you succeed more than anyone, so promise me that you won't mess it up."

Trystan laughs and folds his arms over his chest. "What makes you think that I want to mess it up?"

"There's a lot of pressure with this life, Trystan. People will always be looking at you, waiting for you to fall apart. Have you noticed your peers—the other young actors and singers who flamed out? You get a lot by taking this path, but you're giving up a lot, too. I know how much you value privacy and that'll be gone. You'll belong to the world. There won't be a quiet moment for weeks on end. Do you think you can handle that life? Because it's so damn easy to reach for something to take the edge off and before you know it, you're constantly drunk or high."

Trystan's shoulders tense as he says it. "I don't drink or do drugs. I'll never drink anything. Do you seriously think that I'd touch that shit after living with my father? He tried to—" Words won't come. They stick in his throat like barbs. "If she hadn't walked in—" He sucks in air, his eyes too wide, and heart beating too fast.

Tucker bumps Trystan's hand and cuts him off. "I don't think you'll do it on purpose, Trystan, but yeah—at some point you're going to need a way to deal with things. You need to know what you're going to do before it sneaks up on you. Unless a person intentionally changes what they're doing, children will become their parents. Which means you'll deal with stress the same way your father did. I know you're saying you won't now, but unless you know what you'll do, it's inevitable. So do us both a favor and decide how to handle your life before you get to that point."

Tucker's words cut through Trystan and pierce his heart. Lots of guys become their father. Trystan swore up and down that he'd never be like his old man, but there's nothing stopping it from occurring. Tucker is the first person to even say that it didn't have to happen, and the way to do that seems so simple. Decide not to drink, decide now what he'll do when life is too hard, and Trystan can get anything he wants to drown his stress. Trystan hates that his father is a part of him. He hates how much the man influenced his life, but Tucker is right.

"I will." The air is thick with things yet to come. There's a slush pile filled with shit that he has to trek through before getting to the other side. If Tucker wasn't here, he wouldn't know what to do.

Trystan smiles awkwardly at the guy. "Hey, I suck at saying things like this, but it needs to be said. Thank you. Thank you for looking out for me and dealing with my shit. I pretty much blackmailed you this year and you just rolled with it. You left the school in the middle of the day to talk to us, and you always do stuff like that. You've done more than I could ever thank you for. I know a good guy when I see one, and I hope I can make you proud. If I can be half the man you are, that'll be amazing."

Mari is smiling at Trystan, and leans in close as he speaks. She knows how hard it is for him to say things like this. It means Trystan's wrong, that someone did care about him all this time, and that he wasn't alone. Trystan couldn't see it before, but it's crystal clear now. It's funny how easy it is to see after the fact.

Tucker has a weird smirk on his face. Shaking his head, he laughs. "Trystan, I'm already proud of you. This stupid smile on my face is pride. You're the kid with the most crap stacked against you and you rose to the top. You finally learned what I was trying to teach you and I couldn't ask for more."

Tucker stands abruptly and smacks Trystan on the back, nearly knocking him out of his seat. "I'll see you before the play tonight and tell you how it goes. And Mari, make plans to stay at Katie's in case I can't pick up your dorm room key until tomorrow." He drops fifty bucks on the table and adds, "Celebrate, both of you. Grab a piece of cake and something for dinner. I'll see you guys later."

CHAPTER 9

~MARI~

Trystan and I go to the diner for dinner. My parents won't show up and I doubt my dad is out looking for me. He'll wait for me to come home and then chew me out. I already called and left a message on the answering machine that I'd be staying with Katie tonight, so I won't have to deal with that mess until tomorrow, and right now tomorrow feels so far away.

I'm staring at the menu way too long. Trystan is sitting across from me in the little booth. He glances over the top of his menu and looks around. "Where do you think they went?"

"Who? The press?"

"Yeah, I thought they'd be harder to ditch."

Seth appears next to me and interrupts, "Well, you can thank me for that. And her, I guess." He jabs his thumb at Katie, who's giggling like a maniac and standing next to Seth.

Trystan scoots in to give Seth room, and I do the same. Katie sits next to me and is trying really hard not to laugh. "Tell them what you did," she says to Seth.

Seth leans back into the booth and spreads his arms across the seatback. "Well, the reporters were hanging around the school, like you'd come back. So me and Katie walk over and ask if they've seen you, yet."

Katie can't shut up. She blurts out, "Seth gave an interview and totally made up a bunch of stuff. The reporters are out at Robert Moses beach looking for you right now. Seth told them that you always go out there before opening night, but that you'd be back in time for the show." Her smile looks so weird, because she's trying to keep herself from laughing. "Tell them the other part—about Brie."

"Oh, yeah. I told them that the Skank is a bit of a psycho and that she's not your girlfriend."

"They believed you?" Trystan asks, looking surprised.

"Nah, of course not. I said I was your best friend, but everyone is pulling shit and trying to get on camera. So I told them to confirm that I was your bro with Brie, which they did. So, Brie says yes, and then they ask her where you go before every performance and she says you don't go anywhere." Seth is smiling like he's the most awesome guy in the world.

Katie jumps in and finishes the story. "So they didn't believe that she's going out with you! They told her to step aside so they could talk to Trystan's real friends." Katie busts a gut laughing and doubles over. Her face comes dangerously close to hitting the table as her body shakes.

Seth reaches forward all of a sudden, and shoots his hand out, placing it between Katie's face and the table just before she smacks into it. "Watch it, bacon girl. You'll knock the few brains you have left out of that pretty head."

Trystan's eyes widen and we give each other a silent what the heck was that stare.

Katie stares at Seth's hand and lifts her eyes slowly, smiling way too hard. "Trying to steal a feel, Sexbot?"

"Only from you." Seth and Katie are in their own little world with their eyes locked. Katie practically swoons when he says that last bit.

"Okay, what the hell is going on?" Trystan elbows Seth in the side, adding, "You're freaking us out. What'd you guys do all day?"

Katie sighs and looks at Seth like she's love struck. "Nothing. Messed with reporters, cut class, toilet papered Brie's car, and stuck pickles on her antenna."

"Pickles?" Trystan and I ask at the same time.

"Yeah, cuz she's a dick," Katie says.

Seth laughs. "I had no idea why you picked up pickles."

"It's because the lunch lady gave me the whole jar. I didn't think of the metaphor until later." They both start laughing again, and it's like aliens came down and snatched Katie's brain while we were gone.

"So," Seth says and looks at us, "Did you guys get stuff worked out? Is our boy going to be a rock star? Because I want backstage passes. I'm going to take a marker and cross out the VIP and write PUS-E on mine."

Katie kicks him under the table. "You will not!"

Seth laughs, "Damn woman, those boots hurt. Stop kicking me!"

"Stop saying dumb-ass stuff!"

"I only said it to get a rise out of you."

"Well, you'll get a boot up your ass if you say it again." Katie's smirk is back. She's flirting with him.

"Uh, Trystan…" I say and scoot away from her a little bit. "I think someone stole Katie's brain. They must have sucked it right out of her head."

"Yeah," Trystan answers with a smirk on his lips, "that dazed look on her face says— ahh! She kicked me!" Trystan's eyes widen in shock and he looks under the table and then back up at my best friend.

Katie folds her arms over her chest and leans back in the booth, smugly. "Sorry, the alien made me do it." She examines the back of her hand, looking closely at her polish before looking up. "What?"

We all start laughing and things feel like they're going to be all right.

———

When we get to the school, the building is surrounded by reporters. Trystan stops in his tracks and his face turns white. His hand slips out of mine as he stares. This will be his life from now on and I'm sure he's questioning whether or not he can handle it. Seth and Katie stop when they notice we aren't following them.

"This is nothing, Scott. We can elbow past them—"

"Or?" Trystan asks as he looks at the news vans again. There are more people here than before. This morning it was manageable, but now there are close to twenty different reporters, plus their crew, and cameras are everywhere. Some of the media people are standing in front of the school, blocking the doors, with a microphone in hand, ready to pounce when Trystan arrives. Since Trystan doesn't want to make the announcement until after the performance, it's an issue.

"Or, we can open the basement door. Come on, Katie. I'll distract them and you sneak through. Knock three times on the door and wait for her to open it. Got it?" Seth doesn't wait for an answer. Instead he walks away with Katie a few paces behind.

Trystan looks over at me. "So."

"You're not ready for this, are you?" He takes my hand and shakes his head.

"I don't think anyone could ever be ready for this. I like the limelight, Mari, but only when I'm on a stage and everyone else is far away. I'm not used to having them in my face and sorting through my personal life. I don't like it." He sighs and pushes his silky hair out of his eyes.

Squeezing his hand, we round the side of the building and head toward the stairwell that leads to the basement. "I know. I wish I could keep them away from you, but I think you need them. They're the ones that'll get you a contract and pay your bills, right? Maybe you could think of it like a show, throw out some personal stuff so they don't go digging for it. I'm not naïve enough to think that'll stop them, but it should slow them down, right?"

"Maybe. The truth is I don't think I'm cut out for this, Mari. I'm an actor. I never planned on signing—"

"But that's exactly why they love you. Trystan, you're real. You aren't someone whose clawed his way to the top. You're the lovesick guy that wrote a girl a song. You're the guy who wanted to stay out of the spotlight, and that's why they love you. You're acting like a normal person, not some larger than life Hollywood type. When they look at you, you give them hope. People like you are rare. Remember who you are and you'll be happy for once. You won't have to scrounge for food or worry about where you're going to sleep." I lean into his arm as I say these things. Trystan has no idea what people see in him. I can hear it in his voice.

Trystan stops and slips his arms around my waist, before leaning in and giving me a peck on the forehead. Smiling, he takes a lock of hair in his hand and plays with the curl, wrapping it around his finger. "You have too much faith in me."

"You need people that love you for you and believe in you, Trystan. You've been denied that basic right. And by the way, this isn't too much faith at all. I know what you're capable of, and I expect you to shine bright and rock this Day Jones thing better than any play you've ever done. You've been handed the performance of a lifetime, and you're going to amaze us all. Wait and see." It's hard to say stuff like that to someone when it isn't true, but with Trystan I have no shortage of words. He's amazing and the whole world is about to know for certain that Day Jones pales in comparison to Trystan Scott.

"Mari," Trystan's lips are parted like he's searching for words, but nothing comes out. He shakes his head with laughter on his lips. "I love you so much. You see this," he points to the ring I gave him, "I'm never taking it off. You're my everything, Mari." He wraps his arms around me and holds me tight.

Katie's voice echoes up to us. "Stop making out and get your asses down here before someone sees you!"

Trystan takes my hand and we run down the metal stairs and into the basement. Katie yanks the door shut behind us and looks up, grinning. "You guys are going to get married and have little rock star babies!" I elbow her in the side, but she keeps laughing anyway. "They're going to have little tiny guitars and chains on their diapers!"

Horrified, I look over at Trystan wondering how much Katie just spooked him. The look of terror that I was expecting isn't there when I glance his way. Instead, Trystan is laughing with her and adds, "Don't forget baby mohawks." He looks over at me. "What? You never thought about what's next for us?"

Shyness pulls my face to the floor like an anchor to the bottom of the ocean. I can't look up if I try. "A little, but not that far." Trystan is still laughing when he yanks me toward him.

"Yeah, I have to go save Seth, otherwise I would love to hear this. Tell him that you want two babies and a little house upstate with a picket fence and a cow that eats your pansies." Katie runs off before I can kill her.

Trystan rests his forehead on mine. "Why does she know that stuff and I don't? And what's with the cow?"

I shrug and look up at him. My stomach dips and I can barely find my voice. "Most guys don't want to hear that stuff."

"Since when am I most guys?"

"You've never been like most guys, but that mask you wore threw me off."

"Masks are sexy, right?" He teases lightly and tugs at the waist of my jeans. "Mari, I'd love to be the guy who gives you the house, the cow, and oh my God, I would love to make babies with you. I'd try very, very hard—"

My face is on fire. Someone shoot me! Trystan laughs and lifts my chin when I try to look away, so I smack his chest. "You can't say it like that!"

"What? Making babies is the fun part."

"It doesn't freak you out?"

"What? That you want a family? No, it doesn't freak me out at all. In fact, I like it. I want to be so insanely in love with someone that I'd have a family with her."

"Really?"

"Truly." The way he smiles at me shoots excitement through my veins. I giggle like a crazy person and throw my arms around his neck, while kissing his cheek. "You're my forever, Mari. We'll get through this. I'll be with you every second I get. And when I'm touring, you can meet up with me during your breaks. Or for a weekend. Or even a day. This will work out."

"How do you know?"

"Because this is love, and I'm never letting you go."

CHAPTER 10

~TRYSTAN~

Tucker waits until they're in costume with their make-up finished before he pulls Trystan and Mari aside. "We can't head to my office because the hallways are filled with people, so let's just find a corner and I'll tell you what I was able to work out."

Tucker walks to the far side of the stage, and stops at the back corner. He checks the side door to make sure it's locked and then huddles them together. Handing Trystan a packet of papers, he says, "As soon as you say the last line of the play tonight, you've graduated. I talked to the principal and few of your other teachers to make sure you had passing grades, and they said you're good. So, that's settled. You don't have to come back here tomorrow."

"What about the play?" he asks, surprised to think that Tucker would let him off the hook like that. Besides, Trystan wanted to do all three performances this weekend.

Tucker shakes his head. "This is the only night. We sold out, like standing room only, so the department made more money from this one show than we usually make all year. It's worked out and the school more than recovered the cost of the production. Having you here, and making the announcement this way is a huge help."

Tucker is holding a large envelope in his hand, and smacks it against his palm lightly before continuing. "Listen, you need to look at these contracts and pick one. There are three offers in here for seven figures, Trystan. They want your songs and there are plans for tours. I made notations and altered things that needed to be changed, such as your lodging requirements, privacy—"

"Seven figures?" Mari gasps and touches her fingers to her lips.

Tucker smiles. "Yes, the smallest offer is seven figures. There's one in here for eight. You're a millionaire, kid." Trystan stands there shocked, unblinking, and unable to speak. Tucker slaps him on the back and laughs. "You didn't know, did you?"

Trystan's shoulders creep up as his jaw drops. His voice is a squeak, "I didn't know. I thought maybe they'd give me ten thousand bucks for the song." He goes to rub his hands over his face and stops because he'll smear his stage make-up. "Holy shit."

There have been times when life snuck up and robbed him. It fucking stole everything, and it happened so often that Trystan just expects it. Fate was cruel, but this—he never expected anything like this. Staggering, Trystan takes a step back and hits the wall. Mari's hand is on his shoulder. She's speaking, but the only thing that he can think is that he won't have to buy semi-perished food from Sam ever again.

His thoughts fall out of his mouth because the shock has disabled the filter between his mouth and brain. "I can buy as much peanut butter as I want." A smile creeps across his unbelieving face as he looks up at them slowly, and laughs.

Tucker and Mari chortle with him. Tucker grabs his shoulder and says, "You can buy anything you want, Trystan."

"Oh my God... Do you know?" His thoughts come out in jagged statements and grow louder. He finally slaps his hands over his lips to shut up. He sounds crazy. Is this how people react when they win the lottery? Trystan giggles behind his hand and then reaches for Mari, pulling her against his side with a huge grin on his face.

"I know it's a lot, Trystan." Tucker keeps talking in the low hurried voice he was using before. It takes a lot of effort for Trystan to stand and listen. Part of him wants to run up and down the school hallways, whooping at the top of his lungs.

Tucker snaps his fat fingers in front of Trystan's face. "Pay attention. I know you're excited, but there's more. If you pick a contract and sign tonight, they'll have a hotel room for you. You can stay there until you buy a house, all expenses paid. It's part of the requirement to sign with them, so all of the contracts have that clause."

Tucker looks at Mari next. "I have a dorm room for you. It's all set and the key is in the housing office. Housing expenses and board are paid until school begins in the fall. And, I talked to the principal about your application for early graduation. It was denied." Tucker tries to keep talking but Mari's smile falls.

"What? Why?" She steps toward him with dread in her eyes.

"Wait. Don't freak out yet. Listen to what I worked out first." His voice is gentle, like he can tell that Mari is going to lose it. Her jaw is locked tight and her thin frame is practically shaking as she tries not to show emotion. "You're short an elective, but it's taken care of. You're going to take a summer class that's offered to high school students at the college. It's a one week class, all day, every day. Finish that and you've satisfied the state requirements. The school will give you a conditional graduation, and you won't get your diploma until after you finish the class. The college knows and has agreed to wait on your final transcript. Everything is already arranged."

"They offered to pay my room and board over the summer, too?" Tucker nods, but his eyes flick away from hers. Mari doesn't notice it, but Trystan does. She sucks in a deep breath and presses her fingers to her lips. "I'm going to college! Trystan, I'm going to college!" She takes his hands and jumps up and down before he pulls her into his arms and hugs her hard.

When Mari steps away, she turns to Tucker and throws her arms around him too. "Thank you so much. I can't even tell you what this means to me. Thank you! Thank you! Thank you!" Her voice is giddy, and he can tell she's trying not to cry.

Tucker peels her off and smiles kindly. "It was my pleasure, Mari. Now, go on and have them check your make-up one last time. I think some of your lipstick came off." Mari races off, skipping backstage and laughing. She's happier than Trystan remembers seeing her. Like ever.

When she's gone, he looks up at Tucker. The man is a better person than he'd originally thought. Tucker hides his kindnesses. Call it a gut feeling, but Trystan knows that Tucker did more than arrange for the college to let Mari into the dorms early.

Trystan leans his shoulder against the cinderblock wall and slips his hands into his pockets. Tilting his chin up, he says, "You paid for her housing, didn't you?"

Tucker gives him a lopsided grin. Surprisingly, he doesn't deny it. "She earned it, don't you think?"

There are people who do good deeds in silence. They come and go like a whisper, and most of the time we think it was luck, but it's so much more than that. Tucker isn't a wealthy man—he's on a teacher's salary—and he just paid a massive bill for a student. Mari isn't his daughter. He doesn't owe her a damn thing, and yet he did this for her. It makes Trystan wonder exactly what Tucker's done for him, and what kindnesses swept by unnoticed, because now he's certain that there have been many.

The words knock around in Trystan's head for a moment before he asks, "Yeah, but why not tell her you paid for it?" It's not that he thinks Tucker should draw attention to it, but he wants to know why the teacher did it and doesn't want credit for his actions. The behavior is so contradictory to everything Trystan experienced growing up that he can't fathom the situation. What would compel someone, an acquaintance at best, to act so selflessly?

The large man doesn't answer at first. Instead, he glances around to make sure they're still alone before leaning in closer to Trystan's ear. "Because ownership of the action devalues the kindness in some cases. It'll make her feel indebted, and that isn't the reason it was done. Well, not that I would know." Tucker grins, and admits nothing and everything with his statement.

Having ideals is one thing, and acting on them is quite another. Trystan knows what kind of man he wants to be and sees a reflection of himself in Tucker. Or maybe it's the other way around. It's possible that the young teacher already rubbed off on him over the years.

Tucker is quiet for a moment and then points to Trystan's packet. "The contract that I think you'll be the happiest living with is on top. There's a pen in the envelope. Congratulations, Mr. Scott."

Trystan pulls the contract out and scans it. Just as Tucker starts to walk off, Trystan says, "There's nothing in here for you." There's no notation of a commission percentage for Tucker. No flat fee. Nothing.

The teacher doesn't stop, look back, or try to explain. He simply acts as if he didn't hear and heads off toward the lighting cage to make sure everyone is where they need to be before the curtain goes up. Trystan watches as Tucker disappears around the corner. He looks at the contracts in his hands and knows what he's going to do.

CHAPTER 11

~MARI~

I've never gone on stage before to do a live performance. Up until now, I was the girl who sat in the shadows, the person that no one knew was there. By intermission everyone knows my name. They'll see me flooded in golden light, standing center stage with Trystan. I've always thought he had charisma. The way he says his lines makes the night feel surreal. It's like we're star-crossed lovers trapped in another time, in another life.

There are more people in the audience than I've ever seen. I peeked between the curtains from backstage before the play started. Now that things are underway, my heart doesn't pound so frantically. Periodically, the glint of a camera lens catches my eye from somewhere in back, but I can't see past the second row. The rest of the audience is swallowed in blackness, which is good, otherwise my nerves would choke me to death and I'd die.

The lights keep me from looking out into the audience. They're blinding, and every time I feel the racing of my heart as I start to panic, Trystan seems to sense it. He touches me lightly—on my cheek or my wrist—and pulls me back to where it's only the two of us. When he does that, I realize that I could go on like this forever. He anchors me, steadies me, and makes me a better person.

We're at the end of the second act, and that steamy kiss is about to happen. My heart pounds as I say my lines. I never thought about him kissing me like this in front of so many people. Sweat trickles down my back and it feels like nothing I've ever experienced before. My head is in the clouds, as my hands tremble. Trystan reaches for me, his eyes locked on mine. Smooth words flow softly from his lips as he leans in, closing the distance between us. His hands tangle in my hair and his mouth brushes against mine. The kiss feels more real, more intense than anything before. I gasp as he pulls away, and my eyes flick to the side—to the audience—as the lights fade to black and the curtain swings shut.

She's here.

I stand utterly still, even after the dim blue stage lights come up so we don't trip as we walk off stage. We have fifteen minutes before the next act. Trystan is smiling. He loves this so much and I don't want to ruin it for him, so I try not to react, but he's already noticed.

"What is it?"

"My mom. She's out there." I stare at the floor, at the way the wood takes on blue tones in the light.

"Is that bad?"

Glancing up at him, I answer truthfully. "I don't know. They said they wouldn't come."

"Your dad said they wouldn't come. Maybe your mom realizes he's been acting like an ass. Mari, you are exceptional. You're dazzling everyone out there. She has to see that."

I smile up at him, but it's forced. Seeing her there makes me question myself. Everything I do is lacking in her eyes and it'll crush me if she thinks my performance is subpar. "She doesn't see much when she looks at me, Trystan. She sees that I'm not what she wanted, and that's about it."

The conversation is cut short when we're shoved off stage, so the crew can change out the set. Trystan walks with me quickly into one the back dressing rooms. "Forget that she's here. Tonight is a new start for both of us. Try to be happy." He leans in and kisses my nose, which makes me smile. It's such a sweet thing, innocent and kind, that I can't help but grin.

Sucking in a deep breath, I nod. "You're right. We both get a new start after this. And honestly, I'm loving every second of it. They love you Trystan. You could hear a pin drop out there, and it's because of you."

Trystan never takes compliments well. He usually boasts or does something silly to deflect or distract people from seeing it, but I know. This time he does neither. His voice is a whisper. His dark lashes lower and he leans into me, holding me in his arms and whispers in my ear. "Thank you, Mari. I couldn't have done this without you." As he pulls away, he pecks the side of my face. "I need to take care of something, okay. You should go get a drink and have your make-up touched up before curtain call."

"Okay, I'll see you in a little bit." I wander around backstage until I find the side door that leads to the water fountain. Pushing through, I head into the only hallway that is blocked off from the public. Still, some people have managed to get backstage, including Brie.

She's wearing a tight little skirt and saunters over to me as I guzzle water from the fountain. "I can't believe they let you on stage. Trystan is totally carrying you. If it wasn't for him, they'd be throwing rotten vegetables at you." She laughs and tips her head back. The bruises under her eyes are half hidden by make-up. She must have rubbed her face and some of the concealer came off. Either that or she's been crying.

I straighten and look her over once, and raise an eyebrow. "I'd rather get hit with rotten fruit than have a rotten soul. Good luck with that." My throat is still dry, so I bend my head to the fountain again, but Brie doesn't leave.

"You think you're better than me? Please!" She cackles and several pairs of eyes turn our way. Some of the actors are lingering backstage with me, waiting for water while others are practicing their lines. They all stop what they're doing and watch. Brie rants, "You're just the spoiled daughter of a rich man. You'll never amount to anything, and as for Trystan, I'll always be his first love. I'll always be the woman who slept with him first and nothing you can do will ever change that." Her words are spoken loudly in a clipped tone, like she's superior.

The urge to punch her in the face courses through my arms, and my muscles tense, but I'm not a fool. Besides, Tucker went out of his way for me and I'm not going to get into another fistfight with her, so I straighten, look straight at her, purse my lips together, and spew. A splattering of water comes out and hits her face right before I start choking. By the time she squeals, I'm doubled over and hacking up a lung.

It looks like she was in the spray zone and the rest of the cast that's loitering down the hallway come over to make sure I'm all right. No one notices Brie, but I do. There's murder in her eyes as she wipes away the smeared make-up. It was childish. Maybe. But I'm not letting people like her talk to me that way anymore. Brie stomps off and disappears into the crowd on the other side of the barricade. I hope she goes home, but I doubt it. She's probably waiting around to see what damage she can do.

There are several sets of hands on my back when I hear Mom's voice. "Mari?" I glance up, horrified that she'll try to talk to me now.

Her gaze meets mine and we stare at each other. Everything within me says to walk away, that talking to her right now is not a smart move, but I can't. There's something about her, about the look on her face, that draws me down the hallway. Soon I'm standing in front of her with only the wooden posts separating us.

Glancing up at her with a stern tone, I ask, "What are you doing here?"

There are people around. Many voices are talking at the same time. A camera pushes its way to the front and soon I can see the man wielding it. He shoves it in my face and I think that Mom will back away, but she doesn't. Rather, she lifts her hand and I can see what she's been holding. A single red rose with a white ribbon tied around it, forming a little bow.

Holding it out to me, Mom offers the flower. "You amaze me, Mari. I never knew you could do anything like this and seeing you up there on the stage…" Her fingers cover her mouth quickly as she swallows a sob. The rose remains between us, an offering not accepted. I can't touch it. I'm frozen in place. Her words hit me like a sheet of water and I'm drowning, dying to hear what she has to say.

Mom continues, "I never knew." She looks down at the rose in her hand. "And I'm afraid I've been holding you back. I'm so sorry, honey."

I nod slowly, too shocked to speak. When I find my voice, I ask, "Where's Dad?"

Mom's spine straightens and her eyes lock with mine, offering an apology that words cannot express. She doesn't have to answer because I know he isn't here. Remorse fills her eyes, like there are more things to say, but not here—not now.

The rose starts to fall to her side, clutched in her hand, but I reach for it, refusing to make the same mistakes my father's made time and time again. Forgiveness is something I want, so it's something I have to offer, and there's no one that I'd rather give it to than my mother.

"This is beautiful. Thank you, Mom." I take the rose and reach over the barricade and hug her quickly before saying, "I need to get back. I'll talk to you after. I have some really exciting news." Hiding my face,

I hurry down the hall. Tears prick my eyes as hope fills my chest.

She's proud of me. My mother is finally proud of me.

CHAPTER 12

~TRYSTAN~

The play is over too quickly. Trystan basks in every moment, willing time to slow, but it doesn't. Rather, it seems to fly by, the minutes passing like seconds. He saw Mari with her mother and the smile on her face as she hurried back toward the stage during intermission. At least she has one parent now. Going through life alone is hard and Trystan wouldn't wish it on anyone. For some reason, blood matters. There isn't a day that goes by that he doesn't wish his mother would show up and say something like that to him, but the woman is a ghost—gone forever.

The last line is said and something inside his chest tugs hard. This is the end of one life and the beginning of another. Most people never get a chance like this, and he knows he should feel lucky, but he's going to miss this place. Trystan will miss his afternoons with Mari, and driving Tucker crazy in class. He'll miss the hallways and Seth's crude mouth. If Trystan doesn't make an effort, he knows the people he holds most dear will vanish from his life.

The curtain swings closed as he stands there with Mari in his arms. He beams down at her and kisses her hard, not holding back a bit of emotion. Without warning the curtain swings open again and a single spotlight shines across the room, illuminating their private kiss.

The audience is cheering wildly, standing and clapping so loudly that he can't hear a thing. Mari and Trystan pull apart. She smiles and covers her lips with her fingers, trying to hide a beautiful, shy, grin. Trystan tugs her forward toward the edge of the stage. The spot light follows the pair until Trystan stops. He holds up their hands and they bow together, which makes everyone cheer louder. The casting call begins and one by one, the entire cast is called out onto the stage.

At the end, Mr. Tucker is called out and applauded. Up until this moment, everything is normal. Now, Tucker would normally take a mic and thank everyone for their hard work, but not tonight. Tucker taps the mic in his hand and clears his throat. "There are members of the press here tonight with a question for one of our students, and I believe he has an answer for you."

Tucker turns to look back at Trystan. This is it. His heart feels like it's going to leap out of his chest. It's a combination of dread and excitement. Trystan steps forward and tugs Mari with him before releasing her hand after a couple of steps.

Trystan taps his mic to make sure it's still on before his voice rings across the auditorium. "A few months ago I was completely and totally in love with a beautiful woman who didn't know how I felt, so I wrote her a song." Trystan reaches for Mari and pulls her to him. "She knows how I feel, now." Trystan laughs lightly as he looks at Mari, and the audience laughs with him.

"And before tomorrow morning, everyone will know everything about me, so I might as well tell you a little bit about who I am. When I was a baby, my mother left. It broke my father's heart and for the longest time, he blamed me. He took it out on me with words and fists. I'm not the guy from the pristine home with the perfect parents. I didn't have that life." Trystan's throat tightens as he speaks, but he pushes through. He lifts his gaze and looks at the reporters and smiles the confident smirk he always wears when things are difficult.

"I'm the kid that cut class and drove my teachers crazy. I'm the guy who fell in love with his best friend." He glances at Mari and squeezes her hand. "And I'm the guy who wrote her a love song and uploaded it to the internet. I'm the guy everyone has been calling Day Jones, and my name is Trystan Scott."

Seth steps onto the stage and shoves a guitar into Trystan's hands. Grinning he says, "Show them," before backing away into the crowd on stage. They're separated from Trystan, watching in awe.

The audience goes nuts when the guitar is brought out. Mari stands to the side as Trystan grabs a stool from Katie. She grins at him as she backs away. The guys in the lighting cage, blink the house lights and then turn them off. As Trystan begins to sing, a single light flips on behind him. There are several gasps and squeals of excitement as people realize that Trystan is really the guy in the video.

Trystan continues to sing, losing himself in the song like he's done so many times before. His dark hair covers his eyes as he looks down at the floor. The music fills the room, rendering the buzzing audience silent. The music fills the room, softly resonating and causing that soft vibration that only a live performance can bring.

When he finishes the song the room goes from complete silence to an explosion of applause. Trystan stands and walks toward Seth who hands him the contracts. Trystan holds up his hand to silence the room. There's joy in his voice when he announces his decision. "I've chosen to sign with one of the record labels and accept their generous offer. Mr. Tucker, will you do the honor?"

Tucker gives him a strange look. This isn't what they planned. Trystan was supposed to announce what he decided. Tucker steps forward and takes the papers. Reading the papers as he speaks, Tucker announces, "Trystan Scott, formerly known as Day Jones, has signed with Harbor House Records with the stipulation that…" his voice fades which makes the audience grow even more excited. Tucker looks up at Trystan and then back down at the paper, and continues reading, "With the stipulation that the school drama department receive a portion of his sales, and that Mr. Tucker will be his representative and receive a standard commission as compensation for his time and expertise." Trystan wasn't certain how Tucker would react. Doing it this way kind of forced the guy to say yes, at least that's what he was hoping for.

Trystan speaks, filling the silence as Tucker stares at him in shock. "There are two people who made this possible—Mari Jennings for inspiring me to write the song, and Mr. Tucker, who negotiated the contract. This guy has been watching my back for years, even though I didn't know it." Trystan's body pulses with excitement. For some reason this part feels more exciting than anything else. He looks out at the crowd, nodding, gesturing for them to join in. "Come on, Tucker. Say yes. You can still teach. There's a lot more I can learn, and I promise I won't cut."

Tucker's jaw is hanging open. Several cameras shift in his direction, waiting for an answer, while the audience cheers for him to do it. A rumble of laugher falls out of his mouth before he speaks. "You amaze me, Trystan. You always have. I'm honored, beyond words…"

Trystan extends his hand. "So, you'll do it?"

"Damn right, I'll do it!" Tucker grabs Trystan's hand and almost rips his arm off as he shakes it hard.

The moment seems to last forever, with endless applause and cheering. Trystan turns to Mari and takes her hand, pressing a kiss to it, as he waves at the people chanting his name. The sound rushes over him as he smiles back.

Until today, they called him Day Jones. No one knew who he was or what hell he endured to get to this point. There was this idealized version of the rock star who wrote Mari's song, but that man doesn't exist. Life makes us what we are. Cruelty and compassion shape us into what we become, and nothing about that is ideal.

Today the fictional life of Day Jones shattered, and by tonight the world will know him for who he really is—Trystan Scott.

DON'T MISS IT

To ensure you don't miss H.M. Ward's next book, text AWESOMEBOOKS (one word) to 22828 and you will get an email reminder on release day.

FREE SAMPLE OF STRIPPED

Turn the page to read a free sample of
Jonathan Ferro's story.

CHAPTER 1

CASSIE

Bruce claps his big beefy hands at us like we're misbehaving dogs. "Come on ladies! Hustle! The bachelor party isn't going to be much fun if we never get there. Damn, Gretchen, you aren't even dressed, yet?"

She laughs like he's funny, even though Bruce is as far from funny as a person could get. He's the bouncer at the club and on nights like tonight, he comes with us to keep the guys from getting handsy. Some rich brat out on Long Island rented us for the night. There are seven of us going to perform on stage, plus the stripping wait staff, and dear, sweet, Bruce.

Gretchen is piling her long golden hair onto the top of her head and securing it with a long bobby pin. She's strutting around half naked, as if we like looking at her. She smiles sweetly at Bruce and waves a hand, bending it at the wrist like he's silly.

"Please, I'll be ready before Cassie even finishes lacing up her corset."

She tilts her head in my direction as I fumble with my corset hooks. Every time I manage to hook one, another comes undone. Whoever invented the corset should be burned at the stake. The stupid thing might look cool once it's on, but getting into it is a whole other matter. Add in the fact that mine is a real corset—meaning it has steel boning—and breathing isn't something I can do either. I got this thing because it was authentic. I thought that meant it had period fabric or grommets or something cool. It turns out that authentic means metal rods built into the bodice, guaranteed to bruise my ribs. Fuck, I hate this thing, but I refuse to throw it away—it cost me three weeks' pay at my old job. Plus, it's not like I wear it every night. We only pull out the good stuff on holidays and for special events like this.

Bruce turns his head my way and looks like he wants to pull out his hair. I'm nearly dressed, except for this contraption. My ensemble includes the candy apple colored corset, lace-topped thigh highs, and a delicate little G-string, coupled with heels that could be used as weapons. If I ever get mugged wearing these shoes, you can bet your ass that I won't run, not that I could. These are the things I think about when I make my purchases. Can this purse do some damage? Maybe I should skip the leather Dooney and grab me that metal no-name bag with the sharp corners. My roommate and I live across the street from a drug den. Don't even get me started on that. I know we need to move, but knowing it and affording it are two different things. In the meantime, I buy accessories that can be used as weapons.

Glaring at her, I reply, "Gee, thanks, Gretch." My fingers push the next bit of metal through the grommet. This one stays put.

She bats her glittering lashes at me. "No problem." Gretchen is tall and lanky with a larger-than-life super model thing going on. I hate her. She's a bitch with a capital B. It's all good, though. She hates me, too. It's difficult to be hostile toward someone that likes you. Gretchen makes it easy to hate her guts.

Me, I'm not a supermodel. I'm nothing to look at—my mom drilled that into my head a million times. I'm completely average with sub-par confidence, but I can act. I can fake it so that once I hit that stage, I'm as good as the rest of the strippers.

No, I didn't dream of being a pole dancer when I was a little kid, but my life took some wicked turns and here I am, dealing with it. There are worse things I suppose, although I won't be able to think of a single one when I'm letting a bunch of pervs rake their lusty eyes over my naked body. The truth is, I hate this. I'd rather be anywhere else, doing anything else. The gynecologist's office, sign me up. Root canal, no problem. I'll be there early and with a smile on my face. Anything is better than this.

Bruce lingers in the dressing room for too long, staring at his watch. His thick arms are folded over his broad chest as he watches the second hand tick off the passing time. He ignores Gretch's gibe at me. I may be newer, but I pull in a lot more cash and that's what the boss likes—lots of money. As long as I keep doing it, I have a job.

I finally get my corset hooked up when Beth walks by. She's already wearing some frilly satin thing. "Hey, Cassie. Do you want me to lace you up?"

Tucking a piece of hair behind my ear, I nod. "Yeah, thanks." She laces me in, pulling each X tightly, cinching me up until I can barely breathe. "Tight enough?"

I try to inhale deeply, and can't because the metal bars inside the fabric won't permit it. I nod and press my hands to the bodice, feeling the supple satin under my hands. "Yeah, tighter than that and I'll pass out— or pop a boob."

She laughs, "You're the only one who worries about stuff like that. You're so cute." She ties off the strings and tucks them in before swatting my back when she's finished. My boobs are hiked up so high that I can't see my toes when I look down. I grab my robe and wrap it around me as we head to the cars. It's going to be a long night.

———

The ride to the party is short. We're on the north shore of Long Island, not too far from the coast. There are tons of old homes with huge lawns and even bigger estate houses nestled out of sight between towering oaks and pines. The place hosting the party looks like a castle. We pass through the gates and drive around to the side of the house. The van stops and we're told the usual—go wait in the servants' wing until it's time.

Beth and I walk inside, shoulder to shoulder, whispering about the garish wealth that's practically dripping from the walls as we walk inside. Gretchen and a few other girls trail behind us, chattering about what kind of tips they'll make tonight. A party like this can line a girl's pockets for a month if it goes well, but for me it'll do more than that. You see, I'm the main event, the mystery girl in the pink room—the bachelor's private-party dancer. While my coworkers are off in the main hall, I'll be earning the big bucks. That's the main reason why Gretchen hates my guts. Before I came along, she was the top stripper around here.

It's getting late, which means the party is well under way. Beth picks up a tiny sandwich off a tray as she walks to the back of the bustling room. "You think this guy knows what's coming?"

I shrug. "Like it matters, anyway? When's the last time we were sent away?"

"Uh, never." She pops the food in her mouth and chews it up.

I'm leaning against a counter top with my elbows behind me, supporting my weight. "My point exactly. Guys are dicks. They commit to marrying a woman, but this kind of crap the night before the wedding is okay." I roll my eyes as I make a disgusted sound, and straighten up. All of a sudden I'm talking with my hands and they're flying all over the place, "Tell me, why would a guy want a lap dance if he's in love? You'd think he'd only want his bride, but that never happens. He's always happy to have an ass in his face."

"Well, your ass is pretty awesome, or so I've heard." Beth smirks at me and glances around the kitchen. We're in the way, but there isn't anywhere else for us to go yet.

"Guys suck, that's all I'm saying."

"I know. You've said it a million times." She makes a *roaring* sound and shakes her fist in the air before turning to me and grunting, "Men. Evil."

"You're an idiot." I smile at her, trying not to laugh.

She points at me and clicks her tongue. "Right back at you, Cassie."

Bruce waves us over to the other side of the kitchen. "Cassie, Beth—follow me." We duck out behind him and follow the guy down the hall and slip into a little room. It's been done up in pale pinks with silver curtains, similar to the room I work in at the club. Since this is a party, Bruce added another dancer and I got to choose. While I work the stage at the front of the room, Beth will work the floor.

Bruce points a beefy finger at the stage and says to us, "Take your places, and remember that this client is the shit. Pull out all the stops, say 'no' to nothing. You got it?"

We nod in unison. The stage is elevated off the floor, with a few steps up at either end. It looks like the stage is new, built just for me. People usually rent those gray, make-shift stages that wobble when walked on, but not this guy. They spared no expense. The walls are lined with pale pink silks and illuminated from the floor. Clear tables flicker around the room with pink flames dancing within. It's seductive. The colors blend together, reminding me of pale flesh and kissable pink lips. As I climb the steps up the side of the stage and head to the silvery tinsel curtain, I call back to Beth. "Who is this party for again? And why is he the shit? I must have missed the memo."

She laughs as she's examining one of the lights within the glass table. It looks like fire, but it can't be since it's pink. She looks up at me. "Dr. Peter Granz, and he's the shit because he's a Ferro. Hence the swank party." Beth looks up when I don't answer.

I rush at Beth, nearly knocking her over. My jaw is hanging open as worry darts across my face faster than I can contain it. "Ferro?"

"Yeah, why?"

I'm in melt down mode. "I can't be here." I glance around the room and look at the door longingly. Before I make up my mind to run, I hear male voices approaching. Fuck! My heart pounds faster in my chest. If he's here, if Jonathan sees me—the thought cuts off before it finishes.

I'm ready to bounce out the window when Beth grabs my wrist and hauls me to the front of the room. She shoves me behind the curtain and hisses in my ear, "If you freak out now, Gretchen will steal your job. Snap out of it. Whoever this guy is, he isn't worth it."

The tinsel curtain in front of me flutters, but it conceals both of us for the moment. The male voices grow louder until the door is yanked open. The curtain rustles and I'm in full freak-out mode. He can't be here. He can't see me like this. At the same time, Beth's right. I can't skip out. Bruce will run me over with the van and there's no way in hell they'll ever give me another cent.

I stand there, frozen, unable to think. Every muscle in my body is strained, ready to run, but I don't move. My bare feet remain glued to the floor as I smash my lips together.

Then, I hear it—that voice. It floats through the air like a familiar old song. Oh God, someone shoot me. I can't do this.

"You don't know what you're talking about. What guy wouldn't want a party like this?" Jonathan is talking to someone in that light, charming, tone of his.

"Uh, your brother, Peter. Do you know the guy at all? He's going to act like he loves it and get the hell out before you can blink." Glancing through the curtains, I can see the second man. He has dark hair and bright blue eyes like Jonathan. The only difference is their posture. Jonathan has all his weight thrown onto one hip with his arms folded across his chest. The other guy's spine is ramrod straight, like he's never slouched in his life.

Peering at Jonathan through the tinsel, I see a perfect smile lace his lips. "Sean, I know him better than that. Pete is going to love this. It's exactly the kind of party I'd want if I was getting hitched."

"Yes, I know." Sean's voice is flat. He glances around the room with disgust, and slips his hands into his pockets. "Don't say I didn't warn you."

"Oh come on! It's Peter. What's he going to do?"

Sean laughs, like he knows something that Jonathan doesn't. "Don't let that English teacher façade fool you, Jonny. He's as hot headed as I am. No one fucks with him. He's going to consider this a slap in the face, an insult to Sidney. Cancel the strippers before he gets here." Sean leaves the room without another word.

Jonathan Ferro lets out a rush of air and runs his fingers through his thick, dark, hair. The aggravated sound that comes out of his mouth kills me. I've heard it before, I know him too well to not be affected by it. That's the sound he makes when he knows he's screwed up, when he sees that he isn't the man he wants to be. There's always been this wall between Jonathan and his family. I guess he still hasn't gotten past it. Jon paces in a circle a few times and then darts out of the room.

"Holy shit." Beth looks at me and hisses, "What happened between you and him?"

It feels like icy fingers have wrapped around my heart and squeezed. I stare after him and utter, "Nothing, absolutely nothing."

CHAPTER 2

JONATHAN

Why does everyone think they know my brothers better than I do? I'm taking advice from Sean. How the hell did that happen? I'm walking swiftly down the long hallway, chin tucked, not watching where I'm going. The golden wallpaper appears to be glowing in the dim light. I run my hands through my hair and down my neck, and smack into someone.

When I look up, I'm ready to snap. "What the— Oh, it's you."

My closest friend, Trystan Scott, is standing in front of me. The guy is the brother I never had. He's not blood, but he might as well be called a Ferro because he's that loyal.

Trystan's wearing ripped jeans, a button down shirt with the top three buttons undone, and has way too much shit in his hair. "What the hell's going on? I thought the waitresses were supposed to be strippers. That was the coolest idea you've ever had. Imagine my disappointment when I rush out of rehearsal—away from the sexiest woman you've ever seen—and get here to find a bunch of chicks still wearing clothes." Trystan smirks and shoves his hands in his pockets.

I don't bother to answer him before resuming full speed down the hall. I have to find the guy from the club and cancel my awesome plan. Damn it, why does Peter have to be so difficult. Who doesn't want strippers at a bachelor party?

Trystan follows behind. "So, how's it going?" His voice has that teasing tone, which means he knows how well it's going.

"Nice hair," I throw back, and glance at him out of the corner of my eyes. Trystan makes a face and tries to smooth it down, but it doesn't move. "What'd they use, glue?"

His dark hair is sticking up all over the place. It looks like a porcupine toupee. "Something like that. I look like a fucking idiot."

"Yeah, but it's not the hair that does it—it's the make-up."

"Awh, fuck." Trystan swipes his hand across his eyes, trying to rub it off. "I forgot. I had somewhere to be—somewhere with strippers—so I ran over here as fast as I could." He smacks my arm with the back of his hand. "So, come on Jon, what's going on?"

"Apparently this isn't Pete's MO. I'm canceling the girls before Peter gets here. Sean said he'd bolt, that titties aren't his thing."

"Titties are his thing, but he prefers a certain pair." Trystan grins and looks over at me, pressing his hand to his chest. "The ways of the heart are—"

"And what would you know about that? You're a goddamn legend. You've nailed every chick from coast to coast."

Trystan's smile brightens, but it's like there's something he's not telling me. Ever since I met him a few years ago, he's been like that. He doesn't talk about his past much, but I don't blame him. From the papers, I know Trystan's dad beat the shit out of him when he was a kid, but that's about it. The guy keeps to himself, but somehow manages to get pussy whenever he wants. A shy rock star is a fucking oxymoron, but the women fall at his feet. What do I know? Maybe I've been doing everything wrong this whole time. I shake the thoughts away and enter the main room.

The music pounds through the air, vibrating through me. The dim lights make it difficult to see the guy I'm looking for. He should be back in the kitchen right about now. I lean into Trystan. "I'll catch you later."

"Whatever you need, man." Trystan grabs my arm and squeezes. He's saying he's got my back, even if no one else does. The guy might be a train wreck, but he's good people under all that shit.

I slap his back, "Thanks. Catch you in a few. We can hit the bar after Pete gets here, because I'm not walking around sober if there's only guys here." Trystan laughs and agrees to get smashed with me later. You got to love the guy.

I weave through the crowd. There are already some strippers posing as wait staff. A woman with a tray and way too much make-up on her face brushes my side and turns toward me. "Champagne?" Her cleavage is up to her neck and the thin white shirt she's wearing does nothing to hide the black bra underneath. Fuck, she's hot. I almost stop and flirt with her—almost—but I keep walking, because I'm not a total dick. This was supposed to be for Pete. I need to fix this before he gets here.

Sean falls in step beside me. "Tell me that I didn't see Scott at the bar?" Sean hates anyone who wasn't born with the name Ferro.

"Fuck off, Sean. He's my friend."

"He's using you." Sean's jaw is locked tight as he scans the crowd. "You're too naïve."

"You're an asshole." I'm not defending my friendship with Trystan or with anyone else. Sean acts like he knows everything, and he might be right most of the time, but he's wrong about Trystan. "The guy has his own millions. He doesn't need mine."

"He's unstable."

"You're unstable." I flick my eyes over to him.

Sean smirks. "Possibly."

"I can't chat about your mental health right now. I need to find the guy before all these girls rip their clothes off. Where's Pete?"

Sean laughs and points across the room. "He just got here."

"Fuck." I take off through the crowd, cutting through the guys, shoving some aside.

When I push through the kitchen doors, I see him. "Bruce! My man—change of plans."

Bruce is a huge guy and doesn't look pleased to see me. There are half dressed girls everywhere, slipping into their tear off waitressing outfits. Damn, this would have been so cool. Bruce has his thigh-thick arms folded over his chest. He glares at me. "No refunds."

"I'm not asking for one." I stand in front of the guy and feel like a toothpick, even though I'm not. Reaching into my pocket, I feel around for a hundred dollar bill. "I need them to keep their clothes *on*."

He gives me a weird look. "They're not supposed to be waitresses, Mr. Ferro.

They're strippers and are expecting the tips that accompany the occupation."

Okay, I grab a fist full of bills and slip them into his hand. Bruce takes it and sees how much I've given him. I ask, "Maybe they could be waitresses for a couple of hours and then head out?"

"Maybe, but this isn't going to help the girls you hired for the private room. They're expecting tips, and if you cancel them out, they'll have left the club for nothing. You have to make good over there." The guy's voice is dangerously deep.

"Done. I'll go take care of it." I reach out and shake his hand.

As I turn to leave he clears his throat. "And if you'd like this kept quiet…"

I reach into my pocket and slap more cash into his fist. Bastard. The large man grins. "My lips are sealed, Mr. Ferro. A suggestion?" he asks, and I nod as my gaze cuts across the room to the clock. "Keep at least one girl in that private room for your guests. This is a party that people will talk about. You don't want them to think you're a pussy. You've got a reputation that people know about. They expect a little something extra at one of your parties."

"And you know this because…?"

"Because I've got ears, Mr. Ferro. Every man here is wondering what your big surprise will be this evening. You need to keep something for them, don't you?"

I don't answer him, because I know he's right. "Fine, I'll go speak to them. You keep the girls out here clothed."

Bruce laughs and leans back in his chair. "Done."

When I get back to the private room, I push through the doors without really paying attention until I hear a voice—that voice. It's like being hit in the face with a wall of cold water. Whatever thought I had in my head is gone. Wide eyed, I look up and scan the room. Two women are tangled together on the floor, fighting. Well, no they're not fighting, not really. I'm not sure what they're doing, and they have no idea I'm watching.

My heart pounds harder as her voice fills my head and I try to see her face. My body responds the way it used to—that hollow spot in the center of my chest aches, along with my cock. I stare in disbelief, watching two strippers wrestling on the floor, and stand in shock because one of them is Cassie Hale.

STRIPPED IS AVAILABLE NOW

COMING SOON

NEW YORK TIMES BESTSELLING AUTHOR
H.M. WARD
BROKEN
promises
A TRYSTAN SCOTT NOVEL

BROKEN PROMISES
A Trystan Scott Novel

Read more about the characters in
the **FERRO FAMILY:**

BRYAN FERRO
~THE PROPOSITION~

*****

SEAN FERRO
~THE ARRANGEMENT~

******

PETER FERRO GRANZ
~DAMAGED~

******

JONATHAN FERRO
~STRIPPED~

******

TRYSTAN SCOTT
~COLLIDE~

MORE ROMANCE BOOKS BY H.M. WARD

DAMAGED

DAMAGED 2

STRIPPED

SCANDALOUS

SCANDALOUS 2

SECRETS

THE SECRET LIFE OF
TRYSTAN SCOTT

And more.

To see a full book list, please visit:
www.SexyAwesomeBooks.com/books.htm

CAN'T WAIT FOR H.M WARD'S NEXT STEAMY BOOK?

⭐⭐⭐⭐⭐

Let her know by leaving stars and telling
her what you liked about
THE SECRET LIFE OF
TRYSTAN SCOTT OMNIBUS
in a review!